## PRAISE FOR *MURDER IN THE COURTHOUSE*

"Nancy grabs the readers by their proverbial throats from the very first paragraph and refuses to let go. She is a terrific storyteller and keeps the twists and turns coming page after page. Her latest thriller, *Murder in the Courthouse*, is sure to please her many fans."

—*Kathie Lee Gifford*

"Nancy Grace fans rejoice! Hailey Dean is back on the case. There's murder and mayhem in Savannah, the lush jewel of the south, a city steeped in mystery, folklore, and romance. Hailey is all business on the bench, but after hours, she falls in love with the dreamy setting and into the arms of a handsome stranger, who woos her with more than a mimosa. Pure escape from Ms. Grace, who knows her way around the law but when it comes to love is at the mercy of the court. A fabulous read, y'all!"

— *Adriana Trigiani*, New York Times *bestselling author of* All the Stars in the Heavens

# MURDER IN THE COURTHOUSE

# MURDER IN THE COURTHOUSE

A Hailey Dean Mystery

## NANCY GRACE

BenBella Books, Inc.
Dallas, Texas

Copyright © 2016 by Nancy Grace
First paperback edition 2017

BenBella

BenBella Books, Inc.
10440 N. Central Expressway, Suite 800
Dallas, TX 75231
www.benbellabooks.com
Send feedback to feedback@benbellabooks.com

Printed in the United States of America
10 9 8 7 6 5 4 3 2 1

Library of Congress Cataloging-in-Publication Data is available upon request.
ISBN 978-1-944648-79-4 (trade paper)
ISBN 978-1-942952-88-6 (trade cloth)

Editing by John Paine
Copyediting by Katie Buniak
Proofreading by Brittney Martinez,
    Jenny Bridges, and Sarah Vostok
Front cover design by Sarah Avinger

Full cover design by Ivy Koval
Text design by Aaron Edmiston
Text composition by Integra Software
    Services Private Limited
Printed by Lake Book Manufacturing

Distributed by Perseus Distribution
www.perseusdistribution.com

To place orders through Perseus Distribution:
Tel: (800) 343-4499
Fax: (800) 351-5073
Email: orderentry@perseusbooks.com

**Special discounts for bulk sales (minimum of 25 copies) are available.**
**Please contact Aida Herrera at aida@benbellabooks.com.**

*Murder in the Courthouse* is dedicated to my father, Walter Malcolm "Mac" Grace, who filled our lives with joy.

Please read this book in Heaven, my sweet dad. You gave me strength to finish it.

# IIIIIIIIIIIIIIIIIIIIIIIIIIIIIIIIIIIIIIII ACKNOWLEDGMENTS IIIIIIIIII

Hailey Dean was born in my heart and mind many years ago. Bringing her to life has been quite a journey, down a very long and winding road full of ups and downs.

Thank you to Glenn Yeffeth, Leah Wilson, Sarah Dombrowsky, Jennifer Canzoneri, Jessika Rieck, and the rest of the incredible crew at BenBella, along with John Paine, for making *Murder in the Courthouse* a reality.

Thank you to my Bama friend and anchor throughout, Dee Emmercson, a.k.a. "Moon Pie." What good is anything without a friend to share it with?

Thank you to my dear friends Dean Sicoli, Eleanor Odom, and Mike Walker, all of whom you can spot in these pages whether named or not.

Thank you to my partner in crime, Josh Sabarra . . . you believed.

Thank you to my sweet twins, who love Mommy even when she's working on her book instead of going on an adventure with them out in the swing or at the playground or under the stars.

Thank you with all my heart to my husband David for his presence throughout these many years. He shares with me the belief that what the mind can perceive, the body can achieve.

Thank you to my mom, who demonstrates the gold standard in perseverance.

And last, thank you, Daddy, wherever you are at this very moment, in some beautiful, magical place just beyond the stars. Thank you for all the love. And for the strength to go on. I know you are turning these pages . . . in Heaven.

There was no warning, no movement inside the darkened garage. The morning was just like every other. He locked the kitchen door, balancing a to-go coffee cup. Adjusting the thick lenses of his glasses, Alton peeked back through the door's small panes. He absolutely had to check the coffee machine. Yes, the little red light was off. He'd unplugged it before leaving, as usual. But always better safe than sorry.

Glancing back into the kitchen was one of Alton's rituals and extremely comforting as he headed to the courthouse and all its jarring noises, jostling bodies in and out of courtrooms, and generally untidy goings-on. He loved thinking his little kitchen was neat as a pin, smelling of coffee and sausage patties.

Turning around, the *thwack* to the back of Alton's head and the slice right to his torso really didn't register as pain . . . at first, anyway. But almost immediately, a searing shot of pain jolted Alton's body like an electric current. Doubling over, he spotted deep red blood spurting out onto the concrete floor.

The rhythmic bursts of blood reminded him of water gushing out of the corner fire hydrant last summer when a neighbor crashed into it while texting. A fixed object! It caused a huge mess. Alton stayed up late into the night, discreetly watching clusters of neighbors, police, and fire department personnel through the curtains of his front window.

Crashing forward face-first, his forehead slammed into the back right-side tire of his Toyota Corolla. He caught a whiff of the tire's black rubber.

It was "Magnetic Metal Gray," a color that the ad proclaimed was "Stealthy and stunning. Drive Magnetic Metal Grey and get

1

noticed!" Alton kept the car in absolute mint condition. But he was never noticed.

He loved taking the car to the Super Wash over on Abercorn. It made the car smell like a piña colada. *"If you like piña coladas, and getting caught in the rain, if you're not into yoga, if you have half a brain . . ."*

Sausage, coffee, the manufactured smell of piña colada all crashed together in his head now pressed against the cool cement.

Alton spotted his garage door hanging over him. Why was it up? He certainly had *not* left it gaping open overnight, begging intruders to come in and steal gardening tools.

The figure that just dragged him by his feet bent down, but Alton could only make out a silhouette. Holding a knife. A ripping sensation tearing across his middle, above his hips, was excruciating, cutting through the haze.

A deep dark pool of blood spread out beneath him like a crimson throw rug. Somehow, the thought made him feel warmer and cozier and that was good, because suddenly, Alton felt very cold.

*Cold to the bone.*

*His thoughts were getting more jumbled* . . . but right now, all he could think of was Mother. Diabetes took her away from him. But he still loved her dearly and missed her practically every minute of every day.

Alton judged all other women by her gold standard. She confided she loved him, Alton, the best . . . even more than she had his father. They snuggled together, the two of them, more nights than Alton could remember . . . huddling against the smell of booze and the crazy rantings of his dad. When his dad beat Alton one time too many, it was Mother who came between them, taking the blows herself.

But oddly, here she was, standing behind the barbecue grill in the corner.

There was that sound again. Alton looked up in time to see the garage door lowering. His left cheek flush against the cool concrete floor, he remembered the ad exactly . . . "When seconds count, count on the Titanium-10! The garage door opener that never disappoints!"

*"Mom, help me . . ."* Now, she was just a few feet away, wearing her favorite short-sleeved, yellow dress, belted at the waist. *Why was she wringing her hands? What was wrong?* Alton hated when Mother cried.

Mother was speaking soothingly to him and he wanted to get closer, to hear what she was saying.

Two strange feet appeared at Alton's eye level and at that precise moment, one foot pulled back and delivered a massive kick to Alton's face. Blood gushed from his head and nose into his eyes.

He could no longer see, but he could hear. He recognized the mechanical sound of the garage lowering. Within seconds, the heavy metal door was grinding into him, severing him exactly in half.

Alton tried to reach out to Mother. She was no longer wringing her hands feverishly together. She was smiling . . . holding her arms open and then . . . Alton felt nothing more.

"Come on, Hailey. It's just three weeks. You're already gonna be there to take the stand as an expert witness . . . right? So why does one more day or so matter? And you don't really have to prepare, do you Hailey? I mean . . . I *never* prepare. I mean . . . what is it this time . . . battered woman syndrome? Fiber evidence? No . . . I remember . . . you do a criminal profile and wow the jury . . . right? You know it like the back of your hand. You've *tried* a hundred of those cases. You don't even have to prepare . . . am I right? You'll have plenty of time to do the *Harry Todd Show*!"

Veteran TV producer Tony Russo was hell-bent on nabbing ratings by sucking the Love story dry, mining every salacious detail he could. It was all for the glory of the *Harry Todd Show*. It was Russo who first "discovered" Hailey, which apparently gave him license to badger her to appear on the show.

"I *do* have to prepare because every set of facts is different. You know that! I'm glad *you're* not on the jury. You stay put right where you are, cooking up stories to get numbers for the network."

"Whatever. Like I was saying, why not kill two birds with one stone? This trial is what you're all about! Don't you see that? A new mother, Hailey, a new mother and her baby. How can you turn your back on a little baby? And get this . . . *they're both dead!* Dead, Hailey! Dead, dead, dead!"

"Will you please stop talking about them like that? I don't like it."

"*Murdered.* And the guy's gonna get away with it. Is that what you want?"

It wasn't what Hailey Dean wanted at all.

His words kept ringing in her ears as her flight touched down at SAV, the Savannah/Hilton Head International Airport. It had taken a lot to get her out of Manhattan, to leave her tiny apartment in the sky, and crowbar her away from her psych patients.

As a friend of the prosecutor, Hailey agreed to fly down and testify, or at least consult for the state, regarding Julie Love Adams's relationship with her husband and what may have affected Julie's decision to stay in the marriage. She would also profile the defendant, Todd Adams; specifically, his behavior just before and immediately after the disappearance of Julie. It was all part of the psychology that would prove Julie's murder.

Criminal profiling, as much of an art as a science, draws on psychology and statistics combined with the profiler's experience, knowledge, and, frankly, good old intuition. Profiling had been around since London's Jack the Ripper.

"Behavioral evidence" was one of Hailey's specialties and had been a marquee element in nearly all of her homicide prosecutions. She could pick apart a killer's behavior, reactions, and responses, or lack thereof, like no other. Behavioral evidence analysis skyrocketed Hailey to become one of the most successful, and hated, prosecutors in the South . . . possibly the country.

Profiling often dealt with what was known but not spoken. In polite Savannah, the wealthy elite hobnob at the oldest country club in town, and "check in" regularly at offices set up by great-grandparents. The Julie Love Adams case had been one of their most salacious topics since Julie first went missing. But there was never mention nor, of course, understanding of the mind of a killer. No juicy conversations addressed warning signals before or clues left behind. It was all just gossip to get them through another bridge game, garden club, or round of golf.

But behavior like affairs, money problems, alcohol, gambling, domestic abuse . . . none of *that* would ever be discussed by clusters of ladies at the Savannah Country Club in the quiet carpeted areas off their powder rooms. Pink-faced matrons "glistening" delicately in their morning spin classes would remain silent on the issue, and forget about it coming up in the men's locker room. No way.

The Adamses were third-generation members of "the Club." Todd's father and his grandfather before him had both sat on the board. Hardly a weekend passed without the parents meeting friends for cocktails and dinner there or the whole clan showing up in their Sunday best to man their usual table in the center of the club's casual dining area near a huge stone fireplace for the predictable fare at Sunday brunch.

For a few weeks after Julie went missing, the Adams continued their regular club visits, but after a while, it was painfully obvious the place was buzzing with gossip about Todd and Julie, so Sunday brunches came to a halt. It was Burger King before 10:30 AM now for the Adamses, a small coffee and folded eggs.

And how they resented it.

Julie Love Adams was murdered, her body weighted down and dumped in deep, swirling, muddy waters. She managed to wash up ashore on Tybee Island along with a chunk of cement block. Her baby ultimately detached from her uterus in the salty ocean water and followed her mommy in the next tide.

The two were buried together in one grave, with Julie Love holding her baby's remains in her arms inside the coffin.

Of course, the casket was closed because there was nothing but bones, hair, and soft tissue left of Julie. No one within Savannah's upper crust discussed it openly.

But they would now.

It would be plastered across the airwaves.

Russo tried his best to convince Hailey that the "liberal media machine" would drown out the voices of the two victims with TV talking heads chanting "innocent till proven guilty" over and over. They'd be whining about the so-called power of the state and making the same old claims that police trumped up murder charges and planted evidence. Maybe pundits would even take potshots at the pregnant victim. Nothing was sacred when TV ratings were at stake . . . Hailey had learned that the hard way.

*What if one juror listened?*

But Hailey knew the truth. Julie and her unborn baby girl were brutally murdered. Extremely faint markings on what was left of neck tissue arguably suggested ligature strangulation. But it was only that . . . arguable.

Cause of death was officially ruled "undetermined" by the Chatham Medical Examiner because by the time her body washed ashore off Savannah's South Channel, Julie Love was mostly just a skeleton.

But as fate would have it, a portion of the thick, protective layer of her uterus remained intact long enough to largely protect her unborn baby. The tiny fetus that would have been baby Lily washed up on the same sandy shore with the very next Atlantic tide, looking almost exactly like a bright and shiny, plastic and naked, store-bought baby doll.

The sight of little Lily brought homicide investigators to tears, and the photos taken that day would likely have the same impact on a jury. Not only that, there was plastic twine tangled around Julie's ankles, and the cement block that washed ashore was the same type block found in Todd Adams's garage.

Not entirely damning, in light of the fact it was also the same type of cement block found at every Lowe's or Home Depot you cared to stop at, four of them in metro-Savannah alone. The twine was explained away as having tangled onto Julie's dead body after being set free from some unwitting fisherman's boat.

Hailey heard about the story when the pregnant twenty-eight-year-old first went missing. Julie was home alone decorating the Christmas tree when she reportedly took her little King Charles Spaniel for a walk to a local park. Then, the nine months pregnant mom just "disappeared."

Her husband said he'd gone fishing off the tip of Tybee Island and was away all day. Months and months of investigation ensued and, predictably, a string of Todd Adams's affairs came to light. But the cops didn't find it on their own.

The tabloids beat the cops to the punch by digging up the truth about Todd Adams and his multiple sleazy affairs. Mike Walker with

*Snoop* magazine and the even more ubiquitous *Snoop.com*, racked up two million clicks in the first thirty-six hours after posting. Walker actually ended up doing a lot of the police's legwork for them.

Walker's salacious headlines instantly translated into millions of dollars of sales. Gorgeous shots of Julie as a high school cheerleader appeared out of nowhere, wedding photos, photos of her in the baby's soon-to-be nursery, of Julie at Christmas parties and at home in front of the couple's Christmas tree, her tummy announcing the imminent birth of baby Lily.

The night before Julie Love went missing, she attended a neighborhood Christmas party by herself, then decorated the family tree all alone. It was later revealed her husband went to a Christmas party of his own . . . with a bleached-blonde girlfriend poured into a tight, red satin strapless cocktail dress. To top it all off, Todd Adams had his left hand planted on the blonde's backside *in the picture*.

Only after *Snoop* dug up the Christmas party photo were police pushed to name a suspect. And they did. Amid press conferences, interviews, and banner headlines, Todd Adams was finally arrested on two counts of murder one. Now, he faced the Georgia death penalty and Old Sparky, Georgia's fabled, and notorious, electric chair.

That one scandalous tidbit, the photo of Todd Adams posed with his hand on another woman's rear end in front of a Christmas tree, juxtaposed with a shot of Julie Love pregnant and alone the very same night, galvanized women across the country. For that reason, the jury had to be handpicked in another county, then bused into Savannah for the trial.

*Why is the plane still just sitting here?* Hailey had already taken off her jacket and opened a newspaper she found in the seat pouch in front of her. The pilot of the commuter plane, a cramped regional jet, cut the AC for some barbaric reason. It was stifling hot. Sitting in her seat out on a hot tarmac, Hailey felt perspiration on her chest melting down into her bra.

Looking out the tiny window of her puddle jumper from Atlanta, waves of heat radiating up off the runway and in the distance, she spotted palm trees intermixed with live oaks planted around the airport. Over decades they'd grown into enormous giants, their branches hanging heavily with Spanish moss, giving them an eerie, almost supernatural, appearance.

Quite the contrast from New York's LaGuardia, where she had taken off that morning. Trapped at 40,000 feet up in the air, Hailey read and reread articles about the double murder, making notes in the margins so she could use them later when testifying, provided the judge let her testimony in evidence. The state had to lay the proper legal and factual foundation first.

Prosecutors flew her down and were putting her up for the government rate at the Savannah Hyatt, on the Savannah River. Farther downtown was the Chatham County Courthouse.

Then, there was the possibility she'd discuss the trial on air following her testimony. She still wasn't sure whether she would, but if it would help sway the public, and possibly even the jury, it was an opportunity she wasn't sure she could pass up.

It would only be a few weeks. Hailey could manage her psych practice over the phone and via Skype. She told herself it would be great to be back home again, or at least a few hours' drive away. She hadn't been in Savannah in a while and the truth was, the Julie Love Adams case struck a chord with Hailey from the very first time she'd read about it.

What type of person could take the lives of his own wife and baby? Then wrap a mom-to-be in a tarp and dump the two of them in the choppy waters of the Atlantic? And then go on a date with his new lover that very night like nothing ever happened?

The last bit of advice Tony Russo blasted into his cell before Hailey took off from LaGuardia hung in the air. "Remember! Most important! I don't care who you talk to or what you find out, never, ever refer to 'Global News & Entertainment.' We're not that anymore. We're GNE. The suits will scream if you even breathe the words 'Global News & Entertainment.'"

"Well, if you're not Global News & Entertainment, then why would I say GNE? GNE stands for Global News & Entertainment."

"*No it doesn't!* Not anymore!"

"Then what is GNE? What does it stand for?"

"Nothing! It stands for absolutely nothing!"

Hailey had paused to let that thought sink in. He went on in a high-pitched voice. "*We rebranded!* That's just it . . . GNE! That's the new name of the network. They thought Global News & Entertainment was too long and boring. So now we're just GNE."

"You think four words is too long?" Hailey almost started laughing out loud.

"Yes! It's absolutely too long! And it's so boring it makes my head hurt! Maybe not for you, Hailey, but four unnecessary words *in TV world* . . . it's way too long! It's practically a novel! Just remember . . . try to wrap your head around this . . . it stands for nothing . . . GNE stands for absolutely nothing."

When he realized Hailey wasn't responding, he went on. "You know, like the Game Show Network is no longer the Game Show Network. It's just GSN now."

"Right. GSN stands for Game Show Network and I've never seen it. What is it?"

"It doesn't matter and *it is no longer the Game Show Network*! It's GSN! That's all! Just like GNE is just GNE . . . nothing more!"

Hailey didn't get the reasoning behind the name "change" or the "rebranding." "You mean you're not embarrassed that the letters for your company stand for nothing? They don't mean anything at all?"

"We're not a company. We're TV, we don't have to stand for anything."

"Listen, I'm in Savannah to catch a killer, not be in a TV studio, so I can't promise anything, but if I can get out of court, I'm happy to."

"I take that as an unequivocal *yes*! Love ya! Bye!" He clicked off.

Hailey resumed rereading the medical examiner's report, but after just a few words, her eyes filled with tears. ". . . *with no evidence of tool marks on the skeletal remains, it is unlikely a saw or butcher knife was used to cut up the body.*" Hailey imagined mother and child-in-womb floating in the cool currents of the Atlantic until washing ashore. As awful as it was, Hailey made herself read on, years of courtroom training allowing her to block out the real-life implications of what she was reading and, instead, home in on words she could use as hard evidence.

Hailey looked out the window into the clouds. Funny how a dead body works. Hailey's tears spilled over the rims of her eyes, trickling down one cheek. Nobody cared if she cried, sitting here tucked away in seat 11A, between the windows and the sky.

Hailey was wrong.

"Man problems? Husband being an a-hole?" Seeing the tears spill, the guy sitting next to her finally had an in. The seats were so tight in coach, he was practically in her lap and tried to spark up various conversations with Hailey ever since he'd grabbed her carry-on to hoist it into the overhead compartment.

Hailey had thanked him politely for the help but extricated herself from what was obviously a pass. But now he had another "in." He'd spotted a tear. Quickly wiping her eyes with the little square napkin a Delta attendant placed beneath her hot tea, she answered, "No, I don't have a husband. I never married."

Poor choice of words. His eyes lit up, and now, her in-flight partner seemed to get a second wind.

"*Not married?* A beautiful young girl like you? I'm in shock! I can't believe it! What . . . are the men in New York City blind as bats? Or just plain crazy?"

"You know I flew from New York?" Hailey's antennae went up.

"Well, ma'am. My name is Cloud Sims and I hail from Nebraska, transplanted a few years ago to Manhattan. I was there at the same gate as you this morning. Delta gate number one. So why's a pretty lady like you crying?" Just then, he tried his best to cross his long legs and managed to kick Hailey with the sharp toe of one of his elaborate cowboy boots.

Hailey was tempted to rattle off the medical examiner's autopsy report verbatim, but that didn't seem right. "Oh, I'm just getting ready for a trial and the facts of the case are a little upsetting."

"A trial? Are you a lawyer? Wow! Brains and beauty! You know . . . I always wanted to go to law school . . ."

He was off. Hailey let him talk. It was easier than having a real conversation about why tears had spilled . . . because the autopsy report had stirred up too many memories of another autopsy report.

*Will's autopsy. Her fiancé . . . Will.* Now, suddenly, here he was again in her mind. His blue eyes sparkling, the straight white teeth behind a beautiful smile, laughing, talking, so alive.

Will was in college studying geology. His world ended and Hailey's exploded in one single moment—he was mugged for his wallet and shot five times in his face, neck, and head. It was just before their wedding, and from that moment she existed as a shell of herself . . . pining for a life . . . and a love . . . she could never get back.

Then there was the trial . . . a hazy, awful blur, but Hailey went every day. Ditching her lifelong plan to open a counseling center in the inner city, instead, she went to law school. To put away the bad guys. And one by one, killers, rapist, drug lords, child molesters, the jailhouse population grew to hate her almost as much as she hated them. But after ten years of crusading on behalf of crime victims, she was saturated with it all: the autopsies, the crime scenes, the packed courtrooms . . . and she took off. To Manhattan, to start over fresh, hanging her counseling shingle at a little brownstone in the Village near NYU. The clients started pouring in, and ever since, she'd tried to put Will's murder and all the years in the trenches fighting violent crime behind her.

". . . and that's when I said, 'Good-bye Omaha and hello New York City!' What about you . . . what did you tell me your name was, pretty lady?"

"Hailey. Now let's see, Nebraska. That's the Cornhusker State, right?" She answered as brightly as she could without revealing she had no idea what he'd been saying. That would be rude.

That was all it took. Off he went again, this guy could go on forever. Staring out at the clouds just outside coach seat 11A, she wondered if Will was out there watching her flight, maybe protecting it as it shot across the top of the sky.

Now sitting on the tarmac, the heat was boring through the metal shell of the plane. Finally, a little bell rang twice, like a doorbell, and everyone stood simultaneously to squeeze into the aisle and out the front door of the jet.

Hailey stood, too. Taking the bag Cloud handed down to her with his big, white smile, she merely said, "Thank you." She knew he wanted to stop for a drink after they deplaned, but the memory of Will was too fresh, so she simply merged into the long line of passengers crowding the tiny aisle.

As much as she'd tried to escape a lifetime of homicide, murder weapons, state's exhibits, and courtroom maneuvering, walking up the jetport . . . here she was. Again.

Looking through the glassed walls of the terminal out at the blue sky and waving palm trees, Hailey felt a familiar feeling . . . a spring in her step. Yep . . . here she was again. And all in all . . . it felt pretty good.

It was nearly 2 PM. Not at all her normal time to exercise, but Kacynthia Sikes was not about missing a workout.

Kacynthia speed-walked. Fists pumping, booty grinding, legs and back at unnatural, upright positions and she'd done it every single day for the last 814 days and was not about to stop now. At sixty-seven years of age, a very private number only her banker knew, Kacynthia was one of the very first Penthouse Pets back when Bob Guccione launched the magazine in the U.S. in 1969.

Her spread had been such a hit that six years later, he invited her back. The "1975 Kacynthia Sikes Pictorial," as she chose to call it, was the first time ever that *Penthouse* had beaten *Playboy* on U.S. newsstands. She took sole credit for that.

Kacynthia was extremely proud of that particular piece of porn trivia. She often mentioned it whenever it fit appropriately (even remotely) into conversations, say, on the elevator at her East Gordon condo—shoehorned in just behind the house where the famed lyricist Johnny Mercer once lived—or in line at Kroger, or when getting her hair care products at Sally Beauty Supply. Basically . . . anywhere.

There would be no way Kacynthia Sikes (she often referred to herself in the third person) was going to let her body go to pot. Nor did she plan on spending time alone in her little condo. There was only one answer.

*Speed walking.* So every morning when she believed the most single "gentlemen" were up and about, possibly heading to the grocery store, the park, to work, out to breakfast, Kacynthia was ready. She arose early in the morning, well before seven, and carefully applied full makeup including eyeliner and individual false eyelashes, top and bottom.

Last in her regime, she combed out her long bottle-red hair, added a firm coat of Chanel Polo Red lipstick (some people thought redheads shouldn't wear red, but Kacynthia disagreed vehemently), slipped on her golden-nude colored support leotard with matching leggings, and off she went.

She walked, perfectly poised, backbone straight as a flagpole, long red hair dangling down her back, all throughout Savannah's business and historical districts. Yes, she was pushing seventy, but it only took one. One man. Life with a rich boyfriend would be a lot easier than life alone in her studio condo.

Kacynthia took the rules of speed walking to heart. The correct posture for power walking was very important as this helped Kacynthia with the task at hand, i.e., finding a man and keeping a tight butt at the same time. She worked hard to follow all the required steps she'd read about in her favorite magazine, *Longevity*.

Above all, Kacynthia had to stand straight up on her right foot, neither bending her back nor leaning forward in the least. She must always look directly ahead while walking and avoid looking downward. She kept her chin absolutely parallel to the ground, neither high nor low.

When walking, generally the hips rock from side to side, but in power walking, such swinging of the hips—no matter how provocative Kacynthia believed her hips to be—would ultimately slow her down. With elbows bent to ninety degrees and kept close to her body, she swung her arms forward, making sure they never crossed her chest. Never, never overstriding, Kacynthia concentrated on every step, dramatically rolling each foot forward, pushing off with her toes. Keeping all her moves synchronized was actually extremely complicated.

Today, however, Kacynthia was trying a revised tactic in her manhunt. The suburbs.

So having parked her baby-blue BMW along a curb in the Williamsburg subdivision, she set out walking, hoping against hope to meet a fellow exercise enthusiast of the opposite sex interested in a relationship with a former Penthouse Pet. He'd also need to have a big, fat bank account, or at least a low mortgage and full insurance coverage.

Several male drivers had in fact slowed down upon spotting Kacynthia strutting along the sidewalk bordering a long procession of three-bedroom, two-bath ranch houses. But they were mostly just puzzled at the shiny spandex legs and the long red hair combined with obvious breast implants. You didn't get much of that in the Savannah suburbs.

The problem was that today was trash day, so she was winding her way through large green Herby Curby trash carts on wheels. All the ins and outs made for an incredible show, which was Kacynthia's original intent, anyway.

Yet two hours into it, no one had even honked the horn or whistled at her. Plus, Kacynthia's mascara was running. She didn't have to see it; she could feel it. Her pink and green Maybelline Great Lash was the best, hands down. It glided on smoothly and gave her the "full lash look" she wanted without clumps or globs.

But unfortunately, Kacynthia opted against waterproof. And now she was sweating like a pig. Rivulets of mascara were running down the corners of her eyes. Mascara stains plus profuse sweating, both big no-nos when trying to attract men.

It was so darn hot! She was close to packing up, heading home, and forcing herself to forget men entirely.

It was then she spotted it. Or them. Legs. Sticking out from under a garage door.

Was this some macabre joke? Were those legs real? At least they were a man's legs. Maybe it wasn't all bad, after all.

Kacynthia took a few steps off the sidewalk toward the legs.

*Was that blood?*

It *was* blood and lots of it, surrounding the two legs in pale tan polyester slacks and dark shoes and socks.

"Sir?" No answer. She knelt down a little lower. "Sir?"

Whipping out her micro-cell tucked into the side of her bra, Kacynthia punched the digits 911.

"Savannah emergency dispatch. What's your emergency?"

"Hello. This is *Miss* Kacynthia Sikes." Even in times of emergency, she remembered to stress the "Miss" part.

"Repeat, ma'am?"

"Oh yes, it is me, *the* Kacynthia Sikes."

"I'm not understanding you. Did you just say 'the swimming pool bites'?"

"No, I did not say 'the swimming pool bites.' I clearly said I am *the* Kacynthia Sikes."

"Oh. I heard you that time. Your name is Cindy Sikes."

Kacynthia recoiled at the sound of her name so debased. "No. I am *not* Cindy Sikes . . . I am *Miss Kacynthia Sikes*. I'm sure you've heard of me. WSAV Channel 3 just did an in-depth one-on-one special on me? The eleven o'clock news? Repeated that following Sunday morning? It was a very highly anticipated special on me."

"Did you just say somebody pulled a Saturday night special on you? You mean a .25 caliber semiautomatic? Somebody pulled a gun on you, Cindy? Where are you? I'm sending a patrol car right now. Where's the assailant? Is he still there? What does he look like?"

"No!" Kacynthia's frustration was mounting. "I was in no way attacked! There is no semiautomated . . . or . . . whatever it is you said. I said I was in a TV special about being a Penthouse Pet! Are you one of those phone reps from another country or are you just deaf and dumb?"

With the deaf and dumb comment, the dispatcher asked no more but stoically sent out a radio call message. "That'll be a 24, en route." Savannah police dispatch immediately changed the nature of the 911 call to a "24," a crazy person.

"In any event, I see a pair of legs in a pool of what appears to be human blood and I'm just trying to report it."

"Yes ma'am, what's your location?"

"I'm in the Williamsburg residential community . . . I think . . . just one house down from the intersection of . . . uh . . ." Kacynthia knew her call would be recorded and possibly played back in future TV interviews featuring her, so she tried her best to articulate.

Straining, she could barely make out the green street signs, but she did it. The thought of eyeglasses was never an option for Kacynthia.

*Thank you, LASIK!* she thought quickly before blurting out, "Randolph and Armory!" like she'd just won the clue on Jeopardy.

"Please stay calm, Cindy. Don't move! We're en route." Dispatch didn't want her to move; nobody in the Williamsburg residential community needed a 24 wandering through their backyard.

"It's *Kacynthia*. Not Cindy." She enunciated carefully and spoke loudly as if she were talking to a deaf person.

*What was wrong with these people?*

Kacynthia Sikes kept her thoughts to herself and promptly dialed WSAV. She pressed *3 for viewers to call in breaking news stories as they happen, and to become part of the story themselves!

Speaking breathlessly into her cell, Kacynthia described in detail the pair of legs and the pool of blood to somebody who answered the phone at WSAV. And this time, she got the street address off the mailbox at the end of the pair of legs' driveway.

"Yes . . . I'm standing here in a golden-nude workout leotard . . . I'm at 3443 Randolph Drive. My name is Kacynthia Sikes . . . your station just did a special on me. Penthouse Pet?"

The cameras would be there any minute. Kacynthia just adored those trucks with the satellite thingies that reached up into the sky.

Wiping away the mascara from under her eyes, almost involuntarily, Kacynthia sucked in her stomach and poked out her chest.

The Savannah airport was so busy it didn't seem that different from the crush of people back at LaGuardia. Pulling her roller board behind her, Hailey wound through knots of travelers complaining about the wait for luggage. Overhearing snippets of their conversations, she was glad she was a light packer.

Just as she cleared the last claim belt, she saw him in the distance . . . a familiar figure with his back to her. But between the six feet three inches of frame, broad shoulders, and a dark fedora, she'd know him anywhere. It was Fincher, Garland Fincher, her longtime investigator and sometimes bodyguard.

Together, the two of them had worked felony investigations from the most filthy and dangerous inner-city housing projects to high-society murders along West Paces Ferry Road. It all raced through her head . . . at the crime lab or murder scene, prepping one case after the next, cruising the strip in an undercover county car, digging bullets out from under a swing set playground in the projects. Combing over crime scenes together, measuring blood spatter, staring in windows, late nights and early mornings at every diner and fast-food stop in metro Atlanta. Coffee, coffee, and more coffee . . . it all blended . . . year after year . . . each case spilling over onto the next.

Together, they forged a reputation as being unbeatable. The Odd Couple—that's what they were called around the Fulton County Courthouse. Fincher was a dark-skinned black ex-Marine, six three, ripped, and wouldn't even drive to church without packing heat, hip and ankle. Hailey barely topped five one, and was slight of frame, blonde, and always unarmed.

Secretly, she still recoiled at the sight of handguns, ever since Will's murder years before. Realizing her own aversion, she forced herself to make target practice a routine, and she ranked as one of the best shots in Fulton County, male or female. She hated them nonetheless and even in court, when guns came in as evidence, she held them lightly only when absolutely necessary, as if they burned her fingertips.

For some reason, though, Hailey had packed her shoulder holster. It was specially designed, made of black, flexible Lycra and Velcro. Leather was often used, but it always bulked up and was easy to spot outside clothing. Not Hailey's.

It all shot across her mind in just seconds. As if he knew she was there, he turned just as she walked up to him.

"Need a ride?" He said it casually, like they'd just seen each other yesterday.

"Yeah. I do." She let go of her roller board and in a split second, he picked her up and whirled around with her as if she were as light as a feather. Landing on both feet, they hugged. It seemed like the longest . . . and the shortest hug she'd ever had.

"Fincher, I don't get it. Why are you here?"

"Same as you, Hailey. The Julie Love murder trial. The prosecutors told me yesterday they needed you on the stand. I'm here because I arrested the whiney little SOB. He was up in Atlanta with his new girlfriend . . ."

"He's out of town with a girlfriend . . . that soon after his wife disappeared?"

"Yep. Adams was in Atlanta for one of those 'weekend getaways' they always advertise in *USA Today*. It's something like a dinner and a weekend stay at one of the luxury hotels. So long story short, Adams had a coupon."

"So he's cheap?"

"Extremely, but he doesn't let his lady friends find that out. He had a coupon for the hotel and a coupon for the swanky dinner he took the girlfriend to. I got him the next morning, getting his hair highlighted . . ."

"His hair highlighted?" She didn't even try to hide the ridicule.

"I knew you'd love that part, Hailey . . . him getting his hair done while search crews are still out looking for his wife and baby. Anyway, so they find the body down off Tybee and send an APB out for Adams. Got a tip about the salon there in Buckhead, some fancy-schmancy place. I race over and make the collar."

"How'd he take it, Fincher?"

"Take what?"

"The arrest. You know, him knowing that somebody, specifically the police, saw through his BS."

"The arrest." Fincher let out a laugh. "Cool as a cucumber, Hailey. Slick would be a better word to describe him . . . tall, good-looking . . . and slick. He'll be a hard nut to crack."

"A hard nut to crack? Fincher, he won't crack."

"Why do you say that, Hailey? I've watched you crack the best of them on the stand."

"Number one, Todd Adams will never take the stand. He could never withstand cross-examination on all his lovers. Plus, his where-abouts the day Julie Love goes missing are just too sketchy. His story doesn't make sense. Then, he places himself too close to where the body eventually washes up! Fishing!"

She thought for a moment before going on. "Second, his whole life is a lie. The whole scholarship story was a lie. He got kicked off the team after one semester. Couldn't cut it. No discipline. All the lies he told his wife and her family, his family, his friends, and all the other women . . . they'll all come crashing down on him like a house of cards. He can't be a liar in front of his own family, his friends. Put money on it. He'll stick to his story no matter what."

"You think?"

"I don't think it, I know it. He's got to save face, so his family and friends can still have the option of believing he was framed . . . that he's wrongly accused."

"So when did you know he was guilty?"

"The first night I heard about the story."

"The first night? How?"

"It was the dog part. You know . . . the dog getting loose in the park while Julie was walking it, but the dog leash was still hanging by the door. She's nine months pregnant. No way would she take the dog to the park without a leash and risk it getting loose. Think of her in that condition, digging through bushes and brambles trying to coax back a dog."

"Ah . . . the dog leash. I get it. So you do want a ride to the Hyatt?"

"How the hay did you know I'm staying there? You know I still have death threats hanging over my head down here left over from my old cases. The guys I put in for twenty to life are starting to get out on early release."

"Hailey . . . I know you always travel under your mother's maiden name. I know all your tricks . . . OK?"

"OK." Hailey smiled.

"You brought your .38, right? I know how you hate to carry, but you made a lot of enemies in the courthouse . . . and the jail."

Hailey winced visibly. Fincher realized he hit a sore spot and felt bad about it. "You hungry?" Switching subjects, Fincher hoisted up her bag over his shoulder with one smooth pull.

"Who's paying?" Hailey flashed a smile.

"The county, baby girl! I got a per diem! Fifty bucks a day!"

"Fifty dollars? Let's go crazy! Pizza or cafeteria?" On county salaries, those two had always been their favorites.

"Pizza. We can even splurge and get a salad."

"Man, Fincher, you sure know how to live!"

The two headed out, side by side, through the automatic door at the front of the Savannah airport and toward the parking deck.

"You're driving the county Crown Vic, I hope?"

"You know it. Nothing like a county-issue Crown Victoria."

"Hey, they're not much on style, but they've got good air conditioners. Don't knock it."

"I'd never knock the Crown Vic! We solved a lot of cases in that old brown Crown Victoria."

"Tell it, Fincher. We sure did."

"We sure did, Hailey."

With their years together hanging between them in the air, they crossed the asphalt lanes in front of passenger pickup, across a concrete island loaded with flowers, and on toward the decks.

Fincher was carrying his police radio in one hand, and the low and monotonous staccato of numbers being called out by police dispatch was the only sound piercing the hot afternoon air. But the shadows were already lengthening; the Savannah sun was just now tipping down toward the horizon. It would be dark soon.

"**M**om, I swear, I didn't do it. I didn't murder her. It wasn't like that at all. I told you what . . ."

"Hush. Shhhhh." She looked around her sharply. "I told you to never mention that . . . that incident again . . . *never.*"

Looking deep into her son's eyes, she held his hand across the table. The trial was set to start tomorrow morning.

Normally, inmates were strictly disallowed to be alone with anyone other than their lawyers, but in this case, the rules had somehow been bent a little. Todd Adams was the most high-profile defendant ever housed at the old Chatham County Jail. So when Adams's mother showed up along with his lawyer, who kept a deep tan year-round and had a penchant for wearing sunglasses indoors and out, the jailhouse guards always gave her a few minutes alone with her son . . . without lawyers hovering around and talking incessantly as lawyers are known to do.

The very last thing this jail needed was a celebrity lawyer like Mikey DelVecchio calling a press conference to complain about jail conditions. That would lead to an "investigative report" on some news magazine show, and the county sheriff's goose would be cooked.

The jail had frequent "incidents" it tried its best to keep on the down low. Just the other day, a murder suspect, "Ninja" Hassan DeMay, nearly beat one of the guards to death. DeMay was allegedly angry over marinara sauce on his chili mac dinner and unleashed on a rookie guard.

Then yesterday a shakedown uncovered a deadly homemade shank, fashioned from weather stripping and the cellophane wrapped around food trays. The aluminum metal stripping had been sharpened to a jagged point by scratching it against the concrete floor.

Just the kinds of things Mikey DelVecchio need not know anything about. Ever since he represented some Hollywood starlet on a shoplifting charge, he'd been in the news, celebrity treatment all around.

And even though the star got convicted . . . no matter. DelVecchio went on to represent another Hollywood A-Lister on DUI, then another for going on a drunk and naked rampage in a fancy New York hotel room with a hooker, then a doped-up pop star. Even when he lost, somehow, the convictions never stuck to DelVecchio, just the "glamour."

Nobody knew exactly how, but likely thanks to *Snoop* vaulting the story to national headlines, Todd Adams's family lassoed DelVecchio into representing their son. The word was that whenever DelVecchio flew into town, he holed up at a five-star hotel, ate and drank like a king, charged it all to Adams's family, and went to his room with two or three girls on his elbows.

Everybody in Savannah seemed to "know" Adams did it. Julie was a hometown favorite. She was the public high school's homecoming queen and everybody remembered it. She was sweet and beautiful and the talk had been, for quite a long time, that Adams ran around on her. But nobody would ever dream of hurting Julie's feelings by even alluding to her husband's unfaithfulness.

Now he was here, in the Chatham County Jail. And with a lawyer like Mikey DelVecchio, nobody could touch him. He got the kid-glove treatment . . . special food, private cell, magazines, books, extra TV time, and perks like this—long visits alone with his mom in one of the inmate-lawyer conference rooms.

"Shhh, baby. No need to go through it all again. I know what happened. I'm your mother . . . I believe you."

"But Mom, why would I kill anybody, much less Julie. She was . . . amazing . . ."

"She was, she was! We all know that, and we all know you would never, never have intentionally harmed her. Why, nobody doubts that you loved Julie!"

"I did, Mom, I did!"

"And the jury is going to see that!"

"I mean Mom, they don't have any proof I ever . . ."

"No! Don't say another word. You've already told me everything I need to know. And I believe you, son! So not another word."

Adams's mother looked over her shoulder and quickly glanced around the room, convinced they'd be overheard. Sheriffs were the worst, always listening, nosy . . . busybodies, no doubt about it. Didn't they have lives of their own? It was none of their business what went on between her and her boy.

"And son? No more outbursts." Tish Adams spoke in an urgent whisper. She cut her eyes toward the guards. "After what happened the other day, we can't afford another slipup . . . No matter how badly you feel about Julie's accident, *it wasn't your fault*. You absolutely *cannot* continue droning on and on back here about it. It will be misconstrued! For instance, that horrible prosecutor could take what you said the other day, no matter how innocent, and twist it and turn it and use it against you! You've got to be quiet back here! And no talking to cellmates anymore! Haven't I told you about that? And these . . . these *guards* . . . they're not your friends!"

Glancing sideways, she was convinced the guard to her left was listening. He'd done it before. He practically had an antenna on the top of his head, craning his neck toward Todd and herself as far as it could physically stretch.

"But Mom . . . I'm not talking about what happened to Julie . . ."

"Didn't you hear me tell you last time to *shut up* . . . these walls have ears . . . are you blind?" Again, Tish jerked her head toward the guards at the door.

"Mom, I'm not talking about Julie now, I'm talking about Cynthia."

His mom stared at him blankly. "Cynthia, Mom . . . Cindy. Remember her from high school? She was in the baton corps? Remember before every football game they'd run out on the field . . . one time she had a baton with fire on the ends and she . . ."

"Stop it! For Pete's sake . . . stop it! Yes, I remember the baton with fire on the ends. And yes of course I remember her, Wallace and Helen Gresham's daughter from the Country Club. She would have been a much better match for you than Julie Love. I tried to tell you Julie was all wrong for you. Yes . . . what about Cynthia? She always wore that little royal blue sequined short set for the dance routines. Too tight and too short, I always told your father that . . . but still. But what does she have to do with anything?"

"I mean Mom, they won't bring *that* up will they?"

"Who? Will who bring up what?" Her eyes furrowed together so closely they nearly created a single brow over her eyes.

"Mom . . ." Todd Adams looked uncomfortably around the tiny room, then past his mom and back toward the guards. "You know . . . that we were, uh, *friends*."

"Who were friends? You and Cynthia? Of course you were, you knew each other from high school. You had lots of friends, dozens of friends, of course you did. You were the most popular boy in school as I recall."

"No Mom, I don't mean that . . . I mean do you think they will bring up that we were . . . um, dating?"

The look on his mother's face was unreadable, like a mask. Not a single nerve moved, she didn't even blink. Not once. She stared straight at him as if she were actually looking through his head at the wall behind him.

"Dating? Cynthia? You dated Cynthia in high school. Yes. I know that. What would that have to do with anything at all?"

"I mean, they could argue it was motive, Mom . . ."

"But that was years ago. That's hardly motive, that doesn't even make sense."

"Mom, it wasn't years ago. It was last year . . ." Adams looked down and to the side, his voice lowered to a whisper.

"Last year? And now you tell me? And is the expression 'dating' your word for holing up at some out-of-the-way motel? You let another girl drag you into her problems? The Cynthia girl is divorced from a pool guy and has three kids. Is that the same Cynthia?"

"He's not a pool guy. He owns his own pool company, Mom . . ."

"Like that makes it better?" She spat it out in a whisper but with the venom of a snakebite. "If you keep your mouth shut, they'll never know."

Why did her son keep getting duped by women who were only after one thing? The Adams money. The Cynthia girl rearing her ugly head now. And on the heels of the flood of Julie Love headlines.

Everyone in town had known it . . . Julie Love was a "catch" at the time the two had gotten engaged. She was the golden girl who made all As, worked at a food bank, and attended church every Sunday with her parents. Little witch was even a Girl Scout. And she was the homecoming queen, which apparently meant something even though it was at the public school. A drama queen as well, always making a big production over her brother. He was handicapped since birth, confined to a wheelchair. Julie Love insisted on carrying him to nearly every major event she attended.

Most groom's mothers did not have a starring role in their son's weddings, which seemed so unfair to Tish. She took it upon herself to plan the whole thing for poor Julie. The girl was hopeless at event planning. Julie had actually started with what she called an "intimate gathering of family and friends." Ridiculous. Why even *bother* to get married? "Intimate gatherings" were not picked up by the *Savannah Chronicle*. Fat chance. The couple wouldn't be able to *buy* their way into the wedding or engagement announcements. Of course, Julie Love insisted that didn't matter.

An "intimate gathering" screamed "shabby and cheap" to Tish. Once Julie was confronted with the Adams guest list, things began to look up. Not another single body could've fit into the sanctuary of the Savannah First United Methodist Church. By the time all the Adams guests were tallied, Julie tearfully announced, *at an Adams family dinner no less*, that her family couldn't afford a big reception. Tish could still remember the moment even now, when Julie conjured fat tears to roll down her cheeks into the linen napkin in her lap. Her voice trembling, she said her mom and dad simply couldn't swing it financially.

What a little liar. Tish and her husband ended up footing half the bill for the party. Tish was still stewing over it. The papers—yes, Tish called in a favor and got the wedding details in the *Chronicle* after all—the papers said Julie Love was a beautiful bride . . . a beautiful *fake* as far as Tish was concerned.

In fact, if only the world could see through Julie Love's façade, they'd realize this whole mess was actually Julie's fault. She was so simpering, so mealymouthed, so saccharine sweet. Tish had watched it for years. In her own mind, she often called it "The Julie Love Show." Everything about the girl was a put-on. Even using her handicapped brother as a prop. Pushing him around at public events, fussing over him as if she really cared. It was a ploy. A ploy to get people to notice her, to love her, to get on all their good sides.

Julie never, not for one second, fooled Tish. She could see through that the first time Todd had brought her over to the house to meet his mother. She had taken Todd away, put on that spectacle of a wedding where Tish was a nothing. Julie never let Todd spend time with his family anymore. Then she tried to lock him into a loveless marriage with a *baby* of all things . . . and now, *this!*

Anybody in their right mind could see what kind of boy Todd really was. Why, he had it all . . . good looks, charm, education, manners, a good job . . . everything!

The truth was, Todd had always been too good for Julie Love. Tish knew it and so did the whole neighborhood. And here they were, all lined up in court and siding against Todd! With friends like these . . .

"But Mom . . ."

"No 'buts.' Everything will work out, you'll see, my precious boy. Now . . . let's talk about what you should wear tomorrow for court. That's *all* you have to worry about. Do you understand?"

He nodded, shutting up so his mom could talk, like always. It was easier that way.

"It's all going to be OK. You just wait and see. You've got the best lawyer money can buy. Listen to me . . . listen to your mother. Now I'm going to get those photos for you to put up in your room."

"It's not a room, Mother, it's a cell. *A jail cell.*"

"I know that, dear, but I prefer to refer to it as your room. And that's how you should think of it too, like a dorm room."

"A dorm room? Are you crazy?"

"Calm down, son. No need for the sheriffs to hear you agitated, is there? Remember, I went to nursing school before I married your father and had you. Want me to get a doctor's order for a sedative?"

"You never finished."

Tish gave her son a look that would've scared anyone else into cold silence before she spoke. "Thank you for reminding me that I gave up a career for you and your father. And no, dear . . . I'm not crazy. I'm just trying to make the best of a bad situation and that's what you need to do, too. Now let's get those pictures of Julie Love up in your room."

"My cell."

"The power of positive thinking, Todd, positive thinking."

"Mother. I'm behind bars on two murder one counts. My trial starts in the morning. They had to bus jurors in from another county. What's positive about that?"

Todd Adams's voice took on a whining quality. His mother didn't notice.

"What's positive? The fact that the world will hear what a wonderful son and husband you are. They'll hear about your golf scholarship, your job, your degree, your beautiful home and family . . . that's what's positive."

"And I don't want those pictures up in my cell."

*"Room."*

"OK . . . room . . . whatever! I don't want those pictures up in my *room!*"

"But why? That doesn't make any sense."

"Because . . ." He paused. "They make me depressed. I'm already miserable in this place. Crappy food, hardly any TV, and it's not even cable . . ."

"But photos of you and Julie Love will remind you of all the happy times—"

"No they won't. They'll remind me that I'm here in jail because she's dead. They'll remind me of home . . . of what I'm missing."

"*Shut up!*" It came out like a hiss. Tish turned in her seat to look back at the guard at the door. He was pale and wimpy. The way he'd kept peering in through the glass door, glaring through a hideous set of thick glasses . . . she was positive he'd eavesdropped on every single word she and her son had so stupidly uttered.

His mother's tone made him sit up straight in his chair and stop the whining.

"How will it look in front of a jury when they find out you don't have a single photo of Julie Love up in your room?"

"Cell. My cell, Mother."

The two sat in sulky silence, each staring the other down. Finally, Tish Adams broke the silence.

"Your father and I didn't work our fingers to the bone to have our son arrested, much less convicted for first-degree murder. This absolutely *will not* happen to our family. Now you listen to me and you listen good. You will put up these photos and you'll keep them up. And remember, no friends. Nobody in this facility is your friend, not the guards, not the inmates, not even the chaplain. You have one friend, Todd, and that's me. Your mother."

He wouldn't look up, instead gazing down at his knees like a corrected schoolboy.

"Now wipe that look off your face. Your father's about to come in to visit and then DelVecchio. I'll get the photos. Understood?"

Todd Adams wouldn't answer.

"I said, *understood*?"

"Understood, Mother."

"Good. You'll see, sweetheart. And don't worry about the Cynthia girl. That will have no bearing on this whatsoever. It was just a stupid mistake on your part, really just careless. It was ancient history . . . all the way back to high school. Nobody cares about that. And, truth be told, if you hadn't been married to someone . . . someone like *her* . . . you'd have never sought a shoulder to cry on. That's all it was really, just a shoulder to cry on. This will all turn out just fine. You'll be out of here in no time and back home where you belong. With your father and me."

Todd Adams said nothing.

Undeterred by her son's lack of enthusiasm, she went on. "Mark my words, son, we *will* hold our heads up high in this town again. We *will* show our faces at church the very first Sunday you are out of this . . . this dungeon, and we *will* march right up the center aisle and onto the front row. You'll see."

"Mom, if you hate this town so much, why don't we just move once this is over?"

The look she gave him should have killed him, but it didn't. In fact, it seemed to have no impact at all.

Looking deftly over her shoulder, she plowed forward a little more loudly and a lot more cheerfully. "I'll bring the pictures of Julie over in the morning. The wedding photo, in particular, will look perfect right over your bed. On second thought, maybe we should go with, I mean, you'd probably want the sonogram."

He looked up at his mother blankly. "The what?"

"The *sonogram . . . of the baby . . .* from the doctor's office, you dolt." The words came out in another hiss that caused the guards to look toward them.

Tish Adams straightened her spine, smoothed down the pale yellow skirt of her matching Talbots sweater and skirt set, and pulled up the corners of a smile. She methodically gathered together her purse, papers, and a gorgeous set of faux tortoiseshell Chanel sunglasses. She stood up to leave. Brushing past the guards, she smiled brightly. "Hello, gentlemen! How nice to see you this morning! Have a *blessed* and *wonderful* day, you two."

Hailey lowered the window to let the breeze blow onto her face and rush through her hair. It was the exact opposite of the canned, recirculated air on the plane. Leaving the airport exit, grass on either side of the I-95 waved gently in the breeze. A lonely seagull flew just ahead of the Crown Vic, floating on a current against a blue sky.

The hot afternoon was interrupted when squawks on Fincher's police radio ripped into a steady stream, the brief jumble of numbers repeatedly followed by an address or a truncated sentence.

Police spoke in a language of numbers, each one signaling a different police call: car accident, burglary, stolen car, and so on. The numeric talk was so pervasive on the job it became second nature, and they often used it in regular speech.

"Turn it up, Fincher."

"No, little girl, this is none of our business. This isn't Atlanta."

"Come on. Turn it up. I can't help it. I have to know!"

"OK. But curiosity killed the cat . . ."

"And satisfaction brought it back!" She had a comeback ready. Fincher reached his right hand across and turned up the volume on his police radio.

"Repeat . . . 48-4 . . . 50-48. 48-4 . . . 50-48." The voice from dispatch sounded urgent.

"Hailey, that's a—"

"I know what it is. Person dead."

Dispatch interrupted again. ". . . 3443 Randolph Drive . . . corner Randolph and Armory."

"All units in the vicinity, signal 63. Repeat . . . signal 63. Code 3. Repeat signal 63."

Hailey felt a shock go down her body and turned quickly to Fincher. "It's a 63, Fincher." A sick feeling burned in the pit of her stomach. 63 meant officer down.

Suddenly, Fincher jerked the wheel to the right, steering the car at the last second across two lanes of speeding cars and up an exit ramp off the interstate.

"What are you doing, Finch?"

"I know that street. I know that address. I've been there. My army buddy's off Randolph. We were in Iraq together."

"And?" Hailey didn't need to finish the sentence.

"And we're going over there."

"Fincher, you just got back from Iraq. Vickie will kill you if she finds out you headed to an active homicide scene you didn't have to go to. Forget you, she'll kill me for letting you go!"

"We have to go. I'm not standing by. It's a cop down. But I'll let you out. I don't want you to be there. You're not even armed."

Hailey unbuckled her seat belt.

"Hey! I'm doing eighty miles an hour! Put your belt back on!" He shouted it across the three feet between them. Ignoring him, Hailey bent over the front seat and reached into the back of the car, and leaning lower, unzipped her roller board.

Fincher took a sharp right turn and Hailey slid backward, her head nearly slamming into the back seat. Reaching deep into her bag, between layers of folded clothes, she yanked out a single item. Not bothering to re-zip the bag, she turned face forward and belted herself back into the passenger's seat. Finch spotted her black Lycra shoulder holster, special-made for Hailey, clenched in her hand.

"Hailey, you can't go unarmed. You don't have a gun for that, do you?"

"I know you, Fincher. You're packing hip, shoulder, and ankle. So don't waste time."

Keeping one hand firmly on the wheel, he reached down to his ankle and with one quick snap of Velcro, handed her a .38.

"You still hate guns, Hailey?"

"I don't know what you mean by that." Hailey tensed, keeping her eyes fixed on the road ahead.

"Every time you see a gun, you think about Will. Just like in the courtroom. The sight of a gun still makes you sick . . . right? I bet you haven't dated one guy more than five times up in Manhattan. Have you? I knew moving to New York and getting out of the business wouldn't change anything. Different place, same Hailey Dean . . ."

She didn't answer, raising her window, looking out as the houses passed, watching street signs knowing Randolph would pop up at any minute.

"This is it. 3443 Randolph."

He was right. Hailey clicked the safety belt and, bending forward at the waist, slipped on the holster made especially for her. Adjusting it over and around quickly, sliding the .38 into place, Hailey unlocked the car door and stepped out into waves of heat.

Hailey felt the old, odd energy in her right hand . . . her gun hand. It felt like a snake inside her was coiled and ready to strike.

*Where was the dead body?*

Passing a WSAV news crew pressing a microphone toward a redhead dressed in spandex, Finch and Hailey walked steadily up the driveway. They found a lone officer bent down on his knees, inspecting two legs protruding from underneath the garage door. For one bizarre moment, Hailey felt like Dorothy inspecting an anonymous set of legs so totally out of place, neatly peeking out.

Pushing all thoughts of Oz aside, she stepped forward. This was no movie in Technicolor. This was the real thing, a dead body. And that body was decomposing literally by the minute in the Savannah heat.

The officer walked over to the corner of the door and started fiddling with a handle. Apparently, nothing was budging.

"Hi, officer." Finch held out his right hand to one of the officers standing on the driveway. "I'm Garland Fincher from the Fulton District Attorney's Office here for the Todd Adams trial. We were driving in from the airport and we heard the call. Came to see if you needed any help."

Finch spotted the other cop glance at Hailey. "And this is a former ADA, Hailey Dean."

But the three turned quickly at the sound of another two squad cars careening into the front yard, one after the next. Hailey actually thought for a moment they'd have a pileup right there on the front lawn.

A third car, unmarked but also sporting a quickly rotating blue light popped onto the front dash, arrived just behind them. Plainclothes detectives emerged.

"Hi, everybody." One of the sheriffs approached and said it calmly, like he was reading a quasi-interesting story out of the Savannah paper over the breakfast table. He didn't seem to be the least bit ruffled by the pair of human legs on the paved driveway two feet from his own.

"You guys don't seem in too much of a hurry to get him out from under there." Fincher said it in a casual way, not at all accusatory.

"Well. He's dead. Plain and simple. No two ways about it. First thing I did after securing the scene was feel his ankle. Cold as a brick. So, no rush. No rush at all. Plus, I can't get the darn door up. Probably need some sort of a tool. Maybe if I jam some hedge clippers in the lift, that'll do it." This guy made Hailey think of Barney Fife. And not in a good way.

Hailey stepped back off the neat cement drive and onto the manicured grass, perfectly edged. She looked not down at the pair of legs, but higher up the garage door.

"Hey, guys. What's this?" Hailey stepped over the legs, careful to avoid the pool of blood in which they were lying, and pointed to a hole in the garage door.

"I don't know. Oh yeah, Trimble's the name." Barney Fife stuck out his right hand to Fincher first, then Hailey.

"Well, don't get the hedge clippers just yet. You may not need them. I don't have a garage door where I live, but I think this is one of those emergency-release mechanisms."

"Huh? I never heard of that." Trimble looked stumped. Fincher was quiet, likely because he hadn't either, but didn't want to admit it to Hailey.

"I don't get it. What's your point? What does it mean to us?" Trimble seemed good-natured, but obviously felt Hailey's observation was a waste of time.

"A lot of people get them for these door openers just in case the electricity goes out, so they'll always be able to get in or out of the garage. It's kind of a lock you install directly onto the door." Hailey pointed up as she talked.

"Maybe I'm crazy, but I still don't get it. This baby's as tight as a drum." Trimble stared up at the garage door.

"If we can make it work . . . I think the way it functions is that a cable, a cord, is attached to the door opener emergency-release lever, and when you unlock this thing, you can pull the cable and it releases the drivetrain belt."

"I'm game." Trimble looked at Fincher, clearly expecting him and Hailey to give it a try. He looked over at the EMTs. "Hey guys, no need for a saw, I got it all figured out. No rush. It's Alton Turner and he's DOA anyway."

Trimble obviously wasn't the oversensitive type.

None of the cops made a move, so Fincher stepped up. "OK. Here we go." Picking up one of the bricks edging the driveway, he gave a mighty heave and knocked the lock off the door. Hailey was right. When Finch grabbed the lock mechanism itself and pulled, the door released.

And there he was, lying there . . . Alton Turner . . . the other half, finally revealed. After an initial, instinctive recoil upon seeing a dead human body, the detectives immediately started to circle it, staying a guarded few feet away. A camera started flashing.

A black standard-issue Saturn pulled into the driveway. When the driver's door opened, out stepped what was obviously an undercover detective. He was definitely a cop. No question about it. He had that look, easily identifiable by fellow cops and, ironically, criminals alike. To a trained eye, undercover cops stood out. The younger officers were buff and muscled from beating the streets day and night. The older cops were pale and soft, parked at desk jobs and counting the days until retirement.

This one was neither young nor old and clearly this was not his first crime scene. He walked up, sized up the whole scene carefully without a word, and then, without acknowledging the rest of them, he turned directly to Trimble.

Keeping a steady gaze on the dead body, he directed his question toward the cop. "So, what do we know, Trimble?" His tone was cool but not cold, businesslike but not impersonal.

"Well, Lieutenant, open and shut. Looks like the poor schmuck caught himself under his own garage door. It ain't an easy way to go, but it's pretty obvious."

The lieutenant looked between Trimble and the body and then, at Hailey and Fincher.

Instinctively, Hailey held out her right hand. "Hi. I'm Hailey Dean, formerly of the Fulton District Attorney's Special Prosecutors Division, inner-city Atlanta."

After a beat a little too long, he held out his own and gave Hailey's hand a warm, firm grasp. "Lieutenant Chase Billings. Good to meet you. I've heard of you, Hailey. What brings you here?"

"I'm here on the Todd Adams trial . . ."

"I'm here for the trial too, but as a witness. I arrested Adams in Atlanta and transported him to Savannah," Fincher chimed in.

"Well, you deserve a medal for the collar on Adams. He did it all right. Julie Love was a sweetheart. Hope they don't blow it at trial." Billings smiled. "But what I meant was, how did you two end up here, on Randolph Drive?"

"To tell you the truth, we heard the 63 and I knew the address. We thought we might be able to help." Fincher looked back at the guy lying there on his garage floor.

"I'm surprised. Lots of off-duty lawmen . . . and ladies," he smiled at Hailey, "would run the other way."

Now Hailey's concern she was intruding began to evaporate. The four of them stepped closer to Alton, lying there, and looked down on his face. It still bore a look of shock, almost surprise, Hailey thought.

Billings's brow furrowed. "Let me understand your theory. So Alton Turner accidentally kills himself on the way to work this morning with a garage door. That's funny . . . he was a very particular kind of guy, if you know what I mean. He kept a desk job . . . sharpened his pencils, crossed his t's and dotted his i's. Very particular, methodical. Probably read the owner's manual over and over. Wonder how this happened."

Not to be outdone, Trimble jumped in. "Just what I said! Yep. That's the way Turner always was, all right. Very particular-like. Must've just got caught under it or something. Just an accident, you know? Probably wasn't paying attention. Had his mind on his coffee cup, I guess."

Lieutenant Billings didn't respond, but instead pulled a spiral notebook out of his jacket and started writing with a yellow number-two pencil that had been stuck down in the spirals. He was intent on his own notes when Trimble piped up again.

"Guess you won't be needing homicide backup. Or the medical examiner's people. It's pretty cut-and-dried. Somehow, Turner screwed up." Trimble took out his radio and held it to his lips to call off further backup. "Trimble to dispatch, Trimble to dispatch . . ."

Hailey couldn't hold back another moment. This was all a colossal mistake. Hailey interrupted Trimble before he could say another word. *Don't call off the ME. It's not an accident. Alton Turner didn't screw up."*

Shoulder radio to his chin mid-sentence, Trimble seemed to freeze with his mouth still half-open. Billings stopped scribbling in his spiral notebook, and all three scrutinized her as if she just sprouted three heads.

"What'd she say? Not an accident? I just don't see, Lieutenant Billings, how Cailee Dean . . ."

"It's Hailey. My name's Hailey Dean." Hailey kept her cool.

"OK. If you say so . . . *Hailey* Dean. How can somebody who knows absolutely nothing about this case or this neighborhood or *Savannah in general*, march onto an active death scene and just announce to me, a seasoned police veteran, that this is *not an accident?*" Little flecks of spittle flying off his lips when he spoke, Trimble was indignant at the suggestion his accident theory could be wrong.

Hailey ignored Trimble's outburst. Looking toward the body, her voice was steady. "This was no malfunction. Accident's all wrong." Hailey stepped around to the other side of the body when she saw it.

"It" being blood. Not the thick, dark red pool, coagulating, surrounding Turner's mutilated body. "It" confirmed what her gut had already told her.

"Look. Look at this." Several feet away from Alton Turner's head, his eyes seemingly staring at the ceiling, Hailey bent down, squatting at the side of Alton's car. Whipping out the silver pen that hung on a cord around her neck, stuck down her bra for safekeeping, she gestured toward the car, pointing but not touching.

"This blood. On the tire of his car. Check out the hubcap. See it?" Hailey pointed toward the hubcap, keeping a few inches away so as not to compromise the evidence.

"So what? So there's blood on the tire. It spattered or something . . ." Trimble's voice trailed off as he struggled to comprehend her point.

"It's not spatter. There's no spatter pattern here or on the garage floor around him. If it had been spatter from the impact of the garage door severing his torso, we'd see spatter elsewhere as well . . . not just on the car's tire. And look at it. It's not a spatter mark. It's a smear. Big difference."

She was met with blank stares.

"My point is, gentlemen, he didn't just 'get caught' under a garage door. That's not what happened. You, yourself, Lieutenant Billings, said he's a very particular guy, probably read the manual over and over. That's what you said, right?"

"Right. I did say that."

"No accident happened here." Hailey stated matter-of-factly and looked Billings in the eyes. "Whatever *did* happen started right here, near the tire . . . not under that garage door." She gestured toward the two halves of Alton Turner.

"Look at the blood pattern close to the car . . . here . . . away from the garage door. That pool of blood wasn't the first mortal wound. That's just a bleed out. The first serious wound was here. He *ended up* under the garage door. You have the blood on the tire and a concentration of blood on the cement here. Something happened to Alton Turner, something awful. And it started here."

The three came over and stood behind her, looking down at the tire.

"Please, Lieutenant. You know it, I know it . . . blood evidence never lies. Call in the ME before we lose more evidence. It's hot out here. The body forensics are being destroyed with every tick of the clock." Hailey looked up from the tire where she was still kneeling.

"She's right. Trimble, radio the ME. Pronto." Billings directed Trimble over his shoulder.

"Will do." Trimble looked miffed, but he did as he was told. Stepping away a few feet, he turned to the side and spoke into his shoulder radio.

"But still, he could have just tripped, fallen, hit his head on the tire . . ." Trimble wasn't ready to give in and continued a steady stream of hypothesizing over his shoulder aimed in their direction.

"Then why would there be blood over here and his body all the way over there?" Hailey pointed to the distance between the bloody tire and the body. "It's a good eight to ten feet away."

"He stumbled?" Fincher interjected.

"Maybe. Maybe he did. And if he did stumble, why? But my guess is, he didn't."

"What did you say you did back at Fulton, Hailey?" Billings wondered out loud.

"She was Chief Special Prosecutor. Ten years. Never lost a case. Over a hundred cases at trial." Fincher answered for her and did so with much more bravado than she would have.

"Never lost a case? In ten years? How'd you do *that*?" Billings gave her a quizzical look as if to size her up.

"Just picked the right juries. That's all. Picked the right juries. They convicted, not me. Plus, they were all guilty." Hailey passed off the compliment.

"Pretty impressive." Billings said it like he meant it.

By now, Hailey was counting off the steps from the bloody tire to where Alton's body lay. She kneeled down and looked.

"Uh-oh. Glad the ME's on the way. Come see." She was looking downward.

Fincher and Billings joined her and squatted down with her beside the body. Both of them squinted at the body in complete silence. Neither wanted to be the first to admit they had no idea what they were supposed to be looking at . . . what she had spotted.

After a few more moments of awkward silence, Billings cracked first. "What do you see that we don't see?"

But he didn't sound the least bit irritated, in fact, he sounded pleased she was there. Lots of lawmen would have booted Hailey from the scene at the get-go out of pure turf protection or simple professional jealousy.

"Well, his head is slightly turned to one side. Look at the back of it. Right there. Do you see it?" Again, without touching anything, she pointed her Tiffany pen toward Turner's head.

The two men peered into Turner's hair toward the back of his head. And sure enough, there it was, under his hair. Blood. Not the same blood from the deep red circle underneath him. This blood was a different color, hidden under Turner's hair, and was clearly from a deep gash head wound.

"See, here? There's a slight abrasion on his forehead, not much but the smudge is the important part."

"The smudge?" Shrugging off all sense of ego, Billings asked the obvious question.

"Yeah, look right here. The black smudge just above his brow. You can make out where he hit his forehead on the tire here, a black tire smudge around it. It's slight, but an abrasion nonetheless."

"So the blood in the back . . ." Billings's voice trailed off. Hailey finished the thought.

"The blood in the back of the head has to be from a blow. The most likely scenario is that he got a blow to the head from behind and fell forward, catching the side of the tire with his forehead. That would account for the black smudge."

They all stood up. She went on. "In fact, I bet he never even made it as far as opening his car door. Is it locked?"

Trimble marched around the far side of the car, reaching out his hand for the driver's door handle.

"*Stop!*" Billings and Hailey shrieked in unison. In a flash, Billings's hand shot out and caught Trimble by the shoulder, pulling him back before he could make contact with the car.

"Don't touch anything! We could ruin potential fingerprint evidence." Billings looked alarmed.

"Fingerprint evidence? Oh, right. Fingerprint evidence." Trimble looked flustered. "I didn't know we *had* fingerprint evidence."

"We don't . . . not yet anyway. But we may, and I don't want the crime techs to report the only prints they find are yours!" Billings gave him a wide smile.

As if by cue, the crime scene investigators pulled up and began to unload from a van elaborately emblazoned with the Savannah Police Department insignia across its side door underneath a depiction of a large, gold police shield. Out they came and headed straight to where Hailey stood with Billings.

They all trouped forward . . . first out was the print team to pick up any latent prints the killer, if there was a killer, may have left behind. In no time, they'd have their dark powder covering every possible surface the killer might have touched, even inadvertently. Light switches, door handles, doorbell, windowpanes and sills, car handles . . . the works.

Fingerprints . . . how Hailey loved them when she was a trial lawyer. If any defendant was stupid enough to leave them behind, they had the same effect as a giant neon sign screaming out "I did it!" for the world to see. They could also match up to hand and palm. Even ridges from the foot could be traced . . . basically comparing the raised portion of the skin, practically invisible to the human eye, but not to the microscope.

Fingerprint impressions could be left behind on surfaces simply by the natural secretions of sweat, ever present on the skin. Even though the word "latent" actually meant hidden, in the crime-scene world it meant any impression left by fingers or palms on a surface, visible or invisible at the time it was left. Different fingerprint patterns, each and every loop, whorl, and arch could be used in evidence at trial.

If crime-scene techs picked them up, that is. If Trimble had wrestled with the door handle, it would have only complicated things.

It was hard enough to ascertain and lift latent prints with no interference whatsoever. Latent prints often exhibit only a portion of the fingertip and can easily be smeared, distorted, or even overlapped by prints from the same or different persons.

The crew converged around Billings.

"Start with the car, the handles, the entire side closest to the kitchen door, then the other side just in case a perp was hiding out over there. Then, of course, the kitchen doorknob, all around it."

"What about the garage door remote?" Hailey suggested it quietly to Billings, who was standing next to her. She didn't want to appear to upstage him.

"Good thinking, Hailey. Any other ideas?" He asked it as if he genuinely wanted her thoughts.

"As a matter of fact, yes." She walked across the garage toward the side of the door, looking up at the door's chain mechanism. "Bet this was an older model, no automatic reverse."

"Right. An automatic reverse," Finch thought out loud as he, too, looked up toward the far upper corner of the door. "The feature that causes a closing door to reverse if it detects something in its path."

"Exactly," Hailey went on. "I can't tell from here whether there is one or not; it would probably be part of the mechanism itself. And if there is an electric eye, like a sensor, it can be programmed to override."

"Anything else?" Billings asked her without the least hint of sarcasm.

"Well, yeah. Look at the lower edge of door itself right above where his body is. The rubber trim is cut away in just that one spot. It's left the sheet metal exposed. If he was simply trapped under the rubber edge of the door, at most he'd have been asphyxiated. But the sharp metal actually cut into the guy's torso. That's an awful lot of coincidences."

Billings was listening intently, jotting more notes in his notebook. She was right. There was a good three feet of the rubber edging gone from the bottom of the door and by the looks of it, it had been cleanly and precisely cut away.

"And what about the manual device, the in-garage mechanism he would have used if things had gone wrong. Maybe the perp used that. And, oh yeah, the driver's side sun visor. I see Turner clipped his garage door remote to that; maybe the perp fumbled and touched the visor. I mean, hey, it's worth a shot . . . you never know where you might just get a fingerprint." Hailey was looking into the car though the front window.

Leaving the immediate vicinity of the car, she began to prowl around the garage, staring intently at everything from power tools to golf clubs to a bicycle pump. Fincher knew what she was doing . . . looking for something . . . anything that might have rendered the blow to Alton Turner's head.

"You're right. Maybe the guy did use Turner's own remote." Billings bent down over her shoulder to look into Alton's car as well.

"Might as well do the whole area around the steering wheel and the window too, just to be safe, don't you think, Hailey?" Fincher weighed in.

"Yep." Billings spoke before she did. He called out the orders to the crime-scene techs over his shoulder. They immediately set their black suitcases—looking for the world like big makeup kits—down on the garage floor, kneeled down, and began unloading the tools of the trade.

Out came the dark powder that would soon be strewn everywhere, made of pure, nearly black ground graphite. Then, the Zephyr brushes, resembling a very delicate shaving brush, would apply the latent powder. Then finally, the precut, one-inch fingerprint lifting tape.

The trick was to dip the Zephyr brush into the graphite, tap its handle gently on the beaker to get rid of excess powder, and lightly brush the powder all over the area in question: in this case, Alton Turner's Corolla, inside and out, the garage door itself, and its remote opener. Then a magnifying glass would be used to determine if there were, in fact, any prints left behind.

Hailey stood watching. She'd always been fascinated with prints and loved producing them to juries. The medical examiner's detectives had also arrived and were busily measuring distances from here to there, the car tire to the body, the body to the kitchen door, the blood on the tire from Alton's bloody, upper torso, and so on.

"Hey, guys. Want to take a look inside with me?"

Billings was heading through the door leading into Alton's kitchen.

"Sure!" They said it at practically the same time.

The three walked carefully into Alton's kitchen, scoping the room to take in every single detail. Finch whipped out a writing pen from his pocket and used it to open the fridge.

"Check this out. Every single thing except the milk is in Tupperware and labeled."

Staring into the highly organized fridge, she checked out the contents. Lettuce in a crisper, butter in its specifically designed niche in the fridge door alongside eggs also in their designated holders, canned drinks stacked in two neat, horizontal dispensers . . . every-thing in its place.

Finch pushed the fridge door shut and turned toward the sink. Hailey followed but something caught her eye. Alton's calendar taped squarely onto the upper right portion of the refrigerator. Today was the 24th. But his calendar said the 25th.

That wasn't like Alton Turner at all, based on what Hailey could surmise. Where was the tear-away sheet for today?

Hailey opened the cabinet under the sink and, predictably, found a plastic kitchen trash can hidden under. Checking in, there was only one thing at the bottom of a white plastic trash can liner. A single paper packet of Dixie Crystals sugar, opened and empty. Alton must have had coffee just before he died.

Hailey turned on her heel to continue on through a largely beige and gold den with dark brown accents. The room was dominated by a dark brown pit group in front of a prefab, built-in fireplace. Fire tools were arranged perfectly at its side even though it featured fixed gas logs. Above the wooden mantel was an oil painting of Alton standing behind his mother, seated in front of him. It looked like one painted from a local church directory photo.

Alton's mom had a really beautiful smile, and the strong similarity between the two was evident. Hailey had the eerie feeling Alton's mom was watching her as she walked toward a narrow hall leading past a pristine guest bath with a night-light on, positioned over the sink beside the door. Just passing the door toward three bedrooms in the back of Alton's house, Hailey passed a simple framed copy of his mom's obit hanging alone in the hall. Her eyes again watched Hailey pass by.

Glimpsing into Alton's master bedroom, she noticed the bed was carefully made. The bedroom next to Alton's was done in shades of lilac and deep purple. Using her pen, Hailey gently pushed open one of the levered closet doors to see clothes that looked like they belonged to Alton's mom. She must have stayed here often before her death.

Heading to the third bedroom across the hall from the guest room, it looked like Alton had turned it into an office of sorts. A blonde wood desk with a desktop computer sat in the center of double windows looking out onto the front yard through sheer, ivory curtains accented by deep gold rayon drapes on either side. A clear plastic carpet cover was positioned underneath a desk chair on rollers pulled in exactly to the center of the desk.

Hailey naturally headed straight to the desk after first using her pen again to nudge open a single closet door beside the desk and peek inside at stacks of office supplies neatly arranged alongside boxes marked for the past ten years' worth of tax returns.

Out of curiosity, Hailey punched the "enter" button on the computer's keyboard with her silver pen. To her amazement, she saw immediately Alton didn't keep his computer in lockdown because the screen promptly lit up and his personal email appeared. The very first thing she noticed was a long list of sent mail to someone with a courthouse addy.

The list was most recently accessed the night before. "Hey, Billings! Better come here!" she called over her shoulder.

The heading of the last email read "Big Meeting Tomorrow." As Billings stepped in behind her, Hailey punched a button and the message appeared. It read: "Left a message with his secretary. All set for 2 PM. Nervous. Call me as soon as you can!"

"Hmm. Wonder what that's all about." Hailey studied the email as if somehow its meaning could mysteriously be extracted from its brief message. Could be anything from a dentist's office for a root canal to buying an RV to a new job interview.

Scrolling farther down, Hailey easily saw a bulk of the messages were to someone named Eleanor Odom. Eleanor had a courthouse address as well. The headings ranged from "the cookies were great" to 'let's meet for coffee in the cafeteria" to "lots of paperwork today!" Many of the emails to whomever Eleanor Odom was remained unopened.

At that precise moment there was a large crash simultaneous with loud male voices. Hailey darted down the hall and out the kitchen door to find Trimble standing at the forefront of a tight knot of officers and crime-scene techs. At his feet was the actual garage door.

Billings flew through the door right behind her. "What happened?" His voice was deep, loud, and harsh. Hailey turned just quickly enough to see barely controlled anger etched on his face.

All the guys looked straight at Trimble.

"I just wanted to see how it was tampered with . . . so I got the guys to loosen a few screws and plugs and . . ." his voice trailed off.

"Don't anyone touch another thing. Evidence is not to be tampered with in any way. Another mistake like this could cost us a guilty verdict. Trimble, go to the station right now and complete the paperwork. Myers, oversee the rest of the photographs and work this scene."

"Yes, sir." A man dressed in light blue jeans with a navy blue CPD crime tech shirt tucked in stepped forward. He was clearly in charge of the techs on the scene.

Without a word, Trimble turned on his heel and stomped across Alton's lawn to his patrol car. In dramatic fashion, he cranked up, reversed, and scratched off.

Not another word was spoken among the rank and file there on the scene as several of the techs moved toward to the garage door lying on the driveway. Hailey spotted two of them pulling out plastic gloves.

The garage door. This would have to be handled very delicately ... and not just the door. Not a word of Trimble's snafu could be openly discussed, as that type of conversation, much less anything put in writing, would absolutely be discoverable at trial by the defense.

They'd have a field day with it and end up making the entire investigation look like Keystone cops . . . Barney Fifes. The whole investigation could be tainted, and when the bad guy was caught, whoever he was, he and his defense team could make a joke of the investigation right in front of the jury.

They all knew it, and the air hung heavy with the thought of it as the crew tried to regroup. Billings started directing the techs in heaving up the door and loading it onto a lean, pristine white sheet of plastic laid squarely onto the floor of a huge evidence transport truck.

Hailey and Fincher turned and headed toward their car, walking across Alton Turner's neatly mowed lawn. Out of respect, Hailey stepped off the grass and onto the white concrete drive.

"Hey, guys, wait up!" Billings called out after them when he spotted them heading toward the Fulton County Crown Vic at the edge of Alton Turner's front lawn. He caught up with them in just a few long strides.

"Where you headed?"

"I'm heading to my hotel and Fincher, where are you staying?" Hailey slowed and asked Finch.

Finch grinned. "I'm not the TV star; the county's putting me up at the Best Western."

"Hey, it's not so bad, close to downtown and there's an IHOP next to it." Billings painted a rosy picture.

"There's nothing like IHOP . . . unless you count the Waffle House. We're going to get a pizza first, aren't we? Do we still have time?" Hailey glanced at the watch on Fincher's wrist.

"Sure. Let's go. We don't have to be at the courthouse until 8 AM. Let's go crazy."

"OK. Let's go."

"OK you guys, see you there in the morning." Billings smiled again.

"You'll be at the trial?" Hailey asked, surprised.

"Sure. Nearly every guy on homicide had a part in the Julie Love Adams investigation. That Todd Adams is a piece of work. What an SOB."

"That's what we hear," Fincher agreed.

"And thanks for the backup."

"Anytime," Fincher answered back. The two headed to the car, leaving footprints as they crossed over Turner's manicured lawn.

"Wonder who did it?" Hailey said it first.

"Todd Adams did it, of course." Fincher answered quickly, surprised she had doubts about the Julie Love case.

"*I don't mean Julie Love, I mean . . . who killed Alton Turner?*"

ailey was one of the first people in the courtroom the following morning. At first blush, it appeared she was the very first. She didn't spot another soul in the cavernous room or milling around outside its giant double doors. But Hailey could tell the prosecutor had been there earlier. The state's counsel table was already covered with notes, books, binders, and stacks of documents. A flash of memory crossed Hailey's mind, back to her trial days when she was pitted against one team of defense attorneys after the next, week after week in the pits of the inner city. Typically, they'd be well-heeled. Representing dopers was a very lucrative enterprise.

The dope lawyers wore hand-tailored Italian suits, expensive shoes, and gold or jeweled cuff links, bracelets, rings, and necklaces gleaming at neck, wrists, and fingers. A single briefcase of theirs alone probably would have cost more than Hailey's old Honda. But as of this morning, nothing was on the defense table. Not yet anyway.

She could guess the explanation. At times, defense lawyers would not prep in the courtroom, but instead remain in the holding cell adjoining the courtroom with their client till the very last minute, trying their best to school them with last-minute instructions on how to walk, talk, and behave in front of the jury. Or better yet, talk them into copping a plea. That was easy money for sure. A defense lawyer could make $50,000 to $100,000 for a plea on a high-level dope case.

The jury in the Adams case had already been selected. From what Hailey could tell from the newspapers, which had already profiled all the jurors exhaustively, the group was made up of jurors bused in from another county southwest of Chatham. In Hailey's opinion, that had been a grave mistake for the defense.

Demanding a change of venue, changing the location of the trial, was SOP, standard operating procedure, for the defense, whether it was smart or not. But be careful what you ask for, for you will surely get it and in this case . . . they did. The judge granted a jury selected from another county. Problem for the defense was that they didn't get to select *what* county.

Adams's lawyers, by rolling the dice and rejecting Chatham County jurors, got Early County jurors instead. Early County was situated about a hundred miles away, at the far southern and westernmost region of the state, directly on the Georgia-Alabama state line. Reputed to be extremely conservative, they'd recently tried to order the electric chair, aka Old Sparky, for a repeat bank robber whose gun jammed when he pointed it at the bank teller's nose. It never fired.

The angry jury had to be offered a steak buffet at the local Golden Corral and talked down by the trial judge. When trying to placate the bloodthirsty jurors back in the deliberations room, the judge, wisely, blamed the lack of sentencing options on the U.S. Supreme Court, and then sent them to the all-you-could-eat steak and salad bar.

Georgia's death row stats backed up the reputation. There were more death row inmates there from Early County than any other county in the state. And the local residents were proud of it.

But reputation alone means practically nothing when striking a jury. Hailey had tried enough cases to know that you could never, ever predict what a jury would do with 100 percent accuracy. There were and would always be wild cards . . . jurors that could hold up a verdict, hijack a jury and cause a mistrial, or, even worse, convince a right-minded jury to do the wrong thing.

Hailey always divided jurors into two simple categories. The first category was the sheep. Sheep could be led along easily without much thinking on their own part, rarely took a stand on anything, eagerly looked forward to lunch and cigarette breaks, and were largely focused on getting home each afternoon. Sheep rarely lost sleep over their part of the picture.

On the other hand, there were the alphas. Alpha jurors were entirely different and had to be selected with the utmost caution. Alphas were those uncommon jurors who not only thought for themselves, but led others to their way of thinking. They came in all shapes, colors, and sizes and could be anything from a single mom of five to a retired vet to the foreman of a shipping dock.

Hailey could spot an alpha a mile away and generally tried her best, depending on their views on the justice system, to put them in the box . . . the jury box. The problem with alphas was that they could trick you during voir dire, or jury selection. Their charisma was obvious, but that charisma could be used for good *or* evil, and once that alpha was in the box, either side would be hard-pressed to get them thrown off the jury.

Simply put, there were leaders and followers. Both could be good or bad.

The courtroom was hushed, although it was slowly starting to fill up. Hailey noticed sheriffs, grim-faced, crossing the front of the courtroom wearing double black armbands, one on each arm. They silently signaled the death of a fellow officer, Alton Turner. Even if Turner hadn't been much of a spitfire, never made a collar, and never sat on a barstool recounting stories of a cop's life on the streets, he was nonetheless a brother. Somebody had to get the glory . . . and somebody had to push the paper.

That somebody was Alton Turner. And he had done so proudly and with dedication, rarely taking a day off and doing whatever had to be done, never believing that any task, no matter how lowly, was beneath him.

Wherever he went, Alton proudly wore baseball hats, Windbreakers, T-shirts, and sometimes all three at once, all emblazoned with the green and gold Chatham County Sheriff's logo. He was always the first one at Chatham County Sheriff charity events, cookouts, and softball games, although he never swung a bat nor caught a grounder. He was proud to be a lawman . . . even though he rarely left his tiny cream-colored cubicle at the Chatham County Courthouse.

From his beloved cube, Alton directed the transfer of inmates from the county jail to the courthouse, inputting inmate names, cell blocks, and arrest warrants then connecting them to indictment numbers. The right indictment numbers then had to be funneled to the correct courtrooms, making sure that each and every one of the thousands of accused felons made it to the right place bright and early come Monday morning trial and arraignment calendars.

It wasn't exciting to many, but to Alton it was. As he was a lawman of sorts, the courthouse was Alton's life.

From what Hailey read just before turning off the bedside light in her hotel room, Alton had never married and remained devoted to his only other surviving relative, the elderly sister of his "beloved mother," his Aunt René.

Hailey's first stop this morning was for a cup of hot tea in the courthouse cafeteria. She could easily overhear several sheriffs at the next table talking about Turner. He had worshipped his mother and bragged to her endlessly about every capture, arrest, and trial as if they'd all been his own. Not in a self-aggrandizing way, he was simply proud to be part of the team and wanted her to be proud of her "boy," although Alton had been pushing forty.

Hailey stared down into her cup of tea. She'd tucked her own tea bag of Irish breakfast into her bra that morning so she'd have it once she got to the courthouse. It was her favorite brand but very hard to find. It was easy to score a bag of English breakfast, but Irish was another matter altogether. It was steaming hot and practically white with skim milk, just how she liked it.

It sounded like Alton Turner wouldn't hurt a fly. Staring down at her tea bag floating in its cup, Hailey couldn't help but wonder who could have murdered him in such a brutal way. The pain must have been excruciating.

Hailey caught a glimpse at a plain round clock above the cashier in the cafeteria. Court would start in a little over thirty minutes and she wanted a good seat. Gulping down the rest of her tea and giving a nod to the sheriffs seated next to her, she made her way to the courthouse bank of elevators and up to the Todd Adams murder trial.

And here she sat, soaking it in. State courtrooms almost universally had the same feel to them, the same smell, the same sounds, and the same vibe. Just being here made her miss her days as a felony prosecutor intensely. Homesick for her other life, waves of what might have been washed over her.

*What might have been.*

Her days fighting drug lords, rapists, child molesters, and killers had left her with an edge . . . quite an edge, as a matter of fact. Ten years in the pit of the Atlanta Fulton County Courthouse, waging war on the bad guys, had forever changed her.

But the reality was she'd never be the fresh-faced girl she was before . . . long before she became a felony prosecutor. Or even a law student for that matter . . . before another killer shattered her dreams. The murder of her fiancé, Will, just before their wedding, had left Hailey Dean broken . . . a shell of what she was and even now . . . a shell of what she could have been. *What she should have been.*

As one of the top litigators in the South, she developed a reputation as the most ruthless and hard-hearted prosecutor to have ever walked the courthouse halls. And she didn't mind it a single bit.

But a part of her was sealed off forever. That part of her was her heart.

After nearly twenty minutes of waiting, the swinging doors in the courtroom opened and in walked a fleet of state lawyers, most of them carrying binders, files, and law books. The two men took seats at the state's counsel table, closest to the jury. The two women, dressed in austere gray and navy blue, sat behind them.

No female lead counsel, Hailey thought. Not unusual. Any further thoughts as to gender bias evaporated into thin air when a side door of the courtroom opened from inside.

Out strode two huge, muscled Chatham County Sheriff's officers, shoulder to shoulder. Behind them came two white, male attorneys. By the look of them, she assumed they were part of the defense team. The cut of their suits and the shine on their Italian leather loafers indicated a far bigger paycheck than a state prosecutor could ever pull in. The two were followed by a gaggle of underlings—paralegals, an investigator, a jury consultant by the looks of her, and two skinny law student types, apparently "interning" under the tutelage of famed defense attorney Michael P. "Mikey" DelVecchio.

Their hair was slicked back with some sort of gel that glistened in hard spikes under the courtroom lighting. They spoke quietly to each other, their heads slightly turned inward, DelVecchio with a smile on his lips. And then, at the end of the defense procession, with his head up, shoulders thrown back, muscled chest puffed forward, and looking like he was walking onto a football field to run a touchdown, came the defendant. Todd Adams.

His dark hair was smooth and shiny and clearly just trimmed for the big day. His suit was blue and tailored, fit him perfectly, and contrasted subtly against the light blue of a crisp, starched Oxford button-down shirt and crimson red silk tie. Adams flashed a perfectly aligned, bright white smile at his family, who settled in to take over the entire first row behind the defense counsel table.

Hailey watched and absorbed the interaction between Adams and his parents, his mom in particular. The two held a long gaze. Looking at Mrs. Adams, it was clear: She adored him, loved him, and, most important, believed him.

A rush of papers and sudden movement at the front of the courtroom was followed by a half a dozen minions rushing in. Then, in came the judge. Sharp-faced and gray-headed, Luther Alverson insisted on presiding over more jury trials than any other judge in the courthouse.

At eighty-four, he was also the oldest judge in the courthouse. So old in fact, he predated the state regulations on mandatory retirement. In order to prove himself still up to the task, he demanded that any and all Chatham assistant district attorneys and public defenders assigned to his court must go on trial every other week. His calendar was rarely backed up, and when a case went on his trial calendar, there would be no last-minute haggling, no eleventh-hour guilty pleas, no cheap deals.

Everyone stood as the judge seated himself with the simultaneous pounding of his gavel with three loud strikes. "Court's in session. The Honorable Luther Alverson presiding."

Like in a church at the end of a hymn, everyone sat back down in their seats in unison. The calendar clerk's seat was positioned directly beside the judge's bench. The clerk stood to read directly from the grand jury indictment, calling out the indictment number, a series of letters and numbers that had significance only to court employees, followed by the announcement "*State v. Todd Adams.*"

As her son's name was read out loud, Tish Adams burst into tears, drawing every eye in the courtroom off her son and onto herself. Hailey immediately checked Julie Love's mother, also seated in the front row but on the other side of the courtroom.

The look Dana Love shot at Adams's mother could have cut stone. It was a look of pure hatred. It was clearly borne of resentment at the long years Adams was coddled by his mom, at the numerous excuses for Adams's bad behavior she made, culminating in a final act of violence.

Adams's defense team made a big stir at their table, scrambling among themselves, as it turned out, for a handkerchief the lead defense lawyer dramatically pulled from his lapel and handed back to Tish Adams. Immediately, prosecutors stood, and striding quickly toward the judge's bench, barked out the word "Sidebar!"

"Counsel, approach the bench! Including you, Mr. DelVecchio."

Hailey knew enough from all her years prosecuting in court that Alverson was already on to the defense ploy of having the jury focus on the grieving mother of the defendant, not the grieving mother of the victim, Julie Love. Thankfully, the prosecutor was on to it too, but Hailey hoped he could cut off DelVecchio next time before the play was made.

As it was, all twelve jurors were still staring sympathetically at Tish Adams, who was now breathing deeply into a clear plastic breathing mask attached to a portable cylinder of pure oxygen.

Ugh. This was going to be a long trial.

Hailey couldn't stop staring either, even though she suspected all the sobbing was a preplanned charade, the defense and Tish Adams clearly in cahoots. As Hailey watched the judge's stern face framed by the suited backs of all the attorneys, they turned and strode back to their counsel table.

To see DelVecchio's face, smiling and preening toward the jury, you'd think he had just won an argument in the U.S. Supreme Court when, in fact, he'd just gotten his first dressing down from the judge. The whole game was new to the jurors, but Hailey knew that soon enough, most of them would catch on to the game Adams's defense was playing.

After the reading of the indictment in which the accusations and a partial description of the deaths of Julie Love and baby Lily were laid out, the jurors repeatedly glanced at Todd Adams as if trying to reconcile the two brutal murders with the good-looking, athletic young man sitting behind the defense table. His mother was still overtly crying, but now silently into DelVecchio's hanky, following the judge's admonition.

The judge turned toward the jurors and launched into a set of typed, pretrial jury instructions to provide somewhat of a road map as to how the trial would go.

The case commenced. The lead prosecutor stood up, pushing his chair back from counsel table, approaching a podium directly centered before the judge. He laid out a stack of paper on which he had handwritten pretrial motions to the judge. He began in a conversational tone, but as the intensity of the story increased, he picked up the pace and pitch. By the time he showed the jury a photo of Julie Love—the one at Christmas time, decked out in her Christmas-red satin pantsuit, her tummy bulging with baby Lily—all twelve jurors plus the alternates were at the edge of their seats. And this was just for motions, openings hadn't started!

But just before the prosecutor, Herman Grant, punched the slide projector button to proceed to the next image up on a slide screen on the other side of the courtroom, DelVecchio stood and loudly shouted out.

"Objection! The state is trying to poison us all against Todd Adams, and I won't have it, Judge! This is so cruel and unfair, to use the life of Julie Love in this manner . . . just to get a conviction!"

Hailey cringed as Grant turned, his face in a rage, and then Julie Love's mother put her head in her hands, leaning on her husband's shoulder.

"Send out the jury!" Alverson said it calmly but Hailey could tell the judge was angry. He couldn't afford to show emotion and jeopardize a death penalty case, but there was no way Alverson was going to let DelVecchio run roughshod over the court with his flamboyant behavior.

"Careful, careful . . ." Hailey muttered to herself. If the judge came down too hard on DelVecchio, it could later be argued that he, the judge, was biased against the defense, even at this early stage of the trial.

The judge's law clerk, hooked up to an audio flow of the court proceedings in his own office next to the judge's, came rushing into the courtroom, up to the bench, and began whispering into Alverson's ear.

The judge visibly controlled himself as the jury headed into the jury room, directly adjoining the courtroom. The judge launched into a reprimand of the defense, but Hailey couldn't help but notice the pleased look on DelVecchio's face. Was he happy the judge was reprimanding him? Or happy he had already gotten the jury to view his client, not Julie Love and Lily, as the victim?

Hailey stood up and slipped out of the courtroom. She took the stairs located at the end of the corridor outside swinging doors to the court. Quickly heading down five flights to the courthouse lobby, past the lines waiting at metal detectors, she pushed through the gigantic front doors of the Chatham County Courthouse, and out into the fresh, salty air.

Hailey breathed it in in big gulps. She hadn't realized the mental images, much less the feelings . . . the raw emotions, being in a criminal court would bring back.

Instead of homing in on exactly what was being said with a razor-sharp focus, her mind had drifted . . . back . . . back to her days in countless felony courtrooms where she had prosecuted the worst of the worst. Fleeting moments of trials, courtroom arguments, crying victims, and blood-spattered crime scenes gave way to other memories.

Memories of Will's murder . . . the trial at which she was a witness . . . the sound of her boots as she stepped down several steps from the witness stand to leave following her testimony . . . the sad look in the jurors' eyes as they watched her . . . passing the defense table where she saw Will's bloody denim shirt lying there. She recognized it and in a blur . . . a numb blur . . . she looked into the face of the defense attorney, seated there beside his client . . . Will's killer.

They both immediately looked down into their laps. They couldn't even look her in the face.

Even now . . . years later . . . she wanted to go back to that courtroom. She wanted to grab Will's denim shirt and run away with it . . . to save it from the defense team . . . to keep them from touching it . . . ever.

Looking out blankly at traffic in front of the courthouse . . . it all came flooding back. Her face was hot. Tears sprang up in her eyes. She clutched the wrought iron handrail flanking the stone steps leading to the courthouse entrance.

*Why would I want Will's bloody shirt?* She almost said it out loud. It didn't make sense. And how was she going to sit through another murder trial if she'd be affected like this?

Just then, Hailey felt a hand on her shoulder. She turned.

It was Fincher.

"I saw you leave the courtroom."

"Shouldn't you be up there? They may call you as a witness."

"Ha. With the show DelVecchio's putting on, it'll be days before they call me. Plus, I overheard one of the bailiffs tell the prosecutor that the judge was recessing for the day. He's so mad at DelVecchio, he thinks it's best to start opening statements in the morning when things cool down a little. If there is a conviction, and that's a big if, nobody wants a reversal because of angry words from the bench. So we're done. For today, anyway."

The two headed across the street to the lot where the rental car Hailey got at the hotel was parked. "Want a ride? I'm heading over to Alton Turner's place to check it out."

"Alton Turner? Are you back on that? Why? Does Billings know?" Finch didn't sound as if he thought this was such a great idea.

"I don't know what you mean by 'back on that,' but whatever that means, I absolutely am 'back on it.' I don't find a severed body and just forget about it. It doesn't work that way with me."

"I'm afraid it doesn't," Finch fired back, rolling his eyes.

"I've got a gut feeling if something doesn't give, they'll chalk it up as an accident. You know, take the path of least resistance. I really think a second look with fresh eyes might help. Know what I mean?"

"Fresh eyes. Oh yeah, I think I do know what that means." Risking her wrath, he went on, "You do know this is not your jurisdiction and it's not your case, Hailey."

Hailey gave him a withering glare in response. He didn't wither. Instead, he just looked right back at her.

"Last I checked the Constitution, it's still a free country, Fincher. I know it's not my 'jurisdiction' and it's not my 'case.' I'm like every other ordinary civilian going about my very own business. I just happen to be curious, that's all."

No response from Finch.

"Listen, I just want to go look at the back windows of the house, just to see if somebody could've gotten in that way. Maybe just look around the outside of the house, no harm in that. Maybe visit with a few neighbors . . . just to get the temperature. Know what I mean?"

"Oh yes, I know what you mean. You're investigating the case behind Billings's back. That's what you mean, Hailey. Don't think I don't know it."

She was silent for a few seconds, then spoke. "OK. Have it your way. I won't butt in."

This was not at all what Fincher expected. "I've never known you to give in that easily. Are you sick?"

"No, I'm not sick but as a matter of fact, I was up half the night studying the Adams case."

"Studying the Adams case? You've studied it for months, you've interviewed witnesses, the Chatham County Medical Examiner, visited the scene . . . and you're still studying? What more is there to know? He had a girlfriend, he wanted out . . . so he killed her. There, case solved . . . you're through studying."

"As I was saying before I was so rudely interrupted—"

"Are you still claiming I interrupt you? I hate to interrupt, but that's absolutely not true."

They both started laughing.

"That's right, you would never be so rude. But yes, I stayed up late studying so I'm going to go crash for a couple of hours. I'll call you in a few."

He gave her a long, hard look. "Promise? Because, in the history of Hailey Dean, I have never once known you to take a nap. You're really going back to the hotel to rest? Because that's just what you need to do, whether you ever do it or not."

"I absolutely am going back to the hotel. I promise I'll call in a couple of hours."

He looked at her face, searching for any sign of obfuscation. There was none.

"OK. I'll see you on the flip side."

"OK. See you!"

Hailey headed to her car. She'd promised, true. But what she'd promised was a different matter altogether. Choosing her words carefully, she'd promised specifically to call him later. She knew it was tricking him, but pulling out of the parking garage and heading into the sunshine, she knew full well he would end up laughing about it.

She Google-mapped Alton Turner's address and headed out of downtown Savannah. Hailey smiled to herself in the rearview mirror. He'd laugh all right. In the end.

The neighborhood where Alton Turner lived looked almost deserted in the middle of the afternoon. Most of the residents of the sleepy little suburb were at work.

Hailey retracked the route she and Finch had taken the first time she'd ever been there. She didn't even need to consult her Google map. How could you forget the first time you ever saw a severed torso lying on a garage floor?

Turning a corner, Hailey spotted Alton's house. It was just as precisely neat as ever. Pulling her rental car into the driveway, Hailey got out and slammed the door just in time to spot a guy on foot with a ponytail walking away from Alton's. He had a huge camera slung over his shoulder and was just turning the curve in the street. Had he just been here? Maybe a crime-scene tech . . . or the *Savannah Morning News*.

Hailey turned from the guy who had now disappeared into the neighborhood and faced Alton's house. She took one step and stopped. Something was wrong.

She stood stock-still, just looking. After a few moments she realized what was out of place. There were pinecones and leaves scattered across the front lawn. Pinecones. Hailey's mortal enemy as a child. The things were little, barbed grenades to the touch and when accidentally pressed against bare feet in summertime . . . oh, the scream that would follow. And Alton's yard was covered with them, thanks to some tall pine trees at the edge of his lot.

Pinecones on his otherwise immaculate lawn? That would've driven Alton Turner absolutely crazy.

Instinctively, Hailey strode across the lawn and, bending over, picked up the ten or so prickly pinecones dotting the yard. There was a group of shrubs surrounding an ornamental willow off to the side of Alton's house with a concrete birdbath and decorative swing nearby.

It was a lovely setting. Hailey imagined Alton landscaping it and knew without being told that he and his mom had sat in that swing together many an evening. The shrubs and willow were positioned in a bed of pine straw . . . a pine straw island so to speak. The perfect place to ditch the pinecones.

Hailey quickly dumped the sharp cones behind the bushes. Just to the rear of the island, she spotted three more cones.

Ugh. Why was she doing this? Cleaning the yard of a dead man she'd never even met? Automatically, a voice answered in her head. *Because I'd want someone to do the same for me.*

Truth be told, Hailey felt like she knew Alton and actually connected with him. Looking through his home, reading his emails, looking at so many photos of him, even looking in his fridge, for Pete's sake, Hailey was convinced she knew Alton Turner . . . and she liked him.

Maybe she was just projecting, but she could feel the pang of loss he'd felt when he lost his mom. Immediately, she recalled a small black-and-white photo she'd seen. It was framed and positioned beside his bed. It was an old shot of Alton and his mom when he was a boy. He was standing partially behind her. She had on a short-sleeved print dress with a white apron tied behind her, covering the front of the dress from the waist down. Alton was hugging the tops of her legs with both arms.

He was smiling and so was she. Hailey paused and it struck her that throughout Alton's home, she hadn't seen a dad . . . anywhere. Not a single photo of him . . . not a trace. His mom was all he ever had. Alton, aside from trying to fit in with the other sheriffs at work, was alone in this world.

Hailey understood. She bent over to get the rest of the pinecones and spotted some trash as well. There was a cigarette butt barely edged with bright red lipstick and a piece of round black plastic, something about the size of a Gatorade bottle top.

Did the Eleanor from the emails smoke? Had she been here with Alton? Hailey tossed the cones behind the bushes and carried the cigarette butt and the plastic back to her car to throw away.

The bits of trash were minute, but Alton Turner would've flipped if he'd seen litter in his yard. Hailey smiled to herself and tossed it into the back floorboard of her car.

Now, to get down to business. She wanted another look around Alton's place. Alone. Without a fleet of crime-scene techs, and Fincher, God bless him, nagging at her with questions.

Cell phone in pocket, Hailey clicked her car locked and headed along the white cement driveway toward the garage. The garage door was back in place and a tiny coil of yellow crime scene tape was curled like a fuzzy caterpillar on the drive at the edge of the garage door. That was all that was left, to the casual eye, of the discovery of a dead body.

But as Hailey walked closer, she could see the dark stain on the concrete at the edge of the door. If a potential home buyer didn't know better, they'd probably think it was an oil spill.

But Hailey knew it was Alton's blood. She was rooted to the spot, staring down at the concrete.

A bird chirping overhead in the pines filtered through her thought process, and she looked up to the green branches and to the blue sky beyond. What really happened to Alton Turner?

Hailey glanced toward the front door, but instead turned left and headed around the side of the house along a path of garden stepping-stones. The grass around and in between the smooth flagstone steps was lush and green.

More fresh pine straw bordered the grass on the side of the walkway nearest the side of the house, and the yard sloped slightly downward as Hailey went to the backyard.

A white ornamental bird feeder resembling a mini Victorian mansion stood planted in the pine straw on a high, white wooden pole. It was extremely intricate and the sides of the mini-mansion were beveled batten siding sloping up to tiny eyebrow gables that peeked out from a dull green roof. Pausing to look at it in detail, Hailey saw the tiny initials A.T. painted on the bottom right side of the bird feeder.

He made this? By hand? It dawned on her that Alton Turner was so much more than the mild-mannered paper-pusher others portrayed him as. Staring up at the miniature mansion, she wondered . . . when did Alton have the time or energy to maintain all this?

Stepping off the flagstone stepping-stones into the pine straw, Hailey ran her fingertips across the edge of the little house. Had he made it for his mom?

Taking a deep breath, she tried to distance herself from *Alton Turner the person* and refocus on Alton Turner's *death investigation*. The birdhouse was firmly attached to a tall wooden pole about six and a half feet tall. And there, just below Hailey's line of vision, was a small, round, dark mark smeared on the pole.

What was that? It almost looked burned. Touching it, Hailey glanced down and saw there in the pine straw built up around the base of the pole was another cigarette butt. It seemed wrong to have a nasty butt just beneath the handcrafted feeder made by a gentle—but dead—man.

What was worse was that judging by the rounded black smudge, somebody actually stubbed their cigarette out on Alton's bird feeder pole. Hailey reached down and picked it up and stuck it in her pocket.

Bending upward, a slight movement, ever so subtle, caught her eye. There, in the window on the side of the house. Had the edge of a curtain moved? Looking carefully . . . what room was that?

Remembering the layout of the home, this had to be Alton's office . . . or was it his mom's bedroom? And who would be in the home? Hailey had definitely looked when she pulled up . . . the garage door was shut tight and there wasn't a single car parked on the street in front of Alton's house. The cul-de-sac was empty, too.

She looked back at the curtain. It was ivory colored, gauzy material with some sort of edging and Hailey was sure, very sure, she'd seen movement. The movement she thought she'd seen out of the corner of her eye was as if someone had pulled the curtain back, spotted Hailey outside, then suddenly let the draped material fall back into place, hanging there at the edge of the window.

But that didn't make sense. Remaining completely still, she continued to look directly at the window. With the sun outside and the room dark on the inside, she had no chance of spotting who may be lurking behind the window.

There was no way crime-scene techs would be here on foot. And why would anyone else be inside a dead man's house? Hailey's mind ticked off possibilities.

Was there a cleaning lady? If so, why would she dart away from the window as soon as she spotted Hailey? And where was her car? And what, for Pete's sake, would she be cleaning?

Just at that moment, it happened again. The curtain moved . . . right in front of her. And this time it was in her direct line of sight, not just caught in the corner of her peripheral vision. There was someone in there . . . she was certain of it now.

The curtain fluttered gently, but this time it kept going . . . it continued to flutter against the windowpane. Unlike before, there was no abrupt movement. And what's more, now the curtain on the *other* side of the window began fluttering gently as well.

Then it dawned on her. Just before the fluttering, she'd heard a clicking sound from around the corner.

Stepping out of the pine straw bed, she kept her eye on the window as long as she could. Following the neatly laid path of flagstone stepping-stones down the side of the house, she rounded the corner to the backyard.

Sure enough, big as Ike, there it was. A central heat and air unit was situated at the corner, segregated from dirt and pine straw in a neat, graveled square held in by a low wooden fence. It was humming a mechanical monotone. The gray behemoth was huge. It must serve the whole house.

Set at a certain temperature, it would automatically turn itself on or off to maintain that specific temperature.

That explained it. The AC simply kicked on. That's what she'd seen. There must be a vent centered in the middle of the window that directed an air current toward the drapes. Mystery solved.

Almost laughing out loud at herself, Hailey made her way across Alton's backyard. As she expected by now, it was beautifully, and painstakingly, landscaped. The grass was thick and green interspersed with several islands of pink, purple, and white azalea bushes, and pink-blossomed cherry trees were artfully positioned in islands of built-up pine straw.

Hailey examined not only the grounds but the windows across the back of the house. Only one door, a basement door, apparently, opened onto the backyard. It had a square concrete stoop with clay pots of green plants on either side of the door.

On instinct, Hailey lifted up the clay pot on the right.

Nothing.

Hailey tried under the left pot too, surprised she was wrong on this. She could just imagine the naïve and trusting Alton Turner leaving a spare key under the pot.

But Alton tricked her! His law enforcement training must have paid off . . . regarding the spare key, anyway. Walking up a low incline, she headed back to the front of Alton's home.

There appeared to be no forced entry anywhere around the house, doors, or windows. Or anything else of much interest, at least forensically. So other than picking up some trash, she didn't really accomplish a whole lot.

Headed back toward her car, Hailey couldn't stop herself from going back to the garage door . . . and the bloodstain on the concrete. Gazing down at it, a myriad of thoughts collided in her head. Something was nagging at her . . . but she couldn't identify it.

Was it possible she was wrong? Was it an accident after all? She'd been so sure at the crime scene. Hailey felt the dull pang of a headache beginning.

"Oh, hello there! *Helloo!*" A woman's voice called out, cutting through the still air of the previously quiet subdivision.

Hailey turned to see a lithe young woman dressed in 1980s-style workout gear. Matching neon pink from head to toe, she sported it all . . . at once. Headband, wristbands, kneepads, short runner's shorts over knee-length tights, all coordinated with a pink and purple lightweight shirt and neon pink sports bra peeking out from the shoulders of her shirt. The ensemble was topped with a vivid pink sun visor.

It was certainly something.

"Hi there! My name's Kacynthia and I'm a walkaholic! I confess it! I exercise in this neighborhood and after everything that's happened, I feel like Alton and I were best friends! Isn't it awful? Absolutely awful! I was the one who actually found his dead body and then, I was besieged, positively besieged by the press. Oh, the media! They are truly unrelenting, aren't they? Just unrelenting! I mean really . . . forget about my own personal privacy. After all, I have no thirst for fame whatsoever! It's Alton I'm thinking of! No respect for the dead! So what do you think? Was it murder? Or an accident? From what I hear in the neighborhood, Alton didn't have an enemy in the world! So it had to be an accident . . . right? You're not the press, are you?"

As opposed to looking shocked at the thought she was spilling the beans to a reporter, Hailey noticed the woman, to the contrary, looked elated at the prospect . . . eager, as a matter of fact, with a big smile showing a mouthful of cosmetic dentistry. Hailey also noticed the woman was not as young as she'd thought at a distance.

She had the body of a thirty-five-year-old, but her face, as artfully disguised as it was, belied her body. Creases, especially around her mouth, along with her neck and hands, gave away her age. This was a grandma, possibly a great-grandma and no spring chicken at all.

And Hailey was convinced she'd seen her before.

"Hi." Hailey smiled at the woman who was now approaching her, walking up Alton's driveway.

"I can tell . . . you're the press! *48 Hours? Nightline? 20/20?* No, *Investigation Discovery?* I can tell! No use in hiding it from me! I'm very familiar with the *media*. Let me tell you. Not to brag, of course, I've been in the public eye for years . . . years! Are you familiar with the name Bob Guccione? I was a *Penthouse Pet*! And not that long ago!"

It was actually in 1969, but Kacynthia withheld that tiny detail.

"In fact, my 'article' did so well, he invited me back! For a special 'pictorial.' But it was really all about the article, you know . . . the *content*."

Hailey nodded.

The woman in Lycra went on about something she called her "career as a Penthouse Pet" until Hailey interjected. "Do you live here in the cul-de-sac?"

"Here? In the *suburbs*? Oh no . . . no, no, no, *no*." The woman let out a short, gentle, but derisive laugh. "I'm more of an in-town girl. I just come out here to the sticks to get in my workout! Less exhaust fumes out here. Oh, no. I don't live here. Have you ever heard of Johnny Mercer? 'Moon River'? I live over on East Gordon in the historical district . . . beside the Johnny Mercer house. It's been in loads of movies . . . the Johnny Mercer house?" She repeated it as if she suspected Hailey was hard of hearing. "One of them even caught the corner of my condo building in it!"

"In what?" Hailey didn't get it.

"*The movie!* A corner of my condo building was actually in a movie! *Midnight in the Garden of Good and Evil*! It won lots of awards!"

"It must be lovely."

Hailey was rewarded for her interest with a broad smile from Kacynthia. Hailey went for it.

"Did you know Alton Turner?" Hailey kept her gaze directly on Kacynthia's face.

One of the woman's carefully drawn eyebrows, the left one, rose just a twitch as her eyes widened. She drew her right palm and fingertips to the center of her chest, seemingly without thinking, and sidestepped Hailey's question.

"*Oh, it was awful!* The blood! I was just minding my own business when I saw them."

"Them?" Hailey continued gazing directly into the woman's eyes.

"The legs. Alton Turner's legs. And the blood." Her voice had taken on a theatrical whisper and she mouthed the words dramatically, her red, glossed lips enunciating perfectly.

This woman was meant for the stage.

"I was the one who found him. I'll never forget it as long as I live. It *haunts* me. It absolutely haunts me." Now, she closed her eyes right there in the driveway as if she were entering a nightmare about Alton Turner's body at that very moment.

"And the press was relentless . . . they wouldn't let me go! I had to tell my story over and over!" It was easy to see the woman was thrilled and, watching her, Hailey finally placed her face. This was the woman Hailey spotted at the edge of Alton's lawn speaking to the press. Hailey had only seen her from behind, but now that she thought about it, the woman was wearing the same, or a very similar, workout ensemble with long red hair down her back.

This had to be her.

"Did you see anyone else around that day? Any cars parked at the house?"

"No. Actually, I had just parked my car around the corner. It's the baby blue BMW over on Magnolia, about three blocks from here." She clearly enjoyed dropping the fact she drove an expensive, luxury import.

"Oh, those are beautiful cars! And expensive!"

The shameless fawning paid off. The woman went on without any prodding at all.

"But even if I hadn't just gotten here, I can tell you, nobody else was here. Nobody was ever here. Ever since this guy's mom died, I heard he never had a single car in the driveway other than his own. And that was when he'd bring it out of the garage to wash it in the driveway."

"Really?"

*"Really."*

Hailey remained silent. As she'd surmised fairly easily, Kacynthia was the type that couldn't stand silence in a conversation and imme-diately filled it.

"Oh, yes. I think the mom visited so much, she finally moved in. Or else spent a lot of time here. They'd sit out there in the yard on that swing in the evenings. That's what the neighbors said. She drove an old silver Buick, I think. She'd park it on the street so's not to get oil on his driveway."

"Wow. You really know a lot about Alton."

"Well, I've come here to walk several hours a day lately."

"You sure are dedicated . . ."

"And it pays off!" Kacynthia turned to the side and patted a completely flat, taut tummy. "This isn't Spanx, if you know what I mean. As I've always said . . . beauty has a price."

"Well, you're in incredible shape!"

"Thank you! I guess I'm what you'd call a fitness enthusiast!" Kacynthia positively beamed.

"So, it was just Alton and his mom, then?"

"Yes. And that day, I didn't see another soul. Just them . . . the legs."

"What kind of guy was he?"

The woman clearly wanted to talk. No qualms about spilling the beans whatsoever.

"Well, I've talked to a *lot of neighbors,* let me tell you." The redhead looked both ways as if someone could possibly be listening. She paused before going on. "He was overly quiet, worked on his car in the garage with the door up a lot. After work. Always working in his yard. Grilled out with his mom a good bit before she passed. Since then, not so much."

"Poor guy. Well, it's nice to meet you." Hailey gave her another smile.

"Oh, here's my contact card if you need an interview, I mean information." In one fluid motion, she reached down into her workout bra and produced a pale pink business card. Glancing down at it, Hailey saw it had her name, Miss Kacynthia Sikes, her address, and home and cell numbers.

"Well, thank you. I'll certainly keep it!" Hailey slipped the card into her pocket along with the trash from Alton's yard.

"Lovely to meet you! Lovely! And I'll see you on the airwaves, Miss *20/20!*" Obviously still under the impression Hailey was with the media, Kacynthia Sikes gave a brilliant smile. Dazzling, actually, again displaying a mouth full of expensive dentistry that could not be acquired in just one sitting.

Turning on her white-heeled Pumas, Kacynthia's red hair swung around behind her. Chest out, tummy in, back straight, she started pumping her fists furiously before she even got out of the driveway and turned onto the paved asphalt street.

Taking a last glance back at the house, Hailey headed back to her rental car. She opened the door and got into the driver's seat. Cranking up the ignition, she reversed down the driveway and put it in drive.

Just ahead of her, she saw Kacynthia Sikes's bobbing head dip below a rise in the street and disappear from sight. The woman had never even asked her name, not anything else. She'd been perfectly contented babbling on practically solo.

Hailey glanced to both sides and in the rearview, taking a last glimpse in search of the ponytailed crime-scene tech. Maybe they could compare notes. But there was no sign of him. But wait . . . since when did a CSI have a ponytail? Not in these parts, anyway.

At that moment, a tingle went across Hailey's face and her mouth went dry. The central air hadn't cranked up outside the first time. When the curtain had dropped abruptly back to the window. She was sure of it. When the curtains began fluttering a few moments later, there had been a loud click, a catch of sorts, when the motor kicked in. *Then* the curtains had fluttered . . . not before. She didn't hear a click the first time . . . or the hum of the motor.

She was sure.

Or was she? Maybe she didn't recall it the first time because she was focused more on the Victorian birdhouse mini-mansion. And the black mark on the pole. And picking up the litter. Maybe she hadn't been focusing on anything else.

Hailey looked back in her rearview mirror at Alton Turner's house getting smaller and smaller as she pulled away from it.

If only those walls could talk.

A thick mist was rising up off the Savannah River the next morning as Hailey drove by. She had a fitful night's sleep, largely because of her return to the scene of Alton Turner's death. It even got into her dreams.

In the dream, she was hovering outside Alton's window looking in at the photo of Alton and his mom. The old one in black and white where Alton was still just a little boy. And then, the curtains at the window would begin fluttering and obstruct her view. In the dream, Hailey kept reaching out, trying to pull them to the side to see who, if anyone, was standing there.

In the end, a hotel wake-up call snatched her out of a dream she couldn't seem to get out of on her own.

Crossing over the river, she caught sight of the gray water churning on, giving no thought to those passing over it. The sky was early-morning gray as well, still cool before the Savannah sun came out to blister everything beneath it. She pulled the car into McDonald's.

"Still on McDonald's coffee? Still won't give in and go to Starbucks?" She looked over at Finch in the front passenger seat.

"Costs too much. And it tastes *bitter*. Actually, I don't see how you stand the stuff. I really wanted my Irish breakfast tea before morning session, but the hotel doesn't have it. So, McDonald's it is."

The two drove through, ordered, and headed downtown on the narrow surface roads leading to the Chatham County Courthouse and the Julie Love Adams trial. But Hailey's head was still at Alton's place.

Alton's cul-de-sac. She didn't know why, but thought it was better if she kept it to herself.

She knew he'd be irate that she went out sleuthing on her own. When they were a trial team, he'd bailed her out often, including one time when she went to see a hostile witness and was met with a shotgun barrel right in her face.

He'd grabbed her and together, they dove straight off the porch into the dirt, the ringing of the shotgun blast in their ears.

Yep. He'd definitely be ticked off that she went out on her own. Better keep that quiet. She gulped down her coffee as Finch wolfed down a huge breakfast sandwich. Glancing over, Hailey could only identify some sort of meat, likely sausage, topped with egg and cheese, all in a biscuit.

It did smell pretty good. She had to admit that. The two kept driving in silence. She wasn't in the mood for music interrupted by tons of local advertisements.

After several minutes, Finch broke the silence. "You heard about the parole hearing, right?"

"What?" Hailey continued looking out at the traffic.

"The parole hearing. It's on the schedule, I heard. You haven't mentioned it."

Hailey flicked on the car's blinker and, looking both ways, deliberately steered the car right. She seemed especially focused on traffic.

"You know he's up for parole, right?"

"Who?"

"Hailey. You know who. Will's killer. They're having a hearing on it. Word is, that because of you, it's turned into a political football. They're saying he's gonna get out because of it. They don't want to look like they're being unfair. You know, holding him behind bars just because you and Will were engaged. No preferential treatment . . . that kind of thing."

Hailey didn't turn or budge, didn't bat an eye. She kept staring out toward cars slowly passing by. But her foot had lifted a tiny bit and the car had slowed considerably.

Still. She held it steady in the road.

"I heard." She said flatly. At that moment, if she had given in to what she was feeling, she was in danger of going into a depression so deep, she wouldn't be able to crawl out of it for months. She couldn't give in to it. She couldn't.

Hailey took a deep breath and shrugged Fincher's hand off her shoulder. It wasn't that she wanted to get rid of him, she just couldn't be close.

She couldn't let go. If she let go, she might just howl at the sky out of pure pain left over from a long time ago, when she was still a fresh-faced girl. Before Will was gunned down. When she thought she would still be walking down the aisle in her beautiful dress. When she still thought one day she would have a family, a home, a life.

Fincher knew enough not to push it. He'd been through a lot with Hailey and he understood her. He sat beside her quietly, waiting, as he had done thousands of times, in court and out.

In a few moments, the dark cloud passed over her. She could almost feel it fade away.

Hailey abruptly turned back to face him.

"Let's just get into the courtroom. OK?"

"OK. Let's go." Finch knew that was always her solution. Don't think about it. Don't feel it. Don't feel anything . . . it might hurt. Just get in the courtroom. Where it's safe. This had been her MO since he first met her. But he also knew not to point that out to her.

Hailey was smarter, sharper, and quicker than anyone he'd ever met. He was pretty sure that Hailey Dean knew what she was doing.

So instead, he went along with her. "Yeah. Let's see what BS DelVecchio is up to this morning. Probably an encore performance of yesterday."

Hailey looked him in the face and smiled big. "Yeah. Let's do that."

Slamming the doors and heading in, they climbed the courthouse steps and went through the metal detector fairly quickly by flashing their badges, allowing them to bypass a long line of people waiting to get through. Heading toward the bank of elevators in the center of the lobby, Hailey went on, talking about anything but the parole hearing.

"You want dinner after court?"

"Yeah. I think I want Cuban. A big, fat Cuban sandwich . . . or maybe some jerk chicken."

"I want sushi. I wonder if they have decent sushi in Savannah."

"OK, fine. If you want to eat some raw fish out of the Savannah River, you go right ahead. It's about three miles from the Savannah nuclear reactor plant, but if you don't mind sushi that glows . . . have at it. I will be having the very *well-done* chicken teriyaki."

"Good. Have a piece of leather. Well-done tastes just like a shoe . . . but if that's what you want . . . eat a shoe."

"Hailey, I've known you over ten years and I can't think of a single time—not even one time—you ever wanted the same thing I wanted for dinner."

"Hey. I was just going to say that myself. Why do you have to be so contrary all the time? But that's because *I* am a foodie and *you* . . . are a garbage disposal."

"I've heard that before . . ."

"But Fincher, forget what you're going to eat for once. I'm worried about this jury. Did you see the way they were looking over at Adams's mom?"

Stepping onto the elevator, the doors closed with a whoosh. Everything was OK . . . back to normal. They were heading back to the courtroom. She was OK . . . at least for now, anyway.

It was a contentious morning session of last-minute motions. Again. Hailey took the stand outside the jury's presence midmorning and it was brutal. DelVecchio tried at every turn to stop her, but Hailey managed to score point after point. She had to totally tune out DelVecchio and Tish Adams as well, who insisted on shooting one murderous look after the other at Hailey.

The lawyers were battling, family was tense, and Hailey was bitterly crossed then recrossed. Todd Adams sat through it all as if he were watching a chess tournament.

Hailey testified straight through until lunchtime, occasionally looking Todd Adams directly in the eyes. At the beginning, he always looked away, but an hour or so into her testimony, he looked at Hailey with pure loathing. She kept at it though until, finally, it ended with DelVecchio dramatically throwing his hands in the air and announcing he had no further questions. The judge ruled immediately; Hailey Dean would be allowed to testify as an expert for the state in front of the jury.

It was well into lunchtime and the cafeteria was crowded. A long line queued up on a gently sloping ramp leading back toward a winding hall that ended at the elevators. The ramp took hungry employees, lawyers, defendants, witnesses, and judges down toward dozens of tables crowded in between two parallel lines of food. There was quite an assortment. In one corner stood a coffee bar, tricked out like a Starbucks, with leaded, unleaded (decaf), and flavored coffee, as well as skim, whole, 2 percent, and even almond milk choices. It was mobbed, of course.

At the other end, a serve-yourself salad bar stood, looking lonely, in the corner of the huge dining hall. Just feet away from lettuce, pale truck-farmed tomatoes, shredded cheese, and gooey dressings stood a long line of hungry courthouse employees as workers in light blue uniforms and hairnets dished home-cooked veggies and meats into small melamine bowls. The employees, in turn, would take the bowl, now full to brimming, place it on their tray, and amble down the line. Starting with red and blue Jell-O with fruit congealed in it, salads and desserts, then to meat and noodle entrees, and finally to veggies, breads, and beverages.

While the sound and smell of it all could be a little off-putting to some, Hailey loved it, and thoughts of DelVecchio's angry face faded away. The comfort of courthouse voices mingling in unison, the smell of steamy home-cooked veggies and fresh-baked bread, the occasional raucous peal of laughter all struck a chord in Hailey, reminding her of the years she devoted her life to putting the bad guys in jail. These were the people who worked together for justice: court reporters, sheriffs, investigators, secretaries, and clerks. And lowly transport officers like Alton Turner.

They'd always have a smile for Hailey as she'd go through the list of inmates just brought over from the jail. Comparing her many pages of arraignment calendar to their list of transports started nearly every Monday morning for Hailey for ten years. She could see them now in their tan and brown sheriff uniforms, clipboard and pen, sharing a morning hello, maybe a cup of coffee, maybe handing her a notepad when she lost her own. A comrade.

Opting for ladling chicken noodle soup into a tall paper cup, she took a few packs of saltine crackers from a basket beside the steaming hot soup, took a cold bottled water from a tall, glass-door fridge, and balanced a cup of hot water for tea on a worn cafeteria tray. Hailey wound through at least a few dozen tables, most of them full of seated occupants chatting, eating, or glued to mobile devices and oblivious to the world around them, making her way to a single seat at a two-top near a far window.

Placing her iPhone, BlackBerry, and iPad in front of her to read the news, she caught a glimpse of a gorgeous old oak tree just outside the cafeteria window. Its arms spread out toward the building and its leaves shimmered in a breeze outside.

In a flash, she was mentally reliving a picnic she shared with Will under a huge tree just like this one. They were so, so happy. Hailey recalled distinctly wanting the moment to last forever. Lying on her back on a blanket, looking up at the leaves above them, she spontaneously asked the question, "Will we always be together, even after we die?" Will answered immediately: "Of course we will. I promise."

Even now, she couldn't imagine where the question came from. Will was murdered the following week and her question under the old oak branches always stuck with Hailey. The sure look in his crystal blue eyes when he'd answered so automatically . . . "*Of course we will . . .*"

Still gazing at the shimmering leaves outside the cafeteria, in Hailey's imagination they morphed into the grand old oak outside the apartment she shared with Will, outside their bedroom window. She'd see it first thing every morning, dancing in the sunshine through her bedroom drapes.

Beside the double windows was their bedroom closet and it was there that her wedding dress hung. It hung there silently, pristine, long, long after Will's murder; no one mentioned it should be returned or, at the very least, that the dress and veil should be carefully folded between layers of tissue paper and put away.

No one dared suggest the dress would never be worn. Of course Hailey would never wear it, and who else would buy it? The wedding dress of a bride who wore black to her fiancé's funeral instead of wearing the ivory dress in the closet to her wedding?

It was actually champagne silk, not ivory. It was off the shoulder, simple . . . not an overdone or ostentatious train, but a train nevertheless. The veil was made of light brocade. The two, gown and veil, were meant to gently sway down a carpeted aisle with flower petals gently scattered in her path, all lit by the golden glow of candlelight. In her wedding gown, Hailey should have been admired by a loving crowd gathered at the ceremony and been the subject of photos handed down to children and grandchildren.

Hailey was yanked to alert by an abrupt clatter of a lunch tray practically thrown onto the other side of the tiny two-top in front of her. On it sat a plate piled high with a greasy cheeseburger and a double serving of courthouse curly fries. Fincher pulled the metal chair back with much scraping and plopped down in front of her, smiling.

"This seat taken?"

"Not anymore!" Hailey pulled her tray closer and gathered up all her mobile devices, tucking them into her bag to make room for Finch.

"Some trial, huh? What an arrogant SOB. Am I right? This jury's gotta see straight through him." He tucked into the cheeseburger, holding it with both hands. The pressure forced a mixture of ketchup and mustard to ooze out the backside.

"That looks good. Nothing's better for you than another pound of red meat sitting in your stomach!" She gave him a gentle jab, handing him one of the paper napkins she brought with her from the lunch line.

A surge of new voices made Hailey look over her shoulder to see another wave of hungry lunch-goers coming down the ramp into the cafeteria. Hailey knew at once they were a pool of about sixty potential jurors. Based on their smiling faces, open laughter, and general good spirits, they were clearly just corralled for a trial, because after hours on end of voir dire, John Q. Publics tended to become irritated and grumpy, ready to go home, and ill at being separated from their iPhones.

Leading the pack were two courtroom bailiffs and a cheery-looking young woman. She was curvy but statuesque in a clingy, wraparound dress, a navy, purple, and shocking pink Diane von Furstenberg knockoff. Her honey-blonde locks fell in gentle curls around her shoulders. The huge stack of papers she was carrying could mean only one thing: She was the calendar clerk for that particular courtroom. Hailey knew the stack contained computer-generated sheets of data about the jury pool trouping along behind her as well as the morning's trial calendar.

That calendar would include anywhere from 100 to 200 names with corresponding indictment numbers and named offenses to be tried that week. About half of the defendants would plead guilty that morning when faced with the prospect of sixty fresh jurors waiting in the courthouse hall just outside the doors to the courtroom. Bravado of weeks and months sitting in the jail bragging about their upcoming jury trials flattened like a punctured balloon when they locked eyes with a jury.

How the calendar clerk could be in such a good mood with sixty jurors trailing behind her and 200 inmates left to process on top of an obviously imminent jury trial to manage was beyond Hailey. The clerk and the bailiffs, though, were the only people the jurors could legally talk to during a trial.

Good thing this bunch was in a great mood! They all shuffled down the ramp, merging into food lines, clutching their free lunch vouchers, all under the watchful eyes of their three guardians. They each wore white stick-on badges announcing they were jurors. Translation: Don't talk to me or risk a jury tampering charge!

It was high drama for a juror to be questioned and possibly thrown off an already impaneled jury because of contact with the outside world. Discussing the facts, or really any aspect of the trial prior to actual jury deliberations, would legally poison the juror, disallowing them from hearing facts and evidence with an open mind.

Hailey watched as the still-happy group ambled through the cafeteria lines. The sheriffs and the clerk split up to follow them like mother ducks. The woman's laughing brown eyes matched the curve of her smile as she plopped her stack of papers down on one of the longer tables that could accommodate a dozen lunch-goers. She then hopped back into her place in the lunch line, which an elderly juror was holding open for her in front of the Jell-O.

More peals of laughter came from the food lines and Hailey turned back to Fincher. "What was it you said about Adams?"

He was right in the middle of a huge bite of hamburger. He chewed a few seconds, swallowed, and took a gulp of soda. "What did I just say? I dunno, maybe that Adams is coming off like an arrogant jerk in front of the jury?"

"I hear you, but I disagree. I think a lot of the jurors are going to find him attractive."

"What? Hailey, I can't believe my ears. You think Adams is attractive? That's a first, that you'd have anything good to say about a man charged with killing his wife and baby." Fincher was incensed at this unforeseen turn of events.

"Fincher, get a hold of yourself. I didn't say I found him attractive. As a matter of fact, I don't. He's too slick for me, too suave, too smooth."

"Then why'd you say . . ."

"To win a case, you have to put your own feelings aside and deal with the facts. The hard, cold facts. And, whether you and I like it or not, we have to face the fact that some members of the jury will think he's attractive. Men and women both."

"What? What was that you just said? Women and men jurors think Todd Adams is attractive? What are you talking about?"

For a split second, Hailey thought Fincher was going to jump out of his seat with outrage, but he settled for dramatically throwing his paper cafeteria napkin onto the table beside his food tray.

"Yes, Finch, that's what I just said. That men and women will find him attractive. Women will love him regardless of their age. He reminds them of the man they think they'd like to be with or the 'one that got away.' Adams is also the kind of guy men jurors connect with as well, depending on their age. Younger male jurors might like to go have a beer with him. For the older men, he reminds them of their so-called 'glory days,' a young guy with a full head of hair, an athlete, in the prime of his life . . . just like they were, or how they think they were. Men jurors may see a little of themselves in Todd Adams."

Hailey was dead serious. Leaning toward Finch over the table, she went on. "That's dangerous, Fincher. That's how killers walk free . . . because prosecutors underestimate unspoken emotions at trial."

Fincher looked shocked, his mouth slightly open, staring at her like she was the enemy. Hailey went on, unfazed by the hairy eyeball Finch was giving her.

"I mean look at him, the thick dark hair swept back off his fore-head, chiseled features, warm brown eyes. He's built like an athlete and he looks great in that Armani suit. His outfit alone costs about $800, $1,000 at the least if you include the shoes, belt, and shirt. Maybe more."

Finch looked as if he had been struck deaf, dumb, and blind. "Face it, Finch, women want to be with him, men want to be him."

Hailey said all of this as if she were simply doing a crossword puzzle, unattached yet intrigued. "I don't care about his looks one way or another, Finch. It's all about the psychology behind it. The behavioral evidence. That's what wins a case."

"It's pretty amazing, Hailey. Just the way you read things, the way you analyze every detail and break it down to, basically, evidence. Even the cut of the guy's suit and the color of his eyes."

Before she could answer, they both looked down when Hailey's iPhone started buzzing with an incoming text. Hailey picked it up and read it.

"Work?" Finch asked, still watching the jurors in line pushing trays along in front of them.

"Yep. It's Billings. He wants to go over the Alton Turner case after we leave court today."

"That'll be late. Hope he throws in dinner. And it better be somewhere good. No drive-through."

"He didn't mention anything about dinner, nothing like Alton Turner's severed torso to ruin your appetite. So let's you and me go somewhere, you pick. Hey, you getting coffee or dessert or anything?"

"I might. Yeah, probably. I did see some peach pie over there . . ." Fincher's voice trailed away as he glanced toward the food line.

"What you saw were canned peaches. They're not fresh. I wouldn't bother," Hailey cut in.

"Now how would you know they're canned?" Finch's question came out mid-bite.

"Because the crust on that peach pie they have up there was already sliced open and I happened to notice all the peaches were cut so uniformly, they had to be from a factory kitchen. I mean, I'm just saying."

"I was all set for some homemade peach pie and a cup of coffee and then you, what with all your analysis, ruined it!"

After giving him one long look, Hailey burst into laughter. "You lose your appetite? You know you're going to eat it anyway!"

"Yeah, I am." He grinned and took a bite of burger. The two sat in friendly, comfortable silence as they both finished their lunches. It was the kind of silence that's unstrained or lacking.

Fincher started in about the trial again. "But how can the jury be so blind? Can't they see he did it?"

"Have you lost your mind, Fincher? What do you mean? 'Can't they see he did it?' See what? The state's still putting up witnesses! We haven't even heard the defense! Or closing arguments for that matter! Talk about putting the cart before the horse . . . I mean, really."

Fincher looked back at her with a sulk. "Well, all I know is this. If you and I were putting the Todd Adams case to a jury, they'd already be rolling their eyes every time DelVecchio stood up to open his mouth. They'd be staring daggers at Adams and groaning every time that mother of his cries into a hanky. That's what I know, little girl."

"Fincher . . ." Hailey's retort was drowned out by a sharp, shrill, high-pitched scream. They both turned just in time to see a woman juror leaping up from her seat to the simultaneous sound of lunch trays clattering to the floor.

The loud scraping of cafeteria chairs against the tiled floor mingled with the scream sent a tingling chill down Hailey's back as she and Fincher jerked their heads toward the center of the room. A female sheriff leaped from her seat and like the juror, let out an ear-piercing scream.

For one discrete moment, the cafeteria went totally quiet as everyone froze in their places, some with forks poised in their hands, midair.

But Hailey and Finch jumped up from their table and began darting between chairs, closing the distance between their seats by the windows to the source of the screams in just seconds.

Breaking through knots of onlookers gathered tightly around the source of the scream, they spotted what the female sheriff and lady juror saw.

There on the cafeteria floor. It was her . . . her arms and legs sprawled out at odd angles. The honey-blonde.

Stacks of papers she just carried down the ramp to the cafeteria were strewn on the floor around her. Her fork and spoon still rested neatly on top of a folded, white paper napkin, but the contents of her lunch, once on her plastic tray, were splattered across her chair and onto the floor. A fruit salad, sweet potato chips, and remains of a veggie plate were hurled onto the tile floor. Lying nearby was a to-go cup of coffee. Checks in black marker were made beside the words "Morning Blend," "Black," and "Half-Decaf."

From where she stood, Hailey saw bright pink lipstick on the white Styrofoam rim of the cup. It barely remained on her lips, but it matched the lipstick the calendar clerk was wearing.

The woman lying on the floor looked very little like the smiling, statuesque blonde that Hailey had just spotted leading jurors toward their prepaid county lunches. Now she was splayed on the floor, her wrap dress askew, mascara and black eyeliner smeared across her face.

Her eyes were wide open, protruding grotesquely from their sockets. Tears, still wet on her face, mixed with eyeliner and made dark rivulets down her cheeks. But that was the least of it.

Her peaches and cream complexion was now almost entirely purple. With a sudden convulsion, her body went rigid, her lips unmistakably turning blue before their eyes.

"Elle! Elle! What's wrong?" The male sheriff who had been leading the jurors along with her to their lunch knelt down beside her. "Eleanor! Say something!"

Jerking off his deputy's hat, he quickly bent over the clerk and tried to administer CPR. Hailey and Finch immediately knelt beside him, Hailey grasping the woman's wrist for a pulse, Finch calling for help on his investigators' radio. Several people standing around whipped out cell phones to dial 911.

The sheriff's CPR effort was clumsy but even had it not been, Hailey could see around his shoulder that when he tried to clear her airway for mouth to mouth, the woman's tongue had swelled to the point where he could do nothing. Elle was either dead or dying.

In moments, courthouse EMTs swarmed the cafeteria. Banging doors and loud voices broke through the cluster of people standing around. But by the time the EMTs arrived, Elle was in full respiratory arrest.

Their first maneuver was to run a tube down her throat so they could push air to Elle's lungs. It wasn't easy. The first several efforts failed because her throat had closed up. There was absolutely nowhere to slide the tube. The EMTs injected her with several syringes full of clear liquid that seemed to have no effect whatsoever.

But they didn't stop. They never stopped trying. Not for a second. Even after Elle was clearly dead there on the floor, they kept frantically trying to revive her.

The sound of ambulance sirens and police cars screamed from outside, down on the street, reaching up the sides of the old building and through the windows. But by the time paramedics ran from their emergency vehicles to the elevators and took the elevators to the cafeteria, courthouse EMTs and the sheriff who tried to save her were sitting on the floor distraught or standing disconsolately, some crying.

She was dead. They couldn't save her. Two of the paramedics quickly knelt beside her to give it another try, complete with chest compressions and then a defib paddle.

Ripping open her wrap dress, they tore off a gold costume necklace that dangled just beneath the base of her throat to apply adhesive electrodes to her chest. One of the paramedics connected electrodes to the defibrillator and Hailey was vaguely aware of the other one screaming for everyone to clear the room.

The adhesive solid-gel electrodes, while easier to use in a non-hospital setting, tend to burn the skin. Once the electrodes were applied in an anterior-apex scheme with the first electrode placed on the right, below her collarbone, and the other over the apex of the heart, on the left side, the electrical surge went through her body.

The crowd remaining barely breathed. They all stood tensed, staring at Elle on the floor, praying and hoping against hope the jolt of electricity would bring her back.

Nothing. The smell of singeing flesh rose in the air as the paramedic called for another round. Still kneeling beside the woman, Hailey looked away.

The EMTs and deputies stood silent until the lead paramedic broke the silence. "What happened? Heart attack?"

"I don't know, I don't know. One minute we were all sitting here having lunch, talking. The next, she grabbed her throat, she tried to stand up. She seemed to sway a little and she fell onto the table, everything went flying and . . . and . . . I tried CPR . . . but she . . . she turned purple and I . . . I . . ." The sheriff, Deputy Marks, had to stop speaking in an effort to compose himself.

From the corner of her eye, Hailey noticed a pale woman in a knee-length plaid skirt slip through the double doors to the cafeteria. Her starched white blouse was tucked in tightly and buttoned up all the way to the collar.

Her thin, fine hair was mousy brown and parted straight down the middle. Wispy bangs coming just halfway down her forehead indicated the strong possibility of a home haircut over the bathroom sink of the old bowl cut variety. While she evidently wore no makeup whatsoever, Hailey could make out pale hazel eyes. Hanging around her neck was a blue lanyard with a Chatham County ID card bearing her name and picture.

The woman's eyes darted around the cafeteria from left to right, then left again until they rested on Deputy Marks, now sitting at a two-top. He was being consoled by one of the pink-faced little old ladies who worked over steaming food in the lunch line. Keeping to the edge of the room, she walked crablike, in a sort of side step, back against the outer tables over to Marks.

"What happened, Deputy Marks? Is it true? Is she . . . dead?"

He didn't move, but looked up at her from his seat at the table. "Yes, Eunah. It's true. I can't believe it. I can't take it in. Elle's passed away . . . she's . . . she's dead." The tears began again as he held a bandanna to his eyes to mop his face.

"Oh, Deputy Marks, I'm so sorry. I'm so sorry to hear . . ."

"Get away from me, Eunah!" Marks abruptly pushed away from the table and stood up, his voice raised. "Don't act like you're sorry, Eunah Mabry. You hated her. Nothing could have made you happier than to find out she's dead. And over what? A married man. Who cares if he's a judge? Go ahead and admit it. The whole courthouse knows about it. Now that she's dead, you won't be happy until his wife leaves him and Bill Regard's thrown off the bench!"

"How . . . *how d-d-dare you!*" She sputtered the words out, stammering, searching for the right denial. "That is absolutely not true! The judge is happily married . . . no matter what that . . . *woman's* . . . scheming designs were on him! And I . . . I never so much as had a dinner with the judge!"

"Not because you didn't want to! Because he never asked you! You've been jealous of Elle since the day she came here. And you can tell your Yale-educated, rich-boy judge that I don't like the way he treated Elle. He's a piece of crap as far as I'm concerned! And I don't care if he knows it! In fact, you tell him Deputy Marks said so—"

The deputy was abruptly cut off by another sheriff who seemed ready for battle, materializing out of scattered tables, chairs, and food lines. "Hey, shut your mouth! She never slept with that pompous ass. That's not true. Don't talk about her like that!" The younger, painfully thin sheriff sporting a sparse, ginger mustache stepped into the mix, his Adam's apple bobbing in anger.

"What do you have to do with this, Marshall?" Deputy Marks gave the younger sheriff a confused and disapproving look.

Marshall stammered. "N-n-nothing! I just, I just thought she . . . she was a nice lady!" He finally spit the remainder of his sentence out and with that, turned on his heel and stalked up the ramp toward the elevator bank.

Marks looked after him, seemingly surprised at the younger man's outburst, but with a look of dawning settling over his features, he realized just how popular Eleanor Odom had been.

Eleanor's body was about to be hoisted onto a gurney. The deputy turned back to the judge's secretary, contempt smeared across his face. "Don't act like you care about her now that she's dead. Get out of my sight, Eunah! You sanctimonious prat! Judging her, the whole time wishing it was *you*! *With him!* You and your judge both make me sick. Get lost . . . you don't deserve to even see her body taken out."

And with that, Deputy Marks stormed out the opposite end of the cafeteria. He blasted through the other set of swinging double doors toward the employee parking deck.

Eunah Mabry stood rooted to her spot, an absolutely mortified look on her now sheet-white face. Her ramrod-straight posture swayed a tiny bit as she glanced around the cafeteria, especially at the group of people closest to her, clearly overwhelmed at the thought they may have heard the accusations against her.

For a moment, Hailey thought the mousy woman might just keel over with embarrassment, but slowly, bright red crept up her neck and across her cheeks. Knowing they'd certainly heard it all, Eunah Mabry quickly turned away from the cluster of people. Maintaining a rigid backbone, she all but ran up the sloping ramp, disappearing through the set of double doors to the elevator banks.

"Who was *that*?" Hailey turned to a sergeant.

"I'm not really sure, but I'm guessing it's Judge Regard's secretary. And I think I know a little too much now. About Judge Bill Regard. Probably more than his wife does."

Hailey glanced around at the sound of unfolding plastic. The paramedics were zipping Elle's body into a black plastic body bag.

"Wait!" shouted a male court reporter Hailey recognized from the metal detector line that morning. Perfectly dressed in a crisp shirt, tie, and slacks, he stood up from his chair near a window. He had been sitting there, holding his jaw in both palms and elbows on the tabletop, watching the shock unfold through his fingers.

He crossed the room to the gurney. Reaching the body, he placed a silent kiss on the first three fingers of his right hand, then gently touched them to Elle's lips as she lay there.

Hailey looked up at Fincher. "So Eleanor Odom's got two sheriffs, one judge, and a court reporter in love with her and she drops dead at age what . . . 36?"

Finch looked quizzically. "Two deputies, one judge, and one court reporter . . . *that we know of.*"

"It's not a crime, Fincher." Hailey responded quickly to the tone in Fincher's voice. They stood, watching as two paramedics rolled out the gurney.

"What's not a crime?" He feigned ignorance.

"Sleeping around. If a man did it, you wouldn't even comment. And if there was, he'd be a hero. So put a sock in it."

"I didn't say a thing!"

"But you were going to! Don't deny it!"

"OK! I was! You're right! I was going to make a joke, but you're right. The lady's dead. Sorry, Hailey."

Walking through the double doors to the outside toward the parking lot, they passed a sheriff, heavily muscled, blonde hair buzzed close to his skull. Neck, face, and arms heavily tanned from riding in his cruiser with the windows down. He was turned facing the wall, his forehead lightly touching it. From his profile, Finch and Hailey could both see tears rolling unabashedly down his cheeks, his nose running profusely. As they passed, Fincher patted him on the back and they kept walking.

"Make that one judge, one court reporter, and *three* sheriffs, Hailey."

There was a long silence between them as they entered the elevator alone. "She obviously lived a very, um," Hailey searched for the right word, ". . . *full* life."

"Hailey?"

"Yes, Finch?"

"You should have been a diplomat. The UN could use you."

"Shut up, Finch."

The doors to the elevator swished open and outside, it looked warm and dazzlingly bright. Heading through the huge oak courthouse doors, they stepped into the sunshine.

"Hey, Finch? Is she the same Eleanor that Alton Turner kept emailing?"

"Oh, darn! I left my bag in there!" Finch and Hailey both stopped in their tracks. They had just made it up several flights of stairs and all the way to their rental car in the courthouse parking deck.

"What's in it, Hailey? I thought you brought it all with you to the cafeteria. I saw your iPad, I know, there on the table." Finch looked over at her as if he couldn't believe that she, Hailey Dean, would ever make a fundamental mistake like leaving anything of value in an open courtroom. A courtroom usually full of criminals.

"Nothing really valuable. And you're right. I did bring my iPad, iPhone, and BlackBerry with me to lunch. But I left my shrug and carry bag of notes in the courtroom to save our seats. The bag is just the old canvas one I've had forever, nobody would want it. Or my notes on the trial . . . nobody would want those . . . but me!"

Side by side, the two headed back down the same flight of concrete stairs they'd just climbed up. It led to a side door to the front entrance. "OK. I'll walk back with you. But one thing . . . what's a *shrug?*"

"You have a wife and two daughters, right? It's a sweater, for Pete's sake!"

"Whatever. I'll go back with you even though you are cutting into our pizza time."

"I never agreed to more pizza. Let's just get that on the record right now." At the top of the granite steps, Finch tried the front center door.

"It's past closing time, Hailey. Door's locked."

"Let me try the one on the side." Hailey twisted the knob of the huge door on the right, one of three across the massive front façade.

The knob turned under her hand, and she pushed the big door forward. The doors opened into an anteroom leading to a massive lobby. Front and center was a huge walk-through metal detector positioned directly in front of the center door. The rest of the lobby was cordoned off, so Hailey and Finch had to go back through the machine again. Sitting beside it reading a magazine was a lone sheriff working the overnight shift.

"Hey, man. What's up?" Fincher greeted him.

"Hey Fincher, Miss Dean. What brings you back to the courthouse so soon? Didn't all the courtrooms adjourn right after Elle . . . I mean . . . did you guys hear about the excitement in the cafeteria?"

Fincher peeled three guns off his body (waist, shoulder, and ankle) to drop them one by one in battered white plastic bowls and put them on a conveyor belt for screening. Hailey put her iPad and phones in a plastic basket that followed along after Finch's guns.

"We didn't just hear about it, we were there," Finch responded as they went, one by one, through the machine.

"Seriously, man? You were there?"

"Yep. We were there." Finch spoke over his shoulder as he scooped his guns out of the plastic bowl and commenced strapping them back on, shoulder holster first. Hailey remained silent, reaching across the belt for her things, having no desire to rehash what she had just witnessed . . . the calendar clerk's untimely death and the futile struggle to keep her alive.

"Yeah, we're all pretty torn up about it. Elle was a nice lady. Always had a smile every morning, same thing every afternoon when she left work. Never had a bad word to say about a soul." The night sheriff looked somber.

"Yeah. We heard she was pretty popular around the courthouse . . ." Finch egged him on and as a result, got a sharp jab to his right side as he bent over to strap his .38 back into his ankle holster.

"Not a word . . . *not a word* . . ." Hailey hissed it low into his ear. She didn't want to pass along pure conjecture about Eleanor Odom's "popularity." Luckily, the night sheriff didn't catch her exchange with Fincher.

"Elle always organized Christmas parties, the annual walk-a-thon for needy kids, Toys for Tots . . . the works." He reminisced out loud but in a lowered voice, still looking downcast.

"We, as a matter of fact," Finch replied, "were in the cafeteria when she had her stroke, heart attack, whatever it was, poor lady, and we walked out without going back to where Hailey left her sweater and notes on a bench to save our seats during lunch. Mind if we go up and get them?"

"What courtroom was it?" the sheriff asked, still sitting in his chair, magazine now folded shut in his lap.

"Hmm. Let me see . . . what courtroom was it, Hailey?"

"Judge Alverson's. Luther Alverson, seventh floor."

"Right. The Todd Adams trial? You guys on that one?" The sheriff's eyes sparked with interest.

"Yep. I made the collar on Adams in Atlanta and Hailey's here as an expert witness."

"For the defense? You're a witness for the defense? You're the lady prosecutor from Atlanta, right?"

"*Was* a lady prosecutor in Atlanta. *Was.*"

"Never lost a case, right? Read about you. You're a witness for the defense now? I hear DelVecchio pays his witnesses pretty good."

Hailey bristled. "I'm a witness for the state. There are some things money can't buy, *officer.*"

He looked embarrassed. "Right. I shoulda known you wouldn't turn coat. I just thought, you know, once somebody's out of the system, they can turn all that time in the trenches around for a lot of money, right?"

Hailey relented. "Right." She threw him a bone, a little smile.

"So, we'll head up to the courtroom if that's OK with you." Fincher switched gears, tactfully, for once in his life.

"Well, yeah, about that. The courtroom's been cleared and locked. If you left anything in there, it's in lost and found now. It's right over there across the lobby in the clerk's office. I'm right out here, so it's still unlocked. I can't leave my post; just walk through those double doors and go straight back through the cubicles. You'll see a sign on the wall. Everything left in courtrooms or elsewhere will be in that big bin under a sign. You can't miss it."

"OK." Finch nodded his head.

"They usually won't let you back there without a courthouse employee, but seeing as you're law enforcement, I guess I don't need to escort you. Just don't steal anything or it'll be my hide."

"OK, thanks, man. We promise not to steal a thing."

"Thanks, Sheriff." Hailey echoed Finch over her shoulder as they headed past austere-looking portraits of decades of past sitting Chatham County judges and across the lobby toward the central elevator bank. Veering left, they came to a set of double doors with a placard reading "Clerk's Office" overhead.

Fincher pushed through and Hailey followed him into a large open office area full of at least sixty cubicles in neat rows divided by carpeted footpaths. More placard signs hung down from a particleboard ceiling, dividing the open area into clerks, sheriff intake, transport, marriage licenses, and certified documents. Each section housed multiple cubicles.

At the far end of the room, just as the night sheriff said, was a big sign reading "Lost and Found" over a huge bin. Arrows pointed down toward the bin. They headed toward it through the maze of cubes, passing row after row of work stations; each, in its own way, a thumbprint, a snapshot of the occupant's life.

Photos, certificates, trophies, and mini-posters adorned every cube. Most of the cubes had nameplates on them on the top corners of the partitions. It brought back memories of Hailey's courthouse days in a rush . . . all these people, so different yet so alike, working for the justice system. Each one a cog in a big, big wheel.

"Oh my stars, look at this, Finch. It's Alton Turner's cube. Look, it's neat as a pin, just like I thought it would be." Finch walked back to where Hailey stood, staring at Turner's workspace, her hands lightly resting on the wheeled office chair pushed under the desktop.

While the space was inordinately neat, several photos were thumbtacked to the dividing partitions making walls of a sort around Turner's space. There were several shots of Turner with other sheriffs, at the shooting range, a softball team, a bowling team, too. Men and women law enforcement officers standing together, smiling at the camera. Looking closely at the smiling faces, Hailey saw the woman in the center holding a team softball trophy next to Alton Turner was none other than Eleanor Odom.

Next to his keyboard was a tickler file of prisoners to be transported to various courtrooms, filed day by day. Beside that was a larger framed photo of Turner and his mom standing in front of the Grand Canyon. Even if Hailey hadn't seen the oil painting in Alton's home, anyone could see their connection. Her eyes, chin, and nose matched Alton's exactly. In this shot, Alton had his arm around his mom's shoulders protectively. They were smiling at the camera, squinting into the sunshine. Another was a shot of her, bust up, taken by a professional photographer that could have easily come from the church directory, like the one over Alton's mantle.

"Look at this. He's across the path from Eleanor Odom." Finch pointed right behind them. Hailey turned around to see two cubicles apparently merged into one large cube. Multiple photos of Eleanor were plastered to its walls. Her in what looked to be a glamour shot, at a Christmas party dressed in a black velvet mini with black heels and a tiny matching clutch, her hair done in a Farrah Fawcett-style 'do. Roller skating with a tall, mustached guy Hailey immediately recognized as the suntanned sheriff crying in the cafeteria hallway.

Another showed her jogging, clearly in a race of some sort, crossing the finish line with other courthouse personnel, including Deputy Marks from the cafeteria. A huge bouquet of long-stemmed pink roses stood in a clear crystal vase to the left of her keyboard, the tiny rectangular card still stuck in a tall plastic fork emerging from between delicate pink blooms. It read, "Lots of love, B.R."

Looking at it carefully, Hailey and Finch exchanged glances. "Guess we know who sent that. B.R. isn't much of a secret. It's her married judge, Bill Regard, right, Hailey?" Finch gazed back at the flowers.

"Yep." Hailey acknowledged his find. "I bet dating a married man is a lonely life. A life you fill up with bowling and softball."

"And toy drives," Finch added.

"Yep, toy drives."

They stood a moment looking at the display. "Hey look, Hailey. Her email's still up."

"Finch, get out of her business! The woman's dead." But even as she spoke, Hailey craned over to see the list of emails up on the screen.

"Check out all these emails from Alton Turner!" Finch exclaimed.

"That doesn't mean anything, they worked together, practically on top of each other." As she said the words, she spotted what Fincher meant. At least twenty to thirty emails, one after the next, from Turner. They had been opened.

"But Turner's been dead for two days now. She was just reading them?"

"Well," Hailey began, ". . . I think she was *re-reading* them. Look." Hailey clicked open one of the emails. "See, she opened this one yesterday, Monday, when she got to work. Look at the date, he sent these the morning before he died."

"So she was re-reading them just before she went up to the cafeteria then. What do they say?"

"Finch, I don't think we should read her . . ."

"OK. In this one, he's just saying they should get a sandwich for lunch. That's innocent enough. But look, now he's telling her she's making a bad decision. It's got to be about the judge. And look, Hailey, here he is asking her if she wants to see a movie. I think he had a crush on her."

"Well, who wouldn't?" Hailey countered. "She's young, she's beautiful, she jogs, plays softball . . ."

"She runs the toy drive and dates a married judge plus one court reporter and three sheriffs that we know of . . ."

"You made your point! I get it! I'm going to stop spying on a dead woman and get my sweater and bag, I hope." Hailey turned and headed down the row toward the lost and found bin and looked in.

It was surprisingly full of items left behind throughout the courthouse . . . jackets; a backpack; a little black beaded shoulder bag just big enough for a few items; several lined notepads covered in scribbled writing, probably lawyers' notes; a kid's green LeapFrog computer; and a brown leather briefcase.

And sure enough, there it was, right on top of the pile of forgotten belongings. Hailey's sweater was neatly folded and placed on her old canvas bag.

"See? Somebody turned it in. There are *still* good people in this world." Hailey called over her shoulder as she bent over to get her things.

"Finch! Get out of her email!" He was still standing at Elle's space when Hailey turned around.

"I'm not in her email anymore! I'm at another cubicle looking at alligators!"

"What? Did you just say you're looking at alligators?"

"Yep. Alligators. I'm at the cubicle next to hers. Look at this inmate transport guy's space! All these postcards and pictures of all sorts of wild animals. And here's an old one of Steve Irwin. And here's one of that other wild animal guy . . . Jack Hanna."

Hailey paused briefly, looking at all the exotic animals and photo safari shots. By the huge stack of inmate transport sheets next to his computer screen, he clearly was not afraid of handling dangerous animals.

"Can we go get dinner now?" Hailey asked in mock desperation. "As much as I love spying on county clerks and transport officers, I'm starved."

"OK, Hailey girl. Let's go get pizza."

"Again, Fincher. I never agreed to *another* pizza night. What about a salad bar? Have you ever even heard of that? They're awesome . . . lettuce, tomatoes, peppers, cheese . . . you know . . . healthy?"

The two headed back through the double doors and into the cavernous courthouse lobby. Nodding at the night sheriff, Hailey held up her canvas bag and sweater, showing him she found her things. They pushed through the side door out onto the courthouse steps and into fresh air, away from the ghosts of the dead and their now-empty cubicles full of memories. The sky over them just barely hinted at nighttime approaching.

Dinner turned out to be a compromise. Not pizza, not a salad bar . . . but Mexican. Fincher chowed down on a huge basket of chips and salsa, two cheesy beef burritos, and a bowl that, according to Hailey, looked like a vat of cheese sauce. It was titled on the menu as Queso Divertido, or cheesy fun. Hailey went with the Veggie Lover's Delight with avocado.

After, Hailey drove her rental car straight back to the hotel where the state was putting her up. It wasn't luxurious by any means, but it had a double window that looked past Savannah's famed River Street and out onto the side bend of the Savannah River.

By night, the water was black and silver ripples mirrored the lights of River Street along its edges. Huge ships, barges, and yachts floated past under the stars. There were container ships from faraway ports gliding by in the dark with writing on their sides foreign to Hailey.

After a hot bath, toothpaste, and makeup remover, Hailey sat in the dark on the edge of the king bed situated against the center of the bedroom wall. Hotel drapes still drawn open, she sat motionless, thinking, legs drawn up under her, watching the dark water and the watercraft passing by on the swelling waters of the Intracoastal Waterway that could take a ship all the way up the Eastern Seaboard.

Rowdy voices drifting up from far below her window on the eleventh floor of the River Street Hyatt broke her train of thought. Restless, Hailey paced past the walnut cabinet housing a flat-screen TV. Reaching into her canvas bag, she pulled out her Todd Adams trial notes and her iPad resting in its eggshell-blue case.

Turning on the iPad, she started by poring over searches of Todd Adams, Julie Love, their wedding, and the trial. She rarely found an entry she hadn't already read.

Staring at the screen's effervescent glow, just for the heck of it, she plugged in the name Chase Billings. Wow, Hailey had no idea about his history. "Sharpshooter of the Year" eight years in a row, "Rookie of the Year," and number one in his class at the police academy. He received the Sheriff's Medal of Valor for storming into an ongoing bank robbery in full SWAT gear, taking down the three thugs inside the bank, and, before it was all done, shooting out the tires of the getaway car. Then there was the National Sheriff's Star.

Three years before that, he was awarded the Medal for Heroism for chasing down a white van driven by a child predator during a high-speed chase. Billings managed somehow to get the nine-year-old little girl out unharmed and take down the perp. Just to top it all off, he graduated summa cum laude from the Wharton School at the University of Pennsylvania.

Hailey cleared the screen. Billings never once let on.

She clicked off Chase Billings and tapped in the words "Eleanor Odom" and "Chatham County." Dozens of hits immediately presented themselves.

Just as the night deputy said, there she was . . . Committee Chairman of Toys for Tots for the past four years running, walk-a-thons, charity runs, you name it, Eleanor Odom did it. The fourth or fifth entry down had a link to Eleanor Odom's Facebook page. Clicking on the link, a virtual encyclopedia of her life revealed itself. Literally hundreds of photos of Eleanor with friends, at dinner, and with pets all came into view on the screen glowing in the dark of Hailey's hotel room.

Posts about jogging, the courthouse, cases, trials, fundraisers . . . it was all there. Her life was an open book. Or was it?

Hailey noticed that while there were plenty of sheriffs peppered throughout the photos, there wasn't a single one of Judge Bill Regard. Hailey looked him up.

The judge's online profile revealed a distinguished-looking guy in his mid-to-late thirties, handsome with dark hair brushed straight back from his face and deep brown eyes that practically crackled with intelligence, even in a photo. He was dressed in his long black judicial robes and seated in front of a wall containing shelves of law books Hailey immediately recognized as the OCGA, the Official Code of Georgia, Annotated.

Other photos showed Regard getting sworn in, his wife, a petite brunette with her hair in a short bob dressed startlingly similar to Jackie Onassis, and their three children. Two boys and a girl stood beside their mother. All three resembled Bill Regard.

Hailey clicked back to Eleanor's Facebook page to make sure not a single picture of Bill Regard appeared. Hailey wondered if Deputy Marks was right. Had she secretly been in love with Regard? And what must that be like? For Regard to mourn in complete secrecy?

The memory of the years of mourning Will's death flooded over her . . . the weeks of no appetite whatsoever . . . the very smell of food would make her nauseated. Crying in the shower, the pain of hearing songs on the radio or even the low buzz of voices on TV. Not being able to even speak Will's name—that would have been unbearable. If Marks was in fact right, that's what Judge Regard was going through at this very moment.

Eleanor Odom had lots and lots of "friends." Hailey started scrolling down more than 400 so-called Facebook friends, recognizing several court personnel. And there, of course, was Alton Turner, decked out in full Chatham County Sheriff regalia.

She had lots and lots of friends . . . but were they really friends? Did any of them ever tell her, as a friend, to stop the courthouse romance with a married man? A judge at that? In the public eye? Hailey thought back to the thin, pale wife, the Jackie O look-alike. Did Mrs. Bill Regard know her husband was cheating? Was that what she was thinking about as she held the Bible for her husband to take his oath as judge?

Hailey minimized Eleanor's Facebook screen and went to Google. Dozens of articles popped up before she'd even finished typing the words "Judge Bill Regard Chatham County." Regard had been a crackerjack trial lawyer before he took the bench, a former death-penalty prosecutor for the state's attorney general's office.

That, in itself, was a rare achievement. Only the best and the brightest were typically entrusted to handle death-penalty cases and the AG was very selective when it came to their trial lawyers. He appeared to be a Democratic Party darling and was rumored to be up for the next available spot on the Georgia Supreme Court . . . or more. Some articles suggested that Regard was considering a run at the Georgia governor's mansion.

Wow. The governor's mansion. It was absolutely gorgeous—a 24,000-square-foot red brick Greek revival palace rising at the crest of a gently sloping hill. The entire eighteen acres of lawn was absolute perfection, adorned by abundantly blooming pink, purple, and white azalea bushes, dogwoods, cherry trees, and plenty of tall pine trees that never seemed to drop a single pinecone on the green carpet below.

The interior was gorgeous but comfortable looking. Ostentatious would never do, but the mansion was the ultimate in classical, muted design, not over the top, but clearly steeped in good taste and expert interior design. It was just a few miles northwest of downtown Atlanta. Hailey had been there several times for law enforcement galas.

Hailey sat on her hotel bed, staring at her iPad. If Bill Regard ever hoped to move himself and his family into that mansion someday, it could never come to light that he had an affair with a calendar clerk behind his wife's back.

That sort of story might play in other parts of the country where the cheater would make a carefully guarded statement, with his wife standing beside him in prescription-drug stoicism as her husband claimed a "sex addiction." He'd then go somewhere posh like Horizons Malibu Rehab and be back cheating again in four to six weeks. But in the Bible Belt, not just cheating—but cheating *and* humiliating your wife—was the kiss of death.

If this came out about Elle, Regard's goose was cooked.

Hailey started to navigate out of the online maze of Eleanor Odom's life, but she paused briefly to look at an absolutely perfect-looking roast turkey. Just barely showing over the top of the evenly browned bird was Elle's smiling face, proud of the big bird she'd basted and cooked to perfection. In the background, Hailey could just make out a Thanksgiving pilgrim decoration in the center of a table set for eight.

Hailey clicked through. Eleanor Odom was quite the cook, sharing dozens and dozens of food postings, maybe close to a hundred or so. Many of them showed her cooking in what appeared to be a small apartment kitchen. Several of the dishes were photographed at various stages of preparation with a gorgeous shot at the end. One was a steamed lobster, completely done and perfectly pink, garnished and sitting staged on the same table as the turkey, but this time set for two.

But for who?

Hailey rummaged through a myriad of recipes, amazed Eleanor had taken the time to post so many. What sort of a woman spends hours and hours not just preparing food, but posing the dishes and taking pictures of them to post online?

There was a beautiful shot of ruby red rhubarb and deep purplish-green kale in two colanders beside the sink. Hailey clicked on a gorgeous peach salad with prosciutto, plum, and amaretto tarts, a blue and white dish of bourbon-poached peaches posed on an antique linen tablecloth. Eleanor had each recipe detailed beside each photo. Hailey paused to read "Eleanor's Delicious Banana Nut Bread Without the Nuts!" The next was a photo of Eleanor in a Christmas sweater with "My Favorite Fruitcake, Fruity Not Nutty!" A different set of postings covered cooking organically, avoiding foods treated with pesticides, and intricate recipes for pastries like napoleons and éclairs.

The time and planning it must have taken to prepare, pose, photograph, then post the photogenic dishes. They were, each and every one, absolutely perfect. Had it become sort of an obsession for Eleanor Odom? Something to fill her time? But then there were softball games, charity functions, work. She didn't need time-fillers.

Or maybe it was Eleanor's desire to create something perfect, something beautiful, something that she alone could control . . .

including its outcome. Was she obsessed not just with the preparation of food, but with creating the perfect family home ... minus the family? The family she'd never be able to have with a married judge?

Exhausted and feeing like she knew way too much about Eleanor Odom now, Hailey turned off the iPad and pulled back the covers on her bed. Settling in, she pulled the blankets over her. Lying on the bed looking out and up through the window, she had an entirely different view. Instead of the black water of the Savannah River, she saw an even deeper black, velvety sky with stars twinkling down through her hotel room window.

Unbidden, photos of Eleanor Odom drifted through her mind. So happy, so vibrant, so alive. The last glimpse Hailey had of her, her face was purple and sweaty as she died on the cafeteria floor. Hailey felt a deep swell of sadness for the woman she hadn't even known. The woman smiling over a roasted turkey, holding a team softball trophy, in love, sadly, with a married man. The woman who probably never even knew Alton Turner adored her.

It was 10:30 AM and the courtroom was packed. Hailey sat with her notebook and pen in hand, she and Fincher touching shoulders, three rows back behind prosecutors. The courtroom never failed to remind Hailey of a wedding: No matter how large or small the ceremony was, lavish or simple, guests invariably sat on either the bride's or the groom's "side." Guests would only be seated otherwise if there were no seats on the "right" side.

Julie Love's blood family, relatives, and friends sat, like Hailey and Finch, behind the prosecution. Todd Adams's family, supporters, and the press sat on the defense's side of the huge, old courtroom.

Once or twice, Hailey spotted Tish Adams casting a quick, surreptitious glance across the center aisle dividing the sides. Hailey caught her looking over, usually, at Julie's mother and once at Hailey herself. When she locked eyes with Hailey, Tish Adams quickly looked away.

Opening statements had commenced at nine o'clock sharp under Luther Alverson's watchful eye. He stared down from the bench, rarely interrupting, but listening carefully. His law clerk, Walter Lovell, according to a desk placard sitting at a solid wood desk to the side of the judge's bench, was a slight, pale young man with a bushy moustache, a high forehead, and pale blue eyes. Lovell also seemed to listen to every single syllable uttered in the courtroom, likely as an aide to Alverson. The judge would do nothing to jeopardize these proceedings.

The state's opening had lasted exactly an hour, and, afraid they'd lose their places, neither Hailey nor Fincher left the room for a break before Mikey DelVecchio began opening for the defense. Not a word was spoken as the lead prosecutor, following his opening, returned to his seat at the counsel table closest to the jury box and sat down, clearly spent of energy.

The courtroom was completely hushed. A long silence ensued. From behind them, Hailey could see Julie Love's father place a protective arm around her mom's shoulders, as if to protect her from what was about to happen.

And he was right.

"Mr. DelVecchio? Are you ready to proceed with opening statement for the defense?" Alverson was not about to allow defense delays this early in the ball game.

"Yes, sir. I am." DelVecchio stood up from his chair, pushing it back as he did. He didn't make a move away from the defense counsel table, but stood there, stock-still, his back erect, perusing the jurors from twenty to thirty feet away.

"Julie Love Adams *slept around*!" DelVecchio practically shouted it like a battle cry.

Gasps erupted throughout the courtroom and a single, audible cry, quickly stifled, tore from the throat of Julie's mother. She quickly covered her face in her husband's shoulder. At the same instant, the man seated in a wheelchair beside the father, obviously Julie's younger brother, Brent, grabbed his dad's other shoulder to keep him seated when he made to spring to his feet in defense of his dead daughter.

"Order! Order in the court!" Alverson beat his gavel on hardwood from the bench. Simultaneously the prosecutor leaped to his feet and yelled, *"Objection!"*

"They can't do that!" Hailey whispered into Finch's ear as he leaned over. "You can't bring in the victim's reputation unless it's, say, for self-defense and the victim's known to be pugnacious or carry a gun . . ."

"Objection, Your Honor! A victim's reputation is inadmissible unless it goes to self-defense!" The prosecutor blurted it out as he continued to stand, now on the defense. He had controlled the courtroom up until now, but in the last fifteen seconds DelVecchio took over.

"It must be a ploy," Hailey whispered again into Finch's ear. "The state won't throw out the jury over this and it's not grounds for a mistrial unless it's directed at the defendant. So what's his game? Poisoning the jury against Julie?"

Another sob escaped Julie's mom. The judge looked over at her as a friend behind her handed her Kleenex across her pew.

"I'm sorry, Judge Alverson, but this *is* our defense." DelVecchio said it in his most sanctimonious tone, as if he hated blurting out that Julie was a tramp . . . but that he had to. Hailey knew that, of course, nothing could please DelVecchio more than destroying Julie's memory, if it meant saving his client and gaining national attention for getting another defendant off on murder one.

"Excuse me, counsel. Are you telling me Mr. Adams's defense to a charge of murder one is that his pregnant wife committed adultery?"

Hailey winced. Every time the charge was repeated in front of the jury made it less explosive. Pretty soon the words "Julie Love Adams" and "affairs" and/or "sex" wouldn't seem so incendiary. They would have heard it so often, they'd be numb.

"Yes, Your Honor. It is. We intend to prove that Julie Adams had so *many* sex affairs behind her husband's back that any number of men may have killed her. And as for being pregnant . . . I mean, *who knows who the biological father may have been?*"

At that, Julie's father sprang from his seat, heading straight for DelVecchio and Todd Adams. Full of rage, he leaped over the three-foot-tall partition between the gallery and the well, where lawyers and defendants sat before the jury.

Sheriffs rushed from the paneled walls around them, closing in on Julie's dad, Malcolm Love, Sr. When they reached him, grabbing him by either shoulder, he first tensed as if he would put up a fight, but glancing back at his wife still seated in the pew they had shared, her head bowed toward her lap, her face buried in a white hanky, he relented. His body relaxed and he let the sheriffs take him by either elbow, one on each side of him and one behind him.

The courtroom was in an uproar, everyone talking at once, press frantically taking notes, thrilled at the turn of events and now talking openly to each other. Several sprang from their seats and out the back door of the courtroom to position themselves on the front courthouse steps for impromptu stand-ups for local news . . . all about how the defense had branded Julie Love, the dead mother-to-be, as an unfaithful wife who was ready, willing, and able to fall into bed behind her husband's back.

All this churning as the sheriffs pulled Malcolm Love out of the courtroom by his armpits. Hailey could barely hear the whoosh of the double wooden doors at the back of the courtroom amid all the chatter.

She leaned toward Fincher again. "So now the burden's shifted. He did it, all in just one sentence."

"Did what, Hailey?"

"He changed the game. DelVecchio just changed the game. It's not about him proving Adams is innocent. Now it's about the state proving Julie wasn't sleeping around. Disgusting."

"I can't believe they'd do this to her. The guy kills her, kills the baby, and now his lawyer drags her name through the mud," Fincher whispered back into Hailey's ear.

"Order! Order!" Pounding his gavel on the wooden block, the judge called out again from his bench, his voice carrying to the very back of the courtroom.

Bailiffs appeared seemingly out of nowhere. Six of them assumed sentinel positions at the edges of the pews on both sides and two more stood at the defense counsel table. One stood staring out into the pews full of people directly between Todd Adams and the spectators. The other sheriff stood facing Todd Adams, positioned between Adams and the judge.

Todd Adams was twisting in his seat, first to one lawyer and then to the next as DelVecchio stood, poised as if posing for a full-length portrait to be painted of himself. He was positioned directly to the left of Adams, between him and the jury.

Soaking up the attention and seemingly unaware of the disruption he'd caused, DelVecchio stood unmoved. But the commotion seemed to be gaining momentum.

*"Order! I said order in the court!"* Luther Alverson rose from his seat behind the bench. More bailiffs poured into the courtroom, now lining up between the pews and the walls.

Julie's mother, Dana, let out a moan, quickly holding her damp hanky to her mouth to stifle further anguish. All eyes turned to her, including the jurors. Not to be outdone, Tish Adams rose from her seat to stand directly behind the wooden railing separating her from her son, as if she were guarding him.

"Bailiff, send out the jury. It's time for our morning break." Alverson ordered his chief bailiff to get the jury out of the room before they were so tainted there would be no way they could listen impartially to the evidence that was to come from the witness stand. Alverson didn't want to start from scratch and handpick a new jury. The state agreed.

DelVecchio would see a mistrial as a victory. And he'd be right. It cost time and money for the state to try a death penalty case, much less import jurors from another county, footing the bill for their room and board. It would be a phenomenal loss if they had to start all over.

DelVecchio couldn't have possibly looked more pleased with himself. He stood, looking solicitously at the jury as they stalked from the courtroom and into the jury room. The looks they were shooting both DelVecchio and the defendant, Todd Adams, could have killed. They apparently didn't take kindly to the slur on Julie's memory.

But DelVecchio didn't seem to mind at all. He had planted the seed in their minds. The seed of doubt that all was not as it appeared . . . that Julie was not who she purported to be . . . that she was not the loving and innocent wife the state portrayed . . . not the expectant mother who wanted nothing more than to give birth to baby Lily and start the family she'd always dreamed of with the only man she'd ever loved . . . Todd Adams.

Could she have been someone totally different? The tiny seed was indeed planted. Now all DelVecchio had to do was nurture it over the next few weeks, water it with innuendo, fertilize it with insinuations, caress it with suggestion, and then . . . watch it bloom into a hung jury or better yet . . . an outright acquittal.

"I'll have the lawyers back for motions in thirty minutes," Judge Luther Alverson announced before he stood to the bailiff's banging of a gavel onto a block.

"Court's in recess. The judge is off the bench!" The bailiff called it out loudly into the courtroom.

There was a moment's silence and then a flurry of noise and activity as everyone began to stir, preparing to leave the courtroom for a break. Papers shuffling, books closing, computers being shut down and closed as spectators stood and began merging into the center aisle leading out the huge doors in the back of the courtroom.

"Well, I guess that's that." Hailey looked over at Finch.

"Yep. That's that. End of court."

"For now, anyway." Hailey returned her gaze to the now-empty bench. Counsel tables were abandoned too. All the lawyers had filed out through an innocuous-looking side door that, like the holding cell door adjacent to the courtroom, blended right into the wood paneling. You'd really have to *know* it was there to even notice it. Located beside the judge's massive bench, between the bench and the far corner rail of the jury box, it led directly to the judge's offices and chambers. He used it to enter and exit the courtroom quickly.

"Hailey, what do you mean . . . *for now?*"

"Oh, I just mean that because of the uproar, the defense will certainly ask for a mistrial now."

*"A mistrial?"* Finch looked shocked.

"Yes, a mistrial," Hailey answered back relatively calmly, given the fact that if a mistrial was granted, the trial would have to start all over again. She had missed four days of work already, was away from home, work, and patients who were extremely needy, and, to top it all off, was footing the bulk of the bill for her trip since the state levels of per diem were pretty sparse.

"A mistrial? This early in the game? It's just opening statements, for Pete's sake!" Exasperated, Finch didn't even bother keeping his voice down. At the sound of his raised voice, a few court watchers turned to look back at them as they inched out of the courtroom along with the crowd.

"I said the defense would *seek a mistrial* . . . not that they'd get it! They'll use anything, any ruse to put the state out, even if temporarily. Alverson is no idiot, Fincher. He didn't just fall off the turnip truck."

At that comment, Fincher began to smile again.

"The law is, if the defense brings about the error at trial, not the state, the defense can't then ask for a mistrial or really even have grounds to object."

"But what would they have *objected to*, Hailey?"

"Malcolm Love making a move toward Todd Adams, for starters. Add on Dana Love sobbing out loud, Tish Adams jumping from her seat to stand guard over her son, gasps, cries, and commotion . . . that sort of thing." Hailey answered him fairly routinely. She didn't let it show the least bit she was deeply upset the whole trial might just be headed down the tubes.

"But . . . but . . ." Finch looked angry again.

"I know . . . but. But it was DelVecchio's fault to start with. He made an outrageous comment that ignited a reaction in court. So it's his fault and he won't get a mistrial declared."

"Man, that was close." Finch looked a little dazed at all the legal mumbo jumbo.

"Well, DelVecchio got what he wanted. If that's his defense, that Julie slept around, even during pregnancy, he will have to put more than just his word for it in evidence. Since I doubt it's true and there are no real lovers, who will testify to it? Todd Adams himself? Does that mean the defendant will take the stand? I hope so . . . the state will carve him up like a Thanksgiving turkey on cross."

She went on. "In the meantime, the jurors are probably pretty miffed at what he said about Julie, but he planted the seed . . . the tiny seed of doubt that *somebody else may have had motive for murder*."

"Some other man?"

"Yep," Hailey answered. "Some other man that didn't want to be found out. So that's his defense. Or at least one of them. DelVecchio's no rookie either and since there probably aren't any real lovers, he'll come up with something else to throw against the wall . . . see if it sticks."

"Like what?" Fincher's curiosity was up.

"Maybe . . . that it wasn't murder at all? That Julie died by accident and ended up in the water? I'm just guessing . . ." Hailey's eyes narrowed.

"Like what accident? *That she went out boating nine months into her pregnancy?*" Finch was really up in arms now, but that was part of what made him such a great detective way back when, when they were partners in court.

"Finch, you should know by now, the defense doesn't have to make sense! It just has to snag up one juror . . . just one . . . and the defense wins. They take home all the marbles."

"But it's a lie, Hailey. It's a lie."

"I know, Finch. It's a lie." Hailey felt tears well up in her eyes. This whole trip had been upsetting, from reminding her of her days in the courtroom and why she had become a lawyer to start with, to the death of Alton Turner. Not to mention Eleanor Odom.

"Sorry, Hailey. Didn't mean to upset you . . ."

"I'm OK, Finch! Let's get out of here."

The reality was that now, instead of asserting a substantive alternate theory as to how Julie Love might have died other than murder at the hands of her own husband, DelVecchio would smear the victim. That *was* the defense.

Suddenly, Hailey felt weary right down to her bones.

"Yeah. Let's go get some lunch." Finch gently touched Hailey's elbow, urging her on.

"And not in the county cafeteria!" Hailey added, mustering a smile, referring back to their last disastrous lunch there and Elle's untimely demise.

"Why do I do nothing but *eat* when we're together?" Hailey gave him a jab in the side.

"Maybe you can jog tonight?"

"We always say that and it never happens . . ."

Once past a bottleneck of court watchers at the doors in the back of the room, they finally got out. "Let's take the stairs, I can see a line for the elevator from here." Finch pointed to a door marked "stairs, fire exit" at the other end of a long hall.

"OK." They turned away from the others, opened the fire exit door, which fortunately did not alarm, and headed down a long flight of concrete stairs to the lobby level.

Emerging into the lobby, they found it packed with people—cops, witnesses, county employees—all headed in different directions. Going past the clerk's office and then around the metal detectors, they exited, pushing though the giant doors and onto the front steps of the old courthouse.

"It's gorgeous out here! Let's eat outside!" Hailey said it first, inhaling a deep lungful of warm air. It smelled a little like honeysuckle with just a touch of salt water.

"OK. Good idea. County cafeteria's out. Food court's out. Let me think . . . eat outside . . . eat outside . . ." Finch rambled to himself.

"Hey, guys!" A man's deep voice made them turn to see Chase Billings bounding up the steps toward them.

"Hi, Billings!" Hailey and Fincher said at the same time.

"How's the trial? Todd Adams guilty yet?" He gave a wide grin that showed off a perfectly white smile.

Hailey realized that in the entire time they'd worked the Alton Turner crime scene, she'd never seen Billings smile. In fact, she only remembered his first name was Chase because she'd read it off his uniform. No one had called him anything other than Lieutenant the night Turner's body was found.

"Ha. Not yet!" Hailey returned the smile.

"Where you guys headed?" Billings asked.

"Lunch. Somewhere outside. Want to come? Know of anywhere we can sit outside?" Finch answered.

"Sure! Let's go. I know this place off the old U.S. highway. Williams Seafood. It's between here and Tybee Island."

Hailey's face lit up. "Oh yeah. Williams Seafood. I remember that. Didn't it . . ."

". . . burn down? Yep. It did. Arson, I heard it rumored. Never proved. But they rebuilt."

"Arson? Wow. Who knew? And hey, you gotta stop finishing my sentences for me!" Hailey laughed. All three of them headed toward the parking garage.

"I'll try. How's the trial? I've been working the Turner case like crazy. Mind if we go through it over lunch?" Billings asked, still smiling.

"Aha! I knew you had an ulterior motive other than shrimp and oysters for lunch!" Hailey laughed back at him.

"Hey! We don't have to talk about Alton Turner. I'd love to take you guys to lunch. No murder talk. It's the least I can do since we missed our romantic dinner the other night, Hailey."

*Romantic dinner?* She and Finch both skipped a beat, pausing ever so slightly as they made their way to the rental car.

"Dinner?" Hailey asked. No one, specifically Billings, had ever mentioned a "romantic" dinner to her. Had she missed something?

"Yeah. I texted you about grabbing dinner and going through the Turner notes."

"Right." Hailey remembered now. Billings had texted that day in the cafeteria, just before Elle collapsed. But "romantic" had not been part of the message. She looked at Billings standing before her. At six four with light brown hair brushed over to one side and deep blue eyes, Hailey could imagine many a woman falling for him. Something about those blue eyes . . . they reminded Hailey of Will.

Billings spoke, interrupting her thoughts. She shook it off quickly and put his looks firmly out of her mind.

"Hailey, I can't seem to turn it off. Like turning off the hot and cold water spigots. Alton Turner . . . he's just in my head . . . you know? You know how that is?"

"Oh, yeah," Hailey answered. "I know how that is. Do I ever." Leaving the bright sunshine and entering the darkened parking deck, her eyes blinked involuntarily.

"Want to ride in the cruiser?"

Hailey recognized Billings's squad car parked just a few spots away from her rental.

"Sure. Maybe we won't get pulled over if we speed," Hailey answered over her shoulder.

"Speaking of dead bodies, Billings, did you hear about Eleanor Odom, the clerk who died in the cafeteria?" Finch cut in.

"I didn't know we *were* speaking of dead bodies . . ." Hailey gave Finch another playful jab, this time in the arm. The bicep was rock-hard and as big as a Virginia ham from all the weight lifting and working out.

"Hailey, come on . . . you and I are always talking about dead bodies . . . even when we're not . . ."

"True," Hailey conceded.

"Yeah," Billings answered. "I heard about Elle. Nice lady. I knew her. She played on the county softball team and the bowling team too. Always brought brownies or something like that to every game."

"It was awful. So full of life one moment, dead lying there on the cafeteria floor the next." Hailey slid into the front passenger seat after Finch took the whole back to himself.

Billings reversed out of the spot, driving the short distance to the employee exit. He swiped a plastic card over a black pad at the parking gate and within minutes, the high-rise buildings of downtown Savannah, Forsyth Park and its famous fountain, the crowds, the courthouse, and the Todd Adams murder trial all melted away.

Heading out toward the old U.S. highway, buildings were magically replaced by tall pine trees, live oaks, azaleas, camellias, and magnificent magnolias bursting with sweet-smelling blooms. Hailey rolled down her window to take it all in. Looking out the window and upward, she saw the canopy of trees above them, draped in a veil of Spanish moss.

The conversation lulled as they drove along, Billings's left arm laying across the driver's window, also rolled down. Even Fincher was uncharacteristically quiet in the back seat, taking in the gorgeous scenery.

And now, she could smell the marsh. Vibrant green and flooded with water at high tide, the tide was out and areas normally underwater were now revealed. The marsh laid bare was full of soft, brown mud and countless birds flying low, searching for an easy meal. The low tide of the marsh had its own pungent smell, and Hailey inhaled it all deeply.

Just beyond the marshes, there it was, old Williams Seafood. Getting out of the county cruiser, Hailey slammed the car door shut behind her and headed across the sandy parking lot to a table under a big umbrella on the outdoor patio. A sign read "Try Our Cheese Grits!" That was exactly what she intended to do.

"I was thinking about Elle last night." Hailey picked up the conversation where they'd left off. "I looked her up on Facebook for the heck of it." Hailey didn't mention she looked up Billings, too.

"And?" Billings dropped into a seat beside her.

"Great gourmet cook by the looks of it, jogged, loved softball, bowling, beautiful, unmarried . . ."

"Yep. All true. I guess she was single. Never thought of that before. Didn't she have a boyfriend? Come to think of it, she was always alone." Billings perused the menu the waitress just handed him, studying it as if he hadn't been to the place a hundred times before. Hailey looked over in the corner and saw an elderly man dressed in all white bearing a striking resemblance to the Kentucky Fried Chicken founder, Colonel Sanders, making his way from booth to booth to table.

"Who's that?" she asked, nodding her head toward the man in the white suit, white shoes, and white shirt.

"It's old man Williams. He always gets decked out in all white and works the crowd."

"Hmm. OK. So back to Elle Odom, what was the official COD? The cause of death? What did the ME say?" Hailey studied the menu too, homing in on the fried shrimp and cheese grits.

"They don't have one yet. I guess they're still sorting it out. Her body's still at the morgue. At first they thought it was a heart attack or a stroke, but it was neither one." Billings added, "I'm having the raw oyster platter. Anybody want to share?"

"No, I think I'm going with cheese grits and a salad. Maybe a fried shrimp starter. Want to split some, Finch?" Hailey was still looking at the menu in front of her.

"Oh yeah. That reminds me," Billings added. "I got a notice. They're looking for her purse. They thought the EMTs must have collected it in the cafeteria, but it's gone."

"They should try the lost and found in the clerk's office. That thing's a treasure trove. We got Hailey's sweater and bag out of it last night."

Hailey looked up over her menu as the waitress set tall, clear plastic glasses filled to the brim with ice water in front of each of them. She gently dropped down three long straws in white paper wrappers in the center of the table next to a metal paper napkin dispenser and several bottles of hot sauce.

"A purse?" Hailey asked, mulling it over. "I didn't see that. Did you, Finch?"

"I don't remember, Hailey. It was all kind of a blur. I was focusing more on the dead lady on the floor. OK, I've decided. I'm having the Captain's Platter. Fried." Finch put away his menu.

Suddenly, pushing back her chair, Hailey stood up, knocking over the tall glass of water in front of her. The waitress came rushing over, producing two handfuls of white paper napkins seemingly out of nowhere to clean up the table, now soaked.

Oblivious, Hailey stared over Billings's and Fincher's heads into the marsh. "Hailey, what is it? Are you all right?" Finch asked her first.

"You OK, Hailey?" Billings echoed.

"Was it a little black beaded carry pouch on a black string, a shoulder strap thing?"

"I don't remember the bead part, but it's black. And it's got her driver's license in it. I guess her family wants it . . . why?"

In a lightning flash, it all fit together. The purple face, tongue so swollen the EMTs couldn't get a breathing tube down her throat, the sudden inability to breathe, the clutching at the throat, the missing purse, the pink lipstick on the Styrofoam coffee cup on the floor . . .

the Facebook photos, the recipe for fruitcake and banana bread. It all raced before Hailey in her mind's eye.

*"Banana bread without the nuts . . ."*

"Hailey, what are you talking about?" Finch grabbed her hand as she still stared straight into the marsh as if she were in some sort of a trance.

*"Eleanor's fruit cake . . . fruity, not nutty!"*

Hailey answered as if she hadn't even heard him or noticed he'd grabbed her hand.

"She wore a little black beaded pouch everywhere. Even when she was at the softball game and the bowling alley. *Elle Odom died of anaphylactic shock.*"

Finch and Billings stared at her. Both their mouths hung slightly open, their faces registering a lack of understanding, as if she were speaking some foreign language.

"Listen to me." Hailey grabbed Billings's hand, urgency in her voice. "Call the clerk right now. Get that purse out of lost and found. Hurry, before it's too late!"

"Too late? Hailey, I don't get it. Too late for what?"

"For whoever took it to find it. And get the EpiPen out of it."

"Whoever took it? What EpiPen?" Finch stood up now, too, as did Billings.

"Eleanor Odom took her EpiPen everywhere: jogging, Christmas parties, bowling, softball. She always had it with her . . . I saw it in all the pictures but it didn't really register. But she didn't take it to lunch? Now it's missing? Not in the cafeteria? Not in her cubicle? Not anywhere she'd be? She wore it over her shoulder so she wouldn't leave it behind."

They all stood there in a moment of shocking clarity.

Billings pulled out his radio. He held it to his mouth and started calling out a series of numbers.

"The point is, if she had left it behind innocently, they'd have found it by now . . . in her cubicle, in the courtroom, in the cafeteria. That means somebody took her purse. We've got to get it before they do. *Eleanor Odom was murdered.*"

"*B*ut who put it there?*"

Billings carefully enunciated the question, yet again, as if in slow motion. Hailey leaned close in to his ear and whispered, "Just because you say it loud and slow, like they're deaf, doesn't mean they're going to remember anything."

Hailey, Billings, and Finch stood beside the lost and found bin, looking down into it. There, where Hailey had first seen it, lay the black beaded pouch. It was still zippered shut with its long, thin shoulder strap resting limply beside it. Two county clerks were standing beside the bin as well, all five looking down at the little zippered pouch.

The clerks they were questioning looked as if Billings was speaking Swahili. The two kept making darting glances at the purse as if it were a small, but deadly, exotic animal about to leap out of the bin and bite them on the neck.

"Lieutenant, we just don't know who put it in here. But I'll ask around . . ." The taller clerk's voice trailed off without finishing the sentence. The armpits of his short-sleeved poly blend were darkening with sweat and his eyes blinked rapidly under Billings's questions. The short, chubby one just stood there, remaining silent, his eyes as wide as saucers at the thought of murder *in their very midst . . . here at the courthouse.*

"Ask around where? And when?" Billings wanted answers, and now.

"I guess, here on the floor?" The tall one's answer came out more like a question.

Hailey elbowed Billings in his side, and none too gently. Leaning into his ear, she whispered again, *"Catch more flies with honey than vinegar!"*

"Snodgrass . . . what's your first name, Snodgrass?" Billings tried to soften his voice.

"Cecil."

"Cecil, do you have access to an 'all-personnel' email?"

"You mean can I write the whole courthouse staff at once? Soup to nuts? The whole shebang?" Cecil Snodgrass's previously dead eyes now seemed to show a tiny glint of life.

"Exactly. *Excellent*. Can you do that?" Billings was still playing good cop. He gave Hailey a *How's that for honey?* look. She rewarded him with a congratulatory smile plus an arched left eyebrow.

"Yes, I can do that. But, uh, what do you want me to suh-say?" Snodgrass had a hard time spitting it out.

"How about 'Urgent. Who found this black beaded bag placed in courthouse lost and found?' and attach a photo of the bag to the email," Hailey interjected. "That's easy. Right?"

"Take a picture and attach it to the email?" Snodgrass was still a little slow on the uptake.

"Yes. A picture. You know, with your iPhone?" Hailey answered. He looked a little dazed. The excitement of telling them he could send an "omni," or all courthouse personnel email, had certainly faded quickly.

"Here. I'll just do it right now for you. It'll only take a second." Hailey reached into her pocket, withdrew her iPhone, and snapped a photo of Eleanor's pouch.

"OK. I've got it. Now, what's your email address?" Hailey plowed forward.

"Why do you want my email address? Why does it have to be mine? I don't want a killer mad at *me*." Snodgrass turned to Hailey, but Billings cut in, exasperated.

"So you can send the picture of the bag out so we can find out who put it in lost and found." Once again, Billings was speaking loudly and in slow motion, mouthing his words carefully as if Snodgrass had to lip-read them.

*"Honey. Not vinegar,"* Hailey whispered to Billings, a little too loudly. She turned back toward Snodgrass with a smile in place.

"Right. OK." Cecil Snodgrass seemed to be absorbing it, slowly. The other clerk stood by, saying nothing, his eyes still darting around nervously between the five of them standing there and the beaded bag.

"Right," Billings answered him.

"And you're sure you think Elle was *murdered*? I thought she had a heart attack. Or a stroke or some kind of seizure. Who would do such a horrible thing? And you say the little bag will help?" Snodgrass was clearly trying to figure out what the pouch had to do with Eleanor Odom having a heart attack.

"That's right. It wasn't a heart attack, and finding out who found her bag and where could help."

"Right," Snodgrass repeated himself, still thinking. Now he was staring down at the purse solemnly, as if he were at a funeral.

"And, uh, when is it you want me to send out the email?"

Finch, Billings, and Hailey paused just a nanosecond, glancing at each other incredulously. What didn't this guy understand?

*"Now!"* They all three practically yelled it, blurting it out simultaneously.

"And offer a reward!" Hailey followed up.

"A *reward*?" Billings asked. *"What reward?"* He turned to give Hailey another *what-are-you-talking-about* look.

"I didn't say how much, did I? Listen, Cecil, we'll go with you to your desktop right now and send out the email. Somebody will probably write back in ten minutes. OK?"

Looking from Billings to Hailey to Finch, Cecil Snodgrass acquiesced. "OK." With that he turned, his shoulders curved downward in a semicircle, and trudged to his cubicle.

His cubicle turned out to be the same one where Fincher had been snooping just twenty-four hours before. Its prefab plastic walls were covered in a vanilla blended fabric nearly to the top, where butterscotch-colored plastic took over. His cubicle's "walls" were covered with photos of exotic animals.

A faux-gold plaque had been glued near the top of his wall stating his name, Cecil Snodgrass, and underneath in smaller engraved letters was his title, "Sr. Inmate Intake Manager."

The pride he must have taken in putting that plaque up . . . Hailey smiled. When Snodgrass plopped down into his chair, it rolled a little to the left. He slid it back into the center of his cube, scooting forward to align himself directly in front of his computer screen. Hailey promptly positioned herself behind him, staring over his slumped shoulders to get a bird's-eye view of what he typed.

"Miss Dean, did you send me the photo?" Snodgrass asked over his shoulder, methodically opening up his screen as he'd done a million times before.

Noticing a tag still hanging down off the seat bottom of Snodgrass's chair, Hailey proceeded with the *honey vs. vinegar* technique she'd recommended to Billings and complimented it. "Nice chair." She had to get this email out pronto.

"Thank you," he responded with a businesslike air. "It's the top of the line for county-issue office furniture. I got to pick it out when I got promoted a few months ago to Senior Intake Manager. It's a Series Two Tone High-Back Racer Executive by Techni. I love it. Like I said, I got to select the one I wanted."

He was obviously very proud.

"What's with the cushion?" Finch jumped in. "Is that wood?"

Hailey immediately punched Fincher in the ribs. She didn't want to slow down the email process.

"As a matter of fact, it is. I found it online. It's made completely of high-quality, perfectly rounded wooden beads," he answered, this time a little smugly.

"Do they hurt? They look painful," Finch asked.

"Hurt? No. They're specially designed to massage your back. And this chair . . . it's ergonomic. Designed to support your lumbar."

"Well, they look like they hurt. I'm just saying."

"Fincher, don't distract Mr. Snodgrass." Hailey said it with a fixed smile but her eyes clearly said, *Shut up!*

"And, oh yes, your email?" Hailey went on.

"It's Cecil . . ." he paused and glanced over his shoulders, rising slightly from his seat to glance over the cubicle wall. He looked back at Hailey. "You know, you can never be too careful with your personal information."

Hailey fought back laughter as Billings nudged her in the back.

"You are so right, Cecil. Now what was that email?" She held her iPhone poised in her hand to type.

"It's CecilM.Snodgrass@chathamcounty.org. Did you get that?"

"I believe I did. I'll send the photo now."

"What's the 'M' for?" Finch asked out of natural curiosity.

Snodgrass reddened. "It's for Merriweather. It's a family name," he added defensively. No one spoke.

"OK! I'll do it."

Snodgrass lifted his fingertips to the keyboard but then paused significantly. Suddenly it dawned on the three of them and they turned away so he could enter his password in privacy.

They immediately heard his fingers typing away.

"Yep. Here's your photo. Now, how would you like the email to read?"

"How about 'Urgent. Reward to thank the person who located this black beaded purse and placed it for safekeeping in the County Lost and Found.' Give your extension here."

*"It has to be my phone number too?"*

"Yes, it does. No one will recognize mine or Fincher's and it should be from someone here in the clerk's office, not Lieutenant Billings. Cecil, remember, we think somebody *murdered* Elle. You *do* want to help, don't you?"

He looked resigned. "Yes. I do. She was a nice lady. In fact, she gave me a ride to my car just a few days ago. Spotted me walking on the sidewalk. Pulled over and asked if I needed a ride."

He sounded resigned to doing his bit. Hailey watched as Cecil Snodgrass typed the message. From her view just inches above his head, Hailey could see how carefully he'd combed his hair over a balding pate. At barely 5'2", she would never have guessed from below. He did a beautiful job, though. The smell of men's hair product wafted up to her nostrils. Maybe Rogaine.

"Where'd you get all these photos and postcards? Are you a hunter? They look like safaris. Man, look at this king cobra. That's just freaky. I hate snakes." Fincher couldn't help himself.

Snodgrass stopped what he was doing and swiveled to look Fincher in the eye. "Actually, Mr. Fincher, I have a deep affinity with the king cobra."

At the king cobra comment, all three jerked their heads back toward Snodgrass. "An affinity? Why is that?" Finch just wouldn't leave it alone.

"Well, it's quite obvious, isn't it? The *Ophiophagus hannah*, its true name, of course, is the poisonous monarch of the jungle. Rarely seen but always present, it stays under the radar for the most part, avoids human confrontation if possible, but is always ready to pounce, to attack. In a nutshell, it's *deadly,* Mr. Fincher."

"And you have, what did you say, an 'affinity' with the cobra?" Finch was fighting back laughter. Hailey only hoped Snodgrass didn't see through Finch's questions, and for her own part, she kept an extremely serious face.

"Well, that's exactly how I see my duties here at the courthouse. Rarely seen, but ready to pounce if necessary." He turned back to his keyboard, allowing several furtive but highly meaningful glances between Hailey, Finch, and Billings.

"And, I am *very* close to getting my black belt in judo, Mr. Fincher."

Hailey couldn't help but think again of Barney Fife and his judo lessons on *The Andy Griffith Show.* But this time, in a good way. Wisely, she remained silent and did not voice her comparison.

"Yes, Mr. Fincher. Many Westerners underestimate the ways of the Far East."

"But not you." Finch really didn't know when to stop.

"No, not me. Remember, Mr. Fincher, 'When you seek it, you cannot find it. Your hand cannot reach it nor can your mind exceed it. But when you no longer seek it, it is always with you.' That's a Zen proverb that could possibly help you."

"A what?"

"A Zen proverb."

"OK. I'll keep that in mind."

Hailey and Billings read over the email contents and its "All Courthouse Alert" address, typically saved for emergencies, weather closings, or other bureaucratic necessities. It was perfectly in order.

"Great, Cecil. Thanks. It's perfect. Please send," Billings said appreciatively.

They all watched intently as he pushed the send button. Just seconds later, they breathed a collective sigh of relief when it showed up as sent email.

"So where do we get the reward money?" Billings quickly moved on to the next obstacle.

"It doesn't have to be a lot. A hundred dollars will do. Don't you have a petty cash fund?"

"I do. And I will let you explain to the sheriff's party committee why we won't have the punch spiked at the Christmas party." He smiled when he said it.

"We catch this guy and I'll buy you the Christmas spirits for the sheriff's party myself."

"Promise?"

"Yep. And you've got two witnesses right here, Finch and Cecil."

"OK, you're on." They shook on it, standing there at Snodgrass's cubicle.

Just then, two Savannah police officers entered the room. With them was Tish Adams, following along behind them, talking in a low but strident voice. "I just don't think Todd should be brought over in the jailhouse bus with all the other inmates every morning. It's simply *too dangerous*."

"Ma'am. Isn't he charged with murder?"

Tish Adams's lips pursed. "Yes. You are correct, officer. But he's innocent. And you'll see that very soon. But that's neither here nor there. My son, Todd Adams, should not be thrown in the pot with convicted felons, dope dealers, child molesters, killers, and I mean *real killers*."

"Mrs. Adams, what do you propose? Do you want to bring him over yourself like he's in second-grade carpool over at Frederica Academy?"

"Sir, I do not take kindly to your attempt at humor. This is my son we are talking about. And no, I am not suggesting I pick him up and bring him. But what about a sheriff's transport van? They've got those, right? A private van?"

"I will look into it, Mrs. Adams."

Tish Adams's voice went stern. "Please see that you do. If anything happens to my son . . . there will be a lawsuit against this county like nothing you've ever seen. That's a promise."

"Yes, ma'am. I will pass that along."

Adams looked around the group, giving them all a stony stare, including Hailey, Finch, and Billings. She then relented and gave a weak smile.

"Thank you. After all, he is my son. You'd do the same, I'm sure, if you were in my position. I hope you understand."

"Yes, ma'am."

Tish Adams looked slowly around her as if she couldn't quite take in that she was really here, in the courthouse, begging on behalf of her son. Straightening her back, she turned without another word and walked through the cubes and out the door, pulling her oxygen canister along with her.

Hailey's heart hurt for the woman.

Oxygen or no oxygen, the officers didn't feel as much empathy for Tish Adams, especially after her threat to sue the county. They gave each other a significant look, shrugged it off, and continued directly over to the lost and found bin. They looked down into it and turned around to spot Billings.

"Hi, Lieutenant. Is this it?" One directed the question to Billings.

"Yep, but make sure you photograph it first, if you don't mind."

"Got it." The younger one pulled a police-issue camera out of a black bag he wore over his shoulder. He started flashing shots of the pouch in the bin and the bin itself.

In the midst of the flashes, another officer came in, carrying a black suitcase similar to a big makeup case. Without a word, he placed it on the carpet beside the bin and kneeling down, clicked open hinges on either side. As he folded it out in both directions, Hailey saw it was a fingerprint kit. He started dusting with the dark powder.

"Hey, Lieutenant Billings. How's it going?"

"Fair, Traylor. Fair. Thanks for coming over. You're the best."

"You really think somebody killed Elle?" He tossed it over his shoulder as he worked, never taking his eyes off the slim edges of the bin as he dusted them carefully with what appeared to be a soft-bristled makeup brush.

"I do," Billings answered with no hesitation.

"But *why?* She was a nice lady."

"Don't know that. Yet, anyway."

"I sure hope you get him. She brought a whole dinner to the house one night right after my wife got out of the hospital last year. Out of the blue. Didn't know she even knew Margie and I had a baby. You know . . . complications."

"I remember. How's the baby?" Billings made small talk.

"He's trying to walk now." The crime-scene tech slowed just long enough to throw a big grin at the three of them, and then turned back to the exacting science of fingerprints.

Hailey watched carefully. The guy knew what he was doing. He not only got the upper edge, but all down the three sides of the bin, all the way down to the carpet, just in case. The fourth side was pushed against the wall.

He then went back into his bag and pulled out what looked like a pair of extremely long tweezers, reached into the bin, pulled out the pouch by its strap with the tweezers, and laid the beaded bag onto a sheet of pristine, clear plastic he'd spread on the floor. It would be hard to get a full print off the beads, but he was trying.

Then, he had a go at the strap and the zipper. "Can I open?" He turned back to Billings.

"Sure, that's what we've been waiting for." Instinctively, the three of them edged forward as the tech, with blue surgical gloves on, took the zipper with a smaller set of tweezers and unzipped the tiny black bag.

Resting inside the beaded pouch along with a single gold tube of lipstick, her driver's license and credit cards held together by a blue rubber band, sat Eleanor Odom's EpiPen. It was small and sleek, no bigger than a writing pen. Hailey was right.

The sight of Eleanor's purpling face, her hands tearing at her own throat, her tongue thick and swollen in her mouth, her eyes bulging as the small blood vessels in her eyes burst from asphyxiation . . . leaped to Hailey's mind. But for this pen. The pen that could have saved Eleanor's life. That *should* have saved Elle's life.

"Hey, guys! We got a winner! Somebody wrote back."

The spell was broken.

"The guy that found the bag! He wrote back already! I told you this would work!" Snodgrass was now standing over his keyboard staring at the screen, looking for all he was worth as if the email and reward had been his idea from the get-go.

"Who is it?" Hailey had just gotten the words out of her mouth and come to peer over Snodgrass's shoulder at the return email when the double doors to the clerk's office inched open extremely slowly. Barely pushing through, first came a double-tiered cart on wheels stacked to the brim with cleaning solutions, stacks of unopened toilet paper, and paper towels, with a tall bunch of multi-colored dusters and mops attached upright at the back.

The cart creaked slowly forward and when the doors whooshed shut behind it, a short elderly man poked his head out from behind the mops. "Hello, everybody. You wanted to know who found the little purse? I did. Last night. But I didn't open it, oh no, I'd a never opened up a lady's purse like that. I just came straightaways here to the lost and found and set it in there. That's just what I did, all right . . . I didn't take a thing from it. You can look and see . . . the Lord knows I'd a never . . ."

"Oh, no sir! We don't think you took anything from it at all! We are just trying to find out where you found it. That's all."

Hailey rushed over to the old man, who had to be pushing eighty. Short to start with, he was stooped over with age and wearing a long-sleeved tan shirt buttoned nearly all the way up with matching tan work pants, brown belt, and shoes. His name was embroidered in half print and half cursive over his shirt pocket. It read "Albert Thomas."

"Mr. Thomas, thank you so, so much for coming down," Hailey went on as Billings and Finch approached the two.

"Up."

"Up what?" Billings asked.

"Oh, the lady said I came down. I actually came up. My locker is down in the basement. So I come up to get here." His big brown eyes rested again on Hailey. "You look familiar to me, Miss Lady. But you don't work here in the courthouse, do you? I know I'd a remembered you for sure."

"No, sir. I don't work here. But I have been here the past few days on a trial. Come sit down." Hailey led him over to the cubicle next to Cecil's and sat him in one of the chairs.

"So, Mr. Thomas, where did you find it?"

"The purse?"

"Yes, sir. The little black beaded purse. You say you found it last night?"

"Yes, ma'am." He addressed her with the title ma'am, although he was much older than Hailey, as was just polite manners in the South, just as she referred to him as "sir" due to his age.

"I was cleaning out the ladies' room over by the cafeteria last night and that's when I found it." He nodded his head up and down gently, as if to emphasize his story, all the time looking between Billings and Hailey, then down to the floor as if nervous or simply timid.

"Interesting. I know where that bathroom is. It's the ladies' room on the right just as you come down the ramp to the food lines?"

"Yes, ma'am. That be the one. Right below Judge Regard's courtoom."

"Where was the pouch sitting? On the floor beside a commode? The window ledge? Left beside the sinks?" Hailey continued as Mr. Thomas seemed to be most comfortable with her. He was now looking up from the floor and directly into her eyes.

"Oh no, ma'am. It weren't out like that. It weren't at all. It were wrapped up in the paper towels and it were shoved down all the way at the bottom of the trash can. I only noticed it when it fell out of the towels when I was pouring it all into my big trash can. I don't know why somebody would do that to such a nice little pocketbook. I guess they didn't want it no more."

The import of his words caught in the air and hung around them. Someone had intentionally hidden Elle's purse—and lifesaving EpiPen—so she couldn't possibly find it. So she would die.

"You called the ME, right? To do the additional toxicology screens?" Hailey's mind had already leaped ahead.

"Yep. Done," Billings answered.

"So, Miss Lady. What's wrong with the pocketbook? Did I do wrong putting it in the bin?" Mr. Thomas looked doubtful and worried again . . . almost scared.

"No! Not at all. As a matter of fact . . . you did a *wonderful* thing, Mr. Thomas." Impulsively, Hailey hugged him tight around his old shoulders. He paused briefly, then held his feeble arms up and hugged her back.

"Mr. Thomas, how long have you worked in the courthouse?" she asked.

"Well, believe it or not, it's going on sixty years now. I joined the county straight out of the military when I was just a young man. Almost had to retire a few years back when they passed the mandatory retirement law, but me and one other was already so old, it wouldn't affect us. I thought I would lose my job."

"Well, thank Heaven you didn't retire!" Hailey responded.

"So, Mr. Thomas, were you wearing cleaning gloves when you recovered the purse?" Billings asked him.

"Well, when I fished it out of the trash I had just finished cleaning the toilets, so yes I was."

All three of them looked relieved. If there were fingerprints, they were safe.

"But then, I took off my gloves when I left the ladies room. I don't believe I had them on when I laid it in the bin over there."

Disappointment had to show on their faces. "Uh-oh. Was that bad?"

"Oh, no sir. It's fine. We are just glad you came forward," Billings reassured the old man, who now looked worried again.

"Was anybody else around when you came in here?" Billings asked.

"No. Nobody was in here, but some peoples was just leaving . . ." He looked at Hailey, his eyes wide.

"Miss Lady! That's where I seen you. You and that man there had just come through the doors heading out when I was leaving." He pointed at Fincher. "I knew I'd seen you somewheres. I never forget a face. I don't."

"So, Mr. Thomas, how long did you say you've worked here?" Finch chimed in.

"Over fifty years now," he answered, smiling up at Finch's face.

"And you said one other was too old to have to retire. Who was that? They gone now?"

"Oh, no sir. They not gone. It was the judge. Judge Luther Alverson. We good friends, the judge and me. We started at the courthouse on the very same day."

It was a small world.

"Just curious, how far is the ladies' room where you found the purse from Judge Regard's chambers?"

"Oh, not too far at all. But Judge Regard and his staff, they have the private bathrooms. They don't wander out to the public toilets too much."

"So, you started out with Judge Alverson?"

"Yes ma'am, I did. He's a pistol all right. Don't get him mad, I always say." The old man smiled up at Hailey again.

"Wow, that's something. A pistol, you say. And you two have worked together all these years."

*It certainly was a small world. Very small*, Hailey thought to herself.

Eleanor's pouch, driver's license, and EpiPen were now safely ensconced in a clear plastic bag. Carefully marked, sealed, and signed by the crime-scene tech who processed the scene, they were safely tucked under Billings's arm. He stood beside Hailey as they helped Mr. Thomas from his seat and prepared to finally leave. Maybe they'd even have that fried fish platter Billings had promised them.

Suddenly, Fincher stopped in his tracks. They'd been walking side by side, but now he grabbed Hailey by her arm just above her left elbow.

"What is it?" Hailey turned. "What's wrong?" She looked up into his face.

"*The reward.* Mr. Thomas didn't get his reward!"

Relieved, Hailey laughed. "That's right, Mr. Thomas. You have a reward coming your way."

"Did you say a reward? For what?"

"For coming forward about finding the purse! Lieutenant Billings has it right here. A hundred dollars."

"Miss Lady, I don't need that. I just did the right thing."

"No. Please take it. We insist." Billings took the cash money out of his wallet and handed it to the old man.

"Well, it will certainly come in handy. I believe I'll take my wife out for a nice dinner with this."

"Your wife?" Finch asked. "How long have you been married?"

"Sixty-five years, young man. Sixty-five years. Lynnette was the prettiest girl in Savannah."

"That reminds me, I gotta call Vickie back home in Atlanta. She'll kill me. I haven't called her all day. I only texted her this morning." Finch stepped away a few feet and punched numbers into the cell phone he pulled out of his jacket pocket.

"Yep. The prettiest girl in all of Chatham County. And oh what a dancer. Oh, my Lynnette could do the jitterbug. And she married me. I believe she deserves a fancy meal for putting up with me for all this long."

Hailey was listening to Mr. Thomas. She glanced back at Finch on the phone with Vickie, his wife. She suddenly felt odd and out of place. She didn't have a soul to call. She wasn't part of what they had. She never would be.

She stood in the center of the clerk's office and thought of Will. She couldn't help it. Albert Thomas was old and stooped, that's true. But this old man had known a lifetime of true love. A love that endured nearly seven decades. Children, grandchildren, even great-grandchildren had been born out of that love.

True, she may have a law degree and jet around the country as an expert witness, she may pop up on TV on various cases, and, yes, she lived in the center of the "capital of the world," New York City. But she'd never have true love. Not in this world, anyway.

Finch punched off his phone and put it back into his coat pocket. The four of them, Hailey, Finch, Billings, and Mr. Thomas, started walking again and this time actually made it through the wide doors into the lobby.

Mr. Thomas headed toward the elevator bank going down to his locker to collect his things. Just as Hailey put her hand on the door to go outside, she froze.

"Guys."

"Oh. I know that tone." Finch's arm held the door above her own. "What's wrong? Did you leave something in the clerk's office?"

"No, I didn't leave anything. But we have to go back."

"What for? I gotta tell you Hailey, I'm starved," Billings jumped in.

"Me too, Hailey. All I can think about is fried shrimp and hush puppies."

"I'm hungry too, but I just realized something . . ."

By now she was six feet ahead of them heading straight back from where they'd just come. Pushing open the doors, Hailey charged back down the lines of cubicles, coming to an abrupt halt at one of them not too far from Cecil Snodgrass's.

The others caught up. "What?" Finch asked first. "I don't get it."

*"Look."* Hailey motioned with her head down at the desk.

"I'm looking. I still don't see anything." Finch stared at the work space. There was nothing at all unusual about it. In fact, it was incredibly neat and tidy.

Papers were squarely placed in a metal mesh intake box, their corners perfectly aligned. A tickler file was carefully set up beside the computer screen with each day's tasks in order. A plastic, industrial-size jug of hand sanitizer guarded the other side of the space. Even the pens and pencils seemed to be lined up perfectly. Almost too perfectly, actually.

"Look again," Hailey insisted.

"OK, Hailey. But look at what?" Billings stared hard at the space.

"All I can see is fried shrimp. They're dancing, two of them, right in front of my eyes. Oops, now they turned into a big, fat fried shrimp po' boy," Finch went on.

"This. Look at this." Hailey pointed at a large white Styrofoam cup on the other side of the computer screen.

"So? It's an old coffee cup. Maybe he recycles."

"Right. Maybe Deputy . . . uh . . ." Billings bent around Hailey's shoulder to read the county-issue, faux wood nameplate attached on the plastic portion of the wall. "Deputy Zilenski . . . maybe Deputy Zilenski is a recycler. Although I will agree, by the looks of his space, he's a bit of a . . . a . . . uh . . . let me see. How would I phrase it? A neatnik! Yes, that's it. He's a neatnik and Hailey's right. Under that theory, an old used coffee cup is definitely out of place. So there, you're both right. But is that why you brought us back in here, Hailey?"

"It's got pink lipstick on the rim." Hailey wasn't really talking to either of them . . . more to herself. She bent over the cup, and then walked around to look at it from a different angle.

"And it's marked *Morning Blend, black, half-decaf.*"

"Morning Blend, black, half-decaf, I understand that. Maybe not the pink lipstick, but . . ." Billings's voice trailed off.

"Finch. Look at the photo."

There was a sprinkling of photos on the desk top. All three had one thing in common . . . a young sheriff, heavily muscled, blonde hair buzzed close to his skull. Neck, face, and arms tanned. One was the sheriff, clearly as a cadet at graduation from the police academy. Another was of him and a man who had to be his father holding a big fish, smiling at the camera. The third shot was identical to one on Alton Turner's desk. It was the softball picture with Eleanor laughing, clutching a trophy in the center of the group.

"So?" Finch shook his head.

"This is the guy, the young sheriff we passed yesterday. He was crying in the hall outside the cafeteria when Elle died."

Finch bent over and squinted at the photos but before he could speak, Hailey went on.

"And this." She pointed at the cup. "This is the cup Eleanor Odom was drinking from *just before she died*."

The two men stood in complete silence, looking from the photos to the Styrofoam cup. Billings spoke first.

"Why do you say that, Hailey? I don't understand why he'd keep a cup from a dead woman."

"She's not just *'a dead woman'* to him. You should have seen him crying in the hall to the café. He was actually pounding his head on the wall. I saw him. It's definitely the guy in these pictures."

"She's right. That is the guy, Billings. I saw him too. He was pretty torn up," Finch backed her up. "But I don't know anything about this cup."

"He kept the cup because it's the very last thing to touch her lips before she died. That's why. *And* I saw the cup on the floor beside the table where Elle was going to eat. Emphasis on 'going to eat.' This is important. Her knife, spoon, and fork were still lying on the napkin at her place. The food tray and the food was all thrown onto the floor." Hailey was talking with her eyes closed shut, her fingertips over her eyelids as if she were trying to block out the present and remember exactly what she had seen in the cafeteria the day before. "So if her cutlery was still untouched on top of a folded napkin, that means she had just sat down or was about to sit down when she had her attack. Or whatever you call anaphylactic shock."

"How do you get that?" Billings asked gently, not wanting to interrupt her thought process. He'd seen Hailey do this before and so had Finch.

"Because, if she had taken a bite of anything, her fork, spoon, or knife wouldn't have still been lying arranged on the napkin like that. Plus one of them would have had pink lipstick on it."

For a moment she was quiet, then burst into reasoning again to herself. "But the napkin . . ."

"What about the napkin?" Fincher was staring at her, not moving an inch lest he throw her off.

"The napkin was folded. If she had sat down, she'd likely have unfolded it and put it in her lap. She also had something messy . . . uh . . . a veggie plate and a fruit salad. Not a sandwich, so she'd need a fork or a spoon. Get it? So the napkin . . . the napkin . . . she hadn't had a bite of her food because she hadn't even picked up her fork or unfolded her napkin!"

Hailey suddenly opened her eyes and looked at them, clearly thrilled.

"And what does that mean? That she hadn't unfolded her napkin and the fruit salad made a mess on the floor?"

"It means, she didn't touch her food! Call the ME's office. Tell them to check for a nut enzyme. We could compare to the new evidence."

She didn't have time to explain further. "Hurry! Call the ME. What if the enzyme dissipates over time? I mean, I don't know . . . drugs can disappear in just a few hours . . . they metabolize . . . maybe this does too!"

"Call the ME and tell him *what?*" Billings asked.

"Tell him this means we finally have a piece of evidence!"

"What evidence?" Now Billings was visibly upset that he couldn't seem to grasp her logic.

"This." Hailey pointed at the cup. "*This* is what the folded napkin means. She didn't eat the poison . . . *she drank it! It means whatever poisoned her was in this cup!*"

Riding on the open road, the wind felt good in her hair. Speeding through the marsh with the window down beside her seemed to drive the image of Eleanor Odom's tongue, swollen and purple, her hands clutching at her throat, far from her mind.

The night was cooling down a little and the sky was gently slipping into Hailey's favorite color, the deep, deep indigo blue just before it turned black. The sky seemed to have a lit projector glowing behind the blue. The stars hadn't yet shown themselves and the green marsh seemed to merge into the sky.

"So, we'll have dinner, but I just radioed for an APB on Zilenski. He's in the street, but I can round him up in the morning and feel him out. Okay?"

"That sounds good," Finch piped in from the back seat. "I don't have the strength to keep on. I need those fried shrimp and those cheese grits."

"So, Hailey. Every time I try to take you to eat, something goes sideways." Billings kept his eyes on the road ahead of him as he talked.

"I don't mind. I actually like talking about cases at dinner." The car slowed and gravel kicked up from underneath the cruiser's wheels.

Billings didn't answer but instead parked the car and got out, shutting his car door firmly. The three crossed the parking lot and headed in, the gravel crunching under their heels with every step. The early evening air was sweet, filled with the scents of magnolia blossoms and marsh water.

But the heavy perfume of magnolia trees was quickly replaced by the mouthwatering smell of sizzling fried shrimp and coastal seafood. And who should greet them just as they stepped through the front door but the very same waitress who had taken their ill-fated lunch order.

"Hey, Lieutenant. How are you tonight? Not gonna run out on me again, are you?" She gave him a big smile.

"Nope. Not tonight. Got anything outside? She likes the sky." He pointed with his thumb at Hailey.

"Sure! We have a patio spot for four left." The blonde waitress led them through a maze of tables, her side ponytail bobbing along as she walked ahead of them.

"Forget the sky. I've seen the sky. All I want is the shrimp." Finch, needless to say, did not need a menu.

They quickly ordered and all three practically cheered when, about twenty minutes later, they spotted their waitress making her way toward them with a single, huge tray balanced high over her head. Hailey was in disbelief such a tiny lady could balance and carry such a huge meal! Hustling behind their waitress was another waiter with more drinks and baskets of homemade sweet, golden corn-bread, white buttered yeast rolls, and Southern-style hush puppies full of fresh corn kernels.

As promised, the food was delicious and the conversation lively. Each of them recounting courtroom war stories, yarns about bumbling defense attorneys, pompous judges, and topping each other with tales of one investigation after the next. It seemed like in no time at all, the sun had long set, dinner was done, and stars were beginning to sparkle in the deep, dark blue sky.

They paid their bill, left a nice tip, especially for being public servants, complimented the chef, and made their way across the graveled parking lot to Billings's squad car. Windows rolled down, Billings zigzagged the causeway across the marsh, dropping Finch off first.

"See you in the morning, Hailey. I'll meet you in the lobby of the courthouse, OK?"

"Sure. See you tomorrow, Finch."

He slammed the door and Billings pulled off, heading down Savannah streets to Hailey's hotel. The night air was like velvet and the old buildings were beautiful in the moonlight as the two drove along without talking.

The car slowed down and Billings parallel parked on the side of a cobbled street. Hailey was pretty sure she could see the tip-top of her hotel a few blocks away.

"Is this the Hyatt?"

"Close to it." Billings walked around the back of the cruiser and opened her door for her, holding out his hand to help her out. "I thought you might like to walk a few blocks along the river. It's beautiful at night. So different than during the day. Like a magic spell comes over it at sundown."

Glancing out across the water just on the other side of the worn, cobblestone street, she saw he was right. It was beautiful. The water was black and silver in the night and the moon shone down on it.

"Hailey, I read about you on the internet," said Billings.

"You shouldn't have . . ."

"Ha. I only read the good stuff . . . not what all the defense attorneys and defendants wrote. Who needs the haters?"

"I've got plenty of them. You know the deal. You can't try felony cases for ten years without making a lot of powerful enemies. It's just part of the job."

Billings looked out over the water. "Yep. Just part of the job."

They contemplated the water in silence until Billings spoke again. "I had no idea one of your favorite songs is 'Moon River.'"

"How'd you dig that up?" Hailey turned to look at him standing just beside her, clutching the old iron guardrail that stood between them and the water below.

"An old *Atlanta Journal-Constitution* article about you. Looked like they were trying to unmask the 'real Hailey Dean,' the woman behind the victories. I guess that was their point."

"Oh, yeah. I remember that. That was a long time ago." Her tone changed. Only if you really knew her would you know it was tinged with remembrance.

"Yeah. So 'Moon River,' huh? It's a beautiful song. I played it last night. The lyrics are pretty deep, though. Think about it . . . 'two drifters.' Is he talking about himself and the river? Drifting down the river . . . see how he used that word 'drifter?' Or two drifters? Like us? Two people caught between two different worlds?"

Hailey turned to him, amazed he had thought about it this much or that he'd think so deeply about anything but crime. And how did he read her so right—she was trapped between two times . . . then, with Will, and the present.

A little taken aback, she didn't know quite what to say, so she said what she thought. "I think he means two actual people, I guess, like us." She kept her eyes on the water.

"I think it's a love song, not just to each other, but to wanderlust. Neither here nor there, but wandering."

"I love that part. And I love the part 'my huckleberry friend' . . ." Hailey smiled. Did he have any idea she and Will had toyed with walking down the aisle to "Moon River"?

He couldn't. No one knew that but Hailey herself. No one living, anyway.

"A Mark Twain reference, I guess." After he said it, Billings threw a stone across the river. It skipped a few times and then was lost beneath the silver water.

"You know the real Moon River's not far from here at all. Want to go see it sometime?"

"Where is it exactly?" The stars were shining so brightly overhead and looking up, they seemed just beyond her reach.

"Not far at all. It's where Johnny Mercer grew up. His home overlooked it. He fell asleep every night with it just outside his window. And even though he moved far away, up to New York City, his heart was still right there, looking out his window at Moon River. Is that how you felt when you moved to New York? Like your heart was still here, in the South?"

Hailey took a long pause. She normally refused to speak of why she left Atlanta. But tonight felt different. Maybe it was the velvet dark sky or the stars or the whisper of the river at their feet.

"I don't know, Billings. It's all such a blur now. Will's death, law school, one case after the next after the next. I guess when he died, I left my heart right there and I haven't thought much about it since then."

She turned to look at him and he turned as well. Hailey could see the stars shining all around his face and hair, his blue eyes looking intently into hers.

"Maybe you haven't let yourself think much about it." He held her gaze.

"Maybe," she answered, barely audible above the sound of the water.

Chase Billings took her into his arms, kissing her gently on her lips. He pulled her to him and held her in a firm embrace.

She didn't stop him but after a moment, pulled back.

"Billings, I can't. It's not you. Believe me. It's not you . . ." Her voice cracked. He looked deeply disappointed.

"Hailey, I'm not hurt. I know what you've been through. It's legend now. It's why you are who you are. But don't blame me if I don't give up."

His eyes were smiling again and a grin lingered at the edges of his lips. Hailey returned the smile. The two walked silently the few blocks to her hotel. His arm rested gently across her shoulders.

"Night, Hailey. I hope you take me up on going to see Moon River. I think you'd see what he saw in it when he wrote the song."

"Maybe I will." She smiled and turned away, heading up to her room near the top of the tall building overlooking the river, dark below.

A fine day for fishing. Cool and solitary out on the water, dark and chilled with gray-white mist rising up off the surface. Cecil Snodgrass very rarely took a day off. Typically, he'd never even think of it.

He even had a root canal done over a series of early Saturday mornings rather than miss work. But when he won the all-inclusive free pass to Gator World and it arrived right there on his desk in the courthouse mail, he had to! Who in their right mind could turn that down?

Between work and the courthouse bowling and softball teams, he hardly had a minute free. But wild animals and anything to do with fishing or safari were his true passion. The closest he normally got to wildlife was watching it on TV or surfing for it on the web. But today would be different.

His idea was to work in a few hours out on the water fishing on the Laura Lee before making his way over for the first Gator World Adventure, as the pamphlet called it. He'd spent quite a bit of time poring over the pamphlet that came in an oversized, white envelope along with the Gator World certified free pass, running his fingers over the little gold seal of authenticity in the bottom right corner. And then, he Googled the place to carefully plan out his trip. He didn't want to miss a thing.

Cecil rigged up his Skeeter the night before and by 3 AM that morning, he was backing down the driveway and wheeling into the darkness of his quiet neighborhood. Taking the southbound ramp for I-95, he eased onto the six lanes that headed to Jacksonville and a little saltwater fishing just off the Florida coast.

It was just over two hours away from the Savannah suburbs and tooling along the interstate around 3:30 AM, he didn't spot a single soul in any other lane. Cecil kept a close eye on the Laura Lee in the rearview mirror. He remembered the day his dad sat under the hot sun out in the driveway painting his mom's name on the side of the boat.

She was a sweet one, all right. His dad bought her used before he'd passed away, and now she was all Cecil's. Good memories with Dad. Practically every Saturday morning they'd head for the Savannah River or, better yet, the Intracoastal Waterway; and more often than not, they'd bring home a nice catch of reds to his mom for dinner.

Sweet really wasn't the right word for the Laura Lee. She was so much more than that. Watching in the rearview, she swayed ever so slightly from one side of the hitch to the other in the darkness of the early morning as intermittent yellow lane lines whizzed by beside her.

She was the last of the old ZT07 Bays, the value model in the Skeeter Saltwater line, but still a premium-quality fishing boat. Measuring 19 feet 7 inches over a beam of 8 feet 2 inches, she could take on some stiff chop. She featured open rod racks on the gunwales, a 42-gallon forward dry storage box, Yamaha analog, flip-flop helm seat, and 8 console rod holders topped off with a stainless steel prop. She was powered by a Yamaha F150 outboard and topped out at over 50 mph. What more could a man want?

He'd get the Laura Lee in the water by 6 AM and after a good catch, he'd clean the fish, put them in his cooler, and head to the main event . . . Gator World. It opened about a year ago, but he'd been so busy, he hadn't taken a single break.

It was really amazing he hadn't been yet. It was everything he could imagine . . . and more. Affordable family fun, true. But the real attraction for Cecil Snodgrass was thousands of alligators and crocodiles, including the shy and slippery leucistic white alligator.

Forget about the free-flight aviary, kids' petting zoo, or animal shows . . . it was the natural alligator breeding flats he was looking forward to, specifically the "Wild Gator Adventure Experience." Usually closed to the public, this was reserved for the few who dared venture into the swamp. He'd be just a few yards away from giant, hungry alligators and create a thrilling feeding frenzy. Then there would be photo ops with his "dinner guests."

His free pass included the Croc-N-Gator Night Time Adventure. He had to sign up twenty-four hours in advance for that. It promised to take him deep into the secretive realm of the world's most celebrated reptile, the gator! With a flashlight and a pack of frozen fish-sticks, he would wind his way across the blackened boardwalks of Gator World's Alligator Breeding Flats.

The pamphlet that came with his free pass guarantees the *nighttime awakens as the rippling waters and fluttering wings are a heads-up you have company!*

The thought of it sent a little shiver up Cecil's spine. Photos of him, Cecil Snodgrass, out on the Croc-N-Gator Night Time Adventure would be awesome on Facebook! He even thought ahead to check out the nighttime photo feature on his camera. And there was always his iPhone. The peeps at work would flip. Now, he wouldn't have just photos of wild and exotic creatures on display on the walls of his cube, he'd be in the photos along with man's greatest saltwater/freshwater threat . . . the mighty gator.

This would prove once and for all he was not a poser in any sense. Cecil Snodgrass was the real deal.

But first, the fishing. One good thing about this time of year, the redfish tended to school up and stay tight in the few patches of cooler water. If he happened alongside an oyster bar, even better! He could easily reel in twenty reds. Of course, they are smaller, but what reds lack in size they make up for in thrills! And who knew? If he could run and gun to different areas and weed through the dinks, he just might score a sheepshead or flounder.

After a few hours on the water, on the way to the gators, he'd scarf down the sandwiches and chips he'd packed in the car. No need to waste money at Wendy's or Burger King, much less Starbucks. The three turkey bologna sandwiches he made last night with baked chips would be perfect. And of course, he packed homemade iced tea with sweet Dixie Crystals sugar in his cooler.

His mind wandered to his courthouse cubicle walls adorned with photos of wild animals, birds, and snakes. Mostly they were carefully cut out of magazines and included a few postcards people had sent him. But with the Feeding Frenzy Thrill and Night Time Adventure, he'd get photos of the real thing . . . with *him in the photo* for a change.

He even bought a selfie stick on Amazon specifically for this trip so he could enhance his arrangement of exotic creature photos. They'd be admired by everyone that passed by, court personnel and civilians alike.

With that in mind, Cecil was wearing his incredible khaki-colored fishing vest today, perfect for action photos to put on display. It had eleven strategically placed pockets with zips or Velcro closures. It had tippet pockets, fly box pockets, back pockets, and two interior zip pockets to keep his essentials totally organized. It had three D rings to keep tools in easy reach.

But best of all, it looked exactly like the one Steve Irwin used to wear before a giant stingray killed him.

Why did the Crocodile Hunter have to go to the great jungle in the sky? And so young, too. With so many wild and wonderful adventures lying before him. Adventures Cecil avidly shared from his living room sofa. That was just wrong.

Cecil had been in a slump for days after Irwin's untimely death was announced. He even called in to work sick so he could watch clips of the funeral on TV.

And then . . . the vest. Cecil spent hours online trying to find the one that looked the most like Irwin's. He even tuned in faithfully to watch Steve's beloved Bindi compete on *Dancing With the Stars*, voting on his cell phone and home phone the maximum number of times allowed (twelve per phone before the *DWTS* computerized phone lines cut him off) and convincing friends and family to do the same.

And Bindi won. Cecil was pretty convinced his little tradition of wearing the Irwin look-alike vest during every *DWTS* episode had something to do with that.

It was the least he could do, right? Right.

Gazing out the driver's side window, he could hardly wait for dusk. The Feeding Frenzy Thrill was advertised on late night local TV the night before. Cecil saw it during a commercial during the eleven o'clock news, and now it was coming true. What a stroke of luck, winning the free tickets to the Feeding Frenzy Thrill and Night Time Adventure. His name had been put in a "lawman's lottery."

He couldn't believe it. He had never won anything in his life, and now here he was off work, headed to a free day at Gator World. The winning certificate specified today and it was all-inclusive. He could see whatever show he wanted. But of course, the crown jewels of Gator World were the Feeding Frenzy Thrill and the Night Time Adventure. The letter said so.

After the Feeding Frenzy Thrill, he'd chill and check the place out until it was time for the Croc-N-Gator Night Time Adventure. But now? It would be sight-fishing at its best in northeast Florida. This was truly as good as it gets.

His heart swelled. Why didn't he take off more often? If he hadn't gotten the *free* pass, he'd be sitting back in his cubicle on the first floor of the courthouse fielding questions and dealing with all the headaches of transporting a few hundred felons from the Chatham County Jail to the courthouse.

Cecil let down his window and amped up the Billy Joel. The salt water tinged the air and he breathed it in.

*Wait!* Did he remember to pack his baits? He absolutely always used nice, soft plastic jerkbaits. Yes, he recalled tucking them in his tackle box. The Rhino twitch shad was his favorite. In skinny water, a lightweight lure wouldn't cause a splash when it hit water. Cecil always cast a few feet in front of the fish in the direction they were swimming. He'd fish the surface if there was plenty of cloud cover and go deep if the sky was bright.

Daydreams of what he might catch ended as Cecil Snodgrass pulled up to the County Road Dock and Fishing Pier. Judging by the empty parking area and lonely dirt road, he was the only one out this early. He happened upon this particular dock a year or so ago.

It was perfect for him . . . 525 feet over the water with a boat ramp positioned back from the pier along a grassy bank.

It took just moments for him to back the Laura Lee to the edge of the ramp, unhitch her, and gently ease the boat into the dark green water at the bank's edge.

Let the fun begin! Goosing the motor once he got past the no wake zone, Cecil sped out onto open water, the sun slyly edging its way up in a cloudless blue sky, salty spray stinging his cheeks.

For the next three hours it was man vs. fish. Quite often, the fish won but in what seemed like no time at all, he reeled in nearly twenty, mostly reds. They were practically jumping into his boat!

Cecil Snodgrass was on a roll! He was riding a streak of good luck and it just wouldn't stop! If he were in Vegas, he'd be cleaning out the craps table . . . he'd be a millionaire right now!

But, glancing at the black plastic sports watch on his wrist, he had to finish up, clean these guys, and head out to Gator World. He didn't want to be late and fish spoil fast once they're caught, but he had a plan.

He pulled the Laura Lee back, hitched her up, and headed to a covered pavilion beside the pier to lay yesterday's newspaper on a low bench. He'd kept the reds wet until he could scale them to make the scales easier to remove. Taking his old fish knife out of a leather holster he kept on his belt, he scaled them quickly and cleanly, the knife blade glinting in the sun along with the shine on the silvery scales of the fish. Their dead eyes seemed to be looking right at him as he ran the sharp edge of the knife against their skin, but neither the blank stares directed at him from the fish's dark round eyes nor the blood running in tiny rivulets down his wrists and hands bothered him at all. He had cleaned fish a million times with his dad. At the end of the fish cleaning was a nice fried fish platter with his name on it, his dad always said.

Spotting an old water faucet on the outer wall of the pavilion, he tested it first to make sure it was working. It was. Drenching the fish well, he quickly stowed them on ice in his trusty Polar Bear cooler.

Following a sign, he located a public men's room on the side of the pavilion, washing thoroughly with lots of gooey pink liquid soap from a rusty metal wall dispenser mixed with warm water all the way up past his elbows. He scrubbed his arms dry with rough, brown paper towels from the white tin container above the old ceramic sink. He did *not* want to smell like a red fish appetizer for the gators that night.

What a morning. Cranking up his Toyota, he headed out the same way he pulled in nearly four hours before. Keeping both eyes on the road, he reached into the car cooler, feeling around for sandwiches wrapped in wax paper and eased onto I-95 heading south.

Cecil's homemade lunch was just the right mix of bologna, mustard, and Kraft cheese slices. He took a long pull on the cold sweet tea. The guitar wailed as he cranked up the volume on *The Essential Allman Brothers Band: The Epic Years*. It was Duane Allman, possibly the greatest guitarist that ever lived as far as Cecil was concerned, just as he hit a crescendo.

But what about Dickey Betts? Tough decision. Betts or Duane. And then there was always Clapton. Something for Cecil to ponder. *"Lord I was born a ramblin' man . . ."* Cecil let down his window and hummed it out into the warm air over the water. Humming under his breath was just fine. He wasn't really the type to sing out loud. Even alone in his own car in the middle of nowhere.

Gator World. Feeding Frenzy Thrill then Croc-N-Gator Night Time Adventure. He played it all out in his mind . . . turning his flashlight out onto the dark water, Cecil would be the first to spot gators' glowing eyes swimming closer and closer to Cecil's camera complete with nighttime photo capability!

The Croc-N-Gator Night Time Adventure started at dusk, when the brave group was to meet at the far south end of Gator World's parking lot.

The place was awesome. They even provided bug spray for the humans and raw hot dogs or dry chow for the gators. Being such an exotic animal aficionado, he couldn't believe his good luck! As a matter of fact, thinking back on it, Cecil Snodgrass had never won anything in his whole life.

Of course, though he secretly hoped for it, he never really expected to win, for instance, the Powerball and instantly strike it rich. Although he didn't expect to win, he still bought tickets religiously, every Saturday morning. Out of pure superstition, he always bought them at the same mini-mart where he had once found an unclaimed twenty dollar bill in the parking lot. Now that was good luck.

To double the good luck, he always went to the same register and at the same time on Saturday mornings. He also always played the same numbers, his mom's birthday and his own date of birth.

But forget about the multimillion-dollar Powerball, he had never even won a lesser lotto, like Crazy 8s or Scratch and Win. He'd never even won a quilt or toaster oven at a church raffle . . . not even a cake at the cake walk game.

And now this. Talk about the jackpot.

By 10 AM the next morning, testimony was already heating up in the courtroom. The state's witnesses could hardly get a word out over the constant barrage of rapid-fire objections by Mikey DelVecchio.

"Why can't DelVecchio shut up and let the people answer? It's getting on my last nerve. I want to slug him every time he stands up," Finch muttered under his breath.

"His tactic," Hailey whispered to Finch, who was seated directly beside her in their usual spot on a crowded bench behind the prosecutors, "is to throw off the prosecution's flow of questioning. He's trying to get under the witnesses' skin, to bother them, maybe make them angry enough to have an outburst in front of the jury or contradict themselves. He'd love to trip them up and make them look like liars. And, of course, he wants to keep the jury from hearing their story uninterrupted."

"Badgering!" The prosecutor finally stood up and yelled out his objection. "He's badgering the state's witnesses and he's been doing it all morning!"

"Well, counsel for the state didn't object until now," DelVecchio responded in his most smarmy tone. He gave a look like he had no idea he'd done anything wrong. And actually, he was right. The lead prosecutor hadn't objected until now.

"He's right, counsel. This is your first objection. I can't rule if you don't object. But I will rule now and sustain the objection. You're badgering. Repeat, objection *sustained*," Judge Alverson repeated his ruling from the bench, looking sternly at DelVecchio, who didn't appear the least bit bothered.

At the judge's stern remonstration, the courtroom quieted back down, the next direct exam ended, and DelVecchio launched what promised to be a scathing cross-exam of Rosario Delgado, the lady Julie Love Adams hired to help her do heavy chores in the last month of her pregnancy. She was slight and pale, her brunette hair barely streaked at the temples with gray, her dark eyes underscored by faint purple shadows.

Delgado began again, describing the moment Todd Adams got the call from Julie's mom that she hadn't seen or heard from Julie since they'd gone shopping the day before. Julie's mom had called Todd Adams while the cleaning lady was there in the kitchen.

The poor lady looked absolutely petrified on the stand. DelVecchio looked at her like a hawk examining a mouse cowering under a bush far below him.

"So, ma'am," DelVecchio paused for dramatic effect, "were you lying the first time when you said Todd Adams did not shed a tear or seem upset when he learned Julie Love was missing or the second time when you said you didn't know for sure? *Which was the lie?*"

*"Badgering! Objection! He's doing it again!"* His face red, the prosecutor leaped from his seat. Finally, after two weeks of timidity, he'd woken up and started objecting.

Once again, murmurs spread across the courtroom. All the local news networks had been having a field day and the story had gone national, exploding ratings through the roof over Adams's demeanor.

It was no secret. It had been on every TV screen in America. Todd Adams tried, but he never cried. He was spotted shopping at a strip mall with his high school girlfriend almost immediately after Julie went missing, he didn't speak at Julie's memorial, and he was caught talking about Julie Love in the past tense within seventy-two hours after she disappeared. That was long before her body washed up on Tybee Island, a fact that threw TV pundits into overdrive.

"It's *behavioral evidence*. It's not hard evidence, direct evidence like an eyewitness or DNA, it's more circumstantial. The law says it carries the same weight as direct, but I always thought it was really stronger. It gives the jury clues, so to speak," said Hailey.

"Hmm." Finch loathed the flamboyant defense lawyer and all his drama. "I don't care what you call it, I still don't like the way DelVecchio treats the witnesses. I hope the jury feels the same way."

Finch had his arms crossed, staring at the back of Todd Adams's head. But in the jury box, none of them looked the least bit concerned for the maid. They all appeared to be watching a TV series with no connection at all.

"Me either. And it looks like the state's too weak to fight back. They're really rolling over."

"They're just sitting there."

"But just watch, Finch. DelVecchio seems to have a free rein and nobody's stopping him. And Alverson won't jump in to save a state's witness if they're not even objecting. But like I said, just watch. Give him enough rope, DelVecchio will hang himself. Or at least trip on it."

DelVecchio tore the state's witness into ribbons. It was like shooting fish in a barrel. The Adams's maid, hired by Julie Love but paid for by Todd Adams's mom and dad, was in tears. Already a tiny woman, she seemed to be shrinking smaller and smaller on the stand under DelVecchio's brutal cross-exam.

DelVecchio paused for effect after his last series of questions, delving into the maid and her husband's financial woes. They lived with their four children in a two-bedroom apartment on the far end of Savannah. They'd already lost the family car, and now both she and her husband took the bus to work. Two months before they'd declared bankruptcy.

"Irrelevant," the prosecutor broke in feebly, not even standing when he spoke.

"Not true, Your Honor. I have every right under the law to cross-examine on the witness's possible pecuniary interest in the outcome of this case." DelVecchio was ready.

"That's true, Mr. DelVecchio. You do have a right to cross-examine on a pecuniary interest, but *are you trying to say she's taking a bribe from the state?*" The judge spoke, obviously very concerned about an allegation of bribery rearing its head in the middle of a death penalty case—a highly publicized one at that.

"No, I was not, Your Honor. But now that you mention it . . . maybe she did!" DelVecchio couldn't hide his glee.

The state did nothing. They just sat there and took it. On the other side of the courtroom, DelVecchio actually seemed to be licking his lips in excitement. He reminded Hailey of a vampire about to suck his victim's blood.

Just then, a short man in the back of the courtroom stood up, his hat in his hands. He looked distraught. Hailey turned at the movement behind her. He had to be Rosario's husband.

The man wearing worn jeans and a plaid shirt tucked in, his baseball cap under his arm, was wringing his hands. He stood alone in the sea of seated onlookers, clearly wanting to speak. No one paid him any attention whatsoever, because all eyes were glued on DelVecchio.

"Mr. DelVecchio! That's an extremely serious allegation. Do you have any evidence to support such a claim?"

For one brief moment DelVecchio paused and the judge interjected. "Mrs. Delgado, you were describing Mr. Adams's reaction there in the kitchen of their home when he received the call telling him his wife, Julie Love Adams, was missing. Did you say he cried?"

"No. He didn't! I saw it with my own eyes. He never cried. And when I fell to my knees there on the kitchen floor, sir . . . I prayed. I looked up. His eyes were open and he had half a smile on his lips . . . just on . . . on the corners, judge. I saw him. I remember it 'til I go to my grave, God help me."

"Stop! You're lying! That's not the question I asked you. Nonresponsive! I object! Your Honor! I insist she be reprimanded!" DelVecchio started to blow and right in front of the jury.

The little woman on the stand sat up in her seat before the judge could rule. She looked at DelVecchio. "He never cried . . . he never prayed for Miss Julie and the baby to come home . . . I don't care what his lawyer tries to make me say! I saw him with my own eyes, as God is my witness."

Reporters rushed again from the courtroom to report the latest climax in court. Rosario Delgado's husband sat back down as

Judge Luther Alverson banged his gavel repeatedly, calling for order, finally sending the jury out and calling for a recess.

"OK. I didn't see that coming. What do you think now?" Finch turned to Hailey.

"I think the state has to come up with more than the fact he never cried. Cause of death would help. Forensics linking Adams to the body would help. But Rosario Delgado's a pretty good start. Hey, let's get out of here. Want to go outside?"

"Yeah, let's go." Finch stood up.

"And no talking about the case 'til we're clear of the courthouse. You never know who might be on the elevator with you. Could be a juror, or worse, a defense team minion." Hailey lowered her voice and spoke sideways to Finch as they pushed through the swinging doors in the back of the courtroom.

In fact, the elevator was packed. Hailey could only see the backs of heads. She and Finch remained silent through the lobby and past the metal detectors.

"Hey, I'm ducking into the men's room in the lobby. I held it the whole morning session and I gotta go! Meet you outside at the corner." Finch threaded his way toward the public bathrooms and water fountains in the far corner.

"OK!" Hailey called after him and headed out into the sunlight and the fresh air blowing off the Savannah River.

Before she could make it down more than a few steps from the courthouse, she was jostled sideways by three men. They seemed to come out of nowhere.

One was short, very round in the middle, his gut straining against a thin T-shirt. His dark, greasy hair hung almost shoulder length, matching the stubble across his cheeks and chin. An LA Lakers baseball cap was jammed low over his face. Hailey noticed that in sharp contrast to his unkempt top half, he was sporting perfectly pristine Nike Air Yeezy Customs. Being a runner, Hailey had seen them before. They had to ring in at over two grand.

The greasy one seemed to be ordering around a taller, skinny one with pale dirty blonde hair parted straight down the middle. He was attempting to grow a goatee of sorts, but the hair had sprouted in thin patches, like sprigs of grass that hadn't quite grown together to form a lawn just yet. A camera slung around his neck, he was holding a Sony camcorder in the palm of his right hand, thumb on the ready.

The third one, a taller white male in his forties, stepped through the other two, who slid to either side without being told. He was obviously the boss and when his face came into view, Hailey recognized him immediately.

It was none other than Mike Walker with *Snoop* magazine. Hailey had dealings with him in the past over the murder of a B-list actress found shot dead in some rich guy's pool house. Walker had the cool good looks other women seemed to love—a chiseled jaw, steely blue eyes—and was by no means an idiot. In fact, he was brilliant at his game. He was the ringmaster, the reporter every tabloid reporter wanted to be. There was no story he couldn't crack and he apparently felt no compunction whether his target was a politician, a king, an actor, or a garbage collector. Whatever sold copy was both his prize and his prey.

Walker's good looks aside, Hailey had always fed him with a long-handled spoon. He covered several of her trials but became a little too involved in her investigation of a string of murders, starting with the actress in the pool house.

Hailey did her homework on Walker and found out that he first did a stint in the air force in Japan, shooting to fame as the youngest-ever foreign correspondent for International News Service, the precursor for United Press International. He hit the headlines as an NBC foreign correspondent. After a few years, he chased down a huge paycheck as a star writer with *Snoop*. With Walker as a lead reporter and columnist, *Snoop* quickly rose to the top as the single largest circulation magazine in the country, over 17 million readers weekly.

Hailey had landed on *Snoop*'s front page when she cracked the murders of a string of fading female stars a while back. True, time had passed, but Hailey remembered the moment, standing in the grocery store checkout line, when she spotted her own face emblazoned across the front of the mag. She was pictured with blood smeared down her left cheek, her arm in a sling, and a bandage on her shoulder.

In the cover photo, Hailey was being helped by a plainclothes cop down the steps of the mammoth GNE building in New York City. Much larger color photos of dead actresses Prentiss Love, Fallon Malone, Leather Stockton, and Cassie Lee were superimposed beside the bloody shot of Hailey.

Hailey cracked the case and nearly died in the process.

And here he was again. Wherever this guy showed up, people dropped dead like flies. Mike Walker emerged between his compatriots with the same movie star smile, the same calm demeanor, as usual, dressed nattily and beaming, fresh as a daisy even on a blistering hot day. His hair was perfectly combed, having been clearly set in place with a light spray, and if his teeth had been any whiter, they'd sparkle.

"*Dear* Hailey Dean! What an unexpected thrill! To meet you here on the courthouse steps!" Walker said it with a flourish.

Translation? He'd been watching for days to nail down her pattern, sent his lackeys to the courtroom to spy, then stalked her to these very steps.

"Hi, Mike. How are you?" Hailey returned the smile, holding out her hand to his already extended toward her. But instead of shaking it, he took a step backward down the courthouse steps and in a mini-bow, lowered his upper half to plant a warm kiss on her hand, grazing her knuckles and lingering a tiny bit.

Quite the showman. And charming. Like a snake.

Masking her surprise, it all rushed back, in an instant, to her mind's eye. Briefly a while back, Hailey had considered him a possible suspect in the D-list murders, but not for long. She could never sort out a decent motive, but, of course, motives for murder were as varied and illogical as the sands on the beach. Did Walker somehow suspect her suspicions way back then? If he did know, he didn't let on.

Just then, a new mass of people churned out of the center doors of the old building. Among them, Hailey spied Tish Adams along with the rest of the Todd Adams defense team pushing through the front doors at the top of the steps.

One of DelVecchio's flunkies held the massive door for Tish so she could maneuver her oxygen tank over the door's threshold. Oxygen tank and all, Tish Adams did manage, in the hustle and bustle, to shoot a distinctly disapproving scowl directly at Walker's sidekick, now thrusting a microphone under Hailey's nose. But in the blink of an eye, Tish Adams blended into the flock that seemed to herd itself down the steps to the sidewalk, then melting into hundreds of fleet-footed pedestrians.

"So, Hailey. Is it safe for me to assume you're here to crack a case? Which one is it? The mild-mannered sheriff's deputy severed practically in half or the lovely young court clerk who dropped dead in the cafeteria? *I hear it was poison?*"

Hailey tried her dead-level best to keep a pleasant expression plastered across her face and hide both surprise and irritation. But . . . how did it leak from the ME's office . . . *again?*

"Poison? Who said poison?" Hailey responded, looking genuinely alarmed. "I'm sure the courthouse cafeteria won't like the sound of that! Better watch out, Mike Walker. You don't want *Snoop* in a lawsuit for slander and defamation, do you?"

For a split second, Walker's eyes widened in an expression of shock, but immediately he resumed his usual affable look of complete and innocent inquiry.

"That will never happen! We at *Snoop* have the utmost respect for the truth!" He feigned mock injury and quickly shifted gears. "But, seriously, Hailey, are you here to crack the case? Locals need your help? If the NYPD needed a sharpshooter, what about the Savannah PD? They're up to their belly buttons in dead bodies? Right? Get it? Alton Turner's belly button? *It's gone!*" Walker actually started laughing, his blue eyes sparkling with merriment at his own joke, made at Turner's expense.

Hailey gave a small smile but refused to laugh along. Instead, she tried to continue through clusters of people down the granite steps.

"So Hailey, who poisoned Elle Odom? A lover? A boyfriend? A jealous wife? I know you're on the case, Hailey! Come on, don't deny it!"

Hailey kept walking. He was hitting way too close to home. How did he do it? Was he just guessing? Posing provocative questions to turn into a headline? She laughed it off in front of Walker and his henchmen, but a tingle crept down her neck to her spine.

No one but her, Finch, and Billings knew. *How did Mike Walker know Elle Odom's real cause of death?*

Walker wouldn't let up. Now he was raising his voice, calling after her to get her to turn around.

"So Hailey, you always order the fried shrimp like your buddies Finch and Billings?"

Hailey paused just for a moment. *Had he been following her?* And worse, she hadn't spotted him. She knew better than to ask him outright because it would cause a scene, and Mike Walker would *never* divulge how he got information. She was certain of that.

"Sure! Come and join us next time." Hailey turned and called it back over her shoulder, just in time to see a camera flash in her eyes. They got a photo.

The flash was bright, but as she stepped away, Hailey was sure she saw the guy from the airplane, the one who hit on her, mingled in the crowd pouring out of the courthouse. What was he doing at the courthouse? She held up her hand to wave, but he turned quickly and headed the other way. Hailey got one last glimpse of his blue jeans, his one-of-a-kind boots, and the back of his head before he disappeared. She kept nudging down the steps because somewhere Finch was waiting on her.

The crowd seemed to close in on her and at just five feet one inch, Hailey couldn't see over the heads of all the people knotted up around the courthouse. She couldn't shake the feeling about Walker. He always came across so innocent, so benevolent. But if that were true, how had he climbed the ranks to make it to the top of a very cutthroat industry?

Hailey remembered the gleam in his eye when he tossed off the joke about Alton Turner being severed in half. Had it actually been merriment? Or something more sinister? Real glee over a gruesome murder and the simultaneous surge in magazine sales and clicks online?

Hailey managed to break away and, winding through the crowd, made her way across the street. Something, she didn't know quite what, made her turn back to find Walker in the crowd. Quickly scanning the whole area, she spotted him.

Disturbingly, he was still standing exactly where she left him on the courthouse steps, his two henchmen behind him. Mike Walker was staring directly at Hailey, and he wasn't smiling.

Standing alone there at the corner, she glanced briefly through the plate-glass window of Lombardi's, a high-end Italian restaurant catering to the courthouse's well-heeled clients and defense attorneys who could afford it for lunch. Near the front was a larger party. Hailey immediately recognized them as the Adams defense team. They were all smiling, even laughing. At that precise moment, a waiter in a white apron walked over and displayed a bottle of wine. They were celebrating, Hailey guessed, the slam-dunk cross-exams DelVecchio just performed in court.

Hailey suddenly had a flashback to many years before, to a scene in a book she'd read in junior high. It was her older sister's book, required reading for eleventh grade. Always starved for something new to read, Hailey filched it virtually the very moment her sister finished and laid it down. It was *Animal Farm* by George Orwell.

In Hailey's mind, DelVecchio's group looked exactly like Orwell's pigs, feasting and plotting against the other animals. Lips slick with grease from the food and horribly obese from their gluttony, the pigs were all seated around a table with the finest food and drink while Boxer and the other animals ate grain from their troughs.

It was stifling hot here on the corner. The tall buildings blocked the cooling breeze off the river. On the corner of the busy intersection in front of the courthouse, with her hand shielding her eyes, Hailey scanned the streets for Finch. Where had he gotten off to?

Hailey stood at the edge of the curb, holding her right hand over her eyes to somewhat block the bright sun overhead. Heat was rising up off the street in waves along with fumes and emissions from the heavy downtown traffic. The light turned green and the cars and trucks gunned their engines, impatient. At precisely that moment, it happened.

A hand, or an arm—maybe an elbow or shoulder—it all happened so fast she wasn't sure which, but someone, or something, pushed her hard from behind. Hailey tumbled forward.

She was off kilter with one hand over her eyes and the other clutching her notebook, iPad, and papers to her chest. She was vaguely aware of them all flying out of her arms and into the air in front of her. For a split second they seemed to hang suspended in the air, and she felt frozen for just that moment . . . in midair.

Then, she saw them crash down onto the street. Somewhere in her mind, Hailey heard the high-pitched screech of brakes, but it was too late. Her body catapulted onto the asphalt in the middle of oncoming traffic. Trying desperately to block her fall, she couldn't quite pull it off.

A swell of oncoming traffic surrounded her, rushing forward like a huge, honking robotic mechanical monster. Landing hard on both bare knees, her palms stung on hot, filthy pavement that somehow, in the wavy heat, looked like it was crawling, slithering underneath the cars and trucks.

For a split second, Hailey looked up just long enough to see the front grill of a huge lime green and white Chatham Area Transit bus bearing down onto her.

Her scream was drowned out by the CAT bus engine, the traffic, the crowd. There was nothing but the motor shrieking and the heat as the massive body of the bus careened sideways in traffic, directly toward Hailey and then, in a screeching, skidding burst, collided.

"OK. Great seeing you, Finch! See you back at the crime lab, man!"

"Sure thing, Kelly. Great to see you, too." Fincher had been waylaid outside the men's room by the head of the Georgia Crime Lab Ballistics Division, Kelly Piper.

Usually a man of very few words unless he was on the witness stand, Piper had chewed Finch's ear off about the intricacies involved in the gangland murder case that brought him all the way from his digs at the crime lab in Atlanta to Savannah that morning.

Finch scanned the front steps. A full hour had passed. No Hailey. He headed back in the courthouse lobby. Had she come back for him? He checked outside the bathrooms and again, no sign of her.

Maybe she left something in the courtroom again. Finch headed up the elevator back to the Adams trial. Entering the courtroom, he saw testimony had resumed. He was sure Hailey would be back any minute. Over her cold, dead body would Hailey Dean ever miss a word of testimony.

The defense had taken over. Again. The judge looked peeved and the state's attorneys were hunched forward over their notes at their counsel table.

The prosecutors were no match for a flamboyant performer like DelVecchio. He was prancing back and forth in front of the judge's bench like a Lipizzaner stallion, whose jumps and maneuvers displayed the highest classical dressage. He was having a field day.

Fincher felt sick. Where was Hailey? She couldn't miss this. He glanced back over heads and shoulders toward the swinging doors at the back of the courtroom. DelVecchio's voice cracked like a whip. Finch jerked his attention back to the front of the room.

"So let me understand more clearly, Dr. Richards. An errant fishing line, plastic, nylon, or otherwise. Could that be responsible for Julie Love's strangulation? Is it *possible*?"

"You mean if a nine-months pregnant mom was out swimming in the choppy waters of the Savannah River and she encountered a fishing line? Are you serious?"

Dr. Richards was clearly not in agreement with DelVecchio's theory as to how Julie had mysteriously obtained ligature marks around her neck. The defense went livid, sputtering and red in the face. He was clearly not used to a government employee, even a medical doctor, fighting back.

"Your Honor, again, I must cut off the witness and ask that you direct Dr. Richards to answer only the question I ask him and not elaborate any further. No musings. I am the lawyer and he is on cross-examination! I have a right under the Constitution for a thorough and sifting cross-examination in order to protect the rights of my client, Mr. Adams. And in so doing . . ."

"Mr. DelVecchio, we've all read the Constitution. That's enough, counsel. Save the speeches. Sustained." The Honorable Judge Luther Alverson, wearing an extremely pained expression, turned toward the Chatham County Medical Examiner, now visibly sweating along his brow and mustache line.

"Dr. Richards," Alverson began wearily, "you have testified in my courtroom many, many times. Defense counsel DelVecchio is correct as a matter of a black-and-white reading of the law. I now direct you to answer his question."

"But, Judge Alverson, I don't want to be responsible for misleading this jury . . ." The medical examiner looked distraught.

"I understand, Doctor. But under the law you may not explain or elaborate upon cross-examination. The jury will decide the truth of the matter. Proceed, counsel."

DelVecchio rubbed his hands together in delight. Fincher imagined a filthy fly poised over a laden dinner table.

"Again, for the record, Dr. Richards." DelVecchio turned with a flourish toward the jury and, leaning over the jury rail, looking directly at the jurors, he repeated his earlier-thwarted grand finale.

"Dr. Richards, how long have you been the chief medical examiner here in Chatham County?"

"Twenty-two years," Richards answered in a flat tone, averting his gaze completely away from DelVecchio. He looked like a POW held hostage by DelVecchio, who in return flashed his bejeweled fingers in a dramatic backward pointing motion at the doctor, never once breaking eye contact with the jurors, who sat transfixed by the debacle.

"And isn't it true, Dr. Richards, that it is *possible* that poor Julie Love Adams could have sustained ligature strangulation markings around her neck from a wayward fishing line as her body floated in the Savannah River? Isn't it possible?"

"It's possible," Richards answered, staring numbly. He obviously still had a little fight left in him though, as he began to add, "But practically imposs . . ."

"*Objection!* Unresponsive!" DelVecchio bellowed it so as to drown out the doctor. "Let the record reflect Dr. Richards responded *it is possible* the ligature strangulation markings around Julie Love Adams's neck came from a dislodged fishing line, netting, or otherwise!"

"So reflected." Alverson looked as though he could use an antacid.

Faring no better, the state's prosecutor looked like he'd just been dealt a knockout punch. Huge, swelling sweat stains darkened the armpits of his navy suit, the perspiration long ago having leaked through antiperspirant, pit hair, a short-sleeved white T-shirt, a dress shirt, and the dark suit. He'd bought it on sale at Jos. A. Bank and was convinced it looked like it was from Brooks Brothers.

Leaning forward and peering between backs, heads, and shoulders, Garland Fincher could barely spot Julie Love's mom and dad seated in the front row behind the state's table. Her father sat stiffly upright with his arm protectively around his wife. His skin beneath his short-sleeved dress shirt was worn and suntanned from years working outdoors on construction sites.

Julie's mom, on the other hand, was bent forward, her face downcast. She was holding a white handkerchief to her eyes with both hands. Although her shoulders heaved occasionally, she made not a sound as she cried silently into her husband's hanky out of fear she'd be ejected from court over an emotional display. The prosecutors had warned her of this before the trial had started.

The pink and sky-blue ribbon she'd worn on her blouse in honor of Julie and baby Lily had been confiscated by the bailiffs. They apologized profusely, explaining DelVecchio had objected to a display of support for the state in front of jurors. The state getting trounced at every turn by DelVecchio wasn't helping. And now, the Chatham County Medical Examiner was being crushed right before her eyes.

Fincher could see Dana Love's shoulders shaking. Thunder raging inside him, he glanced across the aisle at the defense supporters. They were taking up the first three rows behind Adams's team. Tish Adams and her husband led the pack and Fincher looked over just in time to see Tish turn toward the jury, a triumphant gleam in her eye. The satisfied look of a winner rubbing it in to the losing team was hard to miss.

"The state requests a recess." The defense attack on the ME had been so thorough, the lead prosecutor didn't bother to stand when he addressed the court.

"So granted." Alverson rose and left through the door beside his bench.

As he left, Finch stood up with the rest of the courtroom and headed toward the exit. Whipping out his cell phone, he immediately called Hailey as soon as he got out into the hall.

After several rings, it went straight to voicemail. That was weird. She'd have to be dead to not pick up a call. Especially during a trial.

Scanning the front sidewalk, no Hailey. Sauntering down the wide granite steps as if he owned the place, Finch looked both ways and then reached into his pocket and glanced at his cell phone to make sure she hadn't called while he was on the elevator.

No good. Not a single call in the last five minutes, anyway.

As he headed toward the parking garage, people that normally moved with the flow of pedestrian traffic suddenly became a human wall, knotted tightly at one corner. Making his way through, he saw why.

Hailey was lying on the sidewalk across the street, surrounded by paramedics. Holding his hand high in the air, hailing traffic to stop, he broke into a full-on run across the street.

Fighting through the group around her, he wedged the paramedics to either side, and kneeled down. "Hailey! Hailey! Can you hear me?"

She didn't answer.

For once, Finch couldn't speak. His mind cycled through all the years he and Hailey had been inseparable. Fighting the bad guys, hitting the streets, casing crime scenes, days at the shooting range, martial arts defense, long days in court, lunches and dinners, driving the city of Atlanta, learning all of its secrets. They were a team that couldn't be stopped.

She'd seen him and his wife through the births of their two children and was godmother to both. She Skyped throughout his deployment in Iraq. She rode along in the ambulance when he was shot in the arm by a doper at a crime scene. She was always there for him, and now she lay at his feet on a hot Savannah sidewalk. He never envisioned this.

With a jolt, Garland Fincher found his voice. And it wasn't pretty. Rounding on the EMTs, he snarled, teeth clenched, "What happened? Does she have a pulse?"

"Well . . . we really don't know for sure . . ." The tallest one scratched the side of his head as another kneeled alongside Finch with her fingertips to Hailey's jugular vein with a look of intense concentration on her face.

A dark purplish bruise was manifesting on Hailey's right jaw and blood was seeping from a gash above her right eye into her blonde hair. The EMT's hands now moved deftly from jugular to eyelids, where she gently lifted Hailey's lids.

Instead of focusing upward and on them all standing over her with her usual piercing gaze, the green irises around Hailey's pupils were rolled back in her head. Seeing that, Finch felt his stomach churn and he lashed out.

Edging even closer to Hailey's body, he roughly elbowed the EMT to the side when she tried to nudge him back away.

"Give her some room, man," one of the EMTs yelled into the air above his head.

"Hell no, I'm not giving anybody any room until my trial partner wakes up." He reached to her neck with his own hand to find a pulse. "She could be dying here . . . if she doesn't pull through this, so help me, you'll have me to answer to. And you mean to tell me you don't know what happened to her? Did a car hit her? Was she coldcocked in the face?"

His voice was now raised . . . he was no longer asking . . . he was bellowing. More onlookers gathered around.

"Nobody saw a thing? Are you for real? Are you people serious? Aren't you people trained, for Pete's sake? They just handing out the EMT uniforms to anybody who asks for one?"

He didn't wait for an answer. "What do you mean you don't know what happened to her? With all these rubberneckers standing around, you haven't asked one . . ."

"Finch."

When he looked back down, he was staring into two green pools. Her eyes were open. A weak smile played at one corner of her mouth.

He grabbed her up under her shoulders, hugging her but trying not to hurt her back or arms in case any bones were broken. "Hailey, what happened? Are you all right?"

"I'm not sure exactly. I was standing on the sidewalk, actually, looking for you across the crosswalk . . . and then, I was out in the street . . . a green bus . . ."

"That was me, lady. I'm so sorry." All of them, Hailey, Finch, and the EMTs, collectively turned to look at a short, thin man standing at the edge of the group. He was twisting a green Chatham Area Transit cap in his hands. His eyes were brimming over with tears.

In one fluid movement, Finch gently disengaged with Hailey, stood, and advanced menacingly on the slight, pale man who was obviously the driver of the bus that had struck her.

"You're sorry? *Sorry?* Is that all you've got to say?" Finch pushed through the group and grabbed the little guy, literally lifting him off the ground by his collar and holding him just inches from his own angry face.

"I swear, mister, she just came outta nowhere. I was looking straight at the street, I was slowing down because we were heading into a crosswalk . . . I didn't want to hit nobody . . . I swear it. It was like one second she wasn't there and the next second there she was. She just kind of lurched out right in front of the bus . . . I'm so sorry lady . . . I'm so sorry you got that shiner . . . I'm gonna lose my job . . ."

With that, the waterworks started and tears streamed down the guy's face. He tried to wipe his nose with his hat.

"Sorry? You're *gonna* be sorry if it's the last thing I . . ."

"Finch. *Somebody pushed me.*" Hailey had fought into a sitting position on the sidewalk, holding out her arm in a nonverbal appeal for Finch to let the guy go.

Not ready to let go, Finch turned to look at Hailey while still holding the bus driver by the front of his collar.

"*Pushed you?* Hailey, are you sure?"

"Finch, I'm positive. It was a sharp push, and it was right in the middle of my back. He pushed really hard . . . I'm almost positive . . . it was definitely somebody's hand and it was definitely intentional."

By now, sirens were screaming and cops were pulling up. Out of nowhere, Chase Billings materialized, cutting through the crowd gathering around Hailey and Finch. Bending down on one knee, Billings asked the same thing.

"Hailey, what happened? Are you all right?"

"I was just telling Finch, Billings, somebody gave me a pretty hard shove. I'm sure of it. The last thing I saw was the bus barreling down on me. I dove away from it, and I hit my head on something, I guess the curb?"

"Yep. It's the curb . . . there's some blood right here where she hit her head." One of the EMTs was bent down examining the concrete curb just a few feet away.

"Hailey. Did you get a look at the guy?"

There was a long pause. "Finch, I didn't. It all happened so fast . . . I . . . I just shot out into the street and the bus was right there and I dove. That's really all I remember. If the bus driver hadn't been watching, I'd be dead right now."

Finch finally relaxed his grip on the bus driver.

"Let's get you to the hospital," the lead EMT broke in.

"No! I want to get back in the courtroom! I have to . . ." Hailey was struggling to get to her feet. Billings held out his hand to help her up.

"Hailey, you have to. You at least need an x-ray. Just to make sure . . ." Billings broke in.

"I don't *have* to do anything. I'm not missing the afternoon session." She was polite but firm and clearly digging in on this one.

"Hailey . . . this is not the right time to be muleheaded . . ." Finch started in.

But looking her in the face, Billings could see it was a lost cause. She wasn't going anywhere but back into the courtroom. He turned his focus to Fincher.

"Finch, she's right. Nobody can physically *make* her go to the ER. You'll stay with her, right? Any dizziness, nausea . . . it could be a concussion."

"You know I will. I can't make her do a thing, though."

"FYI, *I can hear you* . . . I'm sitting right here!" Hailey looked at the two of them accusingly.

"I guess she *is* OK." Billings grinned.

"Yep. Sure sounds like it!" Finch grinned too, obvious relief flooding his face.

Billings turned to the two sheriffs standing at his elbow. "Guys, work the crowd for witnesses. Order the crossing surveillance video. Get the bus driver's statement. I'll get a statement from Hailey later. Thanks."

"OK. Look, thanks for rushing over . . ." Hailey looked up into his face, mustering a weak smile.

"I wouldn't want to be anywhere else but here, and, listen, watch out for speeding buses."

"Very funny," she said it sarcastically, but delivered it with a smile.

Billings turned and headed back across the street. Hailey watched until he disappeared, blending into all the foot traffic outside the courthouse. She glanced back up at Finch, only to spot a completely dumbfounded look on his face.

"What?" Hailey asked him. "What is it?"

"What's with him? *'I wouldn't want to be anywhere but here'* . . . What does *that* mean?"

Hailey paused. Looking back toward where he'd melted into the courthouse throng, she murmured, "I don't know, exactly, what that means."

She wobbled a little and grabbed the arm he held out.

"Sure you're OK, Hailey?"

"I'm positive. Thanks for asking that, but you can stop. I promise to let you know if I feel lethargic, dizzy, nauseous, itchy, scratchy, hungry, sweaty, or basically anything else."

"Always the funny one. Where to?" he asked, stalling just a little to make sure she was stable on her feet.

"The courthouse. Where else?"

"You're kidding. You get run down by a bus and you want to go back for the afternoon session? Seriously?"

"Technically, I did not get run down by a bus. I fell out into the street in front of a bus, but the bus didn't hit me. I bumped my own head on the curb . . . and I'm absolutely fine. Nothing and nobody's going to stop me from hearing Todd Adams's mom on the stand."

Finch just stared at her as if she were speaking a foreign language.

"Don't look at me like that. I'm going back in that courtroom and I'm going right now come hell or high water, Garland Fincher."

After one more hard look at her, his gaze lingering on the rapidly forming bruises, one on her chin and the other circling the cut above her right eye, he shook his head. And off they went.

The Feeding Frenzy Thrill was totally awesome. Nearly three hundred snarling, snapping gators jumping over one another, attacking each other, competing for food. Cecil would never forget it as long as he lived . . . the noise, the splashing, the hissing, the insane chomping of giant, lethal jaws. It was gators galore! In fact, he got so close to the gators, he could see long, gooey strings of saliva draping from tooth to tooth inside their huge mouths.

A stern voice kept reverberating in his head as he threw chunk after chunk of raw meat into the murky water. The voice insisted that feeding gators from twenty or thirty feet away on a boarded pier violated every law of nature and, of course, the regs of zoos, parks, and humankind in general.

Rules such as A, Don't feed alligators. They are mega-carnivores and you, the pathetic, tiny person, are likely to lose an arm at the very least. Plus, feeding them like they're sheep at a petting zoo makes the gators even bolder, encourages the monster meat-eaters to seek out people, and trains them to associate humans with food.

His head went on . . . and B, Even when not throwing caution to the wind and feeding the leathery monsters, keep your distance! Although gators look slow and awkward, they're extremely powerful and can move with startling bursts of land speed.

Cecil knew this because he had actually stayed up late the night before to Google how best to escape an alligator on land. Somewhere during the eleven o'clock news last night, he'd read and reread the classic adage that you can always outrun an angry, or hungry, alligator just by running in a zigzag pattern.

Although he was planning on at least two or three dozen awesome selfies portraying himself as a great and fearless outdoorsman,

Cecil Snodgrass actually took great comfort in the simple but unbeatable plan to outpace a gator. Run zigzaggedly.

But upon further research, Cecil became agitated to learn the zigzag theory was just a myth. In fact, nobody knew where it came from or how it started. This startling development totally blew Cecil's escape plan.

Much to his dismay, he learned that gators actually run in a straight line, and zigzags present absolutely no problem for the gnarly beasts. That was certainly a nasty surprise.

But according to everything on the Gator World website and all the signage at the park, he and all the other adventure seekers were 100 percent absolutely and perfectly safe.

But still, there was no getting around it. The American alligator weighs in at around half a ton . . . a honking thousand pounds of nothing but teeth and hide. The gator's armored body is superbly embedded with bony plates on the back and four short legs with five toes on the front feet and four on the back. They were water beasts all right, and wicked nasty ones at that.

The teeth alone were enough to send a chill down his spine. Eighty fully serrated teeth in all including a freaky extra-large fourth tooth in the gator's lower jaw that fits perfectly into a socket in the upper jaw and remains invisible when the mouth is closed as opposed to the snaggly ones hanging out over the lips . . . if you could call them lips.

So obviously, no way would Cecil be putting even his pinky toe into the old $H_2O$ with a couple of gnarly flesh-eating machines. Gators were much faster swimmers than runners. They could swim at about twenty miles an hour and their attack tactic was to sneak up on prey in the water. The watery Frankenstein fiends, amazingly, were totally silent in water and with their freaky little eyes set on the very top of their heads, they could actually swim while watching what was happening on the surface at the same time.

Because gators have a long, snout-like nose with upward-facing nostrils at the end, they can also stay in the depths for up to one hour. A human wouldn't have a chance against a gator in the water.

But that's what made the whole thing so thrilling. Right? It was man vs. gator.

At the very outset, though, Cecil had to make a big decision. What to feed the gators. There were three feeding options: huge trash cans full of dried food, live mice, or raw chicken. He couldn't help but notice a big sign warning that it's a serious health hazard to feed the alligators live "animal food items" such as mice, frogs, or snakes.

He also noticed the warning mentioned nothing about having your arm ripped off by a gator's triangle-shaped teeth. Instead, the concern was more geared toward the possibility of transmitting a harmful disease or parasite from the raw or live food. A severed artery seemed more likely to Cecil Snodgrass, but that's what the sign said.

There was also alligator food pellets for those less hearty souls too squeamish to feed live mice or raw chicken to snapping alligators. The placard over a huge green trash can full of dry food claimed the hard chunks contained all the vitamins, minerals, and protein necessary for the gators' immune systems.

As if they needed it. From what Cecil had witnessed on YouTube, the gators' immune systems seemed just fine.

Taking a look into one of several big scratched-up, white plastic barrels, there were at least 200 live white mice mixed with what looked to be gray rats, all crawling over each other in futile attempts to scamper up and over the sides of the barrels. They all squeaked frantically, clawing at each other in what must be, in their rodent brains, a getaway to freedom.

Cecil went with the raw chicken. He didn't relish the idea of reaching into a barrel of live mice and throwing them by their tails into the mouths of snapping alligators. The others there for the Feeding Frenzy Thrill didn't seem to be bothered. Suiting up in long gloves that vaguely resembled oven mitts, several of the men laughed uproariously at the mice twitching and squirming.

He was no rat lover. Even the thought of all those nasty rodents writhing on top of each other in the plastic bin totally skeeved him out. Still, the idea of them being thrown by their tails into the mouths of chomping gators made Cecil's stomach churn and he felt hot all over. He had to physically look away from the barrel of mice.

Poor little guys.

So while Cecil loved wild animals, sacrificing live mice, even rats, was not exactly what he had in mind. But when it comes to feeding alligators, was there really any alternative?

Reaching deep into a plastic bin with pale, watery blood trickling in rivulets down the sides, Cecil pulled out a big handful of raw chicken. Although the smell of possibly rancid raw meat permeated the air, he could tell some of it still felt frozen through his own oven mitt thingies.

With the slight breeze on the edge of the boardwalk, he could see the ripples in the water in the sunlight and knew that just beneath the surface, they were waiting. Just feet away from him, they could already smell the raw meat.

Just then, several sets of eyes emerged over the water and instinct kicked in. Cecil Snodgrass, never an athletic child, pulled back his right arm and drew up his left leg like he was Sandy Koufax on the pitcher's mound at Dodger Stadium. With all his strength, he clutched a handful of raw chicken chunks, oozing blood on the edges, and hurled it, catapulting the pale glob of meat out into the dark water.

At once, two giant gators dove out of the water and toward the raw meat, grappling with each other for a single fistful of frozen chicken thigh. There was no doubt about it, these two bags of leather and teeth had to weigh an even ton each.

A surge of electricity went through his body, replacing the tingling fear that had stuck in his legs and pelvis when he first saw the gators' eyes rise up from the water. He, Cecil Snodgrass, had the power. Because he, Cecil Snodgrass, had the chicken thighs.

They were the puppets and he was the puppeteer. He spent the next hour and a half lobbing glob after glob of bloody chicken until his right arm ached. When the Feeding Frenzy Thrill was over and all the chicken, and sadly the mice as well, were gone, the gators still circled the boardwalk. The barrels of food were probably just appetizers for these monsters.

Looking down, Cecil saw his own clothes splattered with chicken blood and guts. He went to the edge of the feeding area and rinsed his hands and arms up to the elbow at an outdoor sink area Gator World had wisely constructed. Following a jungle-themed dirt path out of the Feeding Frenzy Thrill area, he couldn't help but spot the Gator Gift Shop across the way.

Who could resist alligator memorabilia?

Strolling across the paved common area, he saw that it opened up to a food court of sorts sporting gator-on-a-stick trucks, "gator tails" akin to elephant ear pastries consisting of fried dough drenched in sugar and cinnamon, and an ice cream truck. By the time he reached the gift shop, he had eaten one of each. He felt so festive after manipulating ton upon ton of wild gators, he couldn't stop himself.

A bell tinkled as he opened the glass door to the gift shop. Front and center on display was a wide range of genuine alligator tooth necklaces, obviously made with the real thing. A handwritten sign over the necklaces guaranteed they were in fact real gator teeth. It also claimed the necklaces claimed to possess "real gator bayou voodoo magic."

Genuine alligator teeth secured on a sturdy leather strap? Seriously? He loved it! Plus, when would he ever see one of these again? He had to have it. Along with the added bonus of obvious good luck.

He browsed through the inevitable . . . hundreds of kids' items . . . plush gator hoodie hats with iridescent yellow eyes on top, gator T-shirts, baseball hats, snow globes, and posters. But it was the adult section that was the real siren's call. Stepping through a roped-off line, he inspected all sorts of powders and mixes made from alligator hides and teeth. Weren't those illegal?

In a long row several shelves high was everything from alligator toilet paper handles to alligator chew toys for cats and dogs. Further down the row were the mysterious cures and antidotes . . . actual alligator blood in vials touted on the label as a new antibiotic for superbugs. One display was several shallow crates of alligator pepper plants in clay pots to cure diarrhea. The shelves were full of medicinal cures . . . alligator pepper to treat diabetes, even alligator pepper oil to treat a host of maladies.

In a refrigerated stand-up cooler Cecil found "Select Florida Alligator Fillet, processed by a needlepoint tenderizer then marinated with Cajun combination spices to enhance the gator's natural taste!" It was nineteen dollars a pound, ninety-three dollars for five pounds, or one hundred sixty-five dollars for ten pounds of the frozen gator meat. There were even frozen gator-on-a-stick in family value packs. Cecil Snodgrass had no idea there was such a demand.

Looking through a glass door with a bell hanging by a string on the door handle, he spotted dozens of outdoor alligator statues on an adjoining covered patio outside. They had little handwritten placards above them on posts, ranging from "Agitated Alligator" to "Snoozing Gator" to "Big Bite Alligator," which was portrayed with its huge mouth wide open and all eighty teeth on display. They ranged from $995 to a whopping $1,500. There was also a bronze alligator fountain reduced to $995 situated beside an aquascape floating alligator decoy.

Wow. He'd love to put the Agitated Alligator statue in his own backyard, but on a courthouse salary he couldn't blow a thousand bucks at the Gator World gift shop.

He kept browsing.

On the next "adult" row, he spied several shelves of alligator-related "performance enhancers" for the bedroom. Some were even labeled triple-X. Ambling along trying to act inconspicuously, Cecil could feel his face getting warm and he knew without looking his neck and cheeks were red.

Creeping up to just barely over the top of the shelves of performance enhancers so just his eyes would show on the other side, he craned to get a look at the store clerk up front, who was wearing a green alligator plush hat and reading a magazine with his back squarely turned on Cecil. Cecil confirmed the guy wasn't watching him. All sorts of mysterious powders, some claiming to be crushed and—

"All the bedroom aids are 30 percent off!"

Cecil Snodgrass was mortified.

"Hey! You . . . in the back."

If Cecil was a turtle, his head would be so far under his shell he'd be chewing his tail. Instead of responding to the muleheaded cashier who clearly had no sense of propriety, Cecil looked to the right and the left as if the clerk was clearly addressing someone else. Anyone else . . . anyone other than himself.

Sadly, Cecil Snodgrass was the only shopper browsing the adult section of the Gator Gift Shop.

"Hey . . . Steve Irwin. Did you get that? You in the Crocodile Hunter vest in the back. The bedroom products are marked down. Just so you know."

Although briefly flattered someone would lump him, Cecil Snodgrass, in with the famed Crocodile Hunter, the words "absolutely mortified" couldn't possibly do justice to Cecil's humiliation. Especially when a young and very attractive redhead with two little boys in tow turned to look at him. "Mom, what are bedroom products? Is it a pillow or a night-light?" the older boy addressed his mom, still staring at Cecil.

"Ok, thanks," Cecil answered feebly. Then he realized the clerk had a closed-circuit camera in front of him, plainly planted catty-corner above the glass entrance door by the front counter. With this revelation, he abruptly ducked out the glass door onto the patio, causing the bell attached to the door to tinkle fairly loudly for a bell its size.

Now caught out on an enclosed patio, Cecil decided there was only one way out—to climb over the fence surrounding the cement alligator statues rather than walk back through the gift shop and possibly bump into the cute redhead who now, there with her two little boys, clearly thought he was a creepy perv.

The fence was some sort of chicken wire strung to wooden poles, each about five to six feet apart, and woven into the chicken wire was green plastic so as to appear, Cecil figured, jungle-esque. Or as much as green plastic strips could resemble the flora alongside the Amazon.

It was just barely too tall for him; he couldn't jump it or crawl over it. Otherwise, he'd risk pulling the whole thing down. Looking around, he got inspiration. From a gator statue.

Trying to appear nonchalant because he'd wisely scoped out another surveillance camera overhead, Cecil sauntered over to the bronze gator fountain creature. He bent down as if he was checking the price and inadvertently saw it was 10 percent off. He briefly considered buying the thing, but the nine hundred dollars or so was reckless spending in Cecil Snodgrass's book. Plus, he'd have to see the redhead again, which conjured up way too many weird and embarrassing mental images in Cecil's head.

He gently pulled the surprisingly heavy faux gator across the concrete surface. It made a grating sound that thankfully no one inside would hear and be alerted to his humiliating escape attempt. Just a few more feet . . . and bingo! Stepping up on the gator's head, he took a mighty leap and . . . he was free!

Tumbling out onto the parking lot behind the Gator Gift Shop, he instinctively reached for his wallet to ensure it was still there and then, fishing in the hidden pocket inside his Steve Irwin vest, his heart thumped . . . his pass wasn't there!

He'd miss the Croc-N-Gator Night Time Adventure without it! Using both hands, he gave himself a frantic pat down. The Feeding Frenzy Thrill was fun, but it was the Night Time Adventure he was longing for . . . the selfies! You had to be on a special waiting list to be allowed in! The Gator World website said so! Without his certificate, he'd miss the whole thing! And he'd been thinking all afternoon of boasting about it at work.

His mind was racing a million miles a minute when his fingers, on their own accord, reached into yet another "secret" pocket, and there it was. Relief flooded his body before he even unfolded it and gazed lovingly at it. His "golden ticket," the All-Inclusive Gator World Certificate of Admission! He hadn't lost it after all.

Miracles do happen.

Heading back to the main entrance of Gator World, which was coincidentally a huge gaping gator mouth complete with all its teeth, crafted of vibrant green polyethylene plastic, Cecil flashed his admission ticket from earlier that morning. Now he had plenty of time to check out the Gator Museum, look around the park some more, and maybe have another gator-on-a-stick and a frozen gator treat.

Oops. Just then he remembered the brown plastic carry tote full of frozen gator meat and yes, a dozen or so small, dark brown plastic bottles of "performance enhancers" he'd left on the floor of the aisle just before he ducked out.

He hoped the redhead didn't find them.

Every time Hailey looked up at Finch, he gave her an "I can't believe you came to court when you could have a concussion" look. He almost seemed mad at her, but she knew better. She knew he was just worried.

But seriously, other than her body being sore, she hardly felt a thing now. But the question did keep running through her mind . . . what exactly happened out there at the corner of the courthouse? She was 100 percent sure at the time she'd felt a stiff push on her shoulder. Was she wrong?

She replayed the whole thing over and over in her mind. She actually wanted to believe she was wrong. Hailey didn't fool herself, she knew she had enemies. But she still wanted to think no one would do such a thing, actually push her in front of a skidding bus weighing in at over fifteen tons.

Rewinding the accident in her own mind came to an abrupt halt when the bailiff strode into the courtroom. He entered from a side door leading from the judge's chambers.

"Hear ye, hear ye. Court is in session, the Honorable Luther Alverson on the bench. Please rise."

Everyone stood up as the judge swept onto the bench, his black robe billowing out behind him. Alverson immediately took hold of his gavel and banged it sharply on a flat wooden block.

"Court's in session. Call the next witness."

The lead male prosecutor turned to the audience in the well and called out loudly, "The state calls Mrs. Tish Adams."

Loud gasps rippled across the crowd of legal eagles and court watchers. All eyes turned on Tish Adams, seated with her husband on the front row directly behind her son and his fleet of defense attorneys.

She remained seated on the inner edge of the row closest to the aisle, visibly clutching the top of her oxygen tank with her left hand, her right hand pressed to her chest. Her expression was stricken.

"Objection!" DelVecchio leaped to his feet, pounding his fist on the counsel table before him.

"On what grounds, Mr. DelVecchio?" Alverson asked it calmly, again refusing to be goaded into a mistrial, much less intimidated by a showboating defense lawyer.

"Your Honor . . . she's the defendant's *mother*!"

"Mr. DelVecchio, is she of sound mind?" Alverson's demeanor was unflappable.

"Yes, Your Honor! Of course she is!"

"Is she in any way implicated in a related criminal matter so as to allow her to refuse to take the stand and exercise her Fifth Amendment right to remain silent?"

Another loud gasp spread across the crowd at the judge's question.

"Absolutely not! Your Honor, this poor woman has never so much as *jaywalked*! She is absolutely shrouded *in decency, broken* with grief over her son's plight, a *pillar* of the Savannah community!"

"The court so notes she has never jaywalked. At least not in this jurisdiction." Alverson was having none of it. "And is she of sound body, Mr. DelVecchio?"

"Well, Your Honor, now that you mention it . . . Mrs. Adams does suffer from a serious pulmonary . . ."

"*Mr. DelVecchio!*"

". . . a lung defect, so to speak . . ." DelVecchio went on. Stupidly.

"Mr. DelVecchio! Let me remind you that while you do not originate from this jurisdiction, you remain an officer of the court and if, *if* Mr. DelVecchio, it appears to this court that you are obfuscating the truth regarding Mrs. Adams's ability to take the stand, I will not hesitate to hold you in contempt and house you overnight in the Chatham County Jail. *Is that understood?*"

"Yes, Your Honor." For once, DelVecchio was silent. For a man who was used to five-star treatment, the thought of a night in the same accommodations as his client was too much for him.

"Then I ask you again, Mr. DelVecchio, is there any reason the state may not call Mrs. Adams to the stand?"

"But Your Honor . . . she's the defendant's *mother* . . ." It was DelVecchio's last resort, having run out of all other rounds to keep Tish Adams off the stand. "Plus . . . she's a defense witness."

"Mr. DelVecchio, do not trifle with this court. Witnesses are not pawns in a chess game . . . they do not *belong* to one side or another. If Mrs. Adams is not infirm in mind or body and has no legal reason to refuse to testify, she can and will be called to the stand."

"We will appeal, Your Honor! For a certificate of immediate review by the state appeals court!"

"Fine, Mr. DelVecchio. You do that. But in the meantime, no more delays. This trial will proceed. Mrs. Adams, please take the stand."

No one moved a hair.

"*Now*, Mrs. Adams."

DelVecchio sat down, defeated, momentarily anyway, beside his client, Todd Adams. Adams's eyes were trained on his mother. Tish Adams slowly rose from her seat and stood momentarily, her hands gripping the wooden rail in front of her, staring at the judge.

Stepping out into the aisle, she relocated one hand from the bench back to the top of her portable oxygen tank, the other hand enabling her to lean heavily on a metal cane. The jury watched, all eyes on Tish as she walked slowly but steadily, dragging the rolling oxygen tank along with her, toward the witness stand. Passing her son seated at the counsel table flanked by his lawyers, she imparted an all-loving look at the boy-turned-man she'd nurtured his whole life, now on trial for murder one.

Tish Adams was showing her age now. Instead of the calculating socialite she'd been at the beginning of Todd's trial, she was now slightly bent over, walking with the use of the quad-cane, a black metallic cane with a four-point, claw-like base.

Her face was gaunt, although she'd carefully applied makeup that morning. Forget about whose party she and her family were invited to during the Savannah social season, forget the debutante ball committees and the high-society fundraisers she chaired . . . now it was all about survival . . . hers and her son's . . . and taking the next step to the stand. The entire courtroom was hushed as every eye was trained on Tish Adams.

Each step seemed a labor. Twice on her way to the wooden steps leading up to the stand, she had to stop to inhale as deeply as she could from the clear plastic continuous-flow nasal cannula that wrapped across her face under her nose to hinge like upside-down sunglasses over her ears.

She made it up the two low wooden steps to the mini-landing where the steps turned right and upward to the raised wooden chair situated directly beside the judge's high bench, positioning the witness between the judge and the jury during testimony. She seemed to struggle to get the oxygen tank up the two steps, although it couldn't have weighed more than seven or eight pounds.

She slowly approached the witness chair, but then, turning to face the courtroom, a scream rose up from a woman in the jury box as Tish Adams's eyes rolled back in her head. Crumbling before their eyes, Tish dived face forward down the low stairs in front of her, careening off the wooden rail and tumbling down onto the floor into a heap in front of the jury box.

The oxygen tank's plastic tubing apparatus was tangled around her neck, hair, and face, the cane beside her. Todd Adams sprang up from his seat, and immediately he was tackled by bailiffs to keep him at the counsel table. But few noticed Todd Adams, focusing instead on his mom on the floor.

*Was Tish Adams dead?*

Tish Adams lay there, completely unmoving, her limbs twisted at awkward angles.

Everyone in the well was on their feet, staring right along with the jury. The bailiffs bent down on the floor with Tish, and the judge had rounded from behind his bench and knelt on the floor beside her body. EMTs appeared out of nowhere.

The bailiffs turned her over gently. Her face was pale and her mouth hung open as if unhinged at the jaws. Reaching down, one of them quickly took her pulse at the neck.

"She's got a pulse . . . it's steady . . . hold on . . ."

Straining while watching his lips, Hailey could just barely make out the low words of the EMT. So she was alive. A female EMT pulled out a tiny vial of smelling salts, ammonium carbonate. Waving it under Tish's nose, she reacted immediately. Anyone would . . . Hailey knew the human body reacts aggressively to the ammonia when it irritates the lung and nostril membranes, triggering a knife-sharp inhalation reflex. Tish's eyes fluttered open and she coughed, sputtering, gasping for air . . . but alive.

"Send out the jury, bailiff," the judge spoke in a low voice, but firmly. Two bailiffs approached the jury and led them from the jury box into the jury deliberations room adjoining the courtroom.

"Ladies and gentlemen of the jury, I believe this is the perfect time for a coffee break in the cafeteria," Alverson called to their backs as the jurors filed into their room. "Bailiffs, please attend to the jurors on the county expense. Thank you." The jurors could be led out another door in the room out into a narrow hallway that opened into the main hallway outside the huge courtroom. A few glanced back at Tish Adams, still supine on the courtroom floor, being tended to by the EMTs.

As the door closed behind the jury, the judge returned to Tish. "Mrs. Adams, how do you feel?"

"Judge, I . . . I . . . I just couldn't seem to catch my breath . . . I don't know exactly what happened."

"We will arrange for you to be transported immediately to the hospital . . ." Alverson went on.

"No! Please, Judge . . . no! Both my parents, both of them, Todd's grandparents, died in the Savannah Hospital. Please . . . one of Mr. DelVecchio's assistants can take me straight to my doctor's office." She looked up at him imploringly, tears filling her eyes.

Watching her, Hailey realized Tish Adams was really just a shell of herself, practically wasting away as the trial progressed over the last weeks.

"Yes, Your Honor. We can do that right now." DelVecchio turned to two of his flunkies who looked at each other as if they'd been ordered to eat spaghetti off the bathroom floor. But they quickly masked their resentment at being ordered out of the courtroom action and approached Tish solicitously.

The EMTs helped her to her feet and untangled the oxygen tubing from her neck and hair. Thanking them weakly, Tish managed to smooth down her clothes and walk gingerly, an EMT and a defense flunky on either side of her, past Todd Adams at the defense table and slowly, slowly from the courtroom.

Just as she approached the swinging oak doors leading into the outer vestibule, she turned. "Son, don't worry about your mother. I'll be fine. I'll be back here with you tomorrow, Lord help me." Smiling at him, she mouthed a gentle kiss his way.

Adams, turned around in his seat, watched the huge doors swing shut behind her. No one in the courtroom moved an inch. There was total and complete silence.

"Court's in recess for the day. Lawyers report to my chambers immediately."

A loud buzz filled the courtroom as the press jumped from their seats and ran out to begin broadcasting the sudden turn of events from the courthouse steps. Print reporters followed on their heels, pulling out spiral notebooks, pencils, laptops, and iPads as they practically jogged through the swinging doors.

In a matter of moments, the courtroom was all but empty. Hailey and Finch sat stock-still then looked at each other without a word.

"Before this trial is over, *another* woman will end up dead . . . Adams's own mother." Finch finally broke his silence. "He'll be the death of her, for sure. I just know it."

Hailey couldn't disagree. Her head suddenly pounded . . . a dull ache where she'd landed on the curb. She had acted as if it was just a simple fall, but now the ache was spreading across the top of her head, as if a machine was gripping her skull in a crushing vise. She inhaled quickly, and then the pain seemed to subside, followed by a dull ache.

The bus . . . she'd almost forgotten in court. But sitting there, her mind shifted back to the hot street outside, turning it over and over in her mind like a Rubik's Cube.

Standing up, she headed out of the courtroom with Finch a few steps ahead of her. Again, she was trying to make the facts fit together in a neat pattern. But she couldn't.

She'd been standing on the corner. She remembered the heat coming up off the pavement, mixed with gas fumes from cars stalled at the red light. A wave of people came from the other side of the street, and she remembered seeing several of them half-jogging to beat the light.

She'd been squinting back at the courthouse, scanning the front steps, looking for Finch. She hadn't been aware, really, of any of the people standing around her, pressing in on her along with all the others waiting to cross.

And then it happened. The stiff arm pushing her forward. Then all she knew was the hot asphalt, the roaring sound of traffic, the insane screeching of the tires, and the squeal of hydraulic brakes.

Everything was swimming in gray and black when she came to, drenched with sweat with people standing over her, some kneeling around her, some trying to ask her questions. At first, their voices and their words didn't make any sense, but then, slowly, it seemed like she settled back into her own skin and her own senses . . . like she had been out of her body and returned without knowing where she'd gone.

By now, Finch had gotten ahead of her and was all the way down the wide hall leading toward the elevator bank. She spotted him mingling with two of Billings's detectives. "Hailey . . . you coming?" Finch called out to her.

She had to breathe . . . to think. Hailey headed straight across the hall to the ladies' room as if she didn't hear or see any of them.

Maybe Finch and Billings were right, after all. Not that she wanted to go to the ER because she was absolutely sure she was fine . . . but maybe she could have listened to someone else, for once, and not come back to court. Tish Adams's testimony would have been irrelevant to Hailey's opinion on the case anyway. Hailey could've just gone back to her hotel and chilled . . . put her feet up for once.

She shut the ladies' room door behind her. She was finally alone. It was cool and quiet and dark in the smooth tiled bathroom. She could feel the pounding in her head, the ringing in her ears subsiding, at last.

It was completely quiet, finally. No lawyers, no Tish, no Todd Adams, no questions, nothing. The street . . . the sun . . . the bus.

She didn't trip . . . she knew it. She didn't trip at all. But she recalled glancing at the crowd crossing over on her right . . . surely she would have recognized someone . . . someone who wanted to kill her.

But she hadn't.

A random kill in the shadow of the courthouse? Even the thought of it railed against every statistic she knew regarding the manner and assessment of homicides . . . it screamed *unlikely*. So then what? She tripped? No, she hadn't. She fell? No, she didn't. She imagined the whole thing?

Hailey paused. Had she finally reached her limit? One dead body after the next. A never-ending parade of homicides, murders, crime scenes, autopsies, ballistics, the rank, musky smell of human blood. Was the so-called "avenging angel," as the press once called her, totally shot? Frayed? Over? Was it even possible Hailey Dean was over and didn't even realize it?

Closing her eyes, Hailey leaned, bone-tired in mind and body, against the wall. But as quickly as she relaxed against the cool tiles, she gasped out loud, instinctively pushing off the wall as if she'd touched a hot stove. A sharp pain in her shoulder smarted.

Curiosity led her over toward three mirrors placed neatly above three sinks in a row. Hailey pulled her shirt down over her arm and there it was . . . a bluish-black bruise just inside the right camisole strap on the back of shoulder.

The words coursed back and forth across her brain, ping-ponging off the inside of her skull, *"I was pushed . . . somebody tried to kill me . . . somebody wants me dead."*

*But who? And why?*

Just when Cecil thought life couldn't get any better, it did. He took a big bite of another gator-on-a-stick dripping with ketchup. He couldn't resist. After the morning Feeding Frenzy, he spent plenty of time in the Gator Museum boning up on gator facts, particularly the gator's uncanny night vision, because at this very moment, he was heading over to the Croc-N-Gator Night Time Adventure.

Or so the pamphlet said.

He reported to the south end of the parking lot just as instructed and couldn't help but notice multiple signs warning no pets followed by exclamation marks. Cecil could only imagine . . .

His train of thought was interrupted by the faint sound of music. Cecil spotted a tall, extremely pale, pimply teenage boy staring at an iPhone from which thumping, metallic music Cecil had never heard before emanated. The teen stared at the tiny screen as if it were the most fascinating and the most intriguing thing he had ever encountered. Cecil wondered briefly how whatever was on the screen could be more exciting than snapping gators.

Kids. The kid was dressed in khaki shorts that came down to mid-calf and a green polo shirt bearing the Gator World logo. Barely glancing away from his iPhone to examine Cecil's gold-trimmed certificate, he passed off a large plastic bucket with a metal handle, a flashlight, and a mini-container of bug spray.

It was starting to get dark. The sun was just barely showing over the trees in the distance.

"Here you go."

"Thanks. Which way?"

Still staring at his iPhone behind the card table, the kid pointed across the parking lot. Cecil spotted for the first time an arch of sorts, made of what looked to be the trunks from palm trees. Hanging from two chains in the upper center of the arch was a wooden sign with the words "Croc-N-Gator Night Time Adventure" in black letters creating a burned-looking effect.

Passing under the arch, Cecil clutched his flashlight and a fresh bucket of raw chicken. Drenching himself in bug spray, he tossed the can into a metal trash can just beside the arches. He followed a path with tiki torches on either side separating the smooth dirt path from the dense foliage surrounding it.

Palm trees, huge palmettos, and sprawling water oaks were draped with hanging sheets of Spanish moss, all growing so thick he couldn't see past them. It was hard to believe all this was right beside the hot asphalt parking lot, now cooling down as the sun set and the moon rose, both sharing the night sky for a brief time. The cicadas hummed rhythmically on either side of him and as loud as they were, he couldn't spot a single one of them.

Where were the others? The pamphlet said there had to be at least five in a group for the Night Time Adventure. As he kept walking, a cool breeze crossed his face and dried the perspiration there. Finally, it was cooling down.

Rounding another curve in the path, a long wooden boardwalk came into view that stretched way out onto what was rapidly becoming dark water. It looked to be maybe eighty or ninety feet straight ahead, then broke off into four different paths like spokes of a wheel.

Standing at the end of the old wooden pier holding his bait bucket, Cecil felt a chill run up his spine. It was completely quiet now except for the hum of the cicadas. He looked up to see the moon, full in all its glory rising up overhead. It was a lonely moon tonight, though. No stars had yet appeared.

The palm trees silhouetted against the sky as the very last bit of sunlight disappeared and the deep, deep dark blue turned into velvety black. It was absolutely incredible.

Still waiting for the others to show, Cecil ventured out onto the boardwalk resting on thick, sturdy beams that obviously went deep, deep into the muddy goo beneath the dark water. Stomping on the boardwalk itself, just for good measure, Cecil determined that yes, it was safe. After all, he'd checked, and there had never been a single accident at the Gator World Croc-N-Gator Night Time Adventure. Not even one.

Peeking over his right shoulder, he glanced back toward the shore. He had to make sure no one could see what he was about to do and peg him as a scaredy-cat. No one was looking so Cecil bent down just enough to quickly check out the circular posts, the heavy wooden pillars, at least two feet or so in circumference each that supported the boardwalk.

Now he felt better.

He was even more reassured when, at a second glance to make sure he hadn't been spotted, he saw another gator lover milling around at the entrance. Perfect. He could get help with his digital camera. The pictures would be so much better than shots that were so obviously selfies or even worse, taken with a selfie stick.

With visions of all the pics he'd soon be posting on Facebook and Twitter dancing through his head, he was even more emboldened. He'd watched at least a half dozen videos gator fans posted during and after the Night Time Adventure and it was like a big gator party! Thinking it through, maybe he'd Periscope as it was happening! That would be extremely cool. He instinctively felt in his Steve Irwin vest's hidden pocket and identified the calming presence of the hard edges of his iPhone. After, he'd post the rest from his car before he hit the road back to Savannah.

This was the moment he'd been waiting for ever since he found out he'd won the drawing. He was ready, too. He clutched the bucket of raw chicken in his hand. This would be totally awesome! The words he read online came floating back to him as he gazed out at the smooth, black water. "An alligator feeding frenzy occurs when mammoth reptiles, feeding in pools, suddenly engage in a savage free-for-all, viciously clashing over prey."

This was it. Showtime!

He headed out toward the far end of the boardwalk. The water was quiet, dark, and beautiful. Infused with bravery, Cecil ventured onto one of the four winding wooden walkways deep into the dominion of Florida's most notorious beast, the mighty gator. Clutching his trusty flashlight and a bucket of raw chicken, Cecil made his way into the gator breeding flats.

He heard a gentle rustle of feathers somewhere in the night sky. Water rippled. He was not alone. He swatted at the back of his right shoulder; somehow a darn mosquito had taken a bite out of him, bug spray or no bug spray. And right through his shirt and the vest, too.

Cecil turned just in time to see that it was no mosquito. It was the gator lover from the shore. He saw the glint of moonlight on a syringe. In a split second and before Cecil even knew what was happening, a hard shove to his chest made him lose his balance.

There was hardly a splash when Cecil Snodgrass hit the water, and even if there had been, there was no one to hear.

After the long-awaited Cuban sandwiches with Finch followed by a hot bath at the hotel, Hailey slept through the night for the first time in weeks. She was so tired, she didn't even close the heavy hotel curtains; and the next morning, she woke up to bright sunshine pouring across the Savannah River and into her room.

The hotel halls were quiet and the traffic far below was muted. She suddenly wanted to go home, not to her apartment in Manhattan but home to her parents' brick house at the top of a long, winding driveway in Macon, south of Atlanta.

It was surrounded by azaleas, dogwoods, tea olives, and purple wisteria hugging the brick and situated in the middle of nothing but soybean fields and tall pine trees as far as the eye could see. It was a place where, in Hailey's childhood, she could ride her bike all afternoon after school, free from fear of stranger danger or maniac traffic, only returning home when the chimes in the little Methodist church steeple nearby rang out that it was six o'clock. By then her mom would be home from work, and supper would likely be on the table.

Lying in the center of the hotel bed with the morning sun on her face, she knew it wasn't just the *place* of home that she was longing for . . . it was the *feeling* of home. Glancing at the bedside clock, it was only 6 AM, too early to call her parents.

What would she ever do without them? They'd been there through thick and thin . . . Will's death, law school, dozens and dozens of high-stakes prosecutions . . . she pushed the thought from her mind and, as if to get away from it, swung her legs over the side of the bed and headed for the shower.

Hailey grabbed her iPhone and her old, trusty BlackBerry as she passed the bedroom desk where they'd charged all night plugged into a lamp outlet. *Can't I even walk to the shower without multitasking?* Hailey thought to herself but then smiled. *No . . . I can't.*

She reached into the huge shower, turned the shiny silver controls, and stood waiting for the water to heat up. Leaning against the faux marble bathroom counter, Hailey glanced down at her emails and texts from overnight. There were several from Billings and Fincher from this morning. The last one from Finch had a red flag beside it to mark it as urgent.

She read that one first. "Heading home to Atlanta to see the family."

Home? He was leaving the trial? What? Then it hit her . . . she scrolled back to the home screen. It was Saturday! No court!

A sense of relief poured through her body. She'd been on autopilot for so many days in a row, she literally didn't even know what day it was! She went back to read the rest of Finch's message. The words glowed at her, "Sleep late! You look tired!"

*Ha, thanks Finch.*

She skimmed down to Billings's message. Similar, except no mention of her looking tired, and he asked her to lunch. Hmm.

The hot shower began to steam up the room so Hailey jumped in. She was just rinsing conditioner out of her hair when she thought she heard someone at her hotel door. Quickly grabbing a towel, Hailey called out, "Yes?"

No answer.

Padding back into the bedroom, Hailey looked through the peephole. Nobody. Opening the door, she looked down. At her feet was a neatly folded copy of the *Savannah Morning News.* Hailey leaned down to get it and came face-to-face with a huge shot of Todd Adams's mom, her eyes lolled back in her head, stumbling forward down the steps to the witness stand.

Above the fold.

Hailey picked it up and began to read the story. The banner read "Heartbroken Mom Tish Adams at Son's Murder Trial."

The banner headline started a slow burn in Hailey's chest. *Heartbroken mom?* What about Julie's mom? What about her? And her heartbreak? Had the whole community forgotten about Julie's body washing up on Tybee Island followed by her unborn baby girl, Lily? What about that?

But looking back at Tish, Hailey felt a pang of sadness. She was heartbroken at the thought of losing her son. All of this was Todd Adams's fault. He had single-handedly left behind a wake of pain that would not soon subside.

Hailey could only hope the Todd Adams jury didn't get a look at this. They were already concerned enough about Tish Adams after seeing her pass out in court.

Empathy for Mrs. Adams lasted just a brief moment because when Hailey unfolded the lower half of the paper, it got worse. There, *under* the fold, was a shot of Hailey Dean! It was a shot of her walking down the courthouse steps with Mike Walker from *Snoop* magazine thrusting a microphone in her face. And Finch had been right . . . she *did* look tired . . . especially in black and white. In the background and also coming down the courthouse steps, Tish Adams could be spotted. She was looking directly down at Walker and Hailey, and Hailey was convinced it gave the distinct message that she, Hailey, was somehow responsible for Tish's suffering.

Nothing could be further from the truth.

Making it worse, the headline over the photo read, "Super Sleuth on the Todd Adams Case!" Hailey scanned the article, which was only a few paragraphs. The gist of it was that the state had brought Hailey Dean on board as a criminologist to save the prosecution— which they likened to a sinking ship, the Titanic specifically. The article rehashed her perfect win record in inner-city Atlanta and, of course, dredged up Will's murder to make her sound like some sort of angry avenger.

Hailey was used to it. It wasn't necessarily true, but it sold more papers. Over all her years in the district attorney's office, she had been both lauded, usually by the newspapers, and villainized, usually by the Atlanta Defense Bar and their related publications. She couldn't honestly say it didn't hurt, because it did. Not hurting and being used to something are definitely two very different things.

It was likely cool this early in the morning. Hailey pulled on her usual black running pants and Nikes, with a V-neck zip-up long-sleeved shirt and an old Fulton County Fire Department sweatshirt wrapped around her waist. Although she rarely carried, she was still trained to keep her hands free just in case. She wedged her driver's license and credit cards bound together by a single rubber band down the left side of her sports bra and a tube of lipstick down the other side. Baseball hat and sunglasses topped it off, and she was out the door carrying only her cells and car keys.

Passing through the hotel's elegant lobby, Hailey paused long enough to get a free Styrofoam cup of hot tea from a table set up for hotel guests. It was laden with various coffees, decafs, hot water for tea, tea bags, and a huge assortment of creamers and sweeteners.

She hadn't thought to grab an Irish breakfast tea bag from the cache she packed in her suitcase and stuff it down her bra, so she went for the English breakfast. Fishing it out of a basket of individually wrapped tea bags, she gave it a stir into plenty of hot water and skim milk, and headed to her car parked on the street.

Passing by the lobby doors, Hailey stopped short. A man with long, blue-jeaned legs stretched out beneath the double pages of the paper's sports section was sitting in a cushioned wingback chair. Although the paper obscured his face, Hailey caught his profile as she rushed by, and the boots alone were hard to forget.

"Cloud! Hello! Nice to see you! What are you doing here?"

He lowered his paper to eye Hailey Dean and broke into a wide smile. "Well, fancy meeting up with you here! And I thought I'd never see you again!"

"Are you staying here, too? That's a coincidence!"

"Well, as a matter of fact, I am! I was just waiting for a ride heading to a meeting. Where are you headed so bright and early?"

"Oh, I'm just going out for a jog. It's beautiful today! Hey, I think I saw you at the courthouse! On the front steps, but I was in such a hurry, I couldn't slow down. I don't think you saw me."

"The courthouse? Here in Savannah? Nope, haven't been there and can't say I want to! Courthouses and lawyers make me nervous!"

Not missing a golden opportunity, he pressed on. "Hey, want to have dinner tonight? I hear there's a great restaurant right on the river. About seven-thirty?"

"That sounds so nice, but I have to work. Sorry!" Hailey did her best to look disappointed. What she needed now was a quick exit.

Glancing up at a huge clock over the hotel registration desk, she feigned surprise. "Oh no! I didn't realize what time it is! I better run. Rain check, OK? Bye, Cloud. Have a great day!" Hailey practically sprinted through the open lobby doors.

That was weird. She was almost positive that had been Cloud on the courthouse steps. Hailey slowed passing the parking deck entrance. She'd always had an aversion to parking garages after prosecuting so many violent crimes that went down there. She avoided them whenever she could and she'd found a spot on the street she could actually see from way up in her room. It was comforting somehow.

Happy to see her car remained vandal-free for another night on downtown Savannah streets, she hopped in. There was a distinct chill in the early morning air, even though she knew that in a matter of hours the place would be boiling. Probably the cool air off the river made everything chilly in the mornings. But it was nice, and Hailey marveled, once again, that it was good to be alive.

Putting her car in reverse and then drive, she caught sight of her own green eyes beneath the red gash on her forehead in the rearview mirror. The red in her eyes was gone and so were the dark circles underneath. She felt great this morning. Everything around her seemed shiny and new, even though she was in the heart of Old Savannah, full of old pirate houses, Civil War homes, and even the home of Girl Scout founder Juliette Gordon Low.

Pulling out onto old cobblestone streets, she drove underneath the arms of huge, ancient live oak trees. Spanish moss hung down low from the limbs like gorgeous, intricate shawls. She could imagine the Wesley brothers, just kicked out of the High Church of England. John preaching here under the oaks and his brother, Charles, on guitar, spreading what would one day become Methodism.

Waiting alone at a red light, Hailey glanced again into her rear-view and took a sip of her hot tea. It was delicious and she could feel it, warm, going down.

Foot on the brake at the red light, Hailey held the Styrofoam cup with both hands, the steam still rising off the hot liquid. She took a tiny sip, testing it to see if it was still too hot to take a big gulp.

Hot tea. Hot tea . . . milk . . . almond milk . . . immediately, Eleanor Odom, Elle, sprang to mind. Then there was the lackluster love rival. She'd never forget the look on the face of the judge's secretary when Hailey first spotted her in the courthouse cafeteria the day Elle died.

She originally looked so . . . so . . . *mousy*. It was the only word Hailey could come up with. But that look on her face . . . that look changed it all.

With dull, thin, light brown hair sticking flat to her head held to the sides with pins, slightly hunched forward . . . but then that look. It was so stark, so real. What was it, though? Jealousy? Hatred, maybe?

Who was the judge? What was his name again? Hands gripping the steering wheel, she willed herself to *think*! As if Providence intervened . . . right there on the corner was a placard . . . a sign on a short, wooden post stuck in the dirt . . . Bill Regard for Governor! That was him! Bill Regard . . . that was his name!

But . . . the secretary . . . Hailey racked her brain . . . *what was the secretary's name?* Staring up through the sunroof glass and beyond to the Spanish moss swaying in the breeze off the river, it felt like the more she tried to think of it, the less she could remember.

And then, quick as lightning . . . it hit her . . . Eunah . . . Eunah Mabry! Bingo!

Foot still on the brake and no one behind her to impatiently toot the horn should she miss a green light, Hailey did a quick Google search. In just a few seconds, up popped Eunah Mabry in her capacity as chairwoman of the local Daughters of the American Revolution chapter. Hmm, Daughters of the American Revolution. She seemed very active in the group, according to Google.

In the most recent posting was a notice of the last DAR meeting ... at Eunah Mabry's house. It was in Ardsley Park, south central Savannah. Wow, that was a surprise. How could a single woman on a civil servant's salary afford Ardsley?

It was truly Savannah's first and priciest suburb. Ardsley Park meant plush lawns, elaborate landscaping, six- and seven-bedroom mansions dating back to the 1920s, all either restored or in mint condition. Bordering Victory Drive and running east from Bull Street to Waters Avenue, it was the movie version of Old Savannah that tourists and movie producers alike came hunting.

*How could she afford all that on a secretary's pay?*

Hailey couldn't help but ask the question again in her mind. And then, in an instant, her plans changed.

Hailey had intended to go jogging in Forsyth Park. One block south of the Johnny Mercer house, the park was a lush thirty-plus acres of live oaks, historical monuments, old park benches, and, the jewel in the crown, the famous three-tiered cast-iron fountain that served as the backdrop for the movie *Midnight in the Garden of Good and Evil*. But all that could wait.

Maybe it was stirring the milk in her tea. Or maybe it was the "Bill Regard for Governor" sign stuck in the dirt on the corner at the red light ... or the photo in the *Savannah Morning News*. Hailey wasn't sure what it was exactly, but suddenly going to the home of the judge's secretary seemed a lot more interesting than a morning jog.

Wait a minute. That *was* Cloud at the courthouse. Now she remembered his boots when he hurried off after she called out to him. Wonder what was up with him? She didn't have long to wonder; the light turned green and Hailey hit the gas. Ardsley Park it was.

Hailey checked the address again. Could this be right? The address she had was 7768 Victory. Driving by slowly, Hailey peered through her window.

There had to be a full acre of front lawn, carefully manicured and boasting beds of azaleas, palmetto, and laurels, with a large, perfectly formed circular driveway leading onto the street. On both sides of the two street entrances were large stone mounts with eighteenth-century Versailles-type lanterns atop them.

Beyond that rose the house. It was lovely. Judging from the street, it was likely a five-bedroom. Out of curiosity, Hailey ran a quick Google search on the address. Within seconds, an article popped up in the *Savannah Seasons*, a glossy, but boring, magazine catering to the doings of Savannah's high society.

Sadly, to get to the scoop on the antebellum behemoth she was spying on at that very minute from her rental car, Hailey had to scroll down through the magazine's table of contents. Let's see . . . "Distinguished Speaker Series with Georgia's First Lady, Betty-Lou Talmadge". . . "Heitzler Cellars Wine Dinner with Third-Generation Winemaker Hendrickson Heitzler". . . oh dear . . . the implications. Hailey's lips subconsciously pursed as she tried to scroll down with her right hand while still driving with her left. She finally pulled into a side street, Washington Avenue, and maneuvered to one side, putting the car in park, engine still running.

Ugh. She was stuck in some sort of a dinner menu . . . Passed Canapés, Seared Sea Scallops, Prosciutto-Wrapped Trotters (what was a "trotter"?), Grass-Fed Beef Tenderloin, and Dark Chocolate Mousse with Crème Chiboust and Cassis Coulis.

She was obviously dining in the wrong circles. Hailey smiled at the thought of suggesting this menu to Fincher. Staring at her screen, she saw each item was paired with a different wine, so obviously she was still stuck in the Heitzler Cellars Wine Dinner event. She kept scrolling.

Let's see . . . there were two full pages dedicated to honoring the life and legacy of world-famous golf course architect Bobby Trent Jones, a ladies golf session, and a golf greens aerification tutorial, as well as hydrostatic body fat testing, a book club discussion, and a dining article featuring something called a Pinot Palooza.

What alternate universe were these people living in? Hailey let out a silent breath of laughter. On the other hand, Hailey thought to herself, if they spent a day in Hailey's iPhone or emails, they'd probably think her world was nothing but wonky.

Hailey had no idea how much of high society revolved around golf and wine. Maybe if they didn't hit the bottle so much they'd have better golf scores. Whatever. In any event, she managed to locate the feature on Eunah Mabry's family home.

Hmmm . . . the article had a shot of the front of the home. There was no mistaking it . . . a large upper balcony was built into the front porch on the home's second floor and situated between two white Doric columns. A quote from the article ran under the photo, " . . . a trophy house by grand architect Olaf Ottoman off Ardsley Park's renowned Washington Avenue . . ."

Well, that could only mean one thing. She looked up at the street sign to confirm. She was in fact on the "renowned Washington Avenue." She shook her head and kept reading.

" . . . a quiet location, the white-columned manse features a front foyer grand staircase, graceful double parlors, and a glass sunroom. Exquisite outdoor spaces showcase a formal garden with a ceramic fountain and covered gazebo."

Wow. That was it, all right. Taking a deep breath, Hailey U-turned the car in the middle of Washington Avenue, turned right onto Victory, and slowly pulled into the circular driveway that cut an elegant swath through the home's front lawn. Hey, Hailey didn't see a "no trespassing" sign, so why not? She repeated this phrase in her mind over and over in case the police were called.

Parking directly in the front behind a silver Audi also parked at the front steps, she got out, closed the car door gently, and made her way up the steps. Hailey pressed the perfectly round doorbell. Through the door, she could hear the bell ringing inside.

No movement. Hailey leaned to the side and peered through clear panes of glass surrounding the front door. Just to the right of the front door in the "entrance foyer" sat an intricately carved Royal Baroque table. Standing on two ornate scrolled legs, the piece was fraught with elaborate foliate scrollwork. It had an equally carved matching mirror over it. Hailey saw in its reflection that an identical table and mirror were positioned directly across the foyer.

But what set the table closest to Hailey apart from its twin across the foyer was the empty wine glass sitting on it. Hailey could see the smear of burgundy still at the bottom of the clear cut glass and lipstick on the rim.

Still no movement. Hailey rang the buzzer again. Nothing. Just then, Hailey caught a movement in one of the twin mirrors, but because they mirrored each other, she didn't know from which side parlor it came.

Eyes trained, Hailey kept watching . . . for what . . . she didn't exactly know. Hailey watched in the mirror as a woman made her way, slowly, gingerly, across the parlor to Hailey's left and toward the door.

Steadying herself with the back of an elegant sofa, Eunah Mabry paused. Was she ill? Hailey quickly surmised she was likely not ill, but Hailey turning up on the front mat must have woken Mabry up. But the bedrooms, according to the article anyway, were upstairs. Did the woman spend the night on her sofa?

Mabry finally entered the foyer and, glancing at the door, gave a weak smile that did not extend to her eyes. The clinking of locks being undone and then, the door swung open.

"Good morning. May I help you?"

"Good morning, Ms. Mabry. I don't know if you remember me. My name is Hailey Dean."

Eunah Mabry gave a confused look as if trying to place Hailey in her own mind. She bent down to retrieve the morning paper off the front stoop and rising, paused. Eunah looked from the paper back to Hailey and then repeated the comparison.

"Well, at first I must say I did not, but now, of course, seeing the morning paper, I do. How can I help you, Ms. Dean?" Her tone was more hollow than frosty, Hailey thought for a split second.

This wasn't exactly how Hailey wanted their introduction to go, but there was nothing she could do about it now. Since when did people get their newspapers on their doorsteps? Guess you had to pay extra for that.

"Right. The paper." Hailey gave the woman her best smile, under the circumstances, and with the words of the sheriff the day Elle died, lashing out at Eunah Mabry, ringing in her ears, Hailey searched for the right words to say. Stupidly, she hadn't planned her intro.

"Ms. Mabry . . ."

The woman looked at her expectantly. This was the woman, according to one of the sheriffs anyway, that absolutely loathed Eleanor, eaten up by jealousy. Over what, though? The judge was a married man . . . had there ever been a relationship between any of them? Or was it all just courthouse gossip?

*Courthouse gossip that ended in murder?*

"I . . . uh . . . I see the judge is running for governor. I'm a lawyer by trade and I think a judge of his standing would be a real asset in the governor's mansion."

Hailey didn't know where that icebreaker came from . . . but if what the sheriff said *was* true, then this woman, Eunah Mabry, may go with Regard to the governor's mansion.

Or if not *to* the governor's mansion full time . . . at least to an office *within* the governor's mansion from nine to five weekdays. Or did she want more?

"You're interested in the judge's campaign?"

Surprise crossed Mabry's face briefly and she opened the door a little wider, maybe just an inch or two. But even one inch emboldened Hailey, who immediately picked up on the slight, nonverbal cue.

"Yes . . . yes I am. And I must say . . . you have a gorgeous home. Didn't I see a shot of your home in a movie? Let me think . . . what was it? Um . . ."

"*Midnight in the Garden of Good and Evil*, probably. But then there was *Forrest Gump*, you know with Tom Hanks . . . that park bench was right here, you know. And Dolly Parton was even here for *Something to Talk About*. Or was it Julia Roberts? Yes, I got to meet them all. Let's see, there have been so many . . ."

"I thought I recognized it! Wasn't *Cape Fear* shot here? And let's see . . ." Hailey racked her brain to keep the conversation going. ". . . now that one was with . . . oh what's his name?"

"Well, of course the first *Cape Fear* had Gregory Peck and Robert Mitchum. I never liked Mitchum much, but Gregory Peck . . . now that's a different thing. I wasn't born yet for that one . . . but then the remake was made here too and there were scenes of the house in it too. Now, that one I remember. That one had De Niro and Nick Nolte."

"Oh, what's he like?" The door widened another fraction of an inch.

"Which one? Nolte or De Niro?"

"You met them *both*?" Hailey inched closer to the door.

"Yes, I did. I remember it like it was yesterday. And oh, it wasn't me they were interested in . . . no . . . I didn't fool myself. It was this house they wanted. But I got to meet them, you know, by hook or by crook as the saying goes." Eunah Mabry glanced down at the Styrofoam cup Hailey still had in her hand. "Would you like some coffee?"

Hailey didn't dare mention she only drank tea. "I'd love some, frankly. Thank you!"

*She was in.*

Eunah shut the door firmly behind Hailey, jiggered two locks into place, and headed past the parlors and toward, Hailey presumed, the kitchen. Hailey followed along behind Eunah but paused passing the double parlors. "Wow. Your home is just as beautiful on the inside as it is on the outside. Did you do the decorating?"

The interior of the old home was nothing Hailey would have ever picked out, much too stuffy, but it was a perfect fit in keeping with the traditional antebellum design. While the double parlors were symmetrically designed, their interiors were different yet compatible. Both were painted Confederate blue with wide, deeper blue crown moldings edged in white. The window treatments were darker blue velvet curtains trimmed in gold pulled away from the panes. Deep blue valances swagged down to form a semicircular top and white sheers hung across the panes, drawn against the morning sun. White Florentine columns stood at strategic points, the floors were highly polished hardwood, and the furniture matched the hardwood floors.

Very impressive.

Passing through a white wainscoted hallway, Hailey saw the walls were covered almost completely by framed family photos starting at about waist high up. They were photos from many varied years, but in nearly all of them, Eunah was pictured with her father. He looked familiar to Hailey.

In several shots the two were on a boat together. Was that the Savannah River? At Eunah's graduation, family portraits, Christmases. Hailey saw just one including a woman who was clearly Eunah's mother. It was a picture of the three of them, Eunah with her mother and father. In this shot, her father was wearing a black robe.

"Your dad was a judge?" Hailey paused to look at the photo. If Hailey was correct, they were standing in front of a portrait of Eunah's father in the lobby of the Chatham County Courthouse.

Eunah paused briefly, then kept walking. "Oh, yes. Daddy was one of the best judges to ever take the bench. Very famous, actually, if you run in those circles."

Hailey looked again at the picture. Now she understood why she seemed to recognize him. His portrait was hanging in the lobby of the courthouse. She'd been passing his face practically every morning since she got to Savannah.

"That was when his courthouse portrait was unveiled. It's absolutely stunning. Absolutely stunning," Eunah Mabry tossed over her shoulder.

Emerging from the hall, they made their way into a large kitchen. It was perfectly in order except the sink was full of soapy water and filled with dishes. Other than that, not a fork out of place or a crumb on a surface could be seen. African violets, notorious for demanding lots of attention, flowered in and around the kitchen window in several ceramic pots.

"Your home is lovely. Did you design it?"

"Me do this designing? Oh, no. I wish I could take credit, but my father built the home and designed the interior as well. He was amazing, my dad. The Honorable Willard Fulton Eugene Mabry. I'm named after him, you know. The Eugene part. They say he wanted a boy, but he got a girl, so it was Eunah instead of Eugene. He's been gone years now, and I still miss him . . . every day." Her voice cracked a little there at the end of her sentence, but given Hailey was following behind her, she couldn't judge Eunah's facial expression.

Intuitively sensing it was not the right moment to shift the conversation to Eleanor Odom, Hailey replied, "He must have been an incredible person, to design all of this."

Eunah gave a shadow of a smile and threw Hailey a bone. "Please, sit down at the table." Hailey pulled back a chair and sat.

To her shock, sitting on the table, face up, of course, was the brand-new copy of *Snoop* straight off the press. The *Savannah Morning News* was bad enough, but now this? And there on the cover page, of all places, was a shot of her, Hailey. It was salaciously morbid, suggesting to the casual eye that Hailey was sprawled dead on the sidewalk. To Hailey's shock, the banner said, "Avenging Angel Risks Death on Hunt for Brutal Killer!" It was an awful picture of Hailey . . . she actually did look dead.

Inside, Hailey did a slow burn. She'd had dealings with Mike Walker before and she knew he was behind this. The man would do anything to sell his magazine.

Hailey was convinced he'd trade his own mother with *"Snoop"* stamped on her forehead if it increased circulation. What a twist of fate that Walker's in town covering the Julie Love Adams murder trial, lands smack in the middle of a courthouse crime wave, and manages to get a photo of Hailey after a brush with the front grill of a speeding bus. Another lucrative coincidence for Mike Walker.

"You said my father must have been incredible. He was. He was, indeed." Eunah Mabry's voice snapped Hailey out of her mental tirade on Mike Walker and back to the here and now. She did, however, turn the cover of *Snoop* facedown and shove it under the stack of mail and magazines sitting on the kitchen table.

"But to call him incredible is an understatement, really." Eunah, her back still to Hailey, began making coffee. The very back of her hair was matted flat, revealing her scalp where she must have slept the night before. Unaware of her mussed hair, Eunah retrieved the milk from the fridge and set it on the kitchen counter beside another empty wine glass, again with dark red residue in the very bottom.

"Now, back to *Cape Fear*. You know Martin Scorsese directed that. The judge is a big fan of his. I got him a meeting."

"With Scorsese?" Hailey's eyes widened.

"With Scorsese! The two had coffee right here at this very kitchen table. They certainly did." Eunah's free hand grazed the top of the old table lovingly, lost in the memory of the moment the three of them, Eunah, the judge, and Martin Scorsese, all gathered around *her kitchen table*.

"Wow! I hope you got a photo!"

"I did, actually. Would you like to see it?"

Hailey didn't know exactly what she was fishing for, but on more than one occasion, a whim . . . a hunch, so to speak, had steered her right during an investigation. Hailey didn't know what, if anything, Martin Scorsese or this house or this woman had to do with the death of Elle Odom. Maybe nothing at all.

"I'd love to!" Hailey answered brightly. She truly did want to see the shot of Scorsese with the judge and Eunah Mabry, but it wasn't about Scorsese. Hailey wanted to see a photo of the judge with Eunah.

She followed behind Eunah, trying not to stare at the bald spot on the back of her head from her bed pillow. Once in the parlor, however, she realized it may not have been the pillow that caused the hair eyesore. There on an ornately carved sofa upholstered in deep blue velvet was a huge photo album of sorts, but stepping closer, Hailey saw it wasn't full of photos.

On each page was a carefully preserved wine label, a description and history of the wine itself, and the date and circumstances surrounding the uncorking. Without actually flipping through the open pages, Hailey judged there to be at least a hundred completed pages . . . so far.

The room was strewn with scissors, tweezers, an ashtray full of cigarette butts, and a third crystal glass smudged with red wine and lipstick. By the positioning of the pillows on the sofa and a throw blanket on the floor, it looked like Eunah Mabry spent the night right here, drinking and scrapbooking about her last bottle of wine.

On the coffee table beside the wine glass was the photo to which Eunah referred. It was enlarged and framed in an elaborate sterling silver frame.

There they were, Eunah, Scorsese, and Judge Bill Regard leaning in toward each other over coffee cups at the kitchen table, smiling. Regard was in the middle as opposed to the famed director. Eunah sat beside the judge, leaning in and almost touching cheek to cheek.

The look on Eunah's face in the photo was unmistakable. She was smiling all right, but not really looking at the camera. She was looking at the judge beside her, just inches from her own face. There was no mistaking it . . . it was the look of love.

Clearly, Eunah Mabry was deeply in love with Bill Regard. Judge Bill Regard, possibly Governor Bill Regard, was, most important, a very married Bill Regard.

"That's a lovely picture. He must be a fine judge. I saw one of his campaign signs at a red light this morning."

"Oh, he is. I mean, he is a fine judge . . . and he is running for governor. Casting his pearls before swine, I say . . . pearls before the swine. That's from the Bible."

"Yes, I believe it is," Hailey murmured back, holding her eye.

"Oh, it definitely is. And truer words were never spoken. Of course, he's too good for the people. They can't possibly appreciate a man of his stature. And now . . . this . . . this *scandal* threatening it all."

Still holding her coffee, Hailey looked up from the photo of Eunah and the judge and took a pretend sip of the vile brew. "What scandal?"

"Why Hailey, you were there that day. I'm positive I saw you. The day that woman, Eleanor Odom, the bottled blonde? The day she threw herself on the floor and passed away right there in the lunch crowd in the county cafeteria. Of course, she went and did it when she had an audience."

"And she was so young."

"Not as young as she'd have you believe, mark my words. That Eleanor Odom is no spring chicken! She's thirty if she's a day!"

Hailey suppressed a smile. In her book, thirty was young. She managed to nod her head. "You think so?"

"Oh, yes, I do. But the judge wouldn't believe it. He was blind to her . . . her *ways* . . . if you know what I mean." Eunah Mabry gave a knowing nod and her eyes narrowed. "You know, always buzzing around his chambers, especially just as court would be ending and everyone going home. I would stay at my desk and catch up on busy work just to keep her away from the judge. Oh, she loved to corner him alone and throw herself . . . *throw herself* at him."

"No!" Hailey really didn't have to say much at all to keep Eunah Mabry going.

"And the makeup and the perfume. She never once set foot at that courthouse without being positively painted up like an Indian on the warpath. The rouge, the eye shadow, the lipstick. It was so overdone. Ghastly, really. And the perfume. I'd know that smell anywhere . . . something cheap."

"Oh, dear." Hailey was actually interested.

She mentally recalled the moment she'd seen Eleanor Odom coming down the ramp to the cafeteria. She wasn't overdone at all. She looked lovely, young, and full of life with a fairly natural beauty and perfectly applied makeup. Nothing like what Mabry was describing, not that Hailey could vouch for how the woman smelled.

"Oh, and there were plenty of times I'd beat the judge in to work and I'd smell it. Oh yes I did, I smelled it."

Hailey leaned forward in her seat across from Eunah on the sofa. "Smelled what?"

Eunah reached out for a cigarette, lit it with a black plastic lighter from the coffee table, inhaled deeply, and, pursing her lips as if she were whistling to her left, exhaled to the side. Her eyes narrowed again, and in the morning light Hailey could easily see the smoker's wrinkles etched forever around her mouth and eyes.

"That horrible perfume. She positively *reeked* of it. I'd know it anywhere. It would be hanging like a shroud in his office." Her words were barely above a whisper now . . . more like a hiss.

"Interesting use of words . . . *hanging like a shroud*. Why do you say that?"

Slightly taken aback, Eunah paused, tapping her cigarette into a china ashtray stuffed with cigarette butts, presumably from the night before when she'd obviously fallen asleep on the sofa with a glass of wine. Or glasses.

"I really don't know why I said that. I guess because . . . I always thought she'd kill the judge before she'd let him go."

"So they were having an affair?" Hailey looked her square in the face when she asked, gauging Mabry's reaction.

"I would never say that about a man as fine and true as the judge! He was too good, too pure, too . . . too . . . *honorable*! But oh, she wanted to! There may have been a moment where he slipped . . . slightly . . . but what man wouldn't when they're chased? Hunted like an animal in the forest?"

Hailey glanced back at the photo of Regard on the coffee table. He looked like anything but a hunted animal. Young, tanned, muscular, and athletic-looking. He had a vibrant smile. His upper lip was thin, his lower curved to accent perfectly even white teeth. His dark brown eyes seemed to glow back at the camera. It was hard to imagine this man being the prey, not the predator.

"I mean what normal, red-blooded man wouldn't give in? After all, he's *only human*. But I assure you . . . it was all her. I assure you. All her!"

Without thinking, Eunah Mabry lifted the wine glass from the coffee table instead of her coffee, held it up as if in a toast, and drained the tiny bit of wine left in the bottom. Hailey stared, saying nothing. Mabry slammed the wine glass back on the table almost defiantly, her anger and loathing boiling just beneath the surface.

The hate in her voice, the sofa-matted hair hanging in scraggly tendrils around her face, the smeared lipstick, the stink of old cigarettes combined with a glint of pure malice in her voice all combined to give Eunah Mabry the appearance of being . . . somewhat maniacal.

Or maybe she wasn't. Maybe Mabry was simply an aging woman, living alone, lonely and disliking it. Likely scorned—or worse, not even noticed—by the man she appeared to have loved for many years, Judge Bill Regard.

"Well, the judge is married, right? His wife must have been livid about Eleanor Odom . . . if she knew about it."

"Oh, that one. Well she's a piece of work herself, let me tell you that. Rich family, new money, you know, showy, private schools, never worked a day in her life. Blind to the man she married . . . couldn't care less. Spends all her time at the country club with the tennis pro and I will say no more. I'm not one to gossip. Evil, foul thing, gossip is. My daddy always said that and he was right."

"Absolutely. And you, Eunah Mabry, strike me as a woman who would never say a false word, let alone gossip." Hailey said it with the straightest face she could muster. Was this woman still drunk? Or just hungover?

"Actually, it's almost lunchtime. Would you care for a cordial? A small glass of wine?"

Hailey glanced over at a grandfather clock standing solemnly in the corner. It plainly said ten-thirty.

Ignoring the drink offer, Hailey went on. "Earlier, you mentioned a scandal?"

"Did I?" Eunah looked almost surprised.

"Yes. Something to do with Eleanor Odom?"

"Oh, of course. The *scandal of it all* . . . to drop dead just before the governor's race really heats up. I mean . . . what if the press connects her back to the judge? Not that there's anything *to* connect . . . but what if they did? It could ruin everything! Everything!"

Hailey didn't answer, merely held Eunah's gaze as if willing her to go on. And she did.

"If someone knew how she chased him and thought they were putting two and two together . . . I mean . . . for him to be connected to a girl like . . . like . . . *her.* What if someone thought he was somehow . . ."

"Somehow what?"

"Somehow responsible. He's not, of course! But having someone like . . . like Eleanor Odom pop up during a political race . . . I mean, after all, the woman keels over one floor directly under the judge's chambers! And, of course, she had to put on quite the performance, even in death. With everyone looking at her. *Just as she always wanted . . . everyone . . . the judge . . . looking at her.*"

Just then, a horn beeped very close by. Eunah leaped from her seat and instinctively turned toward a mirror hanging on the wall beside them, patting her hair into place. With her two index fingers, she wiped the corners of her mouth where lipstick mixed with red wine had gathered and crusted over.

"Oh dear, it might be the judge! He's here to pick up some letters and orders I finished up for him last night at the courthouse."

She practically flew to one of the front windows, pulled the gauzy white sheers to one side, and peeked out. *"It's him!"*

Eunah Mabry hurried over to a hardwood secretary, eighteenth century by the look of it, and pulled back the roll top to scoop up a good eight inches of stacked papers. Several yellow stickies stuck out on the sides with handwritten instructions on them.

The doorbell rang. Hailey remained seated, but she could easily hear the conversation at the door.

"Well, good morning, Eunah! You must have slept like a baby . . . you look absolutely gorgeous this morning!"

"Judge! How you go on! Please, won't you come in for a cup of coffee?"

"Well, I, uh . . ." the judge stalled.

"Or a glass of wine? I have your favorite, you know!"

"Eunah . . . nothing, absolutely nothing, would please me more than to come in and have a glass of wine with you and just visit. You know, I miss that. Just visiting with you. We've just been so busy with the upcoming race and all . . . and . . . to tell you the truth . . ." he paused.

"Yes, Judge?" Desperation was creeping into Eunah's voice.

"Well, I can't lie to you, Eunah. You know me better than I know myself. I've got Mrs. Regard in the car with me. She has a tennis tournament at the club and she's in a hurry. And . . . you know how she is, Eunah."

On cue, the horn blew as if ordering the judge to hurry up. It wasn't a little toot, either. It was a much longer, agitated blow, like a jab to the back or an elbow to the rib. It was a subtle but important difference in horn blowing that anyone in the South would recognize and immediately take issue with.

"I understand, Judge. Maybe next time?" Her voice actually quivered.

"Absolutely next time. It's a date, Eunah. I'm looking forward to it."

No wonder Eunah Mabry fell in love. This guy was certainly a charmer. Hailey paused. Wonder who else was in love with him?

Hailey stood up from the sofa almost involuntarily. She silently stepped over to the window. Looking out between the sheers, there in the circular driveway behind Hailey's rental sat a metallic baby blue Mercedes convertible SL65. The new ones listed at more than $200,000. Hailey let out a low whistle. That wasn't cheap and it certainly wasn't affordable on a county judge's salary.

The top was down and Hailey could easily see Victoria Regard in the passenger's seat. She had pale white skin, dark silky hair cut in a bob curling in around her neck, and black Jackie O glasses.

Victoria Regard reached her left hand over. The horn blew again. Hailey noticed she didn't bother to look up at her husband and Eunah across the front porch at the front door.

"Gotta run, Eunah. But I'll see you Monday morning, OK?"

"Of course, Judge. I'll see you . . . Monday morning." Eunah's voice was noticeably thin, almost cracking.

"Promise? You won't run off with the mailman? We'll have coffee like we always do? You make the best coffee in the world. I wish you'd give tips to Mrs. Regard; hers tastes like poison!" Hailey imagined he had the same inviting smile he wore in the photo with Scorsese, thin upper lip, full lower one, curved up at one corner.

"Promise," she said it so quietly that Hailey could barely hear her.

Hailey quickly left the window and settled back at her seat before Eunah returned. She heard the front door close quietly, followed by the Mercedes's motor gunning and the sound of gravel churning as the car scratched off.

Eunah Mabry came around the corner and into Hailey's view. She gripped the side of the wall with one hand as if she needed support. She held the fingertips of her other hand to her temple.

"Miss . . . ah . . ."

"Dean. Hailey Dean," Hailey interjected quickly to save her the embarrassment of having forgotten her name.

"Yes. Miss Dean, I seem to have developed a terrible headache. Would it be too rude if I asked you if we could continue our conversation about the judge's campaign at a later time?"

"Of course! I'm so sorry to have barged in on you like this. And thank you for the coffee and the conversation. It's such a pleasure to meet you and see your lovely home."

"Yes. How kind. And please visit again."

Hailey was pretty sure, regardless of what she'd just said, another visit from Hailey Dean was the last thing this woman wanted.

Rehashing the relationship between Eleanor Odom and Judge Regard along with Eleanor's death obviously struck a nerve.

The headache seemed real. But whether it was from all the wine and sleeping on ornamental sofa pillows or from the sight of Bill Regard with his wife . . . Hailey wasn't exactly sure.

Eunah Mabry closed the ornate front door gently. Hailey practically bounded down the front steps and back out into the sunlight. She paused before she got back into the driver's seat of her rental car.

Looking up at the sky through the branches of the live oaks, she suddenly couldn't wait to get away from the mansion, beautiful as it was. The stale smell of cigarettes, the sticky wine glasses, the loneliness of it all hung on her like a heavy, wet cloak. She turned the ignition and pulled out of the driveway and back onto the two-lane. The wind rushed through her hair.

The disappointment that lived in Eunah Mabry's mansion faded in the sunlight.

The sun broke through the heavy oaks like strobe lights as Hailey sped down Victory Drive. Huge gnarled arms with Spanish moss draping down like choir robes made a canopy over her head the length of the avenue. Hailey kept inhaling the fresh air, instinctively almost, gulping it down like a dog hanging its head out the open window.

Only when she escaped the mansion Eunah Mabry's daddy built did she realize she felt she could barely breathe inside. She knew, in her head, that she could in fact breathe perfectly normally in the beautiful old home. It was all in her mind, the constriction of the chest, the claustrophobic feeling . . . even though every room was huge and appointed to a tee. Yes, her head knew it . . . but her heart didn't.

There was something sad and aching and . . . venomous lurking there. And it wasn't the home itself.

Tooling down Victory Drive, Hailey glanced over when her iPhone buzzed and lit up. It was Billings. She put it on speaker.

"Good morning! How are you?" She had a smile on her face.

"Good morning, Miss Hailey Dean! What trouble are you stirring up today? And how do you feel?"

"I feel great. A little achy, but overall great! Thanks for asking. Oops, hold on. A cop's on my tail and I don't want him to see the phone in my hand!"

"Just tell him you know somebody . . ."

"But what if he asks who? He may not like you!" Hailey started laughing as a Savannah cop cruiser passed her and kept going.

"You're in the car? Where are you?"

"Victory Drive heading back to downtown."

"Really? What interests you on Victory Drive?" Hailey could hear the curiosity in his voice.

"You'll never guess. Eunah Mabry. Name ring a bell?"

"It does, actually. Eunah Mabry . . . Eunah Mabry . . . who is she?"

"Judge Bill Regard's secretary. None other."

"Hailey! Are you out investigating a case in my jurisdiction?" She could actually see the twinkle in his eye and the smile playing the corners of his lips.

"I take the Fifth!" She just made it under a yellow light and kept going.

"Well, it just so happens that I'm at Victory and Abercorn. Let's get coffee."

"I don't drink coffee. Unless I have to."

"Then you watch me drink coffee and I'll get you hot tea. How's that?"

"One condition," Hailey answered, checking her rearview.

"What's that?"

"We get it to go. I'll even let you drive."

"Deal! Where are we going?" He was an unusually good sport.

"The Savannah Country Club. There's a ladies' tennis tournament I want to watch."

"Uh-oh. I smell trouble."

Hailey could tell he was still smiling, even though she couldn't see him. He was smart, too. That was a dangerous combination, as far as Hailey was concerned. Good-looking, smart, and a good sport.

Within just minutes, Hailey spotted Billings in her rearview mirror. He put on the blue lights for effect and Hailey started laughing.

Her cell buzzed again. "You're headed to the Savannah Country Club? Is that what you said?" Billings asked immediately, no hello.

"Yep. That's where I'm headed!"

"OK. That's what I thought you said, but I was a little afraid to ask why." She caught his eyes in the rearview.

"I told you! There's a tennis match I want to see! Come join me! Maybe it will help me get in. And I bet you can get a cup of coffee there, too."

"I bet I can," Billings answered. She could see in her rearview that he was still smiling. That was good.

"Hey, you're a lawman. They may even give it to you for free. Now that's incentive . . . right?"

"From what I know of the Savannah Country Club, the last thing they want to see is a sheriff showing up . . . that means trouble. Blue bloods don't like even the suggestion of cops . . . or trouble. They'll give me a gallon of hot coffee to leave!"

"I hear you. But they'll be way too polite to actually come right out and ask you to leave! Agree?" Hailey had a point.

They certainly weren't club members, but Billings's uniform could get them in the door and to the tennis courts. Hailey had the idea she was on to something and she didn't want to slow down now. She had to get a closer look at Bill Regard and his wife.

"Yep . . . they only want a cop uniform on the premises if he's directing parking for a society event. You know the deal, Hailey. It's all right. I get it. It's not like I could afford the membership fees anyway."

"I know the deal, Billings. I know the deal for sure."

"So, Hailey. What's with the tennis match?"

"How about I tell you over our free coffee? Or in my case, tea? I'd hate to get busted for driving while distracted by cell phone. Hee-hee."

"OK. I guess I'll have to trust you. But let me in front. You just took a wrong turn."

"See? You distracted me!"

Billings pulled around in front, and in no time they were there. A guard in a security house waved them through as soon as he saw Billings's patrol car. Hailey noticed the security guard began speaking into a walkie-talkie when they passed. Probably alerting the club a cop had showed up.

Hailey parked beside Billings and hopped out of her car, locking it instantly with her keychain remote. "This place is pretty swanky, huh? I looked it up at a red light. It says it's the oldest golf club in the country. 1894. Could that even be true? It says the golf course was actually built along old Confederate war fortifications."

"Thanks for the history lesson, Hailey. But I don't think you came here for the historical value. So what's up?"

"Well, you know Judge Bill Regard was having an affair with Eleanor Odom. You saw the autopsy report, right?"

"I saw it." His smile faded.

"She died of a severe reaction to a pretty serious nut allergy, and I'll bet your bottom dollar it came from that coffee cup, the one with her lipstick on it. She was fine when she walked in . . . she hadn't eaten a bite, she got a cup of coffee, and then, boom . . . she's dead."

"Yes, I recall you gave me that scenario over the lost-and-found bin at the courthouse."

"Well . . . in case she didn't *accidentally* poison herself . . . then who did?" Hailey's question dripped with sarcasm, and it wasn't wasted.

"I know. I've already been working it. The state crime lab got me a rush on the cup . . . it was simple coffee . . . with a large helping of almond milk."

"I knew it! So either Elle accidentally used almond milk versus regular milk at the coffee bar, or somebody switched the canisters or somehow doctored her coffee itself. Or they could have simply added almond milk to the milk sitting out at the coffee bar. But it's too late to test those, right? They were probably cleaned out by the time we figured out the real cause of death wasn't a heart attack or stroke."

"Exactly."

"What about cameras in the cafeteria? Any trained on the cash register?" Hailey stopped mid-stride.

"I hadn't thought of that, but I can find out right now." Billings pulled his shoulder radio out and radioed to the courthouse, asking a bailiff to check the cafeteria. "So what does the courthouse cafeteria have to do with a tennis tournament at the Savannah Country Club?"

"Well, if the rumors of Elle's affair with the judge are true, I wanted to see Mrs. Regard . . . in action. She's playing today. I got it from the horse's mouth."

"You talked to her?"

"Nope. I heard it from the judge."

"Her husband? Bill Regard? I'd call him more of a jackass than a horse. You talked to him?"

"*I* didn't talk to him . . . Eunah Mabry did and I heard every word."

"Hmm. I'm not even gonna ask how you managed to overhear *that*. And if any laws were broken in order for you to eavesdrop . . . I don't even want to know about it."

"Don't worry! No laws were broken . . . that I know of."

Billings shot her a look just as the two rounded the corner of a huge stucco building with a pinkish-red tiled roof. They'd headed toward the sounds of tennis balls and they were right. Laid out beautifully in front of them were at least a dozen USTA tennis courts, seven Fast-Dry clay courts, and four Novacushion hard courts. Benches surrounded the courts, and for the tournament today, low bleachers had been erected.

The two blended in as best as they could. Climbing up to the back row, they actually managed to wedge in behind a group of female tennis players in tennis skirts and visors. At first, Hailey thought their constant chatter would be distracting in her search for Mrs. Victoria Regard, but it only took a matter of minutes to realize their play-by-play covered more than an analysis of the tennis game in front of them.

On the court nearest them, four women gathered at the net. They quickly dispersed, and as the shortest of the four turned to the baseline to serve, Hailey immediately recognized Victoria Regard. She was slim and muscled. Her dark hair swung when she moved. Her makeup was perfect, even in the morning heat at a tennis match, and her tennis outfit was coordinated, bearing a Nike logo on every spot possible. Facing the stands, she flashed a perfectly even, bright white smile at the crowd.

"I saw Vickie managed to drag Bill here today," one of the women, a brunette with her long, silky hair pulled back in a severe ponytail flipping out the back of her visor, commented. The sound of the tennis ball being slammed by Regard's racket punctured the air. "Nice serve."

"Seriously? He's here? He managed to get away from all that *work* at the courthouse?" a blonde whose hair was bleached almost white answered, sarcasm dripping nastily from her words.

"Yes . . . all that work is just *piling up* . . . if you know what I mean. It takes lots of late hours working to attend to it all . . ." All four of them started laughing at the inside joke.

"Hey. Didn't you guys read the paper? There's one less . . . let me say . . . legal problem the judge has to worry about . . . she's dead!" The blonde on the end couldn't wait to share the news.

The tennis match was heating up. It seemed like Victoria Regard and her doubles partner were winning. Hailey was straining to hear the rest of the conversation in front of her while appearing to be intent on the match, but the four women were so oblivious to everything but themselves, Hailey needn't bother acting.

"*What?*" the other three exclaimed almost in perfect unison. "*Dead?*"

"As a doornail!"

Hailey had to suppress a grimace as the four ghouls in front of her nonchalantly laughed off Eleanor Odom's death. But that certainly didn't stop her from eavesdropping a second time that day. Her ears were practically aching she was straining so hard to hear over the crowd in the stands.

"What happened?" Ponytail asked first.

"I think she had a stroke or an asthma attack or something like that. I don't really know. It happened at the courthouse. But I do know one thing, it's a good thing the girl had an asthma attack . . . or whatever she had . . . because Vickie would have killed her!"

"I believe it! Nothing is going to get in between Victoria Regard and the governor's mansion, and I mean nothing. And certainly not some little secretary at the courthouse. No way."

"You know her parents were dead set against the marriage and she's going to prove them wrong come hell or high water."

"Oh, I heard the two of them have it out last Saturday," Ponytail piped up again.

"What happened?" the short one with curly brown hair on the end asked. A ripple of applause went through the crowd and Hailey glanced up to see the other side had won a point. Victoria Regard didn't look quite as cool, calm, and collected as she had at the beginning of the match.

"They were out on the patio . . . you know the one outside for casual dining, it looks out over the big pool?"

"That one looks out over the kiddie pool."

"Right . . . the kiddie pool one. Well, anyway, whatever pool, they were out on the patio and she was letting him have it about being embarrassed he chases every skirt that walks by and if he didn't end it pronto, she'd blow it all to the *Savannah Morning News* and divorce him to boot." Ponytail spoke so rapidly and with such enthusiasm about Victoria Regard's potential divorce, she actually sprayed spit on the tanned leg of the woman next to her. But it didn't stop her.

"As if she'd ever divorce him. Fat chance with the primaries coming up. This is her ticket and she's going for the ride." They all nodded in unison, not wanting to derail the gossip train with interruptions.

"So she cursed him out and he acted sorry, but he never really admitted to anything. Said he loved her and blah, blah, blah, you know the drill . . . things would be different and he wanted to start over . . . you know, the same things they all say."

"So, she knew about it the whole time? She never let on a thing and I play bridge with her in the ladies' lounge every Thursday! She didn't even tell me!" Mousy Brown actually acted hurt.

"Knew about it? *She's known about them all!*"

Hailey and Billings gave each other a meaningful look. They obviously both thought the same thing. *Knew about them all?* The implications were countless. But just then, a loud crack came from the court and all eyes were back on the match. Victoria Regard had just thrown her racket onto the court in anger. The match was over. She lost.

Without bothering to get her racket or speak to the other players, she abruptly turned and flounced off the court in a show of bad sportsmanship.

Hailey watched as Vickie Regard stalked out of the tournament area. Bill Regard appeared from somewhere in the stands and followed behind her for a few moments until she turned. Even at a distance, Hailey could tell his wife rounded on him and said something. Regard immediately took a right turn toward the parking lot and let her go off on her own.

Trouble in paradise. To put it mildly.

"Well, that was some tennis match!"

Hailey and Chase Billings sat through the next match, but the Chatty Cathys sitting in front of them disbanded. Two went to play in the following match and the other two wandered off together, headed toward the bar.

Hailey and Billings didn't say a word about what they'd seen and heard until they slammed the door shut to Billings's squad car. "That's an understatement!" Billings responded, cranking up the ignition.

The two made their way out of the jam-packed country club parking lot and past the gatehouse. "So, the Jackie O look-alike wife has political ambitions . . . for her husband, anyway." The squad car was baking. Billings rolled down his window.

"And I'm afraid Elle Odom could've just been a speed bump along the way." Hailey did the same as Billings, rolling down the window to let the breeze fill the cruiser.

"Hey, Chase, let's go check out the courthouse cafeteria. I just want to figure out the logistics of entries, exits, where the coffee bar is situated . . . you know . . . the general lay of the land."

"Wow. That's a major development." Billings didn't look away from the two-lane in front of him as he talked.

"Are you kidding? Wait . . . is that sarcasm? You don't think Elle was poisoned? You think it was what . . . an accident? Almond milk was accidentally put in the milk container at the coffee bar? Or do you think a direct dose into her coffee cup is logistically impossible?"

Billings turned to look at her across the front seat and smiled. "No . . . I wasn't talking about Eleanor Odom."

"Then who *were* you talking about?" Hailey looked at him, confused.

229

"You." His eyes went back to the road. "I was talking about you, Hailey Dean."

"Me? What major development has to do with me?"

"You called me Chase."

"Yeah . . . and? I don't get it . . ."

"I don't know . . . I think it's pretty major. That's the first time you've ever called me by my first name."

For one of the few times in her life, Hailey searched for words. None came. It was too simplistic to say she was a little embarrassed. It was more than that. She'd let her guard down. And it was completely unintentional.

This guy, this . . . Chase Billings . . . was like a friend, someone who got her . . . someone who knew her history, understood where she was coming from, and didn't want her to be anything more . . . or different . . . than what she was. Plus, he was funny, smart, a consummate lawman. He knew sports, fishing, cars, and every dirt road and farmhouse in Habersham County in the Georgia mountains and the very beginning of the Appalachian Trail straight down to Glynn at the shore. And he wasn't afraid of a Broadway play or, more important, her win record in court.

But out of the blue, he saved her. "Hey, I know it's no big deal, but it was to me. I don't mind if you do it again someday."

He was met with silence, and Hailey looked out the window instead of at him. "You know, you said you were going for a jog earlier. I've got a change of clothes and I need to get my blood pumping. Let's see if I can outrun Hailey Dean. How about, uh . . . wanna go to Forsyth Park and see the fountain? How about the Waving Girl down by the water?"

"Isn't the Waving Girl a little sad? Isn't she waving good-bye to her dad or her brother or her sweetheart . . . something like that?"

"I always thought she was waving hello." Billings took his eyes briefly off the road and looked at Hailey. In that moment, they locked eyes and something, she wasn't sure what exactly, clicked inside her, almost like a key turning a lock. She could practically hear it.

"I'm pretty sure she's waving hello, Hailey."

"Yes . . . let's go there, then." The moment had passed, fleeting as it was, but the feeling did not.

The water on the river rippled in the morning breeze as they set off on foot, jogging along a brick path winding along beside the dark water. The waterfront still seemed sleepy, the Friday night revelers still in bed.

The party crew might still be asleep, but River Street vendors were wide-awake. The minute Hailey got out of the car, she was hit by the smells of Cajun food, caramel pralines cooking, and funnel cakes frying. Larger-than-life tall ships glided by on sun-dappled ripples.

Then Hailey spotted her, the Waving Girl, her arms held up in the breeze, waving a bittersweet message with her kerchief at the towering ships passing. Hailey paused to look at the young girl, her face to the horizon, and a deep sadness washed over her. A sense of longing, of loss, of yearning for something she couldn't name filled her chest.

Billings jogged up behind her and stopped as well. Intuitively, he remained silent beside her.

"She's lovely, right?" Hailey broke the silence.

"She is," he responded simply.

"Who is she exactly? Do they know?"

"Oh, yes. She's a celebrity of sorts, around here anyway. She's Florence. Florence Martus. She was a sergeant's daughter, used to live in a cottage with her brother at the harbor entrance, but then he got lighthouse duty over at Elba Island. It's pretty remote. She started waving at every single boat with a handkerchief, a tablecloth, whatever she could find . . . she was fascinated with the ships . . . at night she'd wave a lantern. She did it for over forty years. The story is, she fell in love with a sailor who never came back."

"What ever became of her?"

"I guess she kept waiting . . . but in the end . . . she died alone. They buried her over at Laurel Grove Cemetery, next to her brother, I think."

A girl who waited her life away. The story tugged at her heart and even though she'd never met the girl who was now buried not too far away from where they stood, tears sprang into Hailey's eyes. She had no idea why. Turning away, she called over her shoulder, "Where to?"

"Straight ahead and around the curve." Billings took off jogging.

They headed up River Street and then beyond. After about forty minutes, they turned and walked back, laughing, commenting on the sights and sounds as the clock ticked on. There was no more mention of Florence, the Waving Girl.

"I'm starved. Do you like creole . . . Cajun?"

"I love it! I love to make a big pot of crawfish etouffee, but it takes me so long! So I hardly ever do it." Hailey was smiling again. The run had done her good. The Waving Girl, the home on Victory Drive, Elle's suspicious death . . . it all went to the edges of her mind, and instead the day was about the sunshine, the river, and all things light and bright.

Hailey followed Billings as he climbed a wooden flight of stairs up the side of a building. "Hey, you sure you know where you're going? Is this a fire escape?"

"Ha! It is not a fire escape. Tip-off—it's made of wood, number one. And number two, yes, I think I know where I'm going." He opened a door for her, stood aside, and gestured her in.

The moment she walked in, Hailey agreed with him—it smelled incredible! "It smells just like the street food on Jackson Square . . . in New Orleans! Or Galatoire's!"

"Wait a minute. You've been to Galatoire's? That's my favorite."

"Me, too. It's old, but awesome. Have you ever had the turtle soup? More sherry than turtle, huh? I love it." They both started laughing and settled into a booth looking out onto the water.

They sat, eating crawfish etouffee, fried crawfish, and gumbo, telling courtroom war stories and laughing. She couldn't remember a time she'd laughed more than she did that afternoon. They sat down at two o'clock and the clock ticked on unnoticed.

It was finally almost six when the waiter politely edged the check on the table and Hailey noticed the crew was changing to prep for dinnertime.

"What time is it?" She scanned the room for a clock.

"Believe it or not, it's almost six o'clock."

"Six o'clock? I can't believe it! I must have been under the influence of crawfish pie! What about the courthouse?"

"You don't have to go. Remember, I radioed back to the courthouse. They emailed me back. I got your answers right here." He patted his iPhone, which was facedown on the table.

"Well, what does it say?"

"Pretty much what we thought. The cafeteria has two public entrances. One's the ramp you said Eleanor Odom came down along with jury members. The other is directly across the cafeteria. It takes you on kind of a winding route out toward the street on the other side of the courthouse."

"You said *public entrances*."

"Good catch. There are two employee-only entrances. One is from a courthouse service elevator. Need a key card for that one because it leads through all the food stores, freezers, machinery. There's also an entrance into that same kitchen area from the hallway, but it takes a key card too."

"Hmm. So two public, two employee. Someone could enter a public entrance or if the perp's an employee, they have a key card. Although somebody could always scoot in behind an employee with a key card. What about the coffee bar?"

"Well, it's portable. They can roll it around. It gets stocked every morning. The cabinets underneath it include mini-refrigerators. That's where all the milk for coffee is stored. Creamer, soy milk, skim, whole, 2 percent, cashew milk, and almond milk. So there you have it."

"So anyone could reach down, get the almond milk, and slip it into the milk canisters? What about cameras? Any surveillance?"

"Yep. Thank you for reminding me. There are two cameras where all the food is stored, one camera trained on the register lines, and two cameras trained on the tables in general. Nobody knows yet whether the coffee bar was in the surveillance shot that day. Does that answer all your questions?"

"Almost. Last question. When are you going to pull the surveillance video?"

"Hailey. I may look like a hick. I might walk like a hick. I might even talk like a hick. But once in a while, I do manage to think like a lawman. I ordered it right after you ran out on me at Williams Seafood. It's coming in this week." The smile on his face was real, not sarcastic.

"I never said you're a hick! Never!"

"Well, maybe I just added two and two. You have been living in Manhattan for several years now. I know how those folks feel about all of us below the Mason-Dixon Line . . ."

"Well, then, you can't add. Don't forget, I grew up on red clay, drinking well water."

"Ha. OK. I won't forget it."

The waiter appeared again. He stood lingering at the corner of the table and finally spoke, clearing his throat first. "Lieutenant, it's on the house. To thank you. I don't know if you remember, but we were robbed at gunpoint last year. You got the guys. They're doing twenty at Reidsville right now. Thanks to you. My fiancée was working that night. The man held a gun in her face. I owe you, man."

"I remember, it was uh . . . Henry Hamilton. That was his name," Billings answered and smiled. "He was a piece of work. A mean SOB, too. Career criminal. His brother too. It's a miracle they didn't kill anybody."

"That's right! Henry Hamilton! I can't believe you remembered his name."

"Yep. They stick with me for some reason. Don't know if that's good or bad. But anyway, thanks for the offer, but you don't owe me a thing. It's my job."

Billings stood up and laid down several twenty-dollar bills on the table. "Thanks anyway, man."

The waiter smiled. "Maybe next time."

"Maybe. Have a good evening."

Hailey and Billings walked out into the cooling air.

"Hey, let's walk back to your hotel."

"But what about your car?" Hailey asked.

"It'll be fine where it's parked. I'll walk back and get it. I want to stretch my legs."

"Me too. We can walk past everything on River Street. I want to send my dad some of those pralines I was smelling before we went running. He loves them."

"They're in Macon, right? About an hour or so south of Atlanta?"

"Yep. An hour and a half." They walked along a narrow sidewalk, looking through all the windows into the brightly lit shops full of candles, souvenirs, bake shops, ice cream parlors, clothing boutiques, and sea-town treasures.

"I bet they're proud of you."

"I hope so." Not really wanting to talk about herself, Hailey changed the subject. "You know what's funny?"

"What's that?"

"I love window shopping but hate actually shopping. I'd rather try a murder case than go into a shopping mall." Billings let out a laugh. He put his hand on her shoulder and steered her into River Street Sweets, where at that very moment, the candy makers were pouring out hot caramel mixed with pecans. The smell was incredible.

"This is the place if you want pralines for your dad."

"Oh my stars. It smells so good! My mom will kill me. My dad has to keep his sugar down, so he never gets any at all. But he loves it! Two pounds of the pralines, please. With pecans. Thanks."

"Obviously, you're not *that* worried about your mom getting mad."

"I'll risk it. Plus, I won't be there when he opens it! I'll be here!"

A bell on the door tinkled as they left and they strolled the streets for the next few hours. They finally reached the lobby of her hotel.

"Thanks for the Cajun. It was awesome."

"Hailey, the pleasure was all mine. I'll see you in court." And with that, he smiled, nodded his head good night, turned on his heels, and walked off into the night.

And he didn't even turn around once. Hailey knew because she watched practically without blinking until Billings disappeared totally around a bend in the street.

Hmm. He didn't even *try* to kiss her good night this time. Not even a peck on the cheek. She surprised herself . . . she actually felt miffed.

Shaking it off, Hailey headed up the elevator to her room. She found it all nice and clean with the pillows fluffed up. One light was on beside the bed and she could see the dark night above the river outside.

Her legs were aching, so she headed straight for a hot bath. She thought briefly of ordering hot tea but was afraid the tiny bit of caffeine would keep her awake. She turned off the bedside lamp and sank into the pillows, not bothering to pull the curtains, choosing instead to look out into the dark.

What a day. She wished Finch had stuck around so she could tell him all about what she'd uncovered, but his family needed time with him, too.

Tired to the bone, a niggling thought came to mind that sleep would, once again, elude her. Hailey pulled out her iPad to read herself to sleep. Lying there in the dark, she thought of the bittersweet Waving Girl.

Out of nowhere, but somehow linked in Hailey's subconscious, the image of Eunah Mabry came to mind. Hailey remembered Eunah's face, alternately full of loathing for Elle Odom and then wistful longing whenever Bill Regard's name was mentioned.

On a whim, Hailey went to Google, her fingers deftly entering the name "Willard Fulton Eugene Mabry." It only took a few seconds for Google to respond. Hailey's iPad screen lit up in the darkened bedroom and she immediately sat up in the bed to read the first entry.

"Aspiring Supreme Court Judge Willard Fulton Eugene Mabry Dead by Apparent Suicide." Hailey quickly scanned the article.

*Judge Willard Mabry found dead in the family's boat docked at the Savannah River Marina. This, following a bitter divorce amid claims of the judge's alleged infidelity with a courthouse employee named in Mrs. Jane Fickling Mabry's divorce documents as a Miss Elizabeth Collins...*"

Hailey sat stock-still there on her hotel bed in the dark room, letting the whole thing sink in. Moonlight poured in through the curtains. Just outside was the Savannah River and not far away, the marina where Eunah Mabry's father committed suicide when his wife left him. The root of the divorce was his affair with a courthouse employee, Elizabeth Collins, according to the *Savannah Morning News*.

All the pieces were fitting together . . . no photos of Eunah Mabry's mother, hero worship of her dad, her father's suicide, drinking herself to sleep as the child victim of divorce and scandal, and then, unrequited love for very married Judge Bill Regard. And now . . . she was reliving all those emotions again. Because of Judge Bill Regard. Or possibly in Eunah Mabry's mind . . . *because of Eleanor Odom.*

The courtroom was tense. It was already dark outside and the night was visible through tall windows flanking the old, giant courtroom. Newer courtrooms were small and compact, the architects jamming as many onto one floor as possible. Not here in the old Chatham County Superior Courthouse.

The jury had been deliberating for two days now, starting at eight-thirty in the morning and now, day two, into the night. Already, the jury deliberations room buzzer had sounded three times so far.

Each time, it caused a free-for-all in the courtroom . . . reporters ducking to their seats, cranking up their laptops and iPads, each preparing to be the messenger that got the verdict out first. Three times so far. But each time, the buzzer had simply signaled a jury question or request. Once was for a copy of the jury charges. Hailey took that as a bad sign for the state. What about premeditated murder couldn't they understand?

The second buzz was a question about the jury charge on credibility, who to believe. The jurors were instructed that if they disbelieved a witness in any part of their testimony, under law they could throw out the troubling portion of the testimony or all of the witness's testimony.

On the other hand, the judge instructed the jury they were to make all witnesses "speak the truth," impugning perjury onto no one. In other words, to try and reconcile the testimony of all the witnesses.

The third request was for the jury to have a TV and DVD player rolled into the jury deliberations room so that they could watch the police interrogation of Todd Adams. That is, until he stopped cooperating with police and demanded a lawyer. Hailey surmised the question on credibility related to whether Todd Adams was telling the truth. It was hard to tell, because he took the Fifth, refused to testify in front of the jury. It would have been deadly to his case to undergo cross-examination, even by the weakest of prosecutors. So all the jury had to go on was his police interrogation tape.

There were several problems with his story to the police. In one sitting, he contradicted his own alibi, first stating he was at work at the time Julie went missing, and then later insisting he was fishing and then at his mom and dad's house.

But later, when Tish Adams had gotten through her COPD spell and taken the stand the next day, she explained away the inconsistencies in her son's story by telling the jury very plainly that he'd called her on his way home from fishing. That Todd Adams simply stopped by his office to pick up some papers after fishing and en route to her home.

And home to her he came, she said. Home for supper, as a matter of fact, because, as Tish Adams indelicately put it, "Julie Love never was much of a cook to start with, and marriage with a child on the way didn't change that."

Tish Adams then topped it off by giving a wry, knowing smile to the jurors and Hailey was quite surprised to see two of the older lady jurors smiling back at Tish, clearly commiserating about unfortunate daughters-in-law.

Hailey also stole a glance at Todd Adams when his mom threw the unnecessary barb at Julie Love, now dead. She could see his jaw clenched, the muscles along his jawbone working.

But the tide turned in the courtroom when the state put up its very last witness. It was the end of a very long courtroom day. The air conditioning was on the blink and started and stopped in fits. The courtroom was warm and the judge had ordered the windows opened to let in what breeze there was to be had. It was nearly four o'clock when the state called its last witness, Dana Love, Julie Love Adams's mother.

Suddenly, all the fanning and the loud sighs, the wriggling and whispered complaints about the heat ceased automatically. Dana Love stood up in her spot on the first pew behind the prosecution.

She looked so much thinner than when the trial had started. Dark shadows were smudged under her eyes. She looked pale.

Today she wore a beautiful yellow suit jacket and skirt with a string of pearls at her neck. Dana Love had once pinned thin sky-blue and pink ribbons curled together on her lapel in memory of Julie and baby Lily, before DelVecchio insisted they be removed, claiming the delicate ribbons were "unconstitutional."

Love made her way slowly, almost regally, to the stand. Passing between the two counsel tables, she paused long enough to direct a look that mirrored pure heartbreak and numbing hurt straight at Todd Adams. Adams met her gaze briefly, and then cast his eyes down in his lap, hanging his head low.

*Did the jury see that?* If a picture was truly worth a thousand words, then that was the single snap Hailey hoped they'd remember . . . Todd Adams looking down, unable to hold Dana's steady gaze. Why? Hailey could only attribute that particular reaction to guilt and shame.

Her testimony started out matter-of-factly, going through Julie's birth, her childhood, high school then college, her daughter's wedding to Todd Adams, and, ultimately, Julie Love's difficult pregnancy and her disappearance. She outlined the fears Julie had about Todd Adams's possible affairs and, once again, the Christmas photo of Todd Adams with his girlfriend in the strapless red satin dress flashed up on a giant overhead monitor.

Dana Love visibly winced at the sight of the photo. "Did Julie know about this woman?"

"Cindy Gresham? Know about her? They went to the same high school together, so in that sense, yes. If you mean did Julie know Todd was cheating with Cynthia during their marriage? No . . . I don't think so. Julie always believed everything Todd ever told her, without fail."

"Objection! Facts not in evidence! This affair hasn't been proven! It's an insult to my client's character, Your Honor! I must object and have it stricken from the record immediately . . ."

"Sit down, Mr. DelVecchio. Motive for murder, while not required under the law, may be presented. Do I need to remind you that Ms. Gresham has come before the jury and testified under oath that she was in fact having an affair with your client during his marriage?" The judge looked at DelVecchio as if he were no more than a gnat buzzing around his head at a barbecue.

"But, Your Honor! My client never confirmed it! It takes not one, but two to tango, Judge!" DelVecchio wouldn't let it go. Hailey smiled . . . now he was making such a stink he was actually drawing more attention to the affair than if he had just sat there and gritted his teeth in silence.

"Overruled."

The prosecutor had Dana Love go through the seemingly normal day Julie had gone missing. They had talked on the phone that morning. Julie's legs were swollen from the pregnancy; baby Lily was due any day. The two had planned to go to a doctor's appointment, then shop for baby clothes later that afternoon after lunch.

As it turned out, mother and daughter went to the doctor's appointment and shopped, but Julie passed on lunch. She'd said, according to Dana, that she was exhausted and wanted to go home and lie down. Julie had driven away, out of the parking lot of Babies-R-Us with a back seat full of bags stuffed with pink onesies, little baby socks that looked like ballet slippers, and even tiny pink ribbons for when baby Lily finally got hair.

Dana never saw Julie alive again.

She testified about the day the doorbell rang. When she answered it, there were two SPD detectives standing there. They didn't smile when Dana opened the screen door for them. She knew right then. Julie would never come home. She was dead.

They'd sat in the home's little living room, Dana clutching a handkerchief, her husband's arm around her shoulder . . . and they told her. A woman's body had washed ashore Tybee Island. Hours later, a tiny baby girl who looked like a shiny pink baby doll in a store had followed her mommy in the next tide.

Dana Love's voice was dead as she remembered the funeral. The two were buried together, with Julie Love gently cradling her baby's remains in her own dead arms inside the coffin.

When her testimony ended, a silence fell on the courtroom like a spell. Even DelVecchio was not brazen enough to follow with cross. The judge sent the jury out and they had shuffled without a sound from their seats and into their adjoining room.

Out of the jury's hearing, DelVecchio announced there would be no cross of Dana Love. Newbies in the audience may have believed his decision was out of respect for Dana Love. But Hailey knew better. He had to know that if he were perceived as attacking Julie's mother, it would only work against his client. For once, DelVecchio voluntarily sat down and shut up without being ordered to. It was a first and, very likely, a last in Mikey DelVecchio's career.

Dana Love was the state's last witness. The defense responded with a string of experts to refute that Julie Love had been killed at all.

They relied on the fact that there was so little of Julie's body left, cause of death could not be determined. They argued that plastic twine tied around the bones that had once been Julie Love's ankles could have become entwined around her in the water . . . twine possibly from a commercial fishing boat.

Ignoring Adams's multiple affairs during the marriage—including the one in which he was engaged at the time of Julie's death—was the only way to address the appearance and testimony of Cynthia Gresham, just one of the so-called "other women." The defense skillfully argued that a cheater does not a murderer make.

DelVecchio carefully avoided pressing too much with his assertion Julie was not murdered at all . . . that being, if she wasn't murdered . . . how *did* she die and end up at the bottom of the Savannah River, washing up on nearby Tybee Island? When Dana had called Julie later on, there was no answer. That was highly unusual. After church the next day, Dana and Malcolm drove over to check on her. Julie's car was there, but when Dana went in with her key she discovered Julie wasn't home. Her dog, Daisy, was gone too, but her leash was still hanging by the front door where Julie kept it handy for walks.

They'd left a message on the front door, assuming she was out walking Daisy. It was only much later, suppertime, around 6 PM, that they'd circled back and called Todd on his cell and, still, no one would answer the home phone. Todd said he got home to find Julie and the dog gone.

At night? It was fast getting dark. Dana knew in her bones something was horribly wrong and it was she, Dana, who called the police, not Julie's husband, Todd Adams. So if all this was true as Todd Adams claimed . . . then what happened?

A nine months pregnant woman was kidnapped from a park two blocks from her house by a stranger, an unknown assailant, and bound at the feet and likely the hands, and thrown into the river? A chunk of cement washing ashore along with her body? Discovered missing by her husband who never called police? Not likely. Statistically almost impossible.

Neither Dana nor Julie's father ID'd the bodies. Police used DNA from Julie's toothbrush to make the identification in order to spare them the pain. There wasn't much left of Julie's body after being underwater for so long.

The jury had to do the right thing. They had to convict Todd Adams. Next would be the death-penalty phase. When a death penalty was sought by the state, the trial was bifurcated, or tried in two halves. First was the guilt-innocence phase. Assuming a guilty verdict was returned, the same jury moved on to the sentencing phase during which the jury would decide his ultimate fate and sentence the defendant themselves. If they locked or mistried at that phase, the judge would either sentence the defendant himself or the state could re-try the sentencing portion of the trial.

Hailey replayed the closing arguments and the testimony of Dana Love again in her mind. There was no way this guy was going to walk.

Just then, a burst of whispers rippled across the courtroom when the calendar clerk went to sit briefly at her position near the judge.

She would be present when any verdict was reached, as it signaled the disposition of an indictment assigned to her courtroom. But it was short-lived. She merely gathered a stack of papers pertaining to another plea and arraignment calendar and left by the same door through which she entered.

At this point, no one, reporters, families, press, or court watchers, dared leave the courtroom or its near vicinity for fear of missing the verdict.

There had to be at least twenty armed sheriffs around the courtroom's perimeter. Stationed in front of every towering window, door, and in between, they kept stern faces, their service revolvers in plain view. Their presence and demeanor only added to the atmosphere.

And then, it buzzed. An electric surge coursed through Hailey's body, lasting less than a second . . . a physical response to her immediate realization. This was it. It wasn't a question, they didn't want to halt deliberations for another day, they didn't want another exhibit brought back to the courtroom, no read-backs of testimony, and no soft drink orders. They had reached a verdict. She knew it in her bones.

There was a moment when everyone and everything seemed to freeze, standing still in their places followed by a mini-pandemonium. Papers rustling, reporters sending frantic emails and texts, movement in general.

The door to the right of the judge's bench that looked exactly like the paneled wall, blending in without so much as a doorknob to suggest it was in fact a door, opened from within. Out came Todd Adams in handcuffs with two armed sheriffs on either side of him. This was typically a time many defendants would make a run for it . . . just before a jury verdict that would likely send them to jail for life. Or in Todd Adams's case, to a punishment-phase trial and about a decade on Georgia's Death Row followed by the electric chair.

But as always, he looked undaunted. Head thrown back, shoulders wide in what looked to be a Gucci suit, he looked for all the world like a winning quarterback strutting across the field. A half smile was playing at one corner of his lips. *What did he know?*

He looked calm, cool, and confident. He didn't seem worried about a thing! Not in the least, actually. Hailey's eyebrows knitted together. How could this be?

Hailey stretched around the man in front of her to check on the Love family. They sat motionless with stricken looks on their faces. Dana Love couldn't stand, draped forward and to the side, crying into a white handkerchief.

On the other side of the well, Tish Adams, clutching the top of her portable oxygen tank as if to bolster herself, steadily held the gaze of her son as he passed just feet from her, his dad's arm around Tish's shoulders. They stood rooted to their spot.

It took only a minute or so before the bailiff pounded loudly with the gavel. "Hear ye, hear ye! The Superior Court of Chatham County is now in session! The Honorable Luther Alverson on the bench! All rise!"

Everyone in the courtroom, without exception, stood as Alverson blew onto the bench, his long black robes billowing out behind him.

Dana Love had to be helped up in order to stand, her husband, Malcolm, keeping a firm arm supporting her waist on her left side, the other holding her at her right elbow. Her head had lolled slightly back, her face white. She looked as if she were reliving her daughter's horrible death, being forced to remember the beautiful, pink, pristine baby girl who'd been set free from Julie Love's uterus underwater.

The baby she'd never hold. The daughter she'd never see alive again . . . all the happy years to come, gone . . . vanished . . . disintegrated like dust that slipped through her hands and into the wind. Gone. Forever.

The pain of reliving it in the courtroom had been too much to bear and now . . . now . . . Todd Adams and his mother both exchanged smiles. No one near the front of the courtroom could miss it. *What did they know?* Hailey wondered again.

"Madame Calendar Clerk, does the jury have a verdict?"

"Yes, they do, Your Honor."

"Sheriffs, bring in the jury."

Two sheriffs headed to the jury deliberations room as the bailiff called out in a low voice that carried across the courtroom, "All rise for the jury."

In they came. All eyes locked on the twelve jurors entering the courtroom. From the moment the deliberations door opened, Hailey's radar went berserk.

They came out in knots of two or three at a time. Two of the middle-aged men actually looked angry. An older man Hailey remembered from voir dire as a veteran was methodically clenching his fists then unclenching them. Hailey had pegged him as a possible foreperson. Two of the lady jurors came out with eyes red and teary. The four alternates were rousted from somewhere deep within the judge's chambers to file into the jury box along with the twelve.

They sat as if exhausted and, in unison, so did the audience. Hailey noticed they did not all sit together as a group but split into groups of two or three, leaving spaces between them.

There was complete silence; Hailey could have heard a pin drop. She and Fincher sat side by side, their backs ramrod straight, eyes on the jury. The judge turned toward them.

"May I ask the foreman of the jury, have you reached a verdict?"

A pale young man of medium height, his dark hair disheveled and sporting a matching goatee, answered from his seat, "Yes, we have."

"You will stand when you address the judge," the sheriff growled out, taking several steps toward the jury foreperson.

The pinched white face of the foreman screwed into a scowl, but facing the angry-looking sheriff, whose face never once collapsed into a smile, stood up. Smoothing down his sweatshirt, he looked irritated he was asked to stand.

"Yes, we have reached a verdict."

"And has it been signed by the foreman?"

"It has." He practically stuck out his tongue at the judge when he answered, his demeanor so irritated. This was a factor Hailey had worried about since she learned at the get-go that this was the foreperson. Who in their right minds would elect such a brat to lead the jury deliberations and why?

The judge seemed to ignore his bratty manner and calmly addressed the sheriff. "Mr. Bailiff, please hand up the verdict to Madame Calendar Clerk."

"Yes, Your Honor." The sheriff did so, taking the indictment which was folded longways in three sections from the foreman and without so much as glancing at it, strode across the courtroom and handed it to the female calendar clerk seated in a low desk below and to the side of the judge's bench.

"Is the verdict in order, Madame Clerk?"

Without responding, the middle-aged woman who had been Alverson's calendar clerk since she graduated from high school stared at the document. She stood and handed the indictment up to the judge.

The judge took the indictment and studied it. Removing his glasses, he looked at it again and then turned a cold, questioning stare on the jury. "I understood you to say you have reached a verdict in the matter of *The State v. Todd Adams.*"

The foreperson, visibly upset that he had to stand again, launched into a diatribe. "We have Your Honor . . . our verdict is . . . *there is no verdict!* You put a bunch of morons out for blood on the jury . . . what'd you expect? I mean . . . this is just a vendetta by the state over some cheerleader . . ."

Sharp screams rose from the Love camp. Dana Love fell back onto the bench and let out a cry of anguish. In stark contrast, clapping and shouts of victory rang out from the other side of the aisle, the Adams camp as well as from the defense table itself.

DelVecchio managed to yell out two words as his fleet of defense minions leaped from their seats around the defense table, surging toward their leader in victory. *"Appeal bond!"* DelVecchio practically screamed it.

"Oppose bond! We demand a new trial immediately!" A beat behind, the state's lead attorney stood at his seat and finally found his voice but he was immediately drowned out by the judge.

*"Silence! There will be order in this courtroom!"*

Luther Alverson was standing at the bench now as sheriffs from all around the courtroom closed in on the defendant and the sources of the outburst. Alverson was looking directly at the lead defense attorney. "And you sir, Mr. DelVecchio, are hereby held in contempt for your outburst in this courtroom. And I will have silence from the foreman!"

"Order in the courtroom! Order in the court!" the chief bailiff shouted out, and suddenly the courtroom quieted. Except for the low moans of Dana Love, not a breath could be heard.

Reporters, TV and print alike, were silently thumbing texts as quickly as their hot little fingers could type on their iPhones's mini-keyboards while Dana Love's moans continued. The whole bunch hardly glanced over at her as she and her husband, Malcolm, now audibly crying, huddled together on the front pew.

While the press didn't bother to notice them sobbing and shaking right in front of them, Hailey couldn't drag her eyes away. Their suffering coursed through her, bringing back the gut-wrenching pain from Will's murder and trial. A pain shot through her chest, and she felt like she had swallowed a big lump of charcoal that stuck in her throat. Hot tears leaped to her eyes.

Before anyone could fully take in what was happening, Michael DelVecchio strong-armed his defense minions away from a jubilant group hug despite the bailiff's demands for order in the court and sprang to the center of the well. "Under threat of jail, I insist, Your Honor! Appeal bond, Your Honor! Appeal bond! This jury has all but exonerated my client ..."

"No! We didn't!" one of the lady jurors who had been crying jumped from her seat, found her voice, and shrieked at DelVecchio. "*We* didn't! *He* did!" She pointed directly at the surly foreman, still sitting in his juror chair, his arms folded defensively across his chest.

He responded by not budging to turn around to look at the lady juror. Instead, he smiled thinly at the courtroom in general.

"*Madame juror! Please be seated.*" Luther Alverson had never, in his forty years on the bench, had such a display in his courtroom.

"You have to know . . . we are sorry, Mrs. Love. It was eleven to one for guilty, but he wouldn't budge! He did it . . . Todd Adams murdered Julie! We are just so sorry . . ." The juror collapsed into her seat and cried unabashedly into a soaked hanky.

DelVecchio took her collapse as his cue to continue the dramatic delivery of his speech. ". . . and we hereby go on record demanding a bond while we appeal a new trial! It would be unconstitutional to hold him while these legal briefs go up to an appellate court!"

"Bailiff, send out the jury immediately! Order! There will be order or every single spectator in this courtroom will be held in contempt!"

Outside, the silhouettes of tall trees were now pitching wildly against the courthouse in the dark as rain dashed the courtroom windows and lightning pierced the night sky. The wind could now be clearly heard whistling and howling outside as a hush fell across the courtroom.

With the jury out of the room, some shred of quiet was restored but electricity charged just beneath the surface. "Your Honor, please do not grant him bond. The state is prepared to re-try him immediately." The state stood at their massive oak table before the judge.

"Object! It could be months, even a year before retrial on a death-penalty case! The jury has spoken." DelVecchio tuned up again.

"Counsel for the state, I have no doubt you will in fact re-try Todd Adams. But meanwhile, I believe the Georgia Supreme Court, knowing them, will demand I set a bond. Cash bond is hereby ordered in the amount of $1 million. *Repeat, cash bond only.*"

In a split second, DelVecchio leaped back on his feet. "But Your Honor, a million dollars cash bond is tantamount to no bond at all! That disallows the family using the family home as collateral! It's in effect denying bond!"

*"We'll do it."* All eyes turned to the audience as a weak voice broke in. Tish Adams stood, leaning heavily on her tank. She inhaled deeply from the clear plastic tube that hung across her cheeks and just under her nostrils.

Before the judge could stop her, she went on, "We'll raise the money tonight and have him out by the morning. I want my son home in his own room where he belongs. Where he's always belonged."

Although she spoke to the judge, Tish Adams only had eyes for her son. In stark contrast, Dana Love's low sobs punctuated Tish Adams's words.

"So be it. The defendant Todd Adams is hereby remanded to the Chatham County Jail unless and until such time as one million dollars cash bond is posted. At that time, he will be released to the custody of his parents Tish and Ron Adams where he shall be on house arrest until the time of his retrial. Conditions of house arrest are that he may not leave the premises of his parents' home except to visit his lawyers' offices and to attend religious services once a week. Court is adjourned." Luther Alverson, barely disguising his disgust at the hung jury, swept off the bench and into his chambers.

There was one moment of stunned silence before the media sprang to their collective feet and rushed out the door to begin live shoots in the dark of night on the front of the courthouse steps for news cut-ins. Hailey and Finch sat stock-still, taking it all in, trying to digest that the culmination of a year of investigation plus weeks of testimony and evidence was nothing more than a hung jury. Hung, apparently, by one surly juror.

The Adamses were now leaning over the rail separating them from the well, exchanging last words and glances before their son was led out of the courtroom. Malcolm Love had managed to get his wife to her feet and, leaning heavily on her husband, she appeared to be physically limping from the pain of the trial's outcome. The two, never looking back, hobbled out of the courtroom, the swinging doors whooshing shut behind them.

"I can't believe it. I just can't believe it. That foreman ought to be tarred and feathered." Finch's first words came as he and Hailey stood and headed out of the courtroom. She still felt numb at a clear miscarriage of justice. She couldn't rid her mind of the image of Julie Love in the grave, her dead arms holding baby Lily in death.

"I can't believe it either. The evidence was overwhelming. The Loves have to be crushed, and all because of one nut job. Wait . . . shh. Here come the Adamses."

Hailey nodded her head back over his shoulder and held the door open as the Adamses slowly made their way through it, the mom dabbing at her eyes with Kleenex. Hailey and Finch waited to let them pass through the doors and out into the hall. They all made their way into the hallway as the crowd just outside the courtroom doors was thinning.

"You know where they're headed . . . home to try and raise a million dollars cash. Hey, let's go get tea or coffee, OK?" Hailey said. The thought of going back to her empty hotel room after a blow like this was too much.

"Coffee? Are you kidding? I need a drink after this!"

"OK. You get a drink. I've got a tea bag with me. I'm gonna duck into the ladies room. You get the car and I'll meet you in front of the courthouse?"

"Sure. Then I'll take you to get your rental car and you'll follow?"

"OK." Hailey pushed the door open to the ladies room.

"And be careful when you come out the front door. I'm sure Mike Walker and *Snoop* are there to ambush you for a sound bite!"

"I'll be ready." Hailey smiled. She was trying her best to hide her shock at the verdict. True, it wasn't a not guilty, but no matter how you sliced it, a hung jury was a huge setback for the state . . . and for Julie and Lily. Much less Dana and Malcolm Love.

She pulled out her cell phone to call home and tell her folks about the mistrial, but suddenly she spotted a lady's feet next to a silver canister on wheels under one of the two stall doors. She clicked off. She didn't want to say what she really thought about the Todd Adams mistrial with his mom in the very next stall beside her.

Hailey went into the remaining stall, balancing all her gear, and heard Tish Adams open the metal door beside her and roll the tank to the sink. The tiny, tiled bathroom was quiet now. The hall outside it was empty.

The night was dark outside the bathroom's one tiny window. It was late, the trial was done, the courthouse closed, and all the court watchers who had, for weeks on end, packed the Todd Adams courtroom were all gone home and back to their lives. The show was over.

Hailey heard the metallic twist of the water faucet over the white ceramic sinks and the sound of water in the sink. Opening the door, Hailey saw Tish Adams looking into the mirror over the sinks. Her face was pale and white in the mirror, her lips the only color on her face. Lipstick in one hand, Tish reached to turn the faucet off with the other and, juggling, her purse slid down her shoulder onto the tile. Its contents—Kleenex, powder, pill bottles, checkbook, and a sprinkling of other items—poured onto the tile. Tish started to lean down to put it all back in when Hailey interjected.

"No, let me, Mrs. Adams."

"Thank you, Hailey," she said it in somewhat of a stiff voice, which Hailey totally understood, given Hailey had been on the state's witness list in her son's murder prosecution. Hailey got it. Nevertheless, she knelt down to help the woman who seemed literally at the end of her rope after the trial.

Hailey picked up the items one by one, placing them back into the purse. The powder compact had come open and the powder puff had gotten loose. Putting it back in, Hailey saw the compact's mirror was cracked.

"Careful, your mirror's cracked." Still on her knees, Hailey looked up at Tish Adams.

Then she saw it. Hailey's green eyes were directly even with Tish Adams's oxygen tank. And it was there. The knob on the top, the twist mechanism on top of the canister . . . she'd seen it before. Not the many, many times she'd watched Tish Adams leaning heavily on it in court or walking around the courthouse with it . . . she'd seen it somewhere else.

Black plastic, about the size of a Gatorade screw top but not quite, with a peculiar edge to it. An image flashed in her mind. An image of the floorboard in the back of her rental car, scattered with trash from the otherwise immaculate yard of Alton Turner. The round rubber cap wasn't a bottle cap. It fit on Tish's tank.

A chill went across Hailey's arms. Tish Adams's open purse in her lap, Hailey looked down into it again, and there, peeking out from under a red leather ladies wallet beside a thin folded yellow scarf, was the pale green and gold edging of a tall pack of Virginia Slims. Hailey looked from the cigarettes to the oxygen tank's hard plastic valve cap, to the coppery-red lipstick on Tish Adams's lips and stood up, looking Adams unflinchingly in the eyes.

"You." Hailey uttered the one word, taking a step back from Adams, whose eyes were no longer tired-looking or teary. They were burning with a light . . . a zeal Hailey had never seen before in what appeared to be a frail and suffering middle-aged woman. A mother, for Pete's sake.

Somehow, Tish Adams was standing up straight now and at full height, no longer stooped over and shuffling, leaning on a portable oxygen tank. She was a good two inches taller than Hailey.

"I *what*, Hailey Dean?" Adams spit the words out, her eyes on Hailey, her lips hardening at the edges.

"You. The cigarette butts . . . the lipstick stains. You were in Alton Turner's yard, spying on him. Behind the trees, at the birdhouse. It was you . . . you all along. You killed Alton Turner . . . and . . ."

It hit Hailey like a brick. In a flash, Hailey saw what she couldn't see before. It all played out in her mind's eye. Alton taking a blow from behind after someone concealed in the yard, watching, waiting for the right moment, enters the garage. As Alton, unsuspecting, balancing his coffee for the commute to work, reaches for his car handle, the blow comes to the back of the head and he's down. Strength isn't required to swing a bat or a golf club.

Once he was down, the rest was easy. It was just a matter of dragging him a few feet to the garage door, slicing his gut open, and—with that rubber safety edging removed—grinding the metal into his torso to look like an accident until he bled . . . to death. It all looked like a stupid accident.

"And make no mistake, missy. I saw you that day. I knew you were on to me . . . you picked up the flowerpot and saw the key was gone . . . you knew it was me, didn't you?" The venom in her voice was pure evil. Her eyes looked totally possessed with hate.

Tish Adams stepped away from the sink and positioned herself between Hailey and the door to the hall. She yanked the thin plastic tubing off her face and threw it, skidding across the floor. Her memory sparked, Hailey recalled the moment she'd checked the flowerpot at Alton's back door just on a hunch . . . a hunch she'd thought was wrong when no key was hidden. But the hunch was right.

"But how would I have ever known . . ."

"Liar!" Adams's voice was now a guttural hiss coming from deep in her throat, her face contorted. "You saw me . . . in the window. Don't lie about it now. You've been gathering evidence . . . to destroy me just like you tried to destroy my son . . . to kill him . . . to burn him to death in the electric chair. You, Hailey Dean . . . you're the one that should die . . . not him! Not my son!"

Hailey instinctively backed away from her as if she were a rattlesnake about to strike. Her back pressed against the metal beam between the two bathroom stalls. She looked quickly around the tiny bathroom but there was nowhere to go.

"Turner had to die. He threatened Toddy . . . our family. We'd be ostracized, kicked out, *laughed at* if Todd was convicted. We'd be *nothing* in this town. I couldn't let that happen."

Hailey stared, unmoving. She could feel sweat pooling, trickling down the front of her chest into her bra.

"I knew he was eavesdropping that day, hanging around, snooping, listening to Todd and I talk. Todd made a mistake . . . a mistake . . . Julie's death was an accident! She must have hit her head when they argued . . . Todd said so . . . and Alton Turner heard him . . . but it was her fault . . . she trapped him! With that horrible baby in her belly! *My Toddy's no murderer!*"

"But you heard it . . . there were marks on Julie's neck . . . she was strangled . . . ligature . . . someone strangled her . . . the autopsy . . ."

Hailey tried to reason with the woman that it was no accident, even though she realized Tish Adams was clearly insane.

"That was a setup! They set him up! It's not true! Turner heard what Toddy told me that day in lockup . . . he was listening! But I followed Turner . . . all through the courthouse halls straight to the DA's office. Oh yes, he couldn't *wait* to blurt out what he had heard. *And what was he? He was a nobody; he was nothing compared to Toddy. Don't you see he had to die?* Just like the courthouse whore. He told her, too, bragging to her sitting in his car in the parking deck that afternoon. I saw them. He thought she was his girlfriend, but she'd been with every man in the courthouse including a judge. Right under his wife's nose. Believe me, I know . . . I watched her."

"But that doesn't mean Alton told Elle . . ."

"He told her the whole thing! The little whore emailed him about his meeting with the DA! I saw it with my own eyes at Turner's house . . . their disgusting emails back and forth about Toddy. She even made a crack that Turner could sell Toddy's 'confession' to that gossip rag *Snoop*! That Toddy confessed to me he did it! Oh it was no joke . . . I knew better! I knew she wanted headlines and money! Her picture on the cover! But all she got was a cemetery plot! Nobody will miss her . . . they're all glad she's dead and out of their hair. You think the judge isn't glad she's gone? Or his wife? They're thrilled. Trust me."

Tish Adams's eyes looked like they'd popped right out of her head and had taken on a glazed-over quality. Her hair fell in dark tendrils around her face. Her lower jaw thrust out as her teeth clenched, giving her a piranha's underbite. She focused on Hailey with a malevolent intensity that hung in the tiny room.

"Then I saw you with *Snoop* on the courthouse steps and I put two and two together—*you were in on the whole thing*. All because of Alton Turner eavesdropping. And that little courthouse tramp Elle Odom. She died all right, like the pig she was . . . on the floor of a cafeteria with her tongue swollen up and her face turned purple. She can rot in hell for what she tried to do to Toddy!"

Hailey couldn't help but glance at the trash can, now full of refuse from the day. Tish followed her eyes.

"Smart girl, aren't you, Hailey Dean? Yes, I hid it. The purse with the EpiPen. Right there in the trash. And the fools nearly let it go to the dump. It was easy enough to find out about the nut allergy. Anybody could read the girl's babbling about herself online. Just go to the cafeteria, dump a little almond milk in the milk pitchers, and voila! Nobody even glanced twice at the coffee bar. Then she goes into shock and dies in minutes. One of the happiest moments in my life was when she choked dead on her own tongue."

Tish Adams's voice was shrill now, her eyes wide and crazy. "And then there was that idiot . . . that moron . . . Snodgrass. They all sat side by side at work gossiping . . . about my Toddy! I saw it myself on Turner's home computer where he emailed Snodgrass he'd be late for work the next morning because *he had a meeting with the DA . . .* that Turner would *'fill him in on the whole thing'* when he got there. But he never made it. And don't think there's an email trail. I watch TV; I deleted them all." She was actually bragging now.

"That sniveling dunce . . . sticking his nose in Toddy's business. Snodgrass was on to the purse, sending that email asking who found it. But I took care of him too . . . it was easy. A fake 'prize' to Gator World, a syringe full of GHB . . . you know what that is, right, Hailey Dean? Gamma hydroxybutyrate. Odorless, colorless, induces sudden sleep? Ring a bell?"

"But . . . how did you . . ."

"I was almost a nurse, Hailey. If I hadn't gotten pregnant, who knows, I may have gone to med school. But that was ruined for me, wasn't it? *Wasn't it?* You think I can't get my hands on a syringe and some meds? Think again."

"The day you fainted on the witness stand . . ." All the pieces were fitting together now.

"Yes! Smart girl. For once, anyway. And you all fell for it, even Alverson. I had to get to Snodgrass by dark. It was the only way. I knew in my gut he was in on it. They were all going to frame my boy. I wouldn't let that happen."

Tish Adams reached down to her purse with ease, showing no sign of the physical ailments she'd been milking in the courtroom. They'd all bought into her act . . . the judge, the jury, even Hailey. Adams reached to the bottom of her purse and from within the yellow scarf, she pulled out a .22.

With sudden clarity, Hailey knew without a doubt Tish Adams was not insane; she was a cold-blooded killer. Nothing and nobody would ruin her life, her social position, her prop of a family.

"Wondering how I got this through the metal detector? Because of the oxygen tank . . . stashed underneath between the wheels! They never even looked under there. The stupid idiot sheriffs felt sorry for me."

A numbness crept across Hailey's face. Enclosed here in the tiny bathroom with her back against a wall, there was nowhere to go.

"In fact, now that I think about it . . . you're all stupid. Nobody will ever miss Turner *or* the whore. And certainly not that moron Snodgrass. Or you, Hailey. Nobody's going to miss you. You think I can let you go now? Think again."

Tish Adams, finger on the trigger, raised the gun to Hailey's face. "Last words? Want to say bye-bye to mommy and daddy? I'm afraid I can't let you do that."

Quick as a snake when it strikes to kill, in one defining moment, Hailey dove hard and down to miss the roaring bullet and grabbed the only thing she could. The tank.

Tish turned on her, cursing, spittle spewing out of her mouth, full of hate like the devil himself.

Heaving the metal cylinder up over her head, Hailey crashed it down with a loud metallic thud onto Tish's forehead. Hailey pulled it back again. Blood flew across the bathroom, spattering onto the white sinks, the mirrors, the floor, the metal stalls. Hailey slammed it down on Tish's face with all her might and then . . . again and again, Tish Adams's nose crunching under the tank, blood spurting out onto the floor, onto Hailey in a gush.

Like an animal gone wild, Hailey pulled back the tank again, holding on to both ends as best as she could and thrust it down again as Tish Adams lay on the floor. It careened off her chin and landed hard on her right shoulder. Tish Adams now lay in a pool of blood, creeping out to form a crimson rug underneath her. Like Alton's body. Teeth were in the blood on the floor beside Adams's face and her mouth hung open against the cool tile beneath her.

Hailey fell back, sitting on the floor of the ladies bathroom there in the Chatham County Courthouse. It was then she saw deep red blossoming, blooming ever bigger on her own chest.

Hailey Dean was shot.

It was unnaturally cool.

Tish Adams stood, her face a black-and-blue pulp and arm in a sling, directly in front of none other than the imposing figure of Luther Alverson. He stared down from his bench at her. Slowly, he read the charges against her.

The indictments for murder had been handed down by a hastily assembled grand jury, rousted from their beds and called to the courthouse. In a bizarre twist of fate, on the first bench behind her, just beyond the rail, stood her son, Todd Adams, now out on bond thanks to Mikey DelVecchio and his new buddies at All-Night Bonding Company.

Across the aisle, on the front row, stood Garland Fincher. He stood stock-still, staring straight ahead of him directly at Tish Adams. His face looked like thunder. His hands in fists. Beside him, still standing, was Hailey Dean.

Her shoulder sported a thick bandage with stitches underneath where a bullet had grazed her, but otherwise not much worse for the wear. On her other side stood Chase Billings. He glanced occasionally at Tish Adams. For the most part, his eyes remained locked on Hailey beside him. It was hard to take in what happened the night before, that Hailey had somehow managed to literally dodge a bullet . . . well, almost. Tish Adams aimed the .22 straight at Hailey. If Hailey hadn't dived onto the floor at that split second, she'd be dead right now.

"Quit staring! Do I look that bad without makeup? It's your fault! I asked to stop at the drugstore for blush and lipstick but you said we didn't have time!" Billings checked to make sure she was smiling when she said it. She was. Actually, she was even more beautiful without the distraction of makeup, but somehow he couldn't bring himself to tell her that.

Her crystal green eyes were like pools of tropical ocean water, almost unnaturally green. They were framed by her light brown brows, and her silky blonde hair fell in waves around her face. Her lips were perfectly shaped and pink without lipstick or gloss to enhance them, and even with all Billings knew she had been through in her short life, her face remained unlined except for two light wrinkles on either side of her lips . . . laugh lines. Hailey Dean seemed to love to laugh and could almost always find something light and funny to say . . . when she wanted to. He loved that about her. She always made him smile . . . and she wasn't the kind of girl that minded laughing out loud, really loud if warranted. And then . . . there were her half smiles, and he loved those too.

*Wham!*

The sound of the judge pounding his gavel snapped Billings out of his daze. "So ordered. The defendant Tish Adams is hereby remanded to the Chatham County Jail until said time when she shall be tried for the murders of Alton Turner, Eleanor Odom, and Cecil Snodgrass, and the attempted murder of Hailey Dean. We now await the district attorney's decision as to whether this will be a death penalty case and at the time that announcement is made, this court will be in recess on this matter. *Court adjourned!*" He pounded the gavel again very loudly, shot a look of contempt and loathing at Tish Adams, and left the bench.

"I've got to hear the whole thing again, and this time, slowly. I only got the extremely abbreviated version at the hospital this morning. And then, the red tape of getting you out and over to the courthouse in time for the grand jury . . . I can't believe the DA moved so fast. He had to have the grand jury in there by 8 AM at the latest to have the indictment handed down and signed in time for the hearing. What time did you testify in front of them, Hailey?"

"The DA swore me in at eight-fifteen, I told my story, and, believe it or not, I was out of there at eight-thirty."

"No questions?" Billings asked, gently holding the back of her elbow on her good side, the left, as they descended the courthouse steps. Finch stood protectively on her right.

"I never fell for her act . . . with the oxygen tank and all . . . the 'poor me' look all the way through the trial . . . always skulking around . . . she put a bad taste in my mouth from the get-go. No wonder the son is such a loser. Apple doesn't fall far from the tree, you know that's right," Finch, glancing to the left and the right as if on lookout, was growling the whole way down the steps, having his own conversation by himself that had nothing to do with what Hailey and Billings were talking about.

"Not a single question. I started with me flying down to profile for the state and pick apart Todd Adams's behavior. I told it just how it unfolded . . . going to Alton's home, the murder scene, going back out there and finding the black plastic valve, Elle's death, and meeting Cecil Snodgrass. Then, I went straight to last night. They didn't ask any questions, but they were all listening and taking notes. We'd only been outside the grand jury room for two, maybe three minutes when they rang the buzzer that they'd voted. The DA went in, was in there about one minute, and came out with the signed indictment."

"Then what happened? Oh, and did they get the oxygen cap out of the back of your car?" Chase Billings, still staring at Hailey nonstop, asked the question standing at the crosswalk to the parking deck.

"They did get it. Amazing I hadn't thrown it out. They got it this morning. Techs got it and took photos. I think they're back out at Alton's right now. So anyway, back to this morning . . . then I walked to the elevator with the DA, we went and filed the indictment at the clerk's office, and then we came to the courtroom."

"Oh." Billings was still staring, Finch still fussing.

"Then, the DA peeled off and went into the judge's chambers and I went into the courtroom. That's when I saw you guys; and before I could really even sit down, the judge came onto the bench and they wheeled Tish Adams in front of him."

"I should have seen it coming. I can't believe I didn't figure it out before the old bag could take a shot at you. You know, the more I think about it, all the signs were there . . ." Finch was in his own world, still muttering under his breath about Tish Adams.

"Hey, Finch! How are you, man? Long time no see!" All three looked at a tall man coming toward them in the crosswalk. It was none other than Cloud Sims, still in jeans and silver-studded cowboy boots, sauntering up.

"Sims! Hey, guy! How are you? What brings you to Savannah?" Finch grabbed Cloud Sims in a big bear hug. Hailey stared between the two of them.

"And Miss Hailey Dean, how are you? And what are you doing with a character like Garland Fincher? You're going to get a bad reputation hanging out with this guy. And lo and behold, the famous Lieutenant Chase Billings! Last time I saw you, you'd just busted up that bank robbery!" The bear hug with Finch complete, Cloud began pumping Billings's right hand enthusiastically.

"Good memory, Cloud. That's right. I'll never forget that one. So what brings you here?"

"Wait a minute, who *are* you?" Hailey asked with a quizzical look, glancing between the three.

"Just like I told you on the plane, I'm Cloud Sims, Cornhusker-turned-NYPD, now private eye! I've run into these two troublemakers more than once. And I'm still not giving up on having dinner with you sometime, Hailey Dean."

Billings immediately jumped in, effectively cutting off discussion of Cloud's dinner plans. "Sims, you never did say what case you're working down here."

"Ah. Right. I had to lie to Hailey about being here, you know, to protect my client. Some judge's wife convinced he's seeing some other lady in the courthouse. You know, same old same old! But it pays the bills and then some! Right?"

"*Oh no!*" all three groaned in unison.

"Not Judge Regard and Eleanor Odom? You're hired by Vickie Regard, right?" Finch asked first.

"Well, normally I wouldn't divulge, but since we're old crime-fighting buddies, I'll spill the beans." Cloud Sims looked around, then lowered his voice a smidge.

"It's Regard all right, but not Eleanor Odom. She knows all about Eleanor. That's old news. Now it's some young public defender straight out of law school. That Judge Regard. He sure gets around. When does that guy have time to sit on the bench?" Cloud burst into laughter.

"Hey, I have to run, guys. I got some recon to do. I'll see you around the courthouse. You, Hailey Dean, I intend to see you one night for dinner! And no, I don't have your number but hey, I'm a PI! I'll find it! Bye, folks!"

With that, Cloud Sims hustled toward the steps. He bounded up them two at a time.

"You're having a date with that guy?" Billings asked as soon as Sims was out of sight.

Hailey started laughing. "I've been trying *not* to have a date with him since I got on the plane from LaGuardia!" The light turned green and the three headed into the crosswalk.

"Hailey, back to Tish Adams, you think it will be a DP?" Billings asked.

Weaving between pedestrians, Hailey gave a brief glance toward where she'd been pushed in front of the CAT bus. "You know what? I should call the DA. I just realized, there should be two counts of attempted murder and agg assault . . . he didn't include the bus!"

"That's right, Hailey. And we just managed to narrow down the exact time yesterday. That camera on the top right corner of the courthouse may just be the ticket. And the parking garage exit camera may help too."

"Really? That's great! I can't wait to see this . . . myself pushed in front of a bus with a not-so-graceful landing."

"We've already sent a subpoena to the parking garage owners for it. That could prove it. You don't need to call him; I'll bring the video over to him myself and he can re-indict. Just those counts. They can play for the grand jury; you probably won't even need to testify again."

"Great!" Hailey responded as they stepped up on the other sidewalk. Both Finch and Billings lifted her under her elbows. She felt she could walk just fine but knew they were dead set on helping her, so she stayed quiet. They both blamed themselves for not being there the night before.

"I mean . . . *why couldn't we see she's pure evil?* I can't believe we all missed it . . ." Finch kept fighting with himself, although he did occasionally glance over at Hailey and Billings as if he half-expected them to answer all his hypotheticals . . . his shoulda coulda wouldas.

"So, Hailey, death penalty or no death penalty?" Billings asked again, totally ignoring Finch's questions.

"I don't think he has a choice. Mass murder's defined in the criminal code as more than one body. Second, you have the murders of not one but two law enforcement officers, Turner and Snodgrass. Third, as if you need a third, you've got the murder of an officer of the court, Elle. And there's a fourth trigger for the DP: They were tortured. Alton was severed nearly completely at the waist, Elle died a painful death from, essentially, poison, and Snodgrass was fed to the gators. I only hope he was fully sedated when it happened. That's three grounds for a death sentence . . . off the top of my head."

"I mean . . . Hailey . . . if you had told me you were going out to Alton Turner's house and I had seen the cigarettes with lipstick on them . . . maybe *I'd* have figured it out." Finch wouldn't stop.

"You would *not* have figured it out. You couldn't. Stop beating yourself up. With her dragging around an oxygen tank, all hunched over like she was near death, crying, gasping for breath every other minute and really loudly in front of the jury . . ."

"Then there was the fake COPD episode when the state surprise-called her to the stand . . ." Finch chimed in to defend himself.

"I thought it was a fake asthma attack. Who said COPD? I'm sure they said asthma in court . . ." Billings cut in.

"*Whatever it was, it was fake!* She had to fake it to get out of court and down to Gator World before dark! That's my point! You couldn't have guessed it with all that acting going on . . ." Hailey managed to get a few words in.

"And with the training in nursing, I mean, the tank, the syringe, the GHB, and she knew where to get 'em and she knew how to use 'em." Finch was trying again to justify how he'd missed the whole charade that played out right under his nose.

"Right . . . an oxygen tank with a loaded .22 stashed under it. I bet they don't teach that at nursing school. This lady's no softie." Billings again.

"And she's no lady, either," Finch snapped.

They headed to the elevator bank at the parking deck and stepped on together. "Hey . . . do you think she's the one who killed Julie? Hailey, do you remember where you left your car?"

"Next to the top, seventh floor. Chase, doesn't it seem like a year ago that I parked the car? But I know it's only been thirty-six hours. Crazy, right?"

"You did it again, Hailey."

Hailey looked at Billings as he hit the button for the seventh floor. "I did what?"

"You slipped up and called me 'Chase.'" He looked at her with a big smile on his face.

"And plus, she kept throwing those evil glares at us in court. *Why didn't that register?*" Finch was so deep in his own self-torture, he didn't even notice what Hailey and Billings were saying.

"I did, didn't I?" Hailey answered Billings. She could actually *feel* the smile on her face, and she couldn't seem to get rid of it. Plus, she didn't seem to want to.

The elevator door opened at the fifth floor. "OK, Finch. You got her from here? I'll get my car and meet you down at the exit. On the street. Then follow me. I got a great place that serves fresh collard greens and cornbread. Plus shrimp and grits. You'll love it." Billings stepped off the elevator and looked back.

"Yeah, man. I think I can get her to seven. I still don't understand why . . ." The door slid closed as Finch continued his soliloquy and Billings disappeared from view.

"What floor are you, Finch?"

"Six. I'll catch it on the way down so I can get you to your car," Finch answered, obviously still wallowing in self-inflicted misery.

The elevator pinged and the door opened on seven. "Finch, stay in the elevator. I can make it. See, there's my car right over there. If you get off, you'll lose the elevator and this is *the slowest elevator* I've ever seen. Trust me, I've been taking it up to the top every morning since the trial started. It's awful."

"OK. You got your footing? You steady?" He held the elevator door for her as she stepped off, pushing against it to make it stay open past its computer-determined time.

"I'm good!" Hailey called over her shoulder as she made her way to her car. She'd parked it in the darkened, shady part of the garage and away from the bright sun. She opened the door. She didn't even need the key; the crime techs had left it open when they got the trash and the tank valve early that morning.

Hailey could hear the elevator buzzing insanely at the door Finch was holding open. "See? I'm safe! I made it to the car all by myself! I'm getting in now! Go! I'll see you outside the exit! Hurry! I'm starved! I haven't eaten in thirty-six hours! You don't want me to faint, do you?" From the car door, she threw him a smile as he finally let the elevator door close in front of him.

Hailey got in gingerly, slammed the car door, checked the rearview mirror, cranked up the car, and checked the rearview again before reversing out. Her shoulder was actually hurting and every time she moved a pain went through it. But she didn't want Finch and Billings to worry any more than they already had. The look on Finch's face when they rolled Hailey out of the courthouse was something she'd never forget. He was in tears.

And when Billings came bursting through the swinging doors at the ER, he was white as a ghost. He'd looked awful and knelt down beside her bed. She was pretty sure he was saying a silent prayer before he stood up fairly quickly and composed himself.

Hailey put it in drive and headed toward the ramp. Chase Billings. That was the issue. She lived in New York; he lived in Savannah. No way could he drop his career here. Her mind wandered back to the night they'd walked along the Savannah River. She slowed down as the car entered the dark area beside heavy concrete columns supporting the eighth, and top, floor above them in order to go back down. Wincing with pain, Hailey had to struggle to turn the wheel and maneuver the car onto the sixth level.

Only a slight movement alerted her. Before she could turn around, she saw him. In the rearview mirror. A man with ladies' panty hose over his face.

"Bitch, you're gonna die, if it's the last thing I do." Hailey screamed out loud just as a sharp cord cut into her neck, pulling her hard back against the seat's headrest. Her foot hit the brake then let go, and the car sped straight ahead, crunching into the concrete wall in front of it.

Clawing at the cord, Hailey tried to scream again. He pulled it tighter. In the back of her mind, she knew she only had a minute or two before the cord would complete its evil dance and she'd run out of air.

She forced herself to stop clawing at her own neck, and her hands searched on their own for anything . . . anything she could use. The cord hurt so much; her hands flew back to it, trying to loosen it for even one gasp of air.

No good. The gun . . . Finch's gun, that he leant her. It was under the seat. She tried in vain to reach down to it.

He kept talking, spitting out the words through the tan panty hose. "You did it. It's your fault. And now . . . you're gonna die. I knew you were trouble the first time I laid eyes on you."

Suddenly she recognized the voice. It matched the dark hair and deep brown eyes. It was Todd Adams, his eyes wild behind the nylon, his mouth a grotesque gash in his face.

"And yeah . . . before you go to hell, Hailey Dean . . . I want you to know . . . I killed her. I killed her. I hated her. I hated her face and her breath in the morning and her swollen feet and her endless dribbling about *the baby this and the baby that.* I hated her with all my heart. I'd rather rot on death row than be married to her. I wrapped a cord around her fat white neck and I strangled her. Just like I'm gonna strangle you . . . dead. You gonna beg, Hailey? *She* begged, Hailey; she begged me not to kill her . . . to save the baby. But that's just what I didn't want. A baby out of her belly. She made me sick. And now . . . it's your turn. You can die knowing that the only people who know what happened to that cow and the baby are all dead . . . including you. This is what you get for messing with my mother. Without you . . . they don't have a case. Kiss it good-bye, Hailey Dean . . . I'll see you in hell."

Todd Adams yanked the cord tight with his fists. Hailey fought with all her might. It was no use but she kept fighting. For one brief moment, she saw Will in front of the car. He was somehow standing between the car and the concrete wall.

He looked straight into her eyes, and it was the moment Hailey had been waiting for all this time . . . since Will was taken away from her. Since he was murdered. They were together again now, finally.

A feeling of complete peace like nothing she'd ever known came over her, and she knew, ironically, the most joy she'd felt since Will died. Their years apart melted away.

In her last moment, Hailey reached out to Will . . . to hold him again . . . to hold him now and forever. Hailey's head slumped over onto her left shoulder; her arms dropped down to her sides.

When her arms dropped, her hand felt the side pocket on the door, stuffed with a map, a water bottle . . . and a pen. Her lucky pen. The Tiffany pen a victim's family once gave her after a guilty verdict during her first years as a prosecutor. It had a black silk cord around it, and she'd worn it around her neck during nearly every jury trial she had ever tried.

There was Will at her car door now. He seemed to be telling her something, gesticulating. She got it. And in one mighty heave, in a surge of power summoning all the strength she had left, she turned and stabbed.

The pen's sharp end made contact, digging through flesh and veins. A shriek came from behind her, the cord loosened, and she jerked it away from her, breathing as deeply as she could. Forgetting the pain in her shoulder and the blood now seeping from the delicate skin around her neck, she turned to look in the back seat.

The car was silent. Deathly silent. Todd Adams was sprawled on the back seat, Hailey's silver pen still protruding from his neck. His mouth hung open against the stocking. The blood didn't make a sound as it pumped, high-pressured, from the carotid artery just under his chin, forming a river of red going down his neck and chest and pooling under him on the car seat and the floorboard below.

With the strength she had left, Hailey went over the seat and clamped both hands hard over the wound, pushing the pen to the side. Blood poured between her fingers and out from the sides of her palms. She pushed harder.

The car doors flew open on both sides of the car, and Hailey was vaguely aware of loud voices.

"Get 911! *Help me! He's dying!*" Hailey screamed. She could hear the words tearing out of her own throat, but they sounded like somebody else, shrill and wild. Inches from his face, she saw the blood was no longer spurting through her fingers. Just a trickle now came from the sides of her hands and then . . . it stopped.

Hailey felt hands under her armpits, pulling her out of the car. Someone strong pulled her completely out and lifted her under her shoulders and knees, laying her gently down on the concrete floor of the parking garage.

"Hailey, he's dead. You're OK. You're alive, Hailey. Todd Adams is dead. It's over, Hailey. It's all over now."

Her eyes focused for just a moment, and in that moment she saw the face of Chase Billings, just inches above her own. And suddenly, he was holding her in a tight embrace, a hug as if it would never end.

He held her tight, there on the oil-stained concrete. She opened her eyes just once more, to look back over his shoulder for Will.

He was gone.

The sun shone into the front seat of the car as the green from the trees mixed with their limbs overhead appeared for just a moment, then whizzed past in a green blur. The wind through the window felt good and the air smelled heavy with magnolias.

"So, this isn't the way to the airport. Where are we going?"

"You'll see."

The sheriff's cruiser slowed and went off the road down a hard red dirt path and then through an opening between the trees she hadn't seen from the road. It was cool and dark off the road with the sun dappling through here and there. She spotted a butterfly ahead.

The car stopped. "We're here."

"Where's here?"

He opened her door and she took his outstretched hand, stepping out of the car and into the tall grass on either side of the dirt road. "You'll like it, you'll see." He smiled.

He led her by the hand through the tall, green grass, across the clearing and through the trees just beyond. She could hear the water now, playing against the rocks, ambling by. It seemed happy.

"It's Moon River, Hailey. I wanted you to see it."

Hailey looked out onto the water, dotted with sunlight. The leaves in the trees and the Spanish moss swayed in the breeze. It was so beautiful, it didn't seem real . . . like a magic spell had taken her away from everything dangerous and evil in her life . . . like a different world far away from her old world.

"Stay, Hailey. You can stop fighting now. You can stop. You've done enough. Have a life here. With me, Hailey. With me. With us. You don't have to go back to that world anymore, Hailey. It can be over."

The world stood still. Her New York apartment, her practice, her patients, the courtrooms, the crime, it all seemed a lifetime away. All there was ... was this ... this moment ... this man ... the water tripping by ... the sun on her face.

"I'll think about it. I promise."

Sadness crossed his face before he could hide it. "Then, I'll be in Manhattan in a few weeks to try and convince you. Can I do that?"

"I hope you do." She smiled at him, close to his lips, but her eyes filled with tears. She didn't know why.

"I've dreaded the moment, Hailey, the moment you wave from the plane. But Hailey, I'll dream of you. You won't be waving good-bye, you'll be waving hello."

When her fiancé was murdered just before their wedding day, **Nancy Grace** abandoned plans to become a Shakespearean literature professor to enter the world of crime and justice. She attended Mercer Law School, graduating *Law Review*, and obtained her LLM in Criminal and Constitutional Law at NYU. Grace then spent ten years in inner-city Atlanta prosecuting violent crimes, compiling a perfect record of more than 100 felony prosecution victories at trial with no losses—and countless plea negotiations. Grace joined Court TV and, for eleven years, covered major trials after cohosting *Cochran & Grace* with famed defense attorney Johnnie Cochran. One of television's most respected legal analysts, Grace headlined the top-rated HLN show *Nancy Grace* and serves as a legal expert for ABC's *Nightline, 20/20*, and *Good Morning America*. She is the publisher of CrimeOnline.com, one of the world's top internet crime report destinations, and is the executive producer of Hallmark's hit movie franchise *Hailey Dean Mysteries*. Grace lives in both New York City and Atlanta with her husband and beloved twins, a boy and a girl (and a dog and a cat, both pound pets).